Readers love the Lions & Tigers & Bears series
by K.C. WELLS

A Growl, a Roar, and a Purr

"As always, K.C. Wells does a great job at character development and she definitely knows how to sex things up, without making the sex the most important part of the book."

—Love Bytes

"In this paranormal romance, Wells explores the shifter and fated mates tropes in this fun action-adventure romp that includes an epic heist and a sweet romantic through-line."

—J.L. Gribble's Book Reviews

"The romance was definitely the key to this story. It leaped off the pages and heated up the sheets."

—The TBR Pile

A Snarl, A Splash, and a Shock

"This novel contains a super range of characters, from the despicably evil, the super good, the conflicted, and more. I found inter-relationship dynamics most amusing. The journeys of Vic, Saul, and Crank made for splendid reading."

—Love Bytes

By K.C. Wells

BFF
Bromantically Yours
First
Love Lessons Learned
Step by Step
Waiting For You

DREAMSPUN DESIRES
The Senator's Secret
Out of the Shadows
My Fair Brady
Under the Covers

LEARNING TO LOVE
Michael & Sean
Evan & Daniel
Josh & Chris
Final Exam

LIONS & TIGERS & BEARS
A Growl, a Roar, and a Purr
A Snarl, a Splash, and a Shock
Visions, Paws, and Claws

LOVE, UNEXPECTED
Debt
Burden

MERRYCHURCH MYSTERIES
Truth Will Out
Roots of Evil
A Novel Murder

SENSUAL BONDS
A Bond of Three
A Bond of Truth

With Parker Williams

COLLARS & CUFFS
An Unlocked Heart
Trusting Thomas
Someone to Keep Me
A Dance with Domination
Damian's Discipline
Make Me Soar
Dom of Ages
Endings and Beginnings

SECRETS
Before You Break
An Unlocked Mind
Threepeat
On the Same Page

Published by DSP Publications
SECOND SIGHT
In His Sights
In Plain Sight
Out of Sight

Published by DREAMSPINNER PRESS
www.dreamspinnerpress.com

VISIONS, PAWS, AND CLAWS

K.C. WELLS

Published by

DREAMSPINNER PRESS

8219 Woodville Hwy #1245
Woodville, FL 32362 USA
www.dreamspinnerpress.com

Visions, Paws, and Claws
© 2025 K.C. Wells

Cover Art
© 2025 L.C. Chase
http://www.lcchase.com
Cover content is for illustrative purposes only and any person depicted on the cover is a model.

Trade Paperback ISBN: 978-1-64108-820-6
Digital ISBN: 978-1-64108-819-0
Trade Paperback published February 2025
v. 1.0

This book is dedicated to my brother, Parker Williams. Okay, so he's a brother from another mother, but that doesn't make him any the less awesome. I couldn't have written any of the books in this series without him.

PROLOGUE

"HE'S COMING, I *know* he is."

Aric Townsend loved Seth's confidence, his unshakable belief, but right then his words didn't perform their usual feat of magic.

They couldn't take away the chill that had settled in around Aric's heart.

"You keep saying that, but if he was coming, he'd have been here by now." Aric shivered. "Admit it, why don't you? We're going to die in here." And here was such a terrifying place, robbed of all joy, all hope....

And yet I found love in the middle of a nightmare situation.

"No!" Seth glared at him. "We *will* be getting out of here, I swear it. But you need to have faith." He lifted the thin sheet. "Come under here. Let me keep you warm."

Aric slipped into bed and sighed when Seth wrapped a slender arm around him.

"I'm not like you. I don't have your optimism, your strength. I mean it. I'm afraid we're gonna die in here," Aric admitted.

"And I promised you we wouldn't." Seth cupped Aric's chin and gazed into his eyes. "Don't you trust me?"

Aric let out another deep, shuddering sigh. "Only with everything in me." He clung to Seth's promise on an hourly basis, whenever his spirits were at their lowest.

It was all he had left to cling to. His old life had been ripped away from him. He'd been torn from his mother's arms, forced to go to this godforsaken hellhole along with all the other young shifters who'd been similarly taken. And it had soon become obvious why they were there. To be examined. Experimented on. Sifted. The wheat separated from the chaff.

Aric knew he was chaff right from the start. He'd always been delicate, with no special talents except the gift of curling up in someone's lap and soothing them with the rumble of his purr. A house kitty was never going to be of use to them, not like the tigers, the lions, the panthers, all those sinewed, lithe, heart-stoppingly fast cats. No, Aric was like the vast majority of shifters in the camp. Not *entirely* useless, however.

They were cannon fodder.

Target practice.

Expendable.

Disposable.

Aric had resigned himself to an early death, caught up in a battle that wasn't his in a struggle he didn't believe in.

Until he met Seth Miles, and it was as if someone had turned the light on, illuminating his dark prison.

For the first time in his life, Aric fell head over heels in love.

What made it perfect?

Seth Miles loved him back.

Their love was the only positive to come out of their capture, but it was a secret. Being physical was out of the question. Staying safe was paramount.

So Aric made do with cuddles hidden by the dead of night, the squeeze of Seth's hand around his when no one could see.

And then a miracle occurred.

They'd been in the camp a month when a batch of new inmates arrived, and one of them captured Seth's attention from the moment he walked toward them. Aric could understand Seth's reaction. Whoever this shifter was, he was Someone.

Not only that, he was Seth's father, Jake Carson, a man Seth had never met—and they shared a staggering gift, one that caught the attention of the camp authorities.

One individual in particular, a man who made Aric's blood run cold.

Aric knew about Seth's gift, and now it seemed to be an inherited trait, one that could be exploited.

Seth stroked Aric's jaw. "Our mate is coming. He doesn't know about us yet, but once he does?" He smiled, and the sight eased the terror bubbling up through Aric. "We will be the center of his world." Then the smile faded, replaced by an expression Aric recognized instantly.

Grim determination.

"Aric, listen to me. We're getting out of here."

He said nothing. He'd heard the words before.

"Aric, we don't have much time. You've heard the rumors going around, haven't you? They're going to take us to a new camp."

"Then let's hope it's better than this one."

Seth frowned. "You don't understand. I… I don't think they're going to take all of us."

Panic flooded through him in an icy wave. "You mean they might—"

Seth stopped his words with a kiss. "You've already helped me try to reach him. Well… I'm going to need you to help him find *me*. Because they're not about to leave me here."

Aric's throat seized, and for a moment he struggled to breathe.

"They're going to split us up. Either you'll be taken someplace different or I will. Right now I can't see which way it will go."

"*What about Jake?*"

Seth bit his lip. "I think they'll keep us together, at least until they work out how they can use us." He stroked Aric's cheek. "Listen, baby. You and me, we have a connection. And there is *nothing* that can break that, you hear?"

Except if they kill you. Or me.

No way would Aric say those words aloud.

"And that connection is what will help bring our mate to me. To us." Seth locked gazes with him. "So you have to make *me* a promise too."

"Anything." Aric gulped.

"You have to stay alive, even if you need to kill to do that." Seth gripped his chin. "*Can* you do that?"

Aric swallowed. "It doesn't seem as if I have a choice, does it?"

"You have to live. Our mate will come here—that much I *can* see— and when he does, you have to tell him about me. About us. Because then the two of you can rescue me."

"So you already know you'll need rescuing?" Aric fixed him with a hard stare. "There's stuff you haven't told me, isn't there?"

Seth kissed his forehead. "Only because I don't want you to worry."

Aric wanted to be angry—to protest that he could cope—but he couldn't, not when Seth held him so close, sharing his warmth.

"Want to try again before we get some sleep?"

Aric nodded. He closed his eyes and opened his mind. He could already sense Seth there, waiting for him. He had no clue how Seth was able to project his thoughts, but then again, he had a feeling most of Seth's psychic abilities lay untapped.

Together they sent out their distress call for a man neither of them had ever seen but believed would come for them—if he only knew they existed.

Save us.

Save us.

Save us.

CHAPTER ONE

HORVAN KOJIK was going to kill Brick.

Then he reasoned he wouldn't need to. Brick was probably going to end up dead very soon if he kept taking chances the way he'd been doing lately.

And then *what will his mates do?*

Horvan didn't want to contemplate how it would feel to lose a mate. What that loss would do to him. Or them, if the worst happened.

The raid had been textbook. Two teams had shown up at almost midnight on a moonless night—his own and one led by one of Aelryn's commanders—and as one they'd surged forward into yet another camp, meeting enemy fire with their own. Horvan had admired Aelryn from the moment they met, not to mention the awe he felt every time he was in Aelryn's presence. Aelryn was a Fridan blue blood, a direct descendant of one of the brothers who'd been the cause of the rift between shifters back when the earth was cooling.

Okay, maybe not *that* long—Vic Ryder would probably know exactly how long ago that was—but there was no denying Aelryn was Someone. His forces were easily the equal of Horvan's, and it was refreshing to work side by side with military people who didn't curl up their lip at the mere *thought* of collaborating with humans. The raids were well planned and precise but were always bloody: Ansger's spear was still wielded with abandon by his descendants. Those enemy fighters who didn't flee were taken into custody by Aelryn's people, and Horvan knew they'd be treated with more consideration than the Gerans had shown toward *their* prisoners.

This last raid had gone like clockwork—until Brick happened.

He can't go on like this.

Brick out of combat was bad enough. He had a wicked temper, and it was all his mate Aric could do to keep that rage below the boiling point. But on the battlefield?

Gloves came off, he shifted, and then teeth and claws got bloody.

Way too bloody, too often.

5

Horvan knew he should make Brick sit these missions out. His friend was becoming more and more erratic, refusing to obey orders, violently taking down anyone who dared to challenge him. But damn it, they *needed* him. They'd only located and raided two camps in the two months since they'd liberated the one in Bozeman, and also closed down another shifter school, this time in Croatia, and yet it *still* felt as though the bad guys were creeping across the globe like kudzu, swallowing up shifters left and right. Making any real headway was harder than hell.

It would be even more difficult without Brick. A Brick who had crawled back to their own camp and stumbled into the main tent, his maw and claws bloodied.

What worried Horvan was the sight of blood from Brick's wounds, marring his pristine white fur. He'd collapsed on the ground, his chest heaving, in the worst state Horvan had ever seen him.

One day Brick might not be able to tell the difference between allies and enemies.

Aric was there in a heartbeat, kneeling beside him on the hard ground. He stroked a hand over Brick, heedless of the blood matting his fur.

"Brick, shift for me so we can tend to your wounds."

The bustle and noise of fighters returning from the routed enemy camp—dirty, bruised, yet with their backs straight and their heads held high, clearly content to have been part of the mission—continued around them.

Horvan could sense no such emotion emanating from Brick. Under Aric's careful hands, the polar bear let out an anguished roar, and Horvan knew what lay at the heart of his distress.

There'd been no sign of their mate, Seth. Or Jake Carson, Dellan's and Seth's father. Or Dellan's half brother, Jamie Matheson.

"Please?" Aric crooned softly. "For me?"

Horvan could understand Brick's anguish. He'd followed Seth's and Aric's voices, which had called to him over miles and miles, only to find one of them had been taken before Brick had had the chance to lay eyes on him. And each raid brought with it the prospect of another chance to find Seth and the others.

Praying they were okay.

Such mental pain would fray anyone's mind.

Aric was suffering too. Being parted from Seth had left him forlorn and withdrawn; he seemed to curl in on himself. The only time he emerged from his protective cocoon was when Brick was around.

God knows what he went through in that camp.

Horvan crouched beside Brick and glared at him. "Come on, Brick. Don't be such a stubborn fucker. Shift, for God's sake."

Brick's body shimmered, becoming smaller but still huge by human standards. When he did, Horvan gasped. Brick was riddled with wounds, mostly from bullets, he guessed.

Horvan clicked his mic. "A medic to the main tent, ASAP. And that means *now*." He leaned in close, noting the number and severity of the wounds. It was a good thing Brick's bear was so big, because that had likely saved his life.

There was another possibility. Maybe Brick refused to be extinguished until his mate was back where he belonged.

"You'd better not die," Horvan grumbled as a medic hurried over to them and began tending Brick's wounds.

"You're only… saying that because… you wanna do the job yourself," Brick wheezed.

"You got that right." He started to rise, but Brick grabbed his arm. Even as hurt as he was, Brick was stronger than Horvan.

"I'm here," Horvan said in a softer voice.

Tortured brown eyes met his.

"I need him, H. I can hear him in my head, pleading with me to find him. To save him. We've never met, but I'm in love with him already. You gotta understand."

Horvan understood all right.

This was a fight they couldn't afford to lose.

"You still having dreams about Seth?"

Brick managed a nod. "He's screaming, H. They're torturing him. And you wanna know the worst part?" He shuddered. "I can hear those screams even when I'm awake."

Horvan wanted to tell him it wasn't real, but Aric had told him and Brick that Seth was psychic, able to project his thoughts to them. Aric had also confided that when he and Seth connected, what made his heart sink was the fear that laced those thoughts. Fear of being alone. Of being unable to find his way home. Horvan knew what that meant.

Home was Aric and Brick.

Aric stared at Brick with undisguised dismay. "You never told me that. How come I didn't know?"

"Because I locked you out." Brick's eyes glistened. "I didn't want you to be upset."

Aric's eyes bulged. "Upset? You hide something like that from me again, and you'll soon learn what *upset* looks like." He glared. "I'll shift and let my kitty shit in your boots."

There was silence for a moment before Brick laughed, even though it obviously hurt him to do so. Aric stared at him, and then he too was laughing.

Horvan snickered as he stood. "I've got this sudden urge to go hide all my footwear." He gazed down at Brick. "When they've finished patching you up? My tent. We need to talk."

Horvan's plate was overflowing right then, bringing the fight to the Gerans, who believed shifters should rule the world. They seemed to be hiding in every corner, under every rock, behind every tree—under every bed.

But if he could stop Brick from doing what amounted to self-harm, he'd consider that a win.

WHEN HORVAN'S done with him, it's my *turn.*

Aric had done his best to remain calm while the medics patched Brick up, but the effort had taken a lot out of him. He'd watched as Brick made his way slowly to Horvan's tent, the flap closing after him. Aric had no idea what Horvan had said to Brick, but whatever it was, the conversation had lasted only minutes before Saul Emory arrived and the team leaders were called into Horvan's tent to be debriefed by the two men. Aric had lingered outside, listening to the deep rumble of Saul's voice. He didn't shout as much as Horvan. But then again, he didn't need to. One hard stare from Saul was enough to have most people quaking.

A man who'd endured what *he* had at the hands of the enemy was owed respect.

There was another side to Saul, a rarely seen side that Aric had encountered the first time he'd shifted in Saul's presence.

The man *loved* kitties.

Aric couldn't be scared of a guy who stroked him the way Saul did.

One by one, the team leaders began to file out of Horvan's tent, and when Aric couldn't wait a second longer, he went against the tide of bodies and hurried inside.

Only three men remained in the tent. Brick was in a chair next to Horvan's bed, his head in his hands, dressings everywhere. Saul and Horvan were deep in conversation, and from the look of it, whatever was being discussed was a bone of contention.

Aric coughed.

"Horvan? Saul? Can I be alone with Brick for a few minutes?"

Horvan blinked. "Sure. We'll get out of your hair."

Saul raised his eyebrows but said nothing as he followed Horvan through the tent flap. Aric waited until he knew they were far enough away, then whirled around to face Brick, his hands clenched at his sides.

Don't lose your cool. Stay focused.

Yeah, *that* wasn't going to happen.

He glared at Brick. "You don't give a damn about me, do you?"

Brick widened his eyes. "What? Where did that come from?"

"Another raid and here you are again. In as big a mess as you were after the last one."

"What the hell does that mean?" Brick lurched to his feet, wincing as he did do. "I'm doing this for you."

"No, you aren't. You're doing it for *you*. I don't know if it's some misplaced sense of guilt that you weren't there to protect us—which you couldn't have been, by the way, since you didn't even know we existed—but whatever the reason, I am sick to death of seeing you come crawling back on the verge of death."

"It's not as bad as—"

Aric narrowed his eyes. "Don't lie to me, Brick. When I'm near you, I can feel your pain. Do you think I don't share it? He's *my* mate too, damn you. You've been cutting me out, running off and doing stupid things like this and—"

Brick grabbed him, and Aric felt his flash of pain. "You don't yell at me," Brick growled. "You *never* yell at me."

"Well, *someone* has to," he cried out. "You need to stop being so... so selfish."

Brick froze. "Define selfish. 'Cause I'm in the dark here."

Aric forced himself to take deep breaths. "I've already lost Seth. So right now you're the only thing holding me together. If I lost you, I would die. And that's not me exaggerating, okay?" He gazed up into Brick's eyes. "I can't live without my mate. If you get your stupid ass killed, my mind, my heart, and my body will all simply shut down, and I'll *die*."

"Aric, you—"

"*Die*, Brick. I'm telling you, I will. A heartbroken cat can lose its will to live. And right now the only thing keeping me going is you." He nudged Brick's chin with his head. "Please, you have to stay safe—for both of us." Tremors rippled through Brick's massive frame, but Aric didn't move.

Finally, Brick sighed, stirring Aric's hair.

"I'll try, but you have to understand. Seth is in my head, begging me to help him. When I hear his voice, I lose all sense of control. All I know is that somewhere out there, my other mate is suffering."

"Then why can't I hear him?" Aric whined. *Damn it, I saw him first. Doesn't that count for* something?

Then he realized how dumb that sounded, and he was thankful he'd kept it to himself.

Brick's hand was gentle on Aric's head. "Maybe he's protecting you? He knows you better than me. Would he want you to know he's in pain?"

Aric wanted to say Seth wouldn't care, but that wasn't true. "He would do everything in his power to keep me safe." His sigh was the equal of Brick's. "Like he always does. If I'm honest, I think he's waiting for you so he can stop worrying so much about me. Once I'm your problem, he'll be a lot happier."

Brick wrapped his hand around the back of Aric's neck and pulled him in. "That's bullshit, and you know it." His gruff voice sent a delicious shiver through Aric, but he pushed down hard on the thoughts that followed it.

Down boy. Uh-uh.

"You said he loves you," Brick continued, "so no way will he dump you on me. He's going to be with us for a very long time."

"Not if you don't stop doing stupid shit." Brick's embrace had had one positive effect; calm had finally returned. He stood on his toes and kissed Brick's cheek. "Look at it this way. If you die, he does too, because no one will find him. So by being this stubborn ass, you could be killing all three of us." He gave Brick a hopeful glance. "I'm not saying don't go out searching for him, okay? But please be smart about it. For all our sakes."

Strong arms enfolded him, and Aric breathed him in. There was the coppery odor of blood, the medicinal tinge of the dressings, but under it all was Brick's scent, warm and earthy and—

Dammit, Aric wanted to be naked *so* badly right then. With Seth and Brick. Learning to pleasure them, cataloging what drove each of them wild. He desperately wanted the chance to be with his mates.

And soon.

"I'll be smart," Brick promised. "Well, as smart as I can be, which probably isn't saying a lot." He kissed Aric's hair. "Now go pack our stuff. We're leaving in about fifteen minutes."

"And you were going to share this information *when?*" Aric scuttled out of the tent.

Another raid over, and hopefully, a lesson learned.

He wasn't thinking about the Gerans—

BRICK ACHED like a son of a bitch. Everywhere hurt.

And for what?

Sure, they'd freed countless shifters and annihilated countless bad guys, but for fuck's sake, how many more of these camps could there be?

He tried to get comfortable, except he knew that was a nonstarter. Transport planes weren't put together for comfort. He glanced at the faces of those around him, seeing his own emotions reflected there.

There aren't enough of us to even make a dent in the enemy's forces.

Maybe someone needed to say that out loud, especially when H and Saul were in earshot.

Someone like Brick, who was long past giving a shit.

"Hey, H?"

Across from him, Horvan raised his head. "You're awake. How's the pain level?"

"Bearable." He managed a smile. "See what I did there?"

Horvan didn't need to see how bad Brick was really feeling. *No one got to see that, not even Aric.*

Horvan groaned. "That was bad, even for you."

"When is Duke gonna find us more men?"

An eerie silence fell as heads turned in their direction.

Apparently Brick wasn't the only one who wanted to know.

11

Saul glanced at Horvan, who nodded. "We've already started recruiting more bodies," Saul told him.

"More mercs? Vets?" Horvan's business partner, Duke, seemed to have a never-ending supply of those.

"Not exactly." Saul cleared his throat. "We're getting a lot of interest from an unexpected source."

When nothing else was forthcoming, Brick glared at him. "Well, don't stop there, Mr. Joint Team Leader. Spit it out."

"When we closed down the school in Massachusetts, I think it shook up a lot of shifters. The fact that the Gerans up and *abandoned* more than nine hundred kids without hesitation…. Word got around. That was maybe a step too far for some folks. And when the same thing happened in Croatia, it created even more waves."

Brick did the math. "Are you saying we've got people wanting to join us who were on the *other side*? Seriously?"

Saul nodded. "We're gonna vet them all rigorously."

Brick blinked. "Oh, I'm *so* happy to hear that. I thought you were all set to give 'em the keys to the armory."

Horvan snickered. "Get you with the sarcasm."

"I'll be helping with the interviews," Hashtag piped up.

Brick snorted. "Great. Now I'm *really* worried."

Hashtag gave him the finger.

Next to Saul, Crank narrowed his gaze. "You're not dissing my mate's leadership abilities, are you, Brick?"

Roadkill cackled. "Now *there* are words I never thought I'd hear."

"All you need to know is that we're intending to double our numbers," Saul concluded. He aimed a sideways glance at Crank. "That was sweet, by the way. Not to mention hot."

A chorus of groans filled the air.

"Get a room."

"Anyone got noise-canceling headphones with them?"

"H, can't you put something in their coffee to cool their jets?"

Horvan laughed. "Hey, if you wanna try that, go for it. Personally, I think Saul and Crank would make mincemeat of you. And God help you if Vic found out, but you're welcome to try."

"Something else we need to discuss." Brick was on a roll. "We have to discover where their main camp is."

Especially if that was where they were holding Seth, Jake, and Jamie. Brick still got the guilts every time he recalled his part in Jamie's disappearance, not to mention Saul's capture.

Thank God Crank and Vic didn't bear him a grudge.

"You got any suggestions as to where we should be searching?" Saul asked. "We're always open to suggestions."

"Yeah, I heard that about you and your mates," Roadkill quipped.

The main camp was never far from Brick's mind. "It has to be somewhere inhospitable. Somewhere it's nearly impossible to get out of."

That might account for the absence of escapees.

"Like Chicago?" Crank asked. When the rest of the team fired bemused glances at him, he snorted. "What? Ever tried to drive there? It's the very definition of impossible."

"Let's talk about this when we get back to Homer Glen," Horvan suggested.

One of the team cackled. "Yeah, it's times like these I'm really glad to be living in the new barracks. I'd hate to be in the same house as you guys."

"You wanna know what's a really great invention?" Hashtag grinned. "Earplugs."

Brick was more than happy to change the subject now that he'd brought it out into the open. Beside him, Aric stirred from his sleep, and Brick chuckled.

"I can't get over what a deep sleeper you are. Must be a cat thing." He put his arm around Aric and pulled him close, breathing in the scent that went straight to his dick, the way it did every single fucking time. Brick leaned in and brushed his lips over Aric's ear.

Aric shivered. "Please, don't do that."

Brick froze. "Why not?"

Aric glared at him. "Because it turns me on," he said in an urgent whisper.

He grinned. "Nothing wrong with that."

"But we can't do anything, remember? We've talked about this."

It had been one of their first conversations, and Brick could recite it word for word.

"We… we can't have sex. I mean, not with each other," Aric blurted.

"Why not?" Brick stroked Aric's chest, heading lower. "Your equipment works, doesn't it? I mean, you don't have a kitty-sized dick. And while I haven't ever been with a guy, I'm a fast learner."

13

All his senses were telling him it wasn't going to be a problem.

"Seth said we need our third—you—to be complete."

"So you and he never—"

"We cuddled, but without you, neither of us could get hard." Aric bit his lip. "Well, we could, but it never stayed around long enough to do much with it."

Was it wrong that the statement made Brick feel ten feet tall? Probably. It didn't stop his chest from swelling, though.

He cupped Aric's cheek. "We'll find Seth, I swear to you. If I have to raid every fucking camp, I will." Brick kissed Aric's forehead. "So what's Seth like?"

"He's a sweet, gentle soul, a pacifist. He'd be a vegan except he needs meat to keep his cat healthy." Aric sighed. "He saw you in his visions. He told me you would protect us. You would be the glue that held us together." He looked Brick in the eye. "Without you, there is no us."

Without you, there is no us. Brick could wait.

Besides, he couldn't help but get excited at the thought of the three of them finally meeting—all of them new to each other, two of them virgins, one of them experienced but a total newbie when it came to gay sex.

Then a rush of cold flooded through him.

How can you even think about sex? When Seth is God knows where, having God knows what done to him?

Yeah, Brick didn't like himself very much right then.

CHAPTER TWO

SETH MILES knew exactly where to find his father. The same place he was every day, making the most of the fresh air before he was taken to the breeding block or the pair of them were dragged to the science building.

Except he thought of it more in terms of the experimentation block.

Jake Carson stood in the center of the exercise yard beneath the camouflage nets, his face upturned to catch the sun as it filtered through, dappling his skin and the ground under his feet. His eyes were closed. None of the other inmates talked to him.

No one talked much at all in the compound, especially if they knew they were being observed. It was as if an invisible layer weighed them down, depressing every positive emotion, suppressing every urge to communicate.

Extinguishing all hope.

Seth walked toward him, taking his time, trying his best to avoid purpose in his stride. This was their only opportunity to meet; the guards kept them in separate blocks at night, and it wasn't possible to talk while they were strapped into chairs, electrodes stuck to their temples, monitors recording their heartbeats, breathing, brain activity....

Times when Seth did his damnedest not to cooperate, even though that meant far worse pain. But in the end they always wore him down.

Wore him out.

Jake turned his head as Seth approached. "You seem tired. Bad night?"

"No such thing as a good night in this place." He studied Jake, noting the dark circles under his eyes. He swore there were more lines in that kind face than there had been when he and Jake had met in the previous camp.

How long ago was that?

Seth had lost all track of time. There were no clocks in the compound, but he'd managed a peek at one of the monitors in the experimentation block. The tiniest peek, but it had been enough to inform him they were now in July.

As to where we are?

That was a mystery. They'd been transported from the last compound in trucks with no windows. All he knew was that there was nothing to see for miles but scrubs and trees.

Pretty much the same view as the previous prison, but with warmer weather.

Hey, look for the positive, right?

There were few positives to be found. The taciturn guards strolled constantly, guns slung over their shoulders, and getting even one of them to show a spark of humanity was a huge task.

Except they're not human, are they?

That made it worse. That shifters could treat their own kind in so… emotionless a manner.

Jake lowered his voice. "How did you do?"

Seth sighed. "I'm not sure. If Aric is with our mate, that might help amplify the signal, for want of a better word." He'd waited until the block had emptied before sitting on his bed, closing his eyes, and opening his mind, striving to reach Aric. "I think he's simply too far away." The fact Seth had located their mate at all was a miracle.

Aric is with him now.

Seth didn't know if that was knowledge provided by his gift or more like wishful thinking. Gods, he missed Aric. Seth brought the sleeve of Aric's tee, which he wore over his shoulders, to his nose, breathing in his scent. Okay, so it had lost Aric's scent long ago, but Seth could imagine, right? He *knew* it was wishful thinking that it still smelled of his mate, but he clung to it anyway.

He was never going to wash it. Not till he was able to give it back in person. And right then it had a job to do—to keep Aric alive in Seth's mind, to help him remember the nights when Aric had crawled into Seth's bed and they'd held each other until dawn, when they had to be in their own bed before the guards checked on them.

Jake's face tightened, and he suddenly appeared every one of his sixty-two years. "They'll be coming for us soon. I know I shouldn't think about it. I should focus on something else, but…."

Seth grimaced. "Easy to say, damn near impossible to carry out."

How long do we have? Minutes? Longer?

Time ceased to have all meaning, measured only in terms *go here, go there, do this, do that, eat, sleep….*

Suffer.

"Tell me about Dellan," Seth asked suddenly. Jake hadn't talked much about his son, but Seth knew he had to be on Jake's mind.

He thinks Dellan could be in danger.

If he was anything like his father, Dellan would undoubtedly be of interest to the Gerans. Unless....

No. The likelihood of Dellan being on the enemy's side was remote. Jake was a noble shifter with a strong sense of right and wrong, and Seth believed such traits to be inheritable.

Jake expelled a long breath. "I can't. My memories are all of a little seven-year-old boy. I was taken from him more than thirty years ago." He smiled, but it was tinged with sorrow. "I wonder if he looks like me. What he's doing right now. Does he have a family? For all I know, I could be a grandfather."

Except Seth knew Jake wasn't thinking about Dellan's possible children—he was thinking of his own offspring. After all these years, there was no telling how many shifters Jake had sired.

"Does it bother you? Knowing you have children out there that you've never met?"

Jake scowled. "Of course it does. I don't care how they came to be—they're still part of me." He gave Seth a sympathetic glance. "I'm sorry, but I have no idea who your mother was. You know how it goes here. We're never allowed to make our own decisions or choices. They'll put us with someone, and we'll never see them again. I do worry about what happened to some of them." His face tightened. "They were so scared, so desperate to get out. I've never seen it, but I've heard the bastards dangle their freedom in front of them like a carrot, but once it's done, they're gone. I sincerely doubt they simply let them leave."

Seth knew all right.

He knew that if Jake refused to cooperate—which he did, frequently—then a shift was forced on him, using that fucking drug. That was an infinitely worse situation. The aftereffects left Jake feeling ill for at least a day. His mom had had no idea who Seth's father was, not that they'd shared cozy chats about Seth's parentage. He still found it hard to believe his mother fell in line with all this shifter superiority crap.

That didn't mean he hadn't hurt the day they'd appeared on his doorstep to take him to the compound. Seth had cried out for her to keep him.

17

What had hurt worse than the blows he'd received from his captors was the fact that she'd let them take him without so much as a blink.

"Hey, where are you?" Jake squeezed his shoulder.

Seth shoved the memories from his mind. "Sorry. I *am* listening."

"I was saying, it's crazy the number of shifters they forced me to mate with." He tilted his head to one side. "Did your mother know about your gift?"

Seth shook his head. "I didn't tell her. I didn't tell anyone except you and Aric." Once he'd learned where her allegiance lay, he'd decided to keep his talents a secret.

There was no way Seth would have given the enemy more ammunition.

"Then how did these bastards find out?"

Seth stared morosely at the ground. "Testing. You should've seen them when they realized I had psychic abilities. At least here I'm not the only one."

Jake sighed. "We're still only two. Which means we're rare enough for them to want to… study us." He shuddered.

"What if we're *not* the only ones?"

Jake stared at him. "What do you know?"

Seth shrugged. "Just a feeling I get sometimes. It might be nothing." Except he hoped it was more than that. Maybe there *were* several of them, all as worn down and depressed as he was. "How long have you known about your gift?"

Jake smiled. "A long time. Like you I kept quiet about it. My mom knew, though. Too much stuff happened that I couldn't hide. And when I went to college, I told someone there. He was a professor, a really cool guy. Bear shifter. But yes, I've always known I could do things few others could. I must say it's given me a few surprises over the years. A few shocks too."

"What kind of shocks?" Seth glanced toward the experimentation block. So far no guards were heading their way.

It was too much to hope they'd be left alone for once.

"When I was younger, I had two best friends." Jake's face glowed. "I married one of them. Her name was Miranda, one of the swiftest, most beautiful tigers I'd ever seen."

"And the other?"

"His name was Nicholas Tranter, and he was a couple of years younger than me. A medical student and also a shifter." Jake chuckled. "I'll never forget the first time he shifted in front of me. I almost fainted."

"Why?"

"One minute he was a slim guy, the next he was an African elephant."

Seth wished he could have seen that. "Was that the shock you mentioned?"

Jake shook his head. "The three of us were close. One time we went on vacation together, to Kansas, and it was there that I saw something I don't think Nicholas meant for me to see."

Seth's breathing hitched. "What?"

Jake fell silent for a moment, his eyes fixed on the horizon. "I think he was in love with me."

"Oh wow. Did he ever tell you how he felt?"

"Not a word. Then again, I wouldn't have expected him to. Nicholas was an honorable man, with integrity, and he knew how I felt about Miranda. What he *didn't* know—because I never told him—was that I was bisexual. Not something I shared with anyone except Miranda. And I didn't really tell her." Jake smiled. "I didn't have to. Nothing seemed to escape her keen eyes. Oh, she was subtle about it—at first, at any rate. She'd often mention that I should invite Nicholas over. That I should ensure our friendship didn't lapse."

"And when she *wasn't* being subtle?"

He smiled again. "When I wouldn't rise to the bait, she told me I should try sleeping with my friend to see if it was something I was missing out on."

Seth chuckled. "Yeah, not so subtle after all."

"Maybe I should have, but it wouldn't have been something I needed to 'find out.' Miranda said she would be willing to share if I wanted a third in our relationship, but—" Jake sighed. "—I only wanted her. But in my dreams? The three of us might have been together. Of course, that was before I found out about true mates."

"Wait a minute. You said Nicholas was in love with you." Seth stared at him. "But you loved him too, didn't you?"

The skin around Jake's eyes crinkled. "Nothing gets past you either, does it?"

"What happened to Miranda? Do you know?"

Jake said nothing for several long seconds, and Seth could feel the waves of sadness and fury rolling off him. "The last time I saw her was at an airport. She was saying goodbye to me before I left to fly to Italy. I hated leaving her and Dellan, but...." He huffed. "There are some requests you can't refuse, and that was one of them."

"You didn't go home?"

"I never got the chance. I was taken before I'd even packed my bags for the return flight." He glanced at his surroundings. "How was I to know that trip was to be my last taste of freedom?" He sighed. "I've spent half my life incarcerated, kept away from the outside world, cut off from any news of what is going on out there. I have no idea where she is, or if she's still alive. I can't bear to think of how my disappearance would have changed her life. How long after it did she finally give up all hope of ever seeing me again?" He raised his chin. "Let's change the subject."

Seth nuzzled Aric's tee. *You know you're going to see him again, don't you?*

He believed that with every fiber of his being. It was all he clung to in order to keep himself from going under, from sinking beneath the waves of despair that continually battered him.

"So have you heard anything else that might tell us where we are?" He and Jake listened as the guards talked, hoping for any clues as to their location.

Jake nodded toward the north of the compound. "Apparently, Canada is thataway."

Seth smothered a snort. "Wow. Now *there's* breaking news."

"No, I mean it seems we're real close to the Canadian border."

"Which means we could be in any one of numerous states." Seth glanced toward the gate of the exercise yard. "Don't look now but we're gonna have company."

Three soldiers approached the gate, followed by five individuals who blinked in the sunlight, their faces haggard.

"They've been kept in the reeducation center for two months," Jake murmured. "I remember when they arrived." Another scowl distorted his handsome face. "Reeducation, my ass. I wonder what they did to end up in there." All five shifters were painfully thin. He glanced at Seth. "Did you hide some bread this morning like you usually do?"

Seth caught on fast. "It's in my pocket, wrapped in a piece of tissue." Hunger had become a part of their daily lives, but the sorry state of the newly released shifters touched him.

Their need is greater.

He watched as they stood in a clump, clearly assessing their surroundings.

Not a lot to see here, guys. And no way to escape.

The guards around the perimeter and in the towers saw to that. True, helicopters and military planes made regular landings at the airfield Seth had spied to the northeast of the compound, but as for getting through the wire and stealing one?

Yeah. Seth wouldn't get more than five feet before he'd be shot.

He could see that knowledge sinking in as the new inmates took stock of the compound. Then he froze. "Jake, one of the newbies is heading straight for us."

Jake didn't turn his head. "What can you tell me about him?"

They were careful not to overshare with others; who knew if one of their fellow inmates could be a plant?

"You need to see this guy," Seth whispered. The newbie was young, in his midtwenties, maybe a little older than Seth.

Jake frowned. "Why?"

"Because he's staring at *you*."

"Describe him."

Seth spoke quickly. "Tall, dark brown hair, nothing that really makes him stand out." Then the guy got closer and Seth scrutinized his face.

Oh my God.

"Jake? I think we have another one."

"Another what?"

Seth gripped his arm. "Jake, he looks like you."

Jake turned slowly. They stood rigid, waiting for the young man to reach them, and Seth knew by the catch in Jake's breath that he'd seen it too.

He had to be another of Jake's children.

The guy stopped in front of Jake, locking gazes with him, and Seth knew what was coming. He'd heard it on numerous occasions since he and Jake had been brought to the compound.

I think we're related.

Are you my dad?

21

The guy stared at Jake. "You... you're Jake Carson." His voice cracked.

Seth blinked. Okay, *that* wasn't part of the usual script.

"How do you know my name?" Jake demanded.

"I saw a photo of you, about two months ago."

"Where?"

"In Illinois. Where I met your son, Dellan."

Jake gasped, and as Seth watched, he crumpled. Seth caught him. "Hold on," Seth whispered. "Don't let them see. Please, Jake."

Jake wiped his eyes and straightened. "You saw Dellan. You're sure it was Dellan?"

The young man nodded. "He was with his mates."

Seth gaped. "Mates?"

Another nod. "He was with a bear and a lion."

"But they said they were mates?" Seth pressed.

He nodded. "Meeting them changed everything."

Jake finally found his voice. "Who are you?"

"My name is Jamie Matheson, and two months ago I learned you were my father and Dellan my half brother." He swallowed. "I also learned my whole life was a lie."

Jake pulled Jamie into his arms and hugged him, and tears pricked Seth's eyes.

When Jake released him, he pushed the hair back from Jamie's forehead. "I have so many questions. How old are you?"

"Twenty-seven. And until a few months ago, I believed shifters were at the top of the evolutionary ladder. We were the dominant species."

Seth stilled. "You're a Geran?"

Jamie smiled. "Correction—I *was*. Meeting Dellan and the others changed all that." He cocked his head. "You... you're a tiger too." His eyes widened. "How the fuck do I know that about you?" Before Seth could get a word out, Jamie stared at him. "Stupid question. I already know the answer to that. Something *else* I learned when I met Dellan and the others."

Jake leaned in close. "This is another half brother, Seth Miles." Jake gave Jamie a watery smile. "I can see we have a lot of catching up to do."

Seth tugged on his arm. "Not now. We're attracting attention. This family reunion will have to wait." Then he glanced over Jake's shoulder.

"Besides, we've run out of time. Those are the guards from the breeding block, and they're heading this way."

Jake squared his thin shoulders. "Here we go again." He glanced at Jamie. "We'll talk more later, okay?" He scowled. "Once I've recovered."

"Don't make them use the drug, okay?" Seth pleaded. "You're always so ill afterward. I know you want to resist, but—" He gestured to Jamie. "—we need you to be alert."

Jamie nodded. "I have so much to tell you, and something to give to you."

Jake managed a tired smile. "And what's that? The key to the compound? You've got a helicopter hidden away somewhere?"

Jamie took his hand and squeezed it. "I bring you hope."

CHAPTER THREE

HORVAN AND Saul stood in front of the world map on the wide screen.

"This is good," Horvan admitted. "Depressing but good." The blue dots were the two camps they'd raided and shut down, one in Montana, the other in Texas.

Only two. And no idea how many more there were.

The twenty-three red dots were the shifter schools still to be closed down. The two black dots were the ones they'd already raided, in Boston and Croatia.

A row of green pins stood in a clump at the corner of the board, waiting to be placed on the map.

Waiting to show the locations of the camps.

Saul snorted. "Depressing is right. What's the good in knowing where all these schools are if we're not in a position to do anything about them? We're not recruiting enough men."

"Patience. We've got a whole new load of wannabes coming for assessment and interviews on Friday."

Saul scowled. "At this rate, if they have a pulse, they're in."

Horvan knew better. Saul was ex-Delta Force, and he wouldn't accept anyone who couldn't live up to his own high standards.

He's the best man to vet the potential recruits.

Even though sharing command had been Horvan's idea, it had taken a while to get used to the reality. He and Saul would bust heads now and then, but they'd compromise in the end. And Saul was still one of the finest humans Horvan had had the privilege of knowing.

He was on a very short list.

Vic Ryder came into the office. "Aelryn wants a meeting. He's on Zoom."

Horvan grunted. "Well, God forbid we keep him waiting." He went over to his desk and stabbed the keyboard. He didn't really mind Aelryn's manner, but he had a feeling he knew what was coming.

He thinks we're losing this battle too.

Except it wasn't a battle—it was a war of epic, horrendous proportions.

24

Aelryn's long dark hair fell past his shoulders, and his glittering eyes focused on the three of them as Vic and Saul stood behind Horvan.

"Gentlemen, we need an army, and we need to be recruiting heavily now."

Horvan nodded. "We're on it."

Aelryn's brow furrowed. "But you're one team. We *all* need to be on board with this, and unfortunately there are those who don't believe that the situation is as grave as we're making it out to be."

"So not all the Fridans are singing from the same hymn sheet," Saul observed.

Aelryn's lips twitched. "Aptly put, Mr. Emory. But I do have an idea how we can… change their minds." He paused. "We need someone to go to the team leaders directly. Someone who's seen what the enemy is capable of." Another pause. "Someone they already know and respect, whose word they would believe."

Horvan smiled. "I agree. And that means there's one obvious candidate." He swiveled in his chair to stare at Vic. "Isn't there?"

"No." Saul moved to stand behind Vic, his hands on Vic's shoulders.

"You know it makes sense," Horvan reiterated.

"No."

"I agree with Horvan." Aelryn smiled. "And I think this is where I withdraw gracefully to let the three of you sort this out. Let me know of your decision." The screen closed.

"Not gonna change my mind, Horvan." Saul gripped Vic's muscular shoulders, and Vic grimaced.

"Hey, easy there, okay?"

"This isn't Saul the ex-Delta talking," Horvan remarked. "This is the Saul who doesn't want either of his mates out of his sight."

Saul released Vic and folded his arms. "Fine. You're right. Happy now? And it's *still* no."

"It's also not your place to make decisions for me," Vic said in a quiet voice. "So here's *my* opinion, even if you don't want to hear it. I agree with Aelryn and Horvan. It's the best option. I've worked and fought with most of the teams, so it makes perfect sense to send me. Not to put down Aelryn, but he's—"

"Royalty," Horvan interjected. "And some people don't like taking orders from a superior, even if he *is* shifter royalty, whereas if an oral historian known the world over shows up, one who's also a fighter, they'd be more inclined to take notice." Saul snorted, and Horvan rolled his eyes. "This is because I said 'oral,' isn't it? You're as bad as your mate."

"I hope you're not referring to me." Vic walked over to the map and stared at it. "They're everywhere, aren't they? They spread like a fucking cancer."

Horvan joined him. "Even more reason why we need to spread as fast as they do. They're the cancer. We're the cure."

"But we still don't know enough about the camps," Saul said as he stood at Vic's side. "How many there are, their locations.... God help us if there are as many camps as there are schools."

"I don't think so," Vic murmured. "At least I hope not. It doesn't help that we have absolutely no intel about them."

"Hey, we found two, didn't we?" Saul remonstrated.

"Sure, but that was because we got lucky," Vic fired back. "Yes, Hashtag located them by hacking into a US spy satellite, but he had an idea where to search both times. Since then, there's been nothing. And to find all the camps, we don't need luck—we need a miracle."

VIC STOOD at the kitchen countertop, vaguely pondering what he wanted for a snack.

Except I'm not really hungry.

He stared through the window toward the lake, where stacks of building materials had begun to congregate. Dellan had moved swiftly, and the plans for Vic, Saul, and Crank's home had been drawn up within a week of getting back to Homer Glen from Montana.

Our own place.

Not that Vic wasn't comfortable in Dellan's home—it was an amazing space—but privacy was a rare commodity, and having two alpha mates who were both incredibly loud when it came to sex had made them the butt of Roadkill's and Hashtag's jokes, which showed no signs of petering out.

Two strong arms enfolded him from behind, and Vic gave himself up to Saul's embrace, leaning against Saul's hard body.

Saul's lips brushed his ear. "You know we're gonna miss you."

Vic turned and looped his arms around Saul's neck. "I'm happy you said 'we.'" A warm mouth met his, and Vic surrendered to Saul's claiming kiss, his dick rising when Saul reached down to cup Vic's ass and squeeze it, pressing Vic to him, molding him against the rock wall of firm flesh that was Saul.

That was all it took to have Vic entertaining carnal thoughts that had no place in a kitchen.

Then again, the countertops were sturdily built and at exactly the right height, and it was Mrs. Landon's day off, so they weren't about to have her walk in on them....

Saul chuckled. *Now you're talking.*

Except the sexy hug took Vic's mind off on a tangent, and he knew what he had to say.

He pulled back and looked Saul in the eye. "One thing. When I go—"

"So you *are* going." Before Vic could confirm, Saul smiled. "It's okay. Aelryn and Horvan were right. You're the obvious choice. And I was thinking with the wrong head."

Vic bit back a smile. "Actually, it's *that* head that I want to talk about."

Saul leered. "Then let's find a flat surface to 'talk' on," he air-quoted. "A bed, a table, a wall...." He shrugged. "I'm easy."

Vic did his best to shove aside the image of Saul plowing into his ass while he was bent over the kitchen table, holding on for dear life.

"When I go," he persisted, "you and Crank—"

"We'll count the days. Our bed is gonna think it's done something wrong, with no action."

Vic nodded. "And *that's* what I want to talk to you about. While I'm gone, I want you and Crank to...."

Saul widened his eyes. "To fuck?"

Vic simply nodded once more.

"But... it's been the three of us ever since we got back."

Another nod. "Which is why I think this is a really good idea."

"But when Crank was here, and we were in Duluth, we didn't fuck. We waited till we were together."

"Of course we did. That was only right. It was our first time, after all. But this is different."

Saul's frown said otherwise.

"Oh, come on. You're both horndogs. You'd fuck three, four times a day if you could." He stared at Saul. "Well? Do I lie?"

"Okay, you got me there."

"So imagine how you'd be if I was gone for months at a time. I'm not saying it will *be* that long, but at this stage, I don't know."

Saul was very still. "Months? With no sex? I'd die."

Vic chuckled. "And I wouldn't want that on my conscience. So what I'm saying is, you and Crank should… get to know each other. Manhandle each other."

I like the sound of that. Crank's mental cackle was evil.

Saul laughed. *I knew you'd be listening in if sex was mentioned.*

Bullshit. You made sure I was listening. Boys? I think you need to get up here ASAP.

Vic groaned as an image filled his mind: Crank's long, thick cock, his hand gently tugging it.

What about your hole? Saul demanded. *Is that on the table too?*

You wanna fuck on the table? Fine by me, but if I fall and break something, on your head be it.

Vic snorted. *The only thing to break would be the table.*

Are we done talking now? Because I've got the lube out, and time's a-wastin'. Get your asses up to our room.

As they hurried out of the kitchen and up the stairs, Vic reasoned that there were some orders you obeyed without question.

IT MIGHT only have been a couple of months since Saul and Vic popped Crank's cherry—as far as sex with guys went—but he hoped the feeling he got every time they were close to each other would never grow old. It was more than the heady rush whenever he slid into Vic's tight little body, or the tingle that trickled down his spine when Saul's tongue danced over his hole, or even the three-way kisses that blew his freakin' mind. It was the rightness of it all, the balls to bones conviction that this was meant to be.

They were meant to be.

He'd lured them upstairs with the promise of his dick, but what he *really* wanted was the best sensation of all—the three of them, connected, locked into an ever-circling spiral of pleasure, desire, and a joy that made his heart want to sing.

After the fastest cleaning session in history, Saul knelt on the bed, Crank facing him, with Vic sandwiched between them. Crank loved the way Saul cupped Vic's jaw as they kissed, while Vic stroked Saul's girthy cock and Crank played with Vic's hole. The noises that poured from all of them stoked the fire already burning in him, but experiencing Saul's enjoyment of Vic's lips, tongue, and hand, reveling in Vic's pleasure when Crank slid slick fingers into his body....

That was hotter than any porn *ever*.

Love you both. Crank leaned in to demand a kiss from Saul, his dick pressed between Vic's asscheeks, the heat of him compelling Crank to take him, just fucking *take* him, the way he knew Vic loved, raw and primal and possessive.

Vic turned his head, his eyes glowing. *Love you too. So much.*

Our boy. Saul reached down to trace the stony line of Vic's shaft. *Our very hard boy.*

Vic chuckled. *And you know exactly what this boy wants.*

Saul met Crank's gaze, and they each moved back a little, allowing Vic to go onto all fours between them. Saul nudged the head of his cock between Vic's lips, moaning when Vic swallowed him to the root. Crank bent down, spread Vic's asscheeks, and began to lick a trail from hole to taint, breathing in the scent that heated his blood and pushed him to forget about rimming and get to the fucking part.

But Crank wanted to take the slow path. He wanted to enjoy his mates while he had the chance.

Saul moved his hands from Vic's shoulders to his chest, tweaking his nipples until Vic moaned around Saul's shaft, turning his face upward to gaze into Saul's eyes as Saul pushed his cock into Vic's cheek.

Fucking love it when you do that.

Vic pulled free. "Good, because I love watching your face while you're fucking mine." Then he went back to sucking Saul's dick, rocking a little as he took him deep.

Saul bent over him and pulled Vic's cheeks apart. *Now, Crank. Make him moan.*

Crank slicked up his shaft, kissed Vic's hole with the head of his cock, and pushed home.

Oh God, yeah. Like that. Vic rocked faster, shuttling between Saul's dick and Crank's thick shaft, and the noises that fell from his lips, combined with the sensations that coursed through his body, almost brought Crank to the edge.

Not yet. Saul leaned toward Crank, who met him halfway, and they kissed, slow, sensual kisses that were the perfect accompaniment to Crank's languid thrusts. Saul's and Crank's foreheads met as they fucked Vic, both of them spearing him with their cocks.

Saul shuddered. *Fuck, that mouth....*

That raised a chuckle from Crank. *I'd love to.* He pulled free of Vic's tight hole. *Turn around, love.*

Vic rose to his knees and turned, but instead of resuming his sucking, he held Crank's face between his hands. *Love. I'll never get tired of hearing that.*

Crank couldn't resist the siren call of Vic's lips, and he took Vic's mouth in a bruising kiss, exploring him with his tongue. Saul joined them, and three mouths met in a tangle of lips, all of them feeding each other's desire. Then Vic went down onto his elbows, and Crank filled that hot wet mouth with as much of his dick as Vic could take, his lips stretched wide around it.

Saul reached over to raise Vic's leg, one foot flat to the mattress, and slid into Vic, going deep as he stroked Vic's rigid shaft.

Crank let it all wash over him: Saul's unfettered joy as he filled Vic over and over again; Vic's explosion of pleasure as he was both fucked and stroked; and their mingled voices in Crank's head, both of them drowning his own ecstatic internal hollers. He leaned on Vic's shoulders, both arms pressing Vic into the mattress, hips pumping as he fucked Vic's mouth.

Vic pulled back with a splutter. *I want to ride.*

Crank had to laugh at the speed with which Saul dropped onto his back, his hand around the base of his shaft, holding it steady. *All aboard.*

Vic straddled Saul's hips and reached back to guide Saul's cock to his hole, impaling himself. Crank loved to watch Vic's body swallow that wide shaft.

His dick wasn't done, however.

Lean back, he demanded. *Show us how flexible you really are.*

Vic laughed and arched his back, almost into a crab position. He held on to Saul's legs as Crank inched his cock into Vic's mouth, Saul tugging on Vic's shaft while he thrust into that glorious ass.

Crank lowered Vic's head to the mattress. *You okay like that?*

Vic's eyes gleamed. *Bring it on.*

Crank straddled Vic's head and thrust into his mouth, hips bucking as he face-fucked Vic, Saul's hands moving leisurely over Vic's thighs, his own thrusts gathering speed.

The graceful arch of Vic's back and the lure of that mouth proved too much for Crank to ignore, and he slid his cock free to bend down and meet Vic's lips in an upside-down kiss. Saul held Vic's hands, and the kiss continued.

Crank didn't want this to end.

Saul stuffed pillows under his head. *Suck me off, please. I want to come in your mouth.*

Vic was on his front in a heartbeat, lying between Saul's legs as he took Saul's cock once more, and Crank mounted Vic, driving his shaft deep, sensing his orgasm wasn't far off. He stared into Saul's eyes as he thrust, and suddenly all three of them were locked into a battle to stave off their impending climaxes.

Saul nodded. *Let go. Push him over the edge. Let him feel that throb he loves. Let me feel it too.*

Crank groaned as Vic tightened his internal muscles around Crank's dick, and that was all it took to have him pulse into Vic's hole, his own body trembling as he came. Saul's eyes widened and Crank relished Vic's moan of pleasure as Saul filled his mouth. Then Crank slid his hand between Vic's legs, squeezing his balls and tugging on his cock.

Vic's muffled groan as he shot onto the comforter was the release of tension Crank had been waiting for.

They ended as they always did, Vic lying between them, his leg hooked over Saul's thigh, his arm up and back around Crank's neck as they kissed. Both Crank and Saul had their hand on Vic's ass, their fingers meeting at Vic's hole where Crank's come trickled and Saul pushed it back into him.

Crank pressed his lips to Vic's neck. *Fucking beautiful.*

Vic turned to smile at him. *More like beautiful fucking.*

Saul laughed. *You're both wrong. Beautiful fuckers.* He claimed Vic's mouth once more before they moved into a lingering three-way kiss. *I fucking love that smell.*

Crank arched his eyebrows. "You talking about my sweat? 'Cause you can shove your face into my pits if you like. Don't bother me none."

Saul chuckled. "I think it's a mates thing. Whenever I'm around you, there's this scent. A mix of spicy and sweet. And it's only you two."

Vic smiled. "I smell it too. So yeah, it has to be a mates thing."

Crank's heart rate slowly returned to its normal rhythm as he stroked Vic's body, dragging his fingers through the sheen of sweat that covered him, appreciating the way Saul's damp chest glowed in the lamplight. He sniffed, and a sweet scent filled his nostrils.

"Oh wow. I never noticed that until now." Crank liked it. Liked it a lot.

"Kiss me again, both of you," Vic demanded.

Crank would spend all fucking day kissing his mates if he had the chance.

"You're sure about this?" Saul said at last.

Crank didn't have to ask what *this* was; he'd heard the whole conversation.

"Are we talking about Vic going on this mission, or you and me fucking without him?"

Vic smiled. "While the shark's away, the humans play. Besides, you might work out some new tricks for when I get back."

Saul's chuckle was positively evil.

"Now you've gone and done it. We'll have to come up with new ways to wear you out."

Crank pressed his chest to Vic's back. "Be safe, okay?" He couldn't contemplate losing either of them. Not now.

Vic kissed him, then Saul. "I will, I promise. Besides, I'm visiting Fridan groups. I'll be perfectly safe."

Even with his limited experience so far, Crank knew it was foolish to say such things.

No one knows what lies around the corner.

CHAPTER FOUR

MILO KEPPLER'S well-ordered, comfortable world was starting to fray at the edges, and he couldn't tell a soul about it, because *Duh.*

People who did that suddenly disappeared, and Milo wasn't about to join the ranks of the Vanished. A year ago he hadn't even realized such a thing could happen. Not that he was one hundred percent sure, but....

There were too many such occurrences to ignore anymore.

I thought I knew my place in the vast scheme of things.

He'd been raised to believe shifters were the superior race. That humans were meant to serve them. That shifters were at the top of the evolutionary ladder, and one day humans would be in their rightful—inferior—place.

Now? He wasn't so sure.

Milo's childhood had been idyllic. The shifter school he'd attended had provided him with fertile soil in which to grow and develop. His athletic prowess had been applauded, his intelligence celebrated. When he reached the age of eighteen, his parents told him about the origins of shifters. Milo's pride knew no bounds when his lineage revealed him to be a direct descendant of Ansger. And when he'd announced that he wanted to join the Geran military, his parents had supported him 100 percent. Joining the human military was out of the question. Physical exams and blood testing made that an impossibility unless someone in the command chain was also a shifter so physical exams could be doctored. Which was easier than anyone might think.

Shifters were *everywhere.*

He could still hear his parents' words.

You can do whatever you set your mind to. You can excel at everything. You are born to lead.

Except once the first cracks appeared in Milo's world, he began to have doubts about the future he was working toward.

Cracks never heal of their own accord. They always widen.

It was during military training that he'd first learned not all shifters are created equal. Gerans were the purebloods. He listened to the stories about

33

the Fridans: How they were inherently weaker because they chose to mate with humans; how they would fail militarily because they were all pacifists at heart.

How Gerans were the elite of the shifter universe.

And now that he knew all this, Milo realized the signs were obvious. He could spot a Fridan with ease. They acted differently, for one thing, though he couldn't pinpoint exactly what that difference was. They lacked the hard edge that defined every Geran of Milo's acquaintance. And rounding up Fridan dissenters to house them in camps had been a logical route. They could still be useful, after all. They could breed to provide foot soldiers, to increase numbers. Any resultant offspring *not* destined to be used in the battles to come were adopted by Geran couples and sent to the same kind of school Milo had attended, to receive an education at the highest level, to be nurtured, cared for, cherished.

They should be grateful. We've given them a future.

Except there were other uglier rumors circulating, rumors that Milo tried to ignore. Ones that said Fridan shifters were being killed.

That had to be propaganda, spread to sow dissent. Shifters did not kill other shifters. The military was there to protect all shifters, regardless which side they'd chosen.

By the age of twenty-seven, Milo had served in most of the camps, rising through the ranks, proving himself time and time again to be a soldier his ancestor would have been proud of. Four months ago, he joined the security force at his present camp, in charge of guarding the inmates. It wasn't long before he was promoted to the position of Head of Compound Security, overseeing the arrival of new shifters and making sure they knew their place, that no one stepped out of line. It wasn't an onerous task— whatever had brought them to the compound had also knocked the fight right out of them. Another indicator of Fridan weakness.

Then the ugliest rumors of all began circulating.

A shifter school in Boston had been raided. That the Fridans would dare to do something so heinous to children was hardly a surprise. It *was* a Fridan force, right? What else did anyone expect of them?

What rocked Milo to his core was what was whispered—that the Gerans in charge of the school had abandoned more than nine hundred kids. Just left them to their fate at the hands of the Fridans.

It had to be a lie, spread no doubt by Fridan sympathizers. It might even have been a thought planted in his head by some of the inmates, the two who were taken daily to the experimental block.

The ones Milo and every soldier under his command were ordered to take extreme care around. The word bandied about was mind control, and that was enough to send a shiver down Milo's spine.

Are there many more like them out there?

Gods, he hoped not.

The terrible news that a camp in Montana had been under siege was seen as yet more confirmation that the Gerans were on the side of truth. Why else would the Fridans attack them?

More news filtered through, and it seemed the Gerans were indeed under attack. Another camp no longer existed, this one in Texas. When rumors that a second school had been targeted, this time in Croatia, and that yet more children had been left—deserted—Milo clung to his belief that it was still lies.

But what if it isn't?

He couldn't speak of this to anyone; he wasn't stupid. But the idea haunted him that hundreds of children could be so easily....

Dumped.

Discarded.

Forgotten.

Whichever way Milo looked at it, that wasn't right.

Then a new rumor started to circulate, one that increased the whispering in dark corners.

Some of the Fridans were claiming to have mates.

The first time Milo heard that fairy tale, he wanted to laugh out loud. *Mates? For fuck's sake.* There was no such thing. The idea that there were people fated to be together, *joined* somehow? Not only physically but spiritually?

Preposterous.

The Fridans must think we're really stupid to fall for that.

But even if it *was* a blatant lie, there was something seductive, even comforting, about the idea that there was someone out there made for Milo, someone who was a perfect fit. He'd had little luck with girlfriends. Dating a guy in the military made for an uncertain future, and what with his shifts, the remoteness of his detail.... Milo wasn't a hookup kinda guy, but that was all there seemed to be on offer.

Maybe that was why the thought of having a mate appealed to him. That didn't make it true.

Once his mind started turning over the rumors, he couldn't stop it. Insidious thoughts snuck into his dreams. He watched the inmates, searching for anything that might provide him with answers. Milo was always ready to act when he saw any signs of insurrection, escape planning, inmates congregating where they shouldn't. Two or three attracted his attention—one in particular—and he resolved to keep a close eye on them.

His resolution shattered with the arrival of Jana.

"SIR? A new batch of inmates has arrived," Coleman informed him. He handed Milo the tablet. "Thirty of them. They're being processed right now."

"Great. Let me know when they're done." Milo had a little speech he reserved for new arrivals. Mostly it was a warning.

Do as you're told and there'll be no problems.

Mess with us and we will mess you up.

Then he'd point to the towers around the perimeter, each topped with a lookout and equipped with guns. *You see those guards up there? If none of my men down here spot you trying to escape, be sure* they *will, and they* will *shoot you dead.*

He skimmed through the details of the newbies, searching for anything out of the ordinary. None of the names were accompanied by the logo of a hand with an eye across the palm—the icon designated for those rare shifters who possessed psychic ability. Because now the Gerans knew such shifters existed, you'd better believe they were searching for more of them.

A resource with unlimited potential, waiting to be tapped.

Milo made his rounds, walking the perimeter of the compound, his eyes ever watchful, his hand resting on his rifle, ready to react to any sign of danger. Not from the inmates, who were already beaten down when they arrived, but from the outside.

If the Fridans really have taken two camps already this year, then we need to be ready for any eventuality.

No one higher up had said as much—in writing, at any rate—but the word was out.

Be extra vigilant.

His earpiece burst into life. "Ready when you are, sir."

Milo headed for the reeducation center, where the new arrivals were always taken after processing. Coleman and three other guards stood at the back of the main room, where inmates sat at tables, heads bowed, silent as the grave.

He walked to the front and faced them. The faces before him all seemed the same—tired, fearful, devoid of hope. That made his job easier.

He cleared his throat and launched into his speech. When he got to the part where he told them this was not some kind of extermination camp, he couldn't miss their relieved expressions. He scanned each row of tables, searching for any potential troublemakers, but he found—

One face stopped him dead in his tracks.

Milo froze. *What the fuck?* He stood rooted to the spot, unable to move.

She was maybe in her midtwenties, with long reddish-brown hair, tied back. She wasn't looking at him, her gaze lowered.

Milo couldn't take his eyes off her, and he had no idea why. There was nothing out of the ordinary about her. Had they met before? He searched his memories and came to an unsatisfying conclusion.

I don't know her.

Then why did some sense keep on insisting that he did?

He consulted his tablet, scrolling through until he found her. Jana Guzek, age twenty-four, originally from New Hampshire. He had to smile when he saw what kind of shifter she was. He didn't think the Geran military would have much use for an otter.

Scrolling further, he noted this was her first internment.

He still couldn't tear his gaze away from her. If anything, the feeling of being unable to look away from her was intensifying.

Move. Move now, *goddammit.*

Milo walked slowly along each row, making sure to make eye contact with every inmate, his heartbeat racing as he drew closer to her. When he reached Jana, Milo stood in front of her, waiting for her to raise her chin.

To see him.

The need for her to meet his gaze consumed him to the point of dizziness. Jana's chin dipped toward her chest, but Milo wasn't going to move on until he'd seen her eyes. Then her breathing hitched, and he froze once more.

Whatever the fuck was going on, she felt it too.

The room was silent, and he knew he was under scrutiny. He had to move on.

Milo continued along the rows before making his way to the front again.

"Some of the buildings in the compound are out of bounds to inmates. Get too close and—" He tapped his rifle. He didn't need to say more. The implication was obvious. "Now you'll be taken to your block. That's where you'll eat, sleep, and wash. When the weather permits, you can go outside." He smiled. "Fresh air is good for you, after all." He paused. "On occasions, some of you will also be taken to the breeding block. Don't try to resist. If you do that, we have the capability to force you to comply, but it's better for you if you simply follow instructions."

One of the guards snickered. "Besides, why would you want to resist that? Only chance you're gonna get to—"

Milo glared at him, and the guard clammed up.

I'll deal with him later.

He returned his attention to the rows of inmates, doing his damnedest not to stare in Jana's direction, but it was as if he was caught up in a web of invisible threads, their ends wrapped around her fingers, and she was tugging on them, pulling him toward her.

Who the fuck are you? What *are you?*

This was getting dangerous.

Milo straightened. "Okay, that's all. If you obey the rules, your time here will run smoothly. You know what to expect if you don't." He nodded to Coleman, who barked out instructions, and the inmates stood, walking in quiet lines toward the door. Milo watched them file out, his heartbeat returning to its normal rhythm.

When the room was empty, Coleman approached him. Before Milo could say a word, Coleman sighed. "You want Hughes up on a charge? He should've kept his fat mouth shut. Again."

"He knows the rules. No one talks to them except you or me. So yes, put him on a charge. And warn him what will happen the next time." Milo smiled. "Because unless he's a polar bear shifter, his nuts will freeze off in a heartbeat up there. Tell him if he doesn't believe that to come see me. I should know, after all. I was stationed there."

He didn't need to expound on *there*. Everyone knew.

"I'll remind him there are far worse compounds to be sent to." Coleman cocked his head to one side. "Are you okay, sir? You seemed a little distracted."

Milo huffed. "I'm overdue for some leave. That must be it." Like about three months overdue. "I need to find someplace warm, preferably near an ocean, where I can unwind for a week or two."

Coleman chuckled. "A week? Yeah, right. My last leave lasted three days."

Milo patted his arm. "The benefits of rank, Coleman. Work your way up to captain and you too can get to enjoy them." He walked out of the room, Coleman's wry chuckle following him.

Outside, heavy clouds had blotted out the sun, and the air had grown chill. Milo strolled across the compound, taking his time.

Searching for her.

Don't. Don't.

The voice of reason was drowned out by another voice, one that clamored for him to find her. Milo scanned the inmates, searching for that reddish-brown hair, the short, slim figure.

And there she was, standing way too close to the perimeter fence.

He hurried over to her, his heart hammering. "You need to move away from there," he called out as he got closer. "See the white line on the ground? Don't cross it again."

Except what he wanted to do was scream at her that she could get shot if she strayed too far.

She turned, and Milo got his first glimpse of warm green eyes that went perfectly with her creamy complexion. Jana stared at him, her chest rising and falling, her breathing as labored as his own.

"Who are you?" she whispered.

He frowned. "I'm Captain Milo Keppler. I just spoke to you all, remember?"

Jana shook her head. "That part I know. What I mean is who are you to *me*?" She shivered. "Okay, this is weird. It's… it's as if I *know* you somehow, but I've never seen you before in my life."

The sun chose that moment to come out from behind the clouds, bathing her features, making her face glow. And something deep inside Milo burst into life, a warmth he'd never known that crawled through him, then *rushed* through him, leaving his skin tingling and his heart pounding.

Holy fuck. Jana Guzek, who the hell are *you?*

CHAPTER FIVE

VIC ZIPPED his bag, then unzipped it again for one last check. He'd gotten his packing down to a fine art after all these years, and he reasoned that if he forgot something, he'd simply buy it.

Which was why Saul teased him—frequently—about the cabinet under the sink in the bathroom, bulging with spare toiletries.

The magnitude of his mission probably accounted for his lack of sleep the previous night. So much was riding on its success. Aelryn had been correct: This wasn't a goal that could be achieved with calls, Zoom meetings, and emails.

They need to know what we're facing.

They need to understand that we have to work together on this.

No pressure, then.

Saul and Crank came into the bedroom. Saul peered at the bag. "All done? You've got everything?"

He chuckled. "Yes, Dad."

Saul kissed his neck. "I still say 'Yes, Daddy' sounds better." He tilted Vic's chin to kiss him, and Crank moved behind him, sandwiching him between them.

Vic closed his eyes and lost himself in the warmth emanating from his mates—mental as well as physical. "I'm going to miss this."

Saul brushed his fingers through Vic's hair. "I know we won't be able to hear you from across the US, but that doesn't change the fact that we love you."

"What he said," Crank murmured.

Vic let out a sigh. "It was bad enough when I had to leave Saul. This?"

Crank kissed his shoulder. "I know. But think of it this way—you get twice the welcome when you come home."

"What he said," Saul added with a smile.

It was no good. Vic had to make a move or he'd stay all day in their arms. He wriggled free of their embrace. "I'll call you tonight from San Francisco."

"Don't call *too* late, will you?" Crank admonished. "Time zones and beauty sleep, remember?"

Vic chuckled. "Neither of you need that."

Crank gave him another kiss. "You know how to make a guy feel good, don't you?"

Saul sat on the bed. "You're gonna put in a lot of miles on this one. You know that, right?"

Vic knew all right. "Which is why I thought we'd spend more time together before I had to leave. Where *were* you two all day?"

"With Hashtag," Crank told him. "We had something that needed doing."

He arched his eyebrows. "Something more important than the three of us in bed?"

"Actually? Yes." Saul reached into his jeans pocket and withdrew a USB drive. He held it out to Vic.

"What's this?"

"We figured you needed an audio-visual aid for your meetings. Something to show those team leaders exactly what we're facing."

"So Saul and I, with Hashtag's help, put this together."

Saul snorted. "If that doesn't convince them, nothing will."

"It has to convince them," Crank remonstrated. "Because if it doesn't, then we've lost."

As if Vic wasn't already feeling the pressure.

He took the drive. "Thank you."

"I think you'd better watch it first, before you show it to anyone." Crank's grave expression sent a frisson of disquiet trickling through him. "Not now—when you get to California."

"Why? There are no surprises in here, are there?"

Saul hesitated before replying. "No, but...."

"I don't think you wanna be watching this in a room full of military types, wiping fucking tears from your eyes, okay? Forewarned is forearmed."

"At least if you know what to expect, you can keep a lid on your emotions," Saul suggested.

Vic stared at the small piece of hardware. "You've got me curious, I must admit."

"Put it away. Now."

41

That note of steel in Saul's voice sent a shiver sliding down Vic's spine. Disconcertingly, his dick reacted too.

Crank sniffed, and Vic had to smile. "You may be human, but I swear, you're developing shifter characteristics every day."

Crank pulled Vic into his arms. "Video calls are gonna feature heavily while you're away."

Saul stood and joined them. "Yeah, you can jerk off while you watch me fuck Crank." He paused. "You can also watch while he plays with my ass."

Vic gaped, amused to see the same reaction from Crank. "What?"

Saul chuckled. "I said I wanted to try bottoming, didn't I? So I figure Crank can show me what I've been missing." He cupped Crank's chin. "But you don't get to fuck me until Vic comes home, okay?"

Crank's eyes gleamed and his lower lip wobbled. "How long did you say you'd be away?"

Vic laughed. He slipped the drive into a zipped pocket inside his messenger bag, then glanced at the clock on the nightstand. "I'd better go."

"I'll take you to the airport," Saul told him.

"*We'll* take him." Crank grinned. "Think of the entertainment value when both of us give him a goodbye kiss before he goes through security."

VIC DROPPED his bag onto the luggage rack before checking his room out. He sighed at the sight of a king-size bed.

How did that song go? Something about a bed being too big without you?

Vic scanned the QR code to see the in-room dining menu and selected a pizza. It was the safest bet. Then he unzipped his bag and removed his toiletries.

I'll take a look at the drive after dinner.

He called Crank. "Okay, I'm here. Dinner's on its way." He huffed. "Pizza. It'll do."

"Good. Call us when you've eaten." Crank cocked his head. "You haven't watched it yet."

"How did you…?" Vic frowned. "You're worrying me."

Saul's head appeared in the frame. "We didn't pull any punches. We thought long and hard about what to include, and Hashtag came up with a few more suggestions."

"There's too much riding on this to pussyfoot around." Crank's brow furrowed.

"We think this'll have the desired impact." Saul's kind smile was a welcome easing of the tension creeping through Vic. "Call us when you've eaten. And enjoy the pizza." He hung up.

The messenger bag on the desk seemed to call to Vic, and he set up the laptop. The temptation to boot it up was enormous.

What on earth have you put together, guys?

The knock at the door startled him. He dove off the bed and grabbed the bills he'd left on the nightstand. After tipping the server, he reinstalled himself, pillows stuffed behind his back as he ate and watched the news, trying not to peek at the laptop.

Fat chance.

Vic ate half the pizza, and that was about all he could manage. He grabbed the laptop, fired it up, stuck the drive into the slot, clicked on the single file on it, and sat back.

Ten minutes later, tears streamed down his face, blurring his vision as he reached for his phone.

Saul appeared, Crank joining him a moment later. Saul's eyes were warm. "You've watched it, haven't you?"

Vic rolled his eyes. "You think I'd cry ugly tears over a disappointing pizza?" He swiped his fingers over his damp cheeks.

"It should have the desired effect," Saul remarked.

"You were right," Vic told him. "If that doesn't convince them, nothing will." He shook his head. "You pulled this off in less than a day? I'm impressed."

"Hashtag deserves all the praise. I'd never tell him—his head is big enough—but I have to admit, he's a fucking genius." Crank stared at him. "You seem tired. When is your meeting tomorrow?"

"Ten."

"Do you want to sleep? Because I can always come up with an alternative." Saul's eyes sparkled.

Vic laughed. "What did you have in mind?"

"Well, you're wearing too many clothes for what *I* have planned."

Vic shucked off his clothing in a heartbeat, his cock already rising at the sight of his mates, who undressed each other on the screen. He set the laptop on the mattress between his legs, settling back against the mountain of pillows, legs spread.

Crank knelt on the bed, knees wide, facing the camera, his hand on his shaft, leisurely working it. "Our boy is hard for us."

"Always," Vic told him, tugging on his dick.

Saul kissed Crank, a hard kiss that spoke of need. "How do you want me?"

Crank blinked. "That depends. Are we—"

"We are," Saul confirmed.

Crank lurched toward the nightstand and grabbed the bottle of lube. "Then we're gonna need this."

Vic's heartbeat quickened. "Make it a good show, guys."

"No internal messages tonight. We want you to hear everything. Right?"

Saul nodded. "We want you to feel included in this."

And Vic did, relishing every moan that tumbled from Saul's lips as Crank slid slick fingers into his hole, every groan when Crank's tongue teased his pucker. He loved the way Saul's eyes rolled back when Crank fucked him with his fingers and sucked his cock. Vic pulled on his own dick in time with Crank, until his breathing was in synch with theirs.

Saul gaped at the small bright pink butt plug. "That's not even gonna tickle," he retorted.

"It'll feel bigger than it looks," Crank assured him. "And you should be grateful I'm working you up to my dick. First thing *I* took up the ass was your humongous cock." Crank grinned. "I think you're getting off lightly."

Vic tugged harder as Crank eased the plug into Saul's ass, his moan matching Saul's as he got a front row seat. Crank brought his phone close enough that Vic could see Saul's hole clinging to the silicone toy.

"Jesus, what did you just do?" Saul yelled.

Crank laughed. "I guarantee your prostate never felt that good during your physical. Want me to stop?"

Saul reared his head up from the bed. "Don't you fucking dare." Then he dropped onto his back, his hand working his shaft. "Keep going. I want Vic to see me come."

Vic's breathing grew labored as he watched Crank push Saul closer to the edge, and when Saul came with a cry, Vic shot hard.

Watching Crank kiss their mate was beautiful.

Saul appeared wiped out. "Oh my fucking God." Then he rolled onto his front and glared at the camera. "You are in *such* trouble when you get your ass back here."

"Me? What did I do? I'm two thousand miles away."

"How come you never told me it felt this fucking good? Talk about missing out."

"Maybe that's why *I'm* here. Ever think of that?" Crank leaned over and kissed him. "By the way... your ass feels amazing. Can't wait to slide my dick all the way home."

"And you still have to wait until *he's* all the way home." Saul gazed at the camera. "Right, Vic?"

"Right."

Vic hoped his mission wouldn't be too long.

Home was Saul and Crank.

VIC WAITED as one by one, the team leaders walked into the hotel room he'd booked for the meeting. Watched as they helped themselves to coffee. Noted the lack of apprehension.

I'm about to light a fuse.

He hoped.

Vic had known what to expect. Aelryn had briefed him on each of the seven leaders. The last thing he'd said before signing off the video call had prepared Vic for the scene before him.

"They don't believe the Gerans are a threat. They're content to protect shifters, defend them.... But as for the idea that an army is being amassed? They believe it's nothing but my overactive imagination.'" Aelryn had looked Vic in the eye. "You have to convince them."

Vic scanned the faces of the five men and two women around the table. There was no hostility toward him, only an overwhelming feeling that he was wasting their time, that they had better places to be.

This is not going to be an easy ride.

Aelryn had indicated which of the leaders would be the hardest to convince, so it was no surprise that Torben Welland was the first to break the silence.

"Why are we here, Mr. Ryder? Not that I'm unimpressed. You've succeeded in bringing together every leader stationed in California, which is no mean feat." His eyes glinted. "I couldn't even manage to bring *that* off."

Vic straightened in his chair. "You're here because we're going to mount an offensive that will involve every Fridan group, not only in the US, but all over the world. You are the first group to be informed."

Stacey Miller frowned. "An offensive? To do what, exactly?"

Vic didn't break eye contact. "To stop the Gerans."

The shocked silence that followed his words was palpable.

Welland arched his eyebrows. "I think you've been listening to too many rumors. Heaven knows there are enough of those out there."

"To stop the Gerans from doing what?" Kyle Danes stared at him. "Look, Aelryn might be a direct descendant of Ansfrid, but that doesn't mean he knows everything. And right now he's taking a couple of incidents and exaggerating their importance out of all proportion."

Vic took a deep breath. "Exaggerating? It's time you all opened your eyes and learned the truth."

Welland's gaze grew flinty. "You may be one of the few oral historians in existence, but that does *not* give you the right to—"

He lurched to his feet. "I'm going to show you what gives me the right." He picked up the remote and aimed it at the ceiling-suspended projector. The white screen he'd had set up was filled with an image that made his stomach clench.

It was Saul in his hospital bed, the sheets drawn back to reveal his terrible wounds.

Judging by the gasps that filled the air, his guests found it as shocking.

Vic paused the video. "This is Saul Emory. Ex-Delta. A few months ago he was involved in a mission to liberate a shifter school in Boston. He was sent to infiltrate the staff to search for information but was captured by the enemy."

"I wasn't aware the Gerans were our enemy." The quiet utterance came from Ben Simmons.

Then you're in for a shock.

"What happened to him?" Rachel Yates was pale.

"I'll let him tell you." Vic clicked the remote, and the next frame revealed Saul sitting in a chair. The time stamp showed it had been filmed the previous day.

Saul stared directly into the camera. "I looked a mess, didn't I? They wanted me to give them access to the shifter archives, which they assumed I could do, seeing as I was in a relationship with Vic Ryder."

Vic's stomach roiled.

"And did he?" Welland demanded.

Vic paused the video and rolled his eyes. "You think he'd have gotten into that state if he'd cooperated?" Then he reconsidered. "You need to understand something. These guys? They're not nice, and they don't play by the rules. Saul knew if he *did* give them the information, they'd have killed him outright." He clicked to continue, not giving a shit if he'd riled Welland.

The guy needed a good shake-up. They all did.

"I didn't give them what they wanted," Saul said, "so they decided to torture me before they finished me off. I was rescued before they could achieve that particular goal. But the torture isn't the shocking part."

Vic's heart pounded, and his hands were like ice.

"My wounds were inflicted by what appeared to be a ten-year-old boy—a shifter. Except I knew he couldn't be more than one year old. The Gerans had engineered him to be a weapon. His hands became lethal claws that delivered a toxin in such concentrated amounts that I'm lucky to be here right now."

Vic stopped the video when Miller made a strangled noise. His heart went out to her. "I know," he said quietly. "It's unthinkable, isn't it? That someone would tinker with RNA sequencing to do this. That someone would even *consider* doing this." He pressed Play, and a new screen appeared. It was a video of Doc Tranter answering Hashtag's questions about how the Gerans might have achieved such a heinous result.

"I know him," Welland murmured. "Military medic, isn't he? We've met a few times." He met Vic's gaze. "You just got my undivided attention."

If seeing Saul hadn't done that, then Welland was an ass.

Then the video moved on to show the huge hall at the Boston school, with hundreds of students sitting there, most of them wearing the same stunned expression.

"Who are they? And where is this?" Niall Coates leaned forward, his eyes wide. "Is that this school in Boston I've been hearing rumors about?"

Vic nodded, pausing the video. "Unfortunately it's no rumor. These kids are all shifters. Their teachers taught them that humans were the lowest of the low, that shifters were born to dominate." He glanced at the leaders. "And then they were abandoned, more than nine hundred of them. Most of their parents refused to take them back, as many of the kids had been adopted. And the scale of these adoptions is staggering. Enough children to fill twenty-five schools, all over the world."

"What happened to them?" Danes asked, his voice quavering.

"Aelryn's team stepped in and took over. As of now every child with nowhere to go has found a new home and is being cared for. Loved. And where did these children come from?" He clicked Play again, and there was Dellan, talking about his more than one year in incarceration, how they'd used a drug to force him to shift, to mate with other shifters, and how his company had been used—in his absence—to develop and manufacture that drug in vast quantities.

"What could the Gerans hope to achieve with this drug? Why would they force shifters to mate?" Welland sounded shell-shocked.

Before Vic could share his suspicions, Miller let out a low cry.

"Oh Gods. They're breeding an army, aren't they?"

Vic sighed. "That was our conclusion too."

It seemed they were finally on the same page.

There were shots of the camp in Bozeman, the terrible conditions in which Horvan's team had found those left there by the Gerans. Hashtag explained in a voice-over how he'd found the camp, and that it had been hidden by manipulating images.

The faces of the inmates told a story all on their own, but Hashtag had included headgear video footage from when Crank had questioned those soldiers who'd been captured. Their words left no doubt as to their beliefs.

Their utter disdain for humans.

Vic stopped the video and turned to face the table.

The silence was oppressive.

Yates choked back tears. "Oh my God. That was...."

"Horrific?" Vic suggested. "I'd agree with that analysis too. Saul Emory is my mate. Well, one of them."

Welland froze. "Mates? I thought that was another rumor."

"Aelryn has found one of his two mates."

Danes's breathing hitched. "Two?"

Vic nodded. "I have two mates—and they're both human. The guy questioning the soldiers? He's one of them. And before you ask, no, I have no idea how this works. I simply accept it." He paused. "So… now you know what we're up against. The kind of shifters we're up against. That only leaves one question. Will you be a part of the coalition?"

One by one, the leaders gazed at Welland.

At last he spoke. "After seeing that? Of course."

Vic wanted to sag with relief, until he realized it was only one meeting down and many more to go.

"You were right." Yates's voice was flat. "We needed to know this. I assume you're meeting with leaders all over the world to share the same message."

"That's the plan." One that daunted him, if Vic thought about it for too long.

"Then we'll spread the word. Hopefully that will pave the way for you." She flushed. "It might also eliminate the kind of reaction you got from us."

Vic figured that was as close to an apology as he was going to get. He couldn't have hoped for a better outcome, however, and he knew he had Saul, Crank, and Hashtag to thank for it.

Way to go, boys. He'd find a way to show his appreciation to his mates when he got home. He smiled to himself. That was a no-brainer. As for Hashtag? *Maybe we should see about getting him laid.*

Vic removed the drive. "Thank you for coming. And I'd say I was sorry for putting a dent in your day, but I'm not."

"Dent or not, this has been a wake-up call." Welland gestured to the USB drive. "Could I have a copy of that presentation?"

"Certainly."

Welland shuddered. "I don't know about the rest of you, but I need a drink after that. And I don't care what time of day it is."

Vic liked the idea, but he had a long way to go.

"I'll pass on the drink. I've got a flight to catch."

And two mates to thank.

CHAPTER SIX

THERE COULD only be one explanation for the turmoil Milo had been through the last three days.

He was losing his mind.

Disturbed sleep, heightened senses, lack of appetite.... He couldn't account for any of it, but that didn't mean he couldn't nail down the moment it had all started—the day Jana arrived at the camp.

He'd had glimpses of her on and off, but they hadn't exchanged words. That didn't seem to matter: Each glimpse set off a reaction inside him, something akin to a nuclear explosion. Okay, it wasn't *that* severe, but Milo's world lurched off balance every time she was near. She had a scent like nothing he'd ever smelled before. What made it worse was that he didn't even have to be near her—it wafted across the compound, into his nostrils, and all the way to his dick. He put that down to going far too long without sex, but he'd never experienced attraction like it.

Jana filled his head, messed up his senses, and drove him to distraction.
I need to talk to the medics.

Except that was *not* going to happen. Such behavior would be seen as a sign of weakness, and weakness was not tolerated, especially in someone of his rank.

Then it hit him.
Maybe she *holds the key to all this.*

It was a long shot, but he'd try anything to get his life back on an even keel.

Milo strode into the administration block. The main office contained six desks, but what dominated the room were the walls covered with images of the inmates, each one with their name, system number, and date of arrival.

One hundred fifty faces took up a lot of space.

Off-duty soldiers used the office as an unofficial recreation lounge. There was no provision for such a thing, which said a lot about the way the camp functioned. Someone had set up a tablet connected to a pair of speakers, and music filtered through the air, low and unobtrusive, because heaven forbid one of the Geran leaders should decide to put in an appearance and take exception to it.

Milo hadn't witnessed any such visits for about three months. The last one had coincided with the arrival of the two inmates whose presence had caused no end of speculation, especially about what went on in the experimental block.

Someone high up was *very* interested in them.

Milo remembered seeing them at the Bozeman camp before he'd taken up his present post. According to their files, they were father and son. Not long after Milo's arrival, the pair were also transferred. What came to mind was the scrawny individual who'd remained at the camp. Milo had an idea there'd been something going on between the two young men.

The soldiers stiffened as Milo walked over to the wall of images, and he waved his hand.

"Pretend I'm not here. And I'm not about to tell you to kill the music, okay?"

He'd been in their position once upon a time, and he would never forget that.

"Thank you, sir." The men relaxed, and the chatting recommenced.

He scanned the faces that were listed alphabetically, searching for Jana. When he found her, he stared at the photo. Even though she wore the same deadpan expression as all the other inmates, those eyes seemed to lock onto his.

Milo prayed she had the answer to his questions.

"Is something wrong, sir?" One of the soldiers joined him.

Milo stabbed at Jana's photo with his finger. "Have her brought to the reeducation center. I want to talk to her."

The soldier snickered. "I wanna do more than talk to her. Been thinking about it a lot since she arrived. You've got great taste, if you don't mind me saying so. And if you want, I'll make sure you're not disturbed—as long as you return the favor." He leered. "I'm sure *she* won't complain."

White-hot rage surged through Milo, and it took every ounce of self-control not to shift and rip the bastard's arms out of their sockets.

"I'm going to pretend I didn't hear you say that, soldier." He kept his voice even, unable to explain his visceral reaction to the idea of anyone taking Jana against her will.

But it's more than that.

Milo didn't want anyone else touching her, and for the life of him, he had no clue why that should be.

The soldier froze, his face pale. "Yes, sir. Thank you, sir. I'll fetch her myself." He scurried out of the room.

Milo glanced at the impassive faces of the soldiers, and he wondered what they were thinking. No one could fault his reprimand; sex between soldiers and inmates was frowned upon, but maybe he'd spoken a little too harshly.

Raised too many eyebrows.

He left the office, walked out of the block, and headed toward the reeducation center, where he'd first laid eyes on Jana. The place was empty.

Obviously no one needs reeducating today.

The walls had posters stuck to them, and they all followed a similar theme: The rules of the camp. The consequences for breaking those rules.

Milo paced, his heartbeat racing, his skin tingling again. The door opened, and Jana entered the room, coming to a halt when she saw him.

"You." Her lips parted, her eyes shone, and there was a glow to her face that made his heart race even harder.

Gods, that same delicious scent still clung to her. He could smell it from right across the room.

Milo gestured to the empty chair in front of him. "Sit, please."

Jana walked slowly, exhibiting not the slightest trace of fear. When she reached him, she sank into the chair.

He'd expected questions.

Why am I here?

What have I done?

Instead, she gazed at him with a serene expression that settled Milo's unease. His heart rate returned to something more like its usual rhythm, and breathing became less of a chore.

When he found his voice, his words surprised him.

"You're not afraid of me."

Jana blinked. "Why should I be? *You* won't harm me."

He stilled. "How can you know that?"

Her smile widened. "Because you're my mate."

For a moment, her reply shook him to his core, but he quickly recovered. "You don't think I'm stupid enough to fall for that, do you? Mates don't exist."

She gazed at him with obvious sympathy. "I felt the same as you, believe me. I'd heard stories, but I thought they were just that—stories. But after meeting you, I realized that was the only explanation for what you do to me."

Milo sagged with relief. He pulled up a chair and sat facing her. "So you feel it too?"

She nodded. Then she chuckled. "I thought I was going mad."

He laughed, and it was as if a huge weight lifted from his shoulders. "Why are you here? What did you do to be brought here?"

Jana shrugged. "Nothing—apart from exist."

"What do you mean?"

She blinked again. "There's no other explanation for it. I'm only an otter shifter. I'm nothing special." Light filled her eyes. "Except that's apparently not true, because I have a mate—well, I've found one of them." Pride rang out in her voice, and she straightened in her chair.

Milo's world came to a dead stop. "One mate isn't enough?" Then he shook his head. "What am I talking about? There's no such thing as mates. It's a fairy tale, a myth."

"What, like humans think shifters are a myth?" She smirked. "We seem pretty real from where I'm standing. So why shouldn't mates be as real? How else do you explain what you're going through right now?" Jana sighed. "All I know is what I've heard. That there are shifters out there who have found not one, but two mates. And if *that* rumor is true, then the other one might also be as accurate."

"What other one?"

Jana held her head high. "That when all three mates find each other, there's a… connection." She flushed. "I'm not just talking physical. Mental and spiritual too."

"Where did you hear this?"

She pointed toward the door. "Out there. I met a guy—he hasn't been here all that long—who told me he'd met three shifters who could talk to each other without even opening their mouths."

Milo gaped at her. "Seriously? It has to have been a trick."

53

"That's what *he* thought too—until they proved it to him." She smiled. "We've found each other. Now all we have to do is find our third." Jana grinned. "Don't they say good things come in threes?"

Milo stood, scraping his fingers through his hair. "You make it sound so easy. Can I remind you that you're incarcerated here, and that I'm one of the soldiers *keeping* you here?"

Jana rose from her chair. "Do you know how difficult it's been to sit here and not touch you?"

"Jana, you're not listening."

"Yes, I am." That serene smile was back. "It's you who isn't listening. To what everything inside you is telling you right this second." She closed the gap between them. "Your name is Milo, isn't that what you told me when I arrived?"

All he could do was nod, his throat tight.

"Well, Milo, what are you?" Her eyes twinkled. "You already know I'm an otter. I think it's only fair to tell me what my mate is."

And there she went again, saying things that couldn't possibly be true. "Milo?"

He couldn't fight the urge to touch her.

Milo cupped her cheek. "I'm a gorilla."

Her eyes widened. "Oh wow." Then she grinned. "That's cool. I do like a hairy man."

"Whereas gorillas avoid large bodies of water and rivers. We're not natural swimmers. *Playing* in it? That's fine."

All the desire to deny what he was feeling fled. Milo put his arms around her and drew her to him. Jana brought her hands to his nape, and their lips met in a soft kiss.

What happened inside him was anything but soft.

Something caught fire, sending heat to every extremity. What filled his mind was the knowledge that this was *right*, that Jana was his. He prolonged the kiss, and that only served to deepen their connection. He couldn't get enough of her, molding her slim frame to his body, aware of the way her hair smelled like sunshine, her lips tasted like wine, her skin felt like silk.

Then a shout came from outside, and the moment shattered. They sprang apart, both breathing hard, her face flushed, his cheeks warm.

Milo took a step back. "Now what?"

He was in virgin territory with no map and no compass.

Jana took a deep breath. "I have to believe I won't be in here forever. So I have to stay alive until we find our third." She sighed. "They're not going to breed me, because I'm not what they need."

"'They?'"

She frowned. "The Gerans. They're only breeding the strongest, the fastest, the most lethal shifters."

"And who told you that?" Cold inched its way through him.

"Every shifter I've met so far who's part of the breeding program."

"I'm sorry to tell you, your source is incorrect. We breed all kinds of shifters here."

Jana became very still. "We?"

He nodded. "That's right. Gerans. Which includes me."

"You're a—" Jana widened her eyes. "I don't understand. Why would they put us together? A Fridan and a Geran? On what planet would that make any sense?"

Milo stroked her cheek, and she calmed visibly.

"I don't know the answer to that," he said in a low voice. "But it seems it does."

"Kiss me again?"

He didn't hesitate, and once again a wave of bright joy rolled over him to have Jana in his arms, have her lips against his.

"We'll work something out," he murmured.

Then it struck him that he truly believed her.

She's my mate.

He couldn't doubt it anymore.

Milo kissed her fragrant hair. "Do me a favor? Keep a low profile? Try to stay out of trouble. Don't go out of your way to aggravate any of the guards. I can't keep an eye on you twenty-four seven."

"I'll do my best to be invisible, how's that?"

He chuckled. "Sounds good to me."

Maybe she had the right idea. *They'll release her one day, right?* And then he and Jana would be free to be together.

He freed her from his embrace. "You'd better go."

"Can we meet again like this?"

Yet another question Milo didn't know the answer to.

"We can't do this too often. It would only arouse suspicion, and that's the last thing we want."

55

Jana let out a heavy sigh. "I know I haven't asked but... do you... have someone?"

He shook his head. "I'm single."

Her face brightened once more. "Me too." Then she chuckled. "Well, I was. Not anymore." She paused. "Milo? Do me a favor, okay? Ask yourself this question: Why would they be *forcibly* breeding shifters? And don't tell me they're not, because I know otherwise." She tilted her head to one side. "Do you believe in rape?"

Her words rocked him. "Why would you even ask that?"

"Because that's what this amounts to." She sighed. "Just... think about it, all right?" And with that, she turned and walked toward the door.

Milo followed. Outside, a soldier waited, and Milo gave him instructions to return Jana to the compound. The hardest thing was not raising his hand to wave at her as she walked away from him.

When she was out of sight, Milo stared at the admin block. Something Jana said had struck a chord, and he needed to investigate.

He strode across the compound, climbed the wooden steps into the block, then headed for the small room where seven laptops had been provided for staff use. Milo took the one in the farthest corner and logged on to the system. After searching for what felt like hours, he was ready to give up.

It seemed what he wanted to know was above his pay grade.

Fuck.

"That was a sigh and a half." Roslyn Ollerton took the chair next to his.

Milo liked Roslyn. She'd transferred with him from Bozeman, and she had a no-nonsense way about her that was refreshing.

Then he remembered where she'd worked at the last camp.

"Do you still work out of the developmental block?" Not that he had a clue as to what went on in there.

Roslyn smiled. "Yup. Why d'you ask?"

"I'm trying to check the records of a particular inmate, to see if she's going to be... involved in anything." It was a pretty vague explanation, and Milo prayed Roslyn didn't get suspicious.

"She?" Roslyn's eyes sparkled. "Ooh, Captain Keppler. Don't tell me you've fallen for an inmate."

He laughed, because that was what she'd expect of him.

Roslyn tapped the keyboard. "Name?"

"Guzek, Jana. Otter shifter."

Roslyn's fingers stopped their dance. "Then I don't need to look her up. We have a plan for all the species like her—otters, beavers...."

"Really?"

She nodded. "We're developing different methods of warfare."

That last word sent ice edging its way through his veins. "Oh? I didn't think they could be of much use."

"Far from it. An otter could have explosives strapped to them and be sent into locations to blow them up."

Holy fuck.

"But wouldn't that also kill the otter?"

Roslyn chuckled. "And your point is?"

For the first time, Milo saw what lay beneath the surface, and his skin crawled.

"But you're right," she continued. "We wouldn't want to lose a valuable commodity. We could have the otter go in, shift, drop the payload, then shift again to escape." She shrugged. "We simply have to accept that the odds of an exploding otter are pretty high." Her eyes gleamed. "Now, aren't you glad you're *not* falling for her? Because that sounds like a relationship doomed from the start."

It sounded that way to Milo too.

It wasn't until he'd left the block and was halfway across the compound that the thought came to him, leaving him reeling.

If one mate dies, what happens to the other two?

CHAPTER SEVEN

SETH DROPPED onto his bed, every ounce of energy wrung from him. He closed his eyes, waiting for the numbing blanket of sleep to settle on him and take him away from all this.

I wish it could take me to Aric and—

Damn, he really wanted to know their mate's name.

"Seth?"

Jake's voice came as a shock, until he remembered.

They moved him in here yesterday. Seth still wondered about that. *Why, after all this time of keeping us apart?* To paraphrase a line from a favorite movie, the Gerans didn't take a dump without a plan. For all he knew, they could have Seth's bed wired for sound, unseen cameras focused on them right this second.

I'm getting paranoid. Little wonder, he was so freaking tired.

"Go away, Jake. I'm exhausted." Then he realized how rude that sounded. Seth opened his eyes to find Jake kneeling beside his bed. "I'm sorry, but that was the longest session yet, and I'm so far beyond tired, it's ridiculous. They've *really* had me jumping through hoops today."

The guys in the experimentation building had come up with a whole *new* trick for Seth to perform.

"You had me worried, you were gone so long." Jake stroked Seth's hair, and the comforting touch brought tears to his eyes. He wiped them away.

"I'm okay. Well, as okay as you can be when they dish out electric shocks to make you comply with instructions."

Jake let out a low growl. "My tiger wants out."

Seth managed to sit up. He glanced around the sleeping block. Apart from a couple of guys at the far end, they were the only occupants. Everyone else was outside.

Seth didn't blame them. Sunlight was infinitely preferable to the dark interior of the cabin where thirty inmates were housed with barely enough room to swing a proverbial cat.

That woke him up a little. *At least* my *kitty is out of this.* The thought that Aric was safe was all that kept him going sometimes.

He took Jake's hand, noting the lines around his eyes, the dark shadows under them, the perpetual air of fatigue that clung to him.

"Tell your tiger to stay put. I can cope with whatever they throw at me." He peered at Jake. "Today was a first." Usually he and Jake were taken to the block at the same time, both of them wired up to some machine or other.

This time Seth had been alone.

Jake huffed, pulling his hand free of Seth's grasp. "I was there, only in another room. And they had *me* doing a few new tricks too." He scowled. "Today is brought to you by the word 'psychometry.'"

He frowned. "What's that?"

"Another 'skill' from the list of extrasensory perception abilities. The dictionary definition would be the ability to obtain information about a person or an object by touch." He shook his head. "They're working their way through the goddamn list, and I'm their performing seal, except there's no fish waiting for me when I do well."

Seth gazed at him with renewed awe. "And how many of these 'abilities' do you have?"

"So far—well, as far as I'm willing to share with them—there's telepathy, which you already know about because that's an ability you and I share, and clairvoyance." Jake snorted. "When I was a much younger man, ESP was frowned upon as being hokum, and telepathy was dismissed as a trick. Take psychometry as an example. Scientists claimed there was no such thing." He snickered. "Those same scientists would have shit a brick if they'd witnessed my testing today."

"What happened? And please, sit on the bed. That floor is hard on the knees, and you're not getting any younger."

As he hoped, Jake chuckled. "Didn't anyone ever teach you never to poke the bear?"

"Sure, but they never mentioned not poking the tiger."

Jake's eyes gleamed. "Same result, believe me." He got up and perched on the edge of the thin mattress. "They kept handing me different objects—a book, a robe, a pen, you name it—and asking me what I could tell them about it."

"And?"

"I played dumb at first, claiming I couldn't tell them a damn thing." His scowl was back. "Except you *know* what happens when they think you're lying to them."

Seth knew, all right. "So you played ball."

"Eventually."

"How does it work?"

Jake shrugged. "It's as if each object has an energy of its own, and that energy is what I pick up on. For example, that robe... I knew it had belonged to an older man. Then when I concentrated, I knew more about him. The fact that he was in pain. Not to mention desperately sad." His brows furrowed. "Yeah, that made them *really* happy."

Jake fell silent, but the faraway look in his eyes didn't fool Seth for an instant.

"What's on your mind?" he asked quietly.

"I guess I've never really questioned why they grabbed me in the first place. I always assumed it had something to do with their fucked-up idea of a breeding program."

"And now?"

Jake studied his clasped hands. "Remember I told you I was taken during a trip to Italy? Well, it occurs to me that maybe my being locked up has something to do with that. I never thought about it before, but all this testing brought it back. And that worries me." He blinked, then patted Seth's hand. "So what new tricks did they have *you* perform?"

"They called it Remote Viewing."

Jake chuckled. "Yet another ability disclaimed by all good scientists. What did they have you do?"

"They gave me a picture of a man, told me to focus my mind on him, then tell them whatever I could glean about him."

"Were you able to tell them much?"

Seth frowned. "Not much, and it took me a while to be able to do that."

"How long is a while?"

He snorted. "An hour. And all I could tell was that he was sitting in a chair, reading. That wiped me out. I thought they'd be angry with me for coming up with so little, but it was quite the opposite. They appeared delighted. I caught some of their conversation after, while I was being unstrapped from the chair. Apparently the reading guy? He was in another camp, and although they didn't say where it was, I did manage to hear the distance I'd crossed." He met Jake's gaze. "More than four thousand miles from here."

Jake stilled. "Oh my God, that's phenomenal."

Seth frowned. "Okay, so it's phenomenal. Now tell me what exactly they can do with that ability. Or with me, for that matter. What am I going to be, some kind of psychic soldier?"

"They can use you to find someone they're after. You could eventually be able to tell them where they are exactly, and then they'd send someone to…." Jake's voice tailed off.

He didn't need to say another word. It was suddenly all too obvious what that power could be used for.

The thought horrified Seth. "What makes them think I'd do that?"

Jake's gaze grew thoughtful. "You might—if they threatened to harm someone in your family unless you cooperated."

He let out another snort. "My mom? Yeah, right. She just handed me over to these fuckers. They can roast her for all I care."

"I wasn't thinking of your mom." Jake's low, deep voice sent a chill through him.

Aw fuck.

"Jake, we have to get out of here." No way was he going to let them harm Aric. Not because of Seth.

"I keep telling you, it can't be done. Don't you think I haven't thought the same thing? How many camps have you been in? Two? Because I've been in a damn sight more than that, and if there's one thing they've all had in common, it's their security." He grasped Seth's hand around the wrist. "But you *have* given me an idea."

There was an undercurrent of excitement in Jake's words, a tingle through him that Seth could feel all the way through Jake's fingers.

"Tell me."

"Maybe you should conduct a little experiment of your own."

Seth blinked. "What kind of experiment?"

"You've tried to connect with Aric telepathically, and so far that hasn't worked." Jake gazed into his eyes. "But what about *dream* telepathy?"

"Communicate with him through dreams?"

He nodded. "You don't know where he is, but that doesn't matter now, not if you can cross such amazing distances. Wherever he is, you might be able to reach him." Jake tightened his grip on Seth's wrist. "Maybe even both of them."

"You could do the same. You might be able to reach Dellan."

Jake shook his head. "I don't share the kind of connection you and Aric have. You *know* him. You can focus on him." He let go of Seth. "Besides, your skill in this far outstrips mine. So try it tonight." He smiled. "But don't kick yourself if it doesn't work the first time. You can always try again."

"That assumes we have the *time* to try again."

Jake frowned. "What do you know that I don't?"

"Nothing. A feeling, that's all."

"Of what?"

Seth shivered. "Impending doom."

The door opened, and a guard poked his head into the room. "What are you doing in here? Get your asses outside."

Seth glared at him. "I'm recovering, that's what *I'm* doing. I've just spent a couple of hours in the experimentation block."

The guard stared at him for a moment; then his eyes widened. "Oh. It's you." He straightened. "Well, I guess I can let you sleep a while." He withdrew quickly.

Jake chuckled. "You're getting bolder. Good man."

"I'm getting pissed, more like."

Jake inclined his head toward the door. "Magnanimous bastard, wasn't he? He only said that because he knows they'll have his ass if he messes with the prize guinea pigs."

Seth gazed at the door. "No, it's more than that. Haven't you noticed? The guards leave us alone." He grinned. "They're afraid of us."

"That might prove useful in the future," Jake acknowledged.

Seth didn't dare utter the words that were *right there* at the tip of his tongue. To do so felt like tempting fate. But he could still think them.

That assumes we have a future.

ARIC OPENED his eyes... and knew he was in a dream. It could only be that because he was standing in the middle of the compound at the Bozeman camp. What made it eerie was the lack of inmates, or guards for that matter. The wind whistled through the fences, and the sound only added to the spookiness of the dream.

Then he heard it, a low-pitched wail. Someone in pain.

Never mind someone—*that's Brick.*

But was Brick in Aric's dream, or was Aric in his?

Aric raced toward the mournful sobbing that grew louder with each step, the sound pulling him, *tugging* him to it. Behind the block where he and Seth had once slept, Brick stood over a guard lying on the ground, his face bloody, his body beaten to a pulp. There was blood smeared on Brick's face, his hands too.

"Where is he?" Brick hollered at the dying man.

Aric walked over to him and touched Brick's arm. "Brick, you need to stop this."

Brick shrugged off Aric's hand. He whirled around, his eyes huge. "What the…? How can you be here?"

Aric gaped at him. "You're asking *me*? *I* have no idea how this works." He gestured to the guard. "Why did you do this?" He knew it was only a dream, but he also knew what Brick was capable of.

"Get out of my head, Aric. It's not a place you should be right now."

As if Aric was going to listen to that. He stood his ground.

"It's the place I *have* to be. You're our protector—mine and Seth's— and that means you need to keep calm. What good would it do any of us if you died?" He touched Brick's arm once more, but this time, Brick didn't shy away from it. "Use your head for something, would you? This anger isn't doing Seth a damn bit of good."

"He wouldn't tell me where Seth is!"

Aric forced himself to speak calmly. "Look where you are. It's the camp where you found me. Seth isn't here. Seth was gone before you even arrived to save me."

Brick let out a growl that made Aric's blood curdle. "I want to kill every last Geran. I want to make them suffer the way they made you and Seth suffer. Except I want to make them suffer even more." He gripped Aric's shoulders. "They killed my parents, and I was helpless to stop them. They tortured you and Seth, and I couldn't do a damn thing about it. All I have left is this rage. It's the only thing keeping me going."

Aric reached up and caressed Brick's cheek. "You have me," he said in a gentle voice. "And we *will* get Seth back, but only if you calm down. Being angry all the time might make it harder to find him, and that helps neither of us." He pointed to the now-dead guard. "Okay, so what if he isn't real? So what if you've just killed a figment of your imagination? How does it make you feel right now?"

Brick gazed at the body. "Guilty for not controlling my emotions. I could've interrogated him instead of biting his face off."

"What you *should* feel is remorse." Aric pressed his finger to Brick's lips. "I know you find that difficult, and I totally get that, but this guy was still a person, and you killed him. This wasn't in battle, was it?"

Brick stared at him, and the seconds ticked by.

Come on, Brick. Be the protector I know you can *be.*

Finally he shuddered, and Aric knew he'd gotten through. "You're right. Even if it *is* in a dream, it was still wrong."

Aric beamed. *"That's* the Brick I love. That's our mate."

"So that's his name. I like it."

Brick scanned their surroundings. "Who said that?"

Aric gasped. "I know that voice. It's Seth!" He scanned their surroundings. "Seth! Where are you?" His pulse quickened.

"How can it be Seth?" Brick demanded. "This is my dream."

"And *I'm* in it, so why not Seth too?" Aric's heart felt as if it was about to explode. "Seth! You still here?"

"Hey, baby. Still here."

"Then why can't I see you?"

Seth chuckled. "I'm working on it, okay? And obviously I need to work a little harder."

"But—"

Whatever else Aric had been about to say was lost when Seth sort of faded into view. He was thinner than Aric remembered, and he seemed exhausted, but it was definitely him.

Aric rushed over to him, only stopping a foot away. "Can I… can I touch you?"

Seth groaned. "Oh Gods, I hope so." He held his arms wide, and Aric was in them in a heartbeat.

"I wish I could smell you," Seth murmured, pressing his lips to Aric's forehead, nose, cheeks, and at last his mouth.

Aric still couldn't believe this was happening. "It's really you," he said with a sigh. "You're here."

"Do I get a hug?" Brick asked from behind them.

Aric sprang apart from Seth, grabbed Brick's hand, and hauled him toward them. Seth gazed up at him, his eyes glistening.

"Oh wow. You're huge."

Brick chuckled. "All over, sweetheart."

Seth's cheeks pinked. "Good to know."

Brick enfolded Seth in his arms, and Aric's heart leaped to see them together. Seth appeared even thinner against Brick's frame, and Aric tried not to think about what had brought him to that state.

Brick held Seth to him, his eyes closed. "Can't believe this is real."

"You and me both," Seth whispered.

Aric joined them, his spirits soaring when both his mates pulled him into their embrace.

Brick stroked his hair. "Seth, where are you? I'll come for you."

"I'd tell you if I knew. All I do know is that it's another camp, and we were brought here in darkness. We think it's near the Canadian border, but that doesn't narrow the field much."

"Are you okay?" Aric couldn't rein in the question a second longer.

Seth kissed him. "I'm fine, baby. But this is wearing me out." He smiled. "Not bad for my first time, though."

"You're asleep too?" Brick asked.

Seth nodded. "But it takes so much energy, even when I'm sleeping."

"Is your dad with you?"

Another nod. "He's okay too." Seth frowned. "I have to leave you."

"Tell your dad we're at Dellan's home," Brick said urgently. "And don't lose hope. We *will* find you, okay?"

Seth gave them a tired smile. "I believe you. I'll try again in a day or two. Brick…." He stood on his toes and kissed Brick on the lips. "Take care of our mate."

"I will. Can't wait to meet you."

Aric leaned in for one last kiss while he had the chance. "Be safe. Love you."

"Love you too." Seth's image grew faint, grew transparent, and then he was gone.

Aric woke up to find Brick sobbing beside him in the bed.

"Don't cry. He'd hate us to cry." Aric's own tears threatened to spill over his cheeks.

"He was in my arms," Brick said, his voice cracking.

Aric nodded, snuggling against him. "And he will be again. We have to believe that." A thought came to him, and he smiled. "And in the morning, we can tell Dellan his dad is okay."

A little drop of joy in an increasingly scary situation.

"Close your eyes," Aric whispered. "Let's go to sleep and dream of Seth holding us."

That sounded like the sweetest dream ever.

SETH OPENED his eyes. The room lay in darkness. He brought his fingers to his cheeks and found them damp.

I did it. I fucking did it.

And if he could do it once, he could do it again.

He debated waking Jake to tell him what had transpired but decided against it.

Dad needs his sleep too.

Then he realized that was the first time he'd referred to Jake in his thoughts as his dad.

Well, he is, isn't he?

Seth couldn't wait to see his dad's face in the morning when he learned Brick and Aric were with Dellan. The connection felt… right.

Whatever else it felt escaped him as Seth struggled to keep his eyes open.

One thing was certain. He would be careful not to let anyone know what he'd accomplished, with the exception of Dad and Jamie.

I don't want to give these bastards any more ammunition.

Who knew where they would use it?

CHAPTER EIGHT

CRANK HATED himself for being so mean-spirited. Everyone in the house was buoyed by the news that Brick and Aric had finally made contact with Seth, even if it was in a dream. And while Crank smiled and congratulated them, while he said all the right things, only one thought consumed him.

I miss Vic.

He wasn't used to this. His adult life thus far had been a series of hot encounters, one-night stands, maybe the occasional relationship that lasted two or three months, tops. Having someone whose absence left a gaping hole in his existence was new.

What shocked him even more was how quickly Vic had become a part of him, as vital as a limb, and how much Crank yearned to have him back where he belonged—in Crank's arms.

In their bed.

Close enough to hear him breathing, to smell him.

He stood at the patio doors, staring out at the lake, recalling some of their many swims, him and Saul frolicking in the water, hurtling through it as they held on to Vic's fin.

Video calls might have been meant to bridge the distance, but for Crank all they did was emphasize how far apart they were.

Behind him, Aric retold the events of the previous night for maybe the third time. Crank couldn't blame him for that. It sounded amazing, and Crank was overjoyed for them.

He was also jealous as fuck.

What would I give to hear Vic in my head right now?

Except Vic was on his way to Europe, putting even greater distances between them. Crank couldn't deny he'd achieved a helluva lot in the short time he'd been away. The coalition force was growing by the day, and that was down to Vic. But that didn't lessen the ache inside him.

A hand touched his lower back. "I miss him too. You've still got me, though."

Crank turned his head to gaze at Saul. He smiled. "Thank God for that."

He meant every word. Saul had also become part of his life, a rock Crank could cling to. *I never thought I needed anyone.*

Vic and Saul had proved him wrong.

Saul leaned closer. "If you don't make a move soon, you're going to miss out on Mrs. Landon's cookies. They're disappearing fast."

"Fuck that." Crank *lived* for her baking, even though he had to work out twice as hard to keep the pounds from piling on. He hurried over to the kitchen table, where Brick, Aric, Dellan, Horvan, Rael, Hashtag, and Roadkill sat, the plastic box in the center emptying before his eyes. Crank grabbed a couple of the raisin cookies, then handed one to Saul.

"Be thankful you did that," Saul muttered. "You wouldn't have liked the consequences."

Crank rolled his eyes. "Gee, I'm *so* scared. What would you have done?"

Saul's lips brushed his ear. "Put you over my knee and spanked your ass."

His dick gave a twitch.

Brick leaned back in his chair. "So how come we can hear our mates' thoughts?"

Rael chuckled. "Don't ask us. We don't know how it works any more than you do."

"We're just glad it does," Dellan added before biting into a cookie.

"Well, *most* of the time, we're glad." Horvan arched his eyebrows when both Rael and Dellan jerked their heads in his direction. "Oh, come on. When you two are in heat—"

Dellan coughed. "Male felines don't experience heat."

"Maybe it's a territorial thing," Rael suggested.

Horvan rolled his eyes. "Okay, then, when you two 'feel territorial'"— he air-quoted—"it can get pretty—"

"Hot?" Rael offered.

"Sexy?" Dellan's eyes sparkled.

Horvan snorted. "I was thinking more along the lines of exhausting."

Roadkill cackled. "Some of us would *love* to be in your shoes. So don't expect sympathy."

Horvan stroked his chin. "Maybe Doc Tranter knows."

"Why him?" Saul asked.

"Because he usually knows more than we do. You can always give him a call and ask."

"That's a call I wouldn't mind overhearing," Crank confessed.

"Then let's do it." Horvan gestured to Hashtag's laptop. "Do your stuff."

Hashtag tapped on his keyboard. "Calling him now." A moment later, he smiled. "Hey, Doc, you got a minute?"

Doc's voice emerged from the speaker. "For you? Several minutes. What's up?"

"Hang on." Hashtag turned the laptop so everyone could see.

The first thing that struck Crank was the fatigue etched across Doc's face, appearing more strongly in the late afternoon sun that lit up his study.

"You okay, Doc?" Horvan clearly saw it too.

Doc waved a hand. "I'm not sleeping too well, that's all. And before one of you says 'Physician, heal thyself' and suggests I self-medicate with sleeping pills? Don't waste your breath. I hate those things. Now... what can I do for you?"

"We're discussing telepathic connections between mates," Horvan told him. "Brick and Aric connected with their mate, Seth, last night for the first time, in a dream."

"That sounds familiar. Didn't Dellan do the same thing with Rael?" Doc asked.

"Yeah, that's right, he did." Rael gave Dellan a smile as bright as the sunlight that poured into the kitchen.

"I see. Then I'm happy for you, Brick, Aric—" Doc gave a tired smile. "—but all I can tell you is... it works."

Crank burst out laughing. "Yeah, thanks for that, Doc. *Really* informative."

Brick let out a noise of pure frustration. "But Doc... *how* does it work?"

Doc's salt-and-pepper whiskers were stark against his pale skin, and Crank estimated he'd lost about twenty pounds since the raid on the Bozeman camp.

Not sleeping my ass. There was more to this than Doc seemed willing to share.

Doc cleared his throat. "Until recently, no one even understood the concept of *mates*. As far as telepathy is concerned, there are theories, but no one has any definitive answers. It could be biological, psychological, or, hell, even mystical." He gave an apologetic shrug. "I'm sorry, but it'll take people far smarter than we are to suss out an answer. For now, at least for me, it's enough that it does work." He peered at Brick. "I'm sure you're grateful for it."

Brick smiled. "Like you wouldn't believe."

"Horvan, are we any closer to locating more Geran camps?"

Horvan let out a wry chuckle. "No, Doc, *we* are not. The well of information seems to have run dry. Vic's met with dozens of Fridan leaders in the last week, and he's going to meet with more. The coalition is growing."

Crank loved the note of confidence in Horvan's voice.

"Then all we need is somewhere to deploy these ever-growing forces. And when we do?" Doc straightened in his chair. "I want in, Horvan. Okay? Include me on any medical teams."

"You sure?"

Doc huffed. "It worked out well with the raid on the camp in Bozeman, didn't it?"

"More than okay. We couldn't have dealt with all those people without you."

"Then that settles it." His gaze focused on Horvan. "I want to do my part."

Horvan nodded. "I'll let Duke know."

Doc gave him a grateful smile. "Thank you."

"Hey, Doc?" Brick turned the laptop toward him. "You knew Jake Carson, right?"

Doc's smile widened. "Yes indeed. He was a dear friend, both him and his wife, Miranda."

"Well, he's still alive. He's with his son Seth—mine and Aric's mate."

Doc's face lit up. "That's wonderful news. Thank you for that. You've just made my day."

"Take care, Doc," Horvan said. "I'll be in touch when I have news about the next mission."

"I'll be waiting for your call." Doc disconnected, and the screen went black.

Horvan helped himself to another cookie, and Rael coughed. Horvan grinned. "Don't worry. I'm sure you can think of a way to help me burn off the calories."

"Several ways," Dellan murmured. He gave Horvan a hard stare.

Crank had never thought to see the day when Horvan appeared discomfited, but those flushed cheeks were a revelation.

Horvan's phone pinged, and he glanced at it. "Saul? Hashtag? Duke says he's lined up recruits for you to interview. You'll be starting next week."

Saul frowned. "Not here, surely."

Crank snorted. "Of course it won't be here. And don't call him Shirley."

Aric's brow furrowed. "I don't get that. Is it supposed to be a joke?"

Brick leaned across and kissed the top of his head. "You don't get it because you're too young to have even *seen* the movie Crank's referring to, and because Crank's an old fart."

Crank glared. "Hey. Less of the old, if you please." He smirked. "I can't comment on the fart bit, though."

"Much as I hate to interrupt this banter," Horvan hollered, and the room fell silent. "Thanks. The interviews will take place at the new barracks. The fewer visitors we have here, the better."

Crank frowned. "Still not sure about this, H. Why the hell would we let Gerans join forces with us?"

Roadkill gaped. "What the fuck?"

Horvan rolled his eyes. "Don't give me that surprised act. We talked about this in the transport home from the last mission, remember?"

"I must've blotted it out." Roadkill narrowed his gaze. "You know, dismissed it as a bad dream?"

"More like a nightmare," Crank muttered. He peered at Saul. "Be careful, okay? You don't know what's in a person's mind. They could be a plant. They could be trying to infiltrate us."

Saul snorted. "Gee, that hadn't occurred to me."

"Hey, Crank?" Rael gazed at him with obvious amusement. "Ever heard the saying 'Don't teach your grandmother to suck eggs'? All that military experience *you* have?" He pointed at Saul. "*He* has just as much. Saul knows what he's doing."

"Hey, what am I? Chopped liver?" Hashtag retorted.

Saul patted him on the back. "No, Peppermint Pâté, you'll be there because I trust your judgment."

Crank frowned. "I don't get it."

Hashtag said nothing, but his face glowed.

Damn, Saul's good with people. Crank's chest swelled with pride.

"And now I need to go work off all that sugar," Saul announced. "If anyone wants me, I'll be in the gym."

"Isn't that a bit excessive? I only gave you one cookie," Crank remonstrated.

Rael cackled. "Sure, but he'd already eaten three before that one. *And* a slice of Mrs. Landon's coffee and walnut cake."

Crank glared, and Saul made a run for the door. "Your ass is mine when I catch you," he yelled after Saul.

"Promises, promises," Saul shouted back.

And now that he came to think about it, the prospect of Saul pumping iron, covered in sweat, muscles rippling and thighs bulging?

"Wait for me. I'm coming too." Crank followed him, heading down to the gym in the basement.

"We don't need to know that part!" Hashtag hollered amid laughter from the others.

A thought slipped into Crank's mind, and he sighed.

Vic would've watched. Hell, he'd have brought popcorn.

CRANK LAY on the bed, naked, enjoying the warm breeze that wafted in through the open window, playing over his skin. Saul had just finished his shower by the sound of it, which only meant one thing.

It was time to fuck.

Since Vic's departure, they'd gotten hot and heavy a couple of times, but it had mostly been reciprocal blow jobs, which was fine by Crank. He was fast becoming an oral addict, and every encounter became a challenge to see how much of Saul's girth he could take.

Crank was always up for a challenge, and with Saul around, his dick was permanently up.

"Are you gonna put some clothes on, or do you intend going to dinner like that?"

Crank glanced toward the doorway where Saul stood, rubbing himself with a towel. "It's a thought," he quipped. "I don't mind showing off what God gave me." He gave his dick a lazy tug.

Saul walked slowly to the bed, his gaze drifting up and down Crank's frame. "You'll only make 'em jealous." He tossed the towel onto a chair and climbed onto the mattress, which dipped with his weight. Saul crooked his finger. "Come here."

Crank knelt up, and to his surprise, Saul put his arms around him and drew him close, ignoring Crank's erect cock. Their lips met, and a shiver trickled down his spine.

Something's different.

Saul kissed him, slow and sensual, while he stroked Crank's back, one hand going lower to squeeze his asscheek. He dipped a finger in Crank's crease, rubbing it over his hole, and Crank's shivers multiplied.

"I hate it when Vic's away," Saul murmured against his lips. Then he pulled back. "But then I realized... you and me? We've never been alone before."

A frisson of excitement swept through Crank. "No, we haven't."

"And Vic did say he wanted us to get to know each other," Saul added.

Crank snorted. "If I remember correctly, the exact term he used was 'manhandle.'" Saul kissed his neck, and Crank let out a low moan, his dick rising, harder than ever. "This doesn't feel like manhandling."

"Good." Saul's breath tickled the delicate skin around Crank's ear. "Because I had something else in mind." He met Crank's gaze. "On all fours, sweetheart."

Crank arched his eyebrows. "*Sweetheart?*"

Saul nodded slowly. "Don't argue. Do it, facing the pillows."

Crank turned himself around, hands and knees planted on the mattress. A groan escaped him when Saul spread his cheeks and licked a leisurely path over his pucker. Crank rocked a little, wanting more.

Saul chuckled. "Patience. We're not in any hurry, and I wanna enjoy you."

Crank bowed his head, his eyes closed as he relished Saul's tongue dancing over his hole. "You can do that all fucking day as far as I'm concerned."

Saul laughed. "Yeah, I'd noticed that about you. You sure love getting rimmed, don't you?" Then he resumed his licking, and Crank reached back to urge him deeper.

Fuck, this was amazing. The wet sound of Saul sucking Crank's balls, sucking his cock, probing Crank's hole with his tongue.... All of it conspired to send Crank's need into the stratosphere.

"Toss me the lube," Saul instructed.

Crank grabbed it from the nightstand and held it out to him. He stared at the headboard. "You know what this needs? A mirror."

He wanted to watch Saul pleasuring his hole.

Saul's rough chuckle sent vibrations through him. "We'll have to see what we can do. Something to bear in mind, though, when we get our own place." He leaned over Crank, his chest warm against Crank's back. "I was thinking more along the lines of mirrors on the ceiling."

Crank opened his mouth to tell him *fuck yeah*, but the words were lost when Saul smacked Crank's hole with the heavy, slick head of his dick.

"Ready for me?"

Crank twisted to stare at him. "I was ready when you strolled out of the bathroom."

Saul smiled. He gave a gentle push of his hips, his hands gripping Crank's waist as he eased his shaft into him. Saul leaned over to kiss the back of Crank's neck.

"Fuck, that feels good," he whispered. "Tight, but good."

Crank gasped. "I thought tight was always good."

Saul tilted Crank's head back, his hand on Crank's throat, and they kissed, lingering kisses that served as the perfect accompaniment to Saul's unhurried movement in and out of his body.

Crank loved it when Saul went to town on his ass. He loved it when Saul pounded him into the mattress.

Saul's languid thrusts and sensual kisses took Crank's pleasure to new heights.

"Roll over," Saul told him.

Crank flipped onto his back, and Saul raised his legs into the air, rolling his ass up off the bed and holding on to Crank's ankles as he filled his hole with that thick cock. Saul gazed into Crank's eyes, his face framed by Crank's calves as he drove his dick all the way home.

Then Saul paused. "How does that feel?"

"Fucking awesome." Crank's voice cracked. He waited for Saul to sit back, to fuck him the way he usually did, both of them ending up covered in sweat.

Except it didn't happen.

Saul covered Crank with his body and kissed him while he slid in and out, like they had all the time in the world. Crank held on to Saul with his legs, making him a prisoner, desperate to prolong this blissful experience that went far beyond their usual sexual encounters.

What made it all the headier were the smoking-hot looks Saul gave him as he made love to him, the constant kissing, the touching, the emotion in every gasp, every cry.

He was *connected* to Saul, body, mind, and soul. And in that moment, Crank knew he truly loved his mates.

Saul raised himself up on his hands. "I'm close, but I want you with me when I come."

Crank could only manage a nod before Saul picked up speed, and then both of them were hurtling toward the precipice, their breathing harsh, their chests heaving, Saul's thrusts short and quick. Crank groaned as Saul filled him to the hilt, reveling in the delicious throb of Saul's cock inside him. It was enough to push him into his own orgasm, warmth pulsing onto his belly, his body trembling.

Saul lowered his head and kissed him, his cock still wedged in Crank's ass. He locked gazes with him. "That wasn't exactly manhandling, was it?"

Crank smiled. "Fuck no. It was way better."

"So it's okay if we do this again?"

He chuckled. "More than okay." Saul eased out of him, and Crank was aware of feeling emptier than he'd ever done before. Saul stretched out beside him, and they kissed and touched, kissed and stroked, talking in low voices, neither of them, it seemed, in any hurry to get dressed.

Crank could get to like this.

"Vic will be calling us in a few hours," he murmured.

Saul kissed him. "We get to do this all over again, show Vic what he's missing." His eyes sparkled. "You never know, that might bring him home to us all the faster." A soft sigh rolled out of him. "I know things were a little... prickly when you and I first met."

Crank cackled. "And the rest."

"Vic telling me we were mates? I have to admit, it knocked the wind right out of my sails."

"And now?"

Saul cupped Crank's chin. "Now, I couldn't imagine my life without you. Either of you."

Crank cradled Saul's head in his hands. "Ditto." He kissed Saul on the lips, a sweet, lingering kiss that seemed the perfect end to their coupling.

Never thought I'd see this day.

A man had just made love to Crank, not to mention made his ass ache in the most delicious way *ever*, and he wouldn't change a fucking thing about it.

CHAPTER NINE

IT DIDN'T matter how many times Vic showed the presentation to Fridan leaders—watching his mate on the screen speaking calmly about what the Gerans had done to him still made Vic's blood boil.

Shifters have no idea what's going on under their very noses.

What saddened him was that for a significant number of them, learning the truth wouldn't alter how they felt. They would still see humans as beneath them, not worthy of their attention.

Such pessimism wasn't like him, but he knew the root of it. This last visit hadn't been an unqualified success, and Vic wanted to go home to his mates.

"You have no idea of the impact your coming here has had."

Vic turned to face Marc Delore, the leader of the Fridan group in Paris. "Kind of you to say, but I think we both know the truth." He gestured to the long table around which were gathered more than fifteen Fridan leaders, some of them not bothering to lower their voices.

The same leaders who glanced over to where Vic stood, doing little to hide their disdain.

"Not all the leaders agree with you." Vic sighed. "I didn't pull any punches, but it doesn't seem to have helped."

Delore peered at the assembled group. "I'm not surprised, if I'm honest. Two of my fellow leaders have always seen the world through rose-colored glasses, and nothing will persuade them otherwise." He patted Vic's arm. "But I for one am grateful, and I know others feel the same. It was truly a cannon shot across our bows, but a well-timed and much needed one."

"And *I'm* grateful no one asked me to deliver my speech in French."

He laughed. "Which was why we had a translator. Some of our leaders here in France are old-school. They think everyone should speak French." He gazed out at the skyline. "It's strange to think of a whole world of shifters out there that has no idea of what is going on."

Vic blinked. "You read my mind." He followed Delore's gaze. "It's a beautiful city, one I've never visited before. When this is all over, I must come back."

A romantic stay in Paris with Saul and Crank sounded wonderful.

"Do you really think this will end?"

He glanced at Delore. "Don't you?"

Delore sighed. "I am older than you. I have seen too much of the world and witnessed too many scenes like the one we just saw, unfortunately." He pointed to the landscape beyond the glass. "I know that even if we were to show our shifter brothers and sisters out there the atrocities that have been committed in their name, all with the aim of smiting humans and establishing shifter superiority, there would still be those who would say we lie. A minority, perhaps, but...."

Vic remained quiet, but it was a relief to hear his own thoughts from someone else's mouth.

It's not only me, then.

Delore had gathered leaders from all over France, to provide Vic with his largest audience yet. And once more, dissenting, doubting voices had been silenced when confronted by the evidence.

Well, most of them. Vic had a feeling he could've put together a comprehensive document detailing all the evidence they possessed, and it would still not have been enough for some of them. Hell, if they had video of the atrocities being committed, that still wouldn't sway them.

"There are those among us who say that shifters originated in Europe," Delore stated.

"I'd heard that." He smiled. "It might even have been here. The Carolingian dynasty ruled here in the eight hundreds, after all, making it one of the oldest countries in Europe."

"And does your knowledge of shifter history go back that far?"

Vic had to admit the deficit in his archives. "There's still so much we don't know, but we're learning more every day. I'm not sure we'll ever have a complete archive, but at least we're trying."

"And what about the Gerans? How far back do your archives go where they are concerned? What do you know of their existence?"

"Only that they came to be after the split between the brothers, about a thousand years ago, some say, and that there's been a chasm between us ever since." It was all Vic needed to know.

Then he realized Delore had gone quiet.

Not only that, he was gazing at Vic in such a thoughtful way that Vic's curiosity was aroused.

"What have I said?"

Delore tilted his head to one side. "Where is your next destination?"

"I'm on a flight to Rome tonight. I meet with Italian leaders tomorrow." And after that, it would be Eastern Europe, and after that, Russia, then China....

He'd get home eventually, but not until he'd traveled around the world at least once. *Thank God for the invention of flight.*

A close second was the internet. Vic lived for his nightly Snapchats.

"You know how Ancient Rome was founded?"

Vic nodded. "According to legend, two brothers—and demigods— Romulus and Remus, had an argument over who would rule the city. Romulus killed Remus and named the city after himself, in April, 753 BCE." Vic smiled. "Yet another argument between brothers. Something shifter history has in common with human history."

"Perhaps." Before Vic could tell him there was no perhaps about it, Delore continued. "Might I suggest that while you're in Rome, you make time to visit the Castel Sant'Angelo. Have you heard of it?"

"Yes, but"—Vic frowned—"I don't have time to go to a museum. This isn't a sightseeing trip."

"The Castel Sant'Angelo was built as a mausoleum for the Roman Emperor Hadrian, and later various popes used it as a fortress and castle. And yes, while it *is* a museum," Delore said, staring at him, "it is also the repository for the oldest known shifter documents of our history. The archivist Luciano Orsini maintains the collection, which contains artifacts from all over the world."

Vic knew the name Orsini, as did every oral historian. "I've always wanted to meet him," he confessed.

"Then make the time," Delore urged. "But...."

"There's a but?"

Delore squared his shoulders. "You need to be prepared."

"For what?" Delore's enigmatic words had piqued his interest.

"To have your beliefs challenged."

Vic stilled. "Which beliefs are we talking about?"

Delore waved his hand. "Perhaps all of them. But I'll say no more. You'll understand when you see the collection and talk to Orsini. By the way, I'll contact the museum and tell them to expect you. I wouldn't want them to mistake you for a tourist." He glanced toward the table. "And now I need to continue the work you have begun here. I'll talk to Aelryn. He will have our support."

"Good luck."

Vic had a feeling Delore was going to need it.

"So where are you tonight?"

Vic lay on his side in bed, his phone propped up against a pillow. "It's Tuesday, so it must be Rome."

"You little jetsetter," Saul teased.

"Less of the little," Vic admonished.

"Biggest thing about you?" Crank lay in front of Saul, their fingers laced against Crank's chest. He smiled at Vic. "Your heart."

Warmth barreled through him at Crank's words. "Love you."

"Right back atcha."

"How did today's meeting go?" Saul asked.

Vic sighed. "Don't ask."

Saul's gaze narrowed. "Do I need to get on a plane to Paris and go crack some heads? They weren't mean to you, were they?"

Vic chuckled. "You make them sound like a room full of schoolkids." Then he grinned. "Actually, that pretty much nails it where some of them are concerned." He shrugged his shoulder. "To expect success every time is unrealistic. It's just frustrating to run smack dab into a wall of apathy when previous meetings had opened the door to future associations." He gazed at his mates. "Wish I was there with you."

All he wanted right then was a night of being held, kissed, caressed….

"Aw, honey, we want that too." Saul gave Crank a gentle push, shifting him onto his back. "Tell you what. You're in charge tonight. You tell us what to do."

Vic smiled. "Seriously?"

Crank nodded. "I might draw a line at some things, though."

Saul peered at him, eyebrows arched. "Such as?"

Crank snorted. "You ain't tying me up, for one thing. And you'd better not be hiding shit like nipple clamps in the nightstand drawer."

Vic laughed. "Sounds to me as though Crank has been doing some research."

Saul guffawed. "Is that what we're calling porn these days?" He leaned in and kissed Crank on the mouth, and Vic's cock stiffened at the low moan that tumbled from Crank's lips. "Don't get your panties in a twist. I had something far more... sedate in mind." He turned his head to stare at Vic. "Wanna watch me fuck our mate senseless?"

Vic's breathing hitched, and then he smiled. "Sure, but after that thirty seconds, what'll we do with the rest of the night?"

"Oh, you guys are so funny," Crank snapped. Then he stood and started stripping off his clothes. "Let's get this show started. I want to see him get all hot and bothered, knowing ten minutes after he gets home, he'll be on his hands and knees between us for hours on end."

"There's nothing I'd like more than to watch the pair of you." Vic smiled. "Other than be there to join in."

VIC STROLLED across the Sant Angelo Castle bridge flanked by statues of angels, thankful he'd taken Delore's advice and come early: There were few tourists accompanying him as he approached the arched gateway to the round fortress set below the battlements, a many-sided tower to the left. The early morning sun sparkled on the surface of the Tiber, and he wished he had time to linger, to gaze into the still waters.

The museum was the oldest building Vic had ever had the occasion to visit. He knew its construction dated back to 139 CE, and that within its walls lay the remains not only of Hadrian, but also Marcus Aurelius, Commodus....

Crank would love this. Gladiator was one of his favorite movies.

He reached the gate and spoke with one of the security guards who stood inside the ramparts. Delore had been as good as his word, and Vic was escorted into the museum.

"Aspetti qui, per favore. Il signor Orsini sta arrivando. Sarà qui a breve."

Vic waited as instructed, listening to the low murmurs of the tourists who followed the signs to the ancient spiral walkway that led up to Hadrian's tomb. From his brief research, he knew Roman walls were still visible from the outside. He didn't want to see ornately decorated halls, their ceilings covered in paintings, the glint of gold everywhere. Vic couldn't wait to gaze on the only antiquities that interested him, ones that could teach him something about the origins of shifters.

Something new.

"Mr. Ryder."

Luciano Orsini was short in stature, dressed in a dark suit. What little hair remained was white as snow, stark against his black skin. Wrinkles lined his forehead and cheeks, and his bright eyes appraised Vic. He sniffed, and his smile lit up his face.

"Welcome, brother."

Vic gave a short bow. "Thank you for agreeing to this. And my apologies for having to keep the conversation in English."

"No matter—I speak several languages. And all oral historians are welcome here. The pity is that few take advantage of that invitation. If you would follow me?" Orsini led the way out of the building, across the courtyard, and down a flight of steps past a niche containing a statue of Hadrian. The lower level was a curved wall, and set into it were small wooden doors and windows, appearing for all the world like a row of terraced houses. Above each door was a terracotta-colored painting of a figure etched into the white wall. Orsini walked past them, under a stone archway, and stopped at an iron gate, beyond which a dark passageway headed lower. He opened the gate, and once Vic had followed him inside, he locked it.

"No one is allowed into the archives except for myself and the occasional visitor." He smiled, his wrinkles deepening. "We don't want tourists down here."

Vic followed him down a flight of narrow, worn steps. The air was cool, a relief after the heat above. At the bottom of the stairs was a simple wooden door.

Vic stared at it, and Orsini chuckled. "You expected something more ornate? Such finery is reserved for the museum above us." He opened the door, and Vic found himself in a small atrium. In front of them was a steel door.

"The archives are kept in a hermetically-sealed chamber. We must pass through two such doors."

Finally they stood in a long, windowless room lit by electric lamps, its floor covered with stone flags made shiny with the wear of time. Some of the walls were covered with wooden doors, and around the perimeter of the room were stone caskets. Orsini pointed to them. "Those contain the artifacts."

"How long have you been the archivist here?"

He smiled. "There has been an Orsini here for more than a thousand years. My family can trace its origins back to the year 998. Each new generation has taken on the noble task of protecting our heritage. My ancestor was a Roman nobleman, and at one point an Orsini married a descendant of Septimius Severus, the Roman emperor who ruled until 211 CE."

"A noble task for a noble family," Vic observed.

Orsini beamed. "A diplomat as well as an historian." He indicated the two armchairs at the end of the room, bracketing a small table. "Please, sit with me. I know why you're here, so we should talk."

Vic sat, and Orsini joined him. Vic knew what his first question would be.

"Then shifters *have* existed for more than a thousand years?" Vic had known there were writings out there that referred to shifters; he'd just never seen any of them.

Orsini leaned back, his fingers steepled. "Longer than that, we believe. No one knows for sure, and there have been many different theories spouted as to our origins. I read an article recently where someone postulated that the eruption of a super volcano seventy thousand years ago introduced something new into the atmosphere, something that caused certain genes to mutate. Others claim we are the creation of a goddess. And there are even those who believe we simply 'appeared' because we were always fated to exist."

"But there's never been any proof to these theories," Vic surmised.

"We have found sketches done on animal skins that would indicate the existence of shifters. Only last year, cave paintings were discovered in Indonesia depicting man-animal hybrids, hunting wild pigs and dwarf buffaloes. Therianthropes, scientists called these hunters. Some had the head or body parts of birds, reptiles…. And the paintings are believed to date back to forty-four thousand years ago." He smiled. "So while such depictions *may* have been the result of taking hallucinogenic substances, or some supernatural encounters, they may also be the first portraits of our shifter ancestors." Orsini sighed. "We may never know, and to be frank, our time would be best occupied studying events from our more recent history, instead of speculating on our ancient past."

"You're talking about the Fridans and the Gerans."

Orsini nodded. "And before you ask, I follow neither group. I prefer to follow the path of truth—when I find it."

"So we do know when Ansger and Ansfrid existed?"

"Yes. We can date them to the year 1000. We can even give an approximate date—1046—to the now-famous argument that caused them to break away from each other." Orsini paused. "But that is where the mystery begins, because that date was *not* when the two splinter groups came into existence."

Vic went very still. "Then when was it?"

Orsini regarded him in silence for a moment. "Would it surprise you to learn there is no true record within these walls of *any* conflicts between shifters until around nineteen hundred? Beyond the usual petty squabbles, of course."

What the—

"That can't be right," he murmured.

"I assure you it is. Of course, there may be artifacts that haven't come to light yet, and they might paint a different picture, but...."

Vic leaned forward. "So what happened in nineteen hundred?"

Orsini frowned. "As far as we can tell, someone resurrected the brothers' disagreement."

"*Resurrected?*" Vic's stomach roiled.

I don't like the sound of this.

Orsini gave a nod, his face grave. "Not only that, they embellished it. We know this from the Missal of Godwin."

Vic frowned. "What's that?" He'd never heard of it.

"The oldest known document in shifter history. It details the argument between the brothers." Orsini peered at him. "Would you like to see it?"

"It's here?" Vic's heartbeat raced. "Yes!"

Orsini rose and went over to the nearest casket. "It was written in 1050 and refers to Godwin's visit to the brothers that took place four years before that. It's the oldest known European document to use paper instead of parchment—that we've found so far." He lifted the lid, and Vic caught his breath at the sight of the pages captured under glass, their aged beige surfaces covered in black writing, and occasionally in red. He recognized the language as Latin.

"Can you read it? My Latin is about as good as my Italian," Vic managed to croak.

This is amazing.

"Certainly. Although I might paraphrase." Orsini chuckled. "Whoever Godwin was, they wrote in a remarkably long-winded style." He removed a pair of glasses from his breast pocket, put them on, and peered at one of the pages.

"My Lord Ansfrid is beloved of his people, counting among those he loves both humankind and versipelli."

Vic blinked. "I've never heard that word. Is that Latin for shifters?"

Orsini nodded before continuing. "But my Lord Ansger shows his countenance to versipelli alone, shunning the company of humans." He fell silent.

"Please, don't stop." Vic stared at him. "That isn't all of it, surely?"

"I understand your confusion. Those few lines are hardly the basis for such a vicious split, correct?" Orsini closed the casket. "Now let me show you this. It purports to be written by Ansger himself." He led Vic to another casket, which contained only one document, a single sheet of browned paper covered in identical writing. He leaned over to read from it, taking his time.

"For so long as you choose to mix the blood of humans and versipelli, my brother, you will bring about our destruction. Mankind is weak, but we are strong. Mankind's place is beneath our feet, but our destiny is to rule. Mankind has tried to eliminate us already, and your weakness for their company would bring us to the brink of extinction. You have chosen your path, my brother, and I have chosen mine. Peace is not the answer, only war. And if you continue along this path, then my war will be against not only mankind, but against you and any who choose to follow your example."

Vic shivered. "That sounds more like what I'd expected."

"I would agree. This document came to us quite by chance. It was stolen from the Spanish house of a Geran leader about fifty years ago. The thief in question was a Fridan, and he had no idea what he had his hands on, so he brought it here, thinking we'd give him a reward. My father was still alive then, and he paid the thief handsomely for it. To think we had actual proof of what caused the rift between the brothers, and why nothing has healed that rift to this day." Orsini paused. "My father was a man of integrity who believed in the good of all men—humans *and* shifters—but I was by nature more suspicious. He accepted the document as being accurate, and it was placed in the archives, where it sat for twenty years. In time he forgot about its existence, but I did not." Orsini gave a graceful shrug. "I cannot tell you why, even to this day. I simply knew I did not accept its validity. So… when I took over my father's position as archivist, I decided to have it tested. Yes, it *was* dated, and yes, it *seemed* genuine, but something in me still did not believe that." He gave a half smile. "Except my methods for establishing its provenance seemed a little unorthodox at the time."

Vic was intrigued. "What did you do?"

"I meet a great many shifters in my work here. Most of them come because they know many of their ancestors came from Europe. And roughly thirty years ago—I may be out by a year or two—I met a professor from your country. We spoke of his students, how he spotted those who were shifters, how he took care of them. And then he spoke of one in particular, a young man with incredible gifts."

"What kind of gifts?"

"He had the power to send his thoughts into the minds of others, and to read what lay in their thoughts too. He could also see events taking place that were nowhere near him. And finally what was of vital interest to me, he possessed the ability to glean information about a person or an object by touch alone."

Vic smiled. "One member of the team I work with? His mate has similar abilities."

Orsini's eyes widened. "Mate? Oh, we must talk further of this. But tell me, how old is this mate? Might he be the same man that I invited to come here?" Orsini was visibly buzzing with excitement.

He shook his head. "Seth is in his early twenties. It couldn't have been him."

Orsini's face fell. "I see. I had to ask. Such gifts are rare. No, this man would be in his early sixties by now." His features tightened. "And if I had known the danger I would place him in, I would never have extended that invitation."

"What danger? What happened to him?"

"Forgive me. I digress. He came to the archive, and I let him hold the document you see here. He told me what I'd already guessed. That it had *not* been written more than a thousand years ago."

Vic scrutinized the paper. "But… it looks the same."

"Yes, it does. It is a really amazing effort on someone's part. But once he confirmed my suspicions, I sent it to be tested scientifically."

"And?" Vic had a feeling he knew what was coming.

"As far as we can tell, this was created in the early twentieth century."

Vic's head was spinning. "A forgery? But… why?"

"To cause a rift. Someone had obviously read the Missal of Godwin and decided to exploit it, to use it for their own ends. It had the desired effect. This document was created, news of it was deliberately spread, and thus the Fridans and the Gerans came to be."

"But if it's a forgery, then tell people! Let them know they're being manipulated." He pointed to the sheet. "This… if this got out, it would *cripple* the Gerans."

Orsini let out a sorrowful sigh. "It is *one document*. And we know from our sources that many similar documents exist. If *this* is a forgery, then I have to believe they are too. I would be one lone voice adrift in an ocean of others."

"But what happened to the shifter who came here? You didn't finish that part of the story."

"He spent a morning with me, he left, and when I tried to get in contact with him, I learned he'd disappeared. No one heard from him after his arrival in Rome, not even his wife. He simply vanished from the face of the earth." Grief contorted Orsini's features. "I did that. Because I have to assume someone learned of our meeting, learned what had passed between us and didn't want that knowledge to be made public."

"You think the Gerans got to him."

Orsini nodded. "It was too big a risk to let him tell others about the forgery."

The light dawned. "That's why you haven't told anyone about it, isn't it? You're afraid the same thing will happen to you."

He glanced toward the door. "I never leave the museum. I have an apartment in one of the little houses we passed on the way here. I dare not set foot outside this place, because I don't know who would be waiting for me."

Orsini's words hit home, and it was like a sucker punch to Vic's gut.

"Oh Gods. What was his name? The shifter who disappeared?"

No, don't say it. Please.

Orsini lowered his gaze. "He was a tiger shifter named Jake Carson."

CHAPTER TEN

ORSINI STARED at Vic. "You know that name."

"Yes. And until recently, no one knew if he was alive or dead."

"But you know now?"

Vic nodded. "He's being held in a Geran camp, but apparently he's okay. We don't know where the camp is located, but the mate I spoke of? He's with Jake." He expected to see some indication of relief, but Orsini's brow was still furrowed. "What's wrong?"

"What troubled me at the time—and troubles me still, if I am honest—is how the Gerans had knowledge of Jake's gifts. More importantly, how they were able to take him once he left the archive. Because as far as *I* was aware, the only people privy to that information were the Fridan leaders I contacted about him when I learned of his abilities. It was they who arranged for Jake to visit me."

"Then I'm troubled too, because that points to only one conclusion." Vic's mouth was suddenly dry. "Someone was feeding the Gerans information, and that someone had to be a Fridan. Maybe even a Fridan leader." He didn't want to believe that.

Orsini stroked his chin. "There is another part to this archive that I think you should see." He rose and walked over to the huge wooden doors that covered part of the wall. Vic watched as Orsini unlocked them and folded them back onto themselves, like shutters on a window, revealing....

Vic got up and went to take a closer look. Two panels lined the wall, and one glance told him he was gazing at the depiction of a family tree. At the top were two names.

His mouth fell open. "These are Ansfrid's and Ansger's descendants?" So many shifters, spreading out like the branches of a tree.

"Not all of them—there isn't enough space for that—but the heads of families, certainly. My ancestor began this work, and each new generation has continued to add to it." Orsini pointed to the foot of the panels. "There is no room left."

Vic peered at the last names. He noted some were circled in red, and others in blue. Then he looked higher up the panel, seeing more such names. "Why are these different?"

Orsini gazed at the panels. "The dates are important."

Vic leaned in. "1904, 1909, 1910...."

He nodded. "Those shifters in blue became leaders of the Fridans, while those in red were Gerans. These details were added during the last century, the result of painstaking research." He pointed to the names at the foot of the panel. "You may recognize some of them."

Vic smiled. "I've met Aelryn."

Orsini smiled. "As have I. Now *there* is a noble man. Do you know what his name means?" Vic shook his head. "*Bright Guardian.*"

There were other names too, ones he'd only heard of. He bent down to peer at the present Geran leaders. "You keep track of these shifters?"

Orsini nodded. "As I told you, I follow neither group, but—"

"But that isn't exactly true, is it? You said you contacted the *Fridan* leaders about Jake."

For a moment, Orsini stared at him; then his face tightened. "I have tried for so many years to be impartial, but you're right. I am lying to myself. Everything I have learned so far leads me to one inescapable conclusion, and that is—"

"There's a war coming," Vic said in a low voice. "A battle between Fridans and Gerans. Someone went to a lot of trouble to fabricate that so-called 'artifact.'" He swallowed. "Someone wanted this war."

"I fear you are correct." Orsini pointed to one of the leaders circled in red. "In which case, remember this person."

Vic read the name aloud. "Theron." He glanced at Orsini. "Why him?"

"His name derives from ancient Greek, and it means *to hunt*. But that is merely a name, after all." Orsini shivered.

Vic laid a hand on his arm. "Are you all right?"

He took a deep breath. "When I was a child, my father used to bring me here to educate me about the artifacts, to teach me what he knew of our history. And then Theron came to the archive." Orsini stared at the panel. "He was not alone, but he was the only one of the visitors that day whose presence touched me. I cannot tell you what it was about him that sent a shiver through me. Perhaps it was nothing more than a child's overactive imagination."

"Or maybe it was instinct," Vic suggested.

"Perhaps that too. All I know is, I have never forgotten him." He expelled a breath. "And now, let us talk of mates. I have so many questions."

Vic smiled. "As long as you understand I don't have all the answers."

He glanced at the panels that Orsini hid once more behind doors. *I'm going to remember those last names in red.*

What did Sun Tzu say? Not that Vic had had many occasions to quote the Chinese military general, strategist, and philosopher, but one saying had stayed with him: "Know thy enemy and know yourself; in a hundred battles, you will never be defeated."

But if Orsini was correct, and the split between the brothers had been blown up out of all proportion, then maybe war could be averted.

If they could convince their fellow shifters it was not the only path.

"WELL? WHAT do you have to report?"

"Vic Ryder left the archive two minutes ago, sir. Do you want me to follow him? Should we eliminate him?"

Theron rolled his eyes. "Oh please. Use your brain. That's all we need—a martyr."

"Sir?"

He should have known better than to employ sarcasm. The foot soldier on the other end of the phone was great when it came to doling out death and mayhem but excelled at little else, especially interpreting the nuances of speech.

"Let him go. We know where he's headed next, after all. If he has useful information, then we'll get to hear it eventually. Right now it's enough that we know he's visited the archivist."

"Yes, sir."

"Return to base and report to your commander." He finished the call.

"Are the Fridans proving a nuisance?"

He smiled at Fielding. "Your source was correct. Ryder went straight from Paris to the archive."

"You don't appear concerned about that."

"That's because I'm not. They may have managed to get their grubby little hands on one of the artifacts, but it's the *only* one they'll ever see." He scowled. "It was a major lapse that they came to possess it."

"And the shifter who lapsed paid for it with his life, if you remember."

"I read the records as you did." He snorted. "As well he should, letting it fall into the hands of a Fridan. And since then, I've taken great pains to ensure they don't get within sniffing distance of any of the others." He gazed at his surroundings. "They certainly won't ever lay eyes on these." He pressed his hand against the glass of the sealed room that contained several stone caskets, and smiled. "No one will ever see *your* contents." The basement, once a dungeon with its vaulted ceilings, was his favorite place to sit. Unlike the two upper floors that had been rebuilt during the late eighteen hundreds, this part of the castle had retained some of its former charm and structure.

The obvious place to build his strongroom.

"There's something I've been meaning to ask." Fielding pointed to it. "Why didn't you destroy them when they were first discovered?"

He arched his eyebrows. "Because they may yet prove useful."

Fielding stared at him. "How?"

Theron sat in the wide chair facing Fielding. "I can understand your confusion. Why keep something that would lead to peace, when we wish to sow nothing but discord and chaos?" He leaned back. "But the day will come when we have won this war. The Fridans will be nothing but a memory, and all shifters will be bereft. *Then* it will be time to 'discover' these artifacts. *Then* we'll tell everyone that we never knew." He placed his hand on his heart and affected an agonized expression. "How could we? The truth had lain hidden, undisturbed for centuries. Can't you just hear the words? 'But *now* we can see that all shifters and humans must work together, as they were meant to. We must strive to forget what has passed, and live in peace and harmony.'" He smiled. "After all the bloodshed and heartache, such words will ensure no one seeks to resurrect the past, and we shall live out our days the way we always intended—as the rulers of all."

"May I congratulate you." Fielding bowed his head. "You have foreseen every eventuality."

"Not quite. Mr. Ryder's decision to visit the Castel Sant'Angelo was unexpected. *We* might be following the enemy's movements closely, but it seems someone else is following ours. We must be watchful."

"What about Carson? You saw the latest reports from the camp?"

Theron scowled. "Indeed I did. Despite his captivity and enforced isolation, his abilities continue to blossom. And now it appears he is not the only one."

Fielding smiled. "Then you agree with me? He has outlived his usefulness?"

"More than that. He is proving far too dangerous, and should there be another raid, the last thing we want is for the Fridans to get their hands on such a valuable and powerful weapon." He gave a brisk nod. "Terminate him."

"As you wish." Fielding cocked his head to one side. "Immediately?"

Theron smirked. "Finish your tea first." That raised a chuckle. Fielding was one of Theron's inner circle, a man he could trust to get things done, and one of the few men who was bold enough to look Theron in the eye, even though his body language told of his nervousness.

Strength was always something to be admired, and a healthy dose of fear was a good thing. It kept men alive.

Theron tapped the tabletop with a finger. "Take care of this matter personally. You're due to visit the camp in a week's time, correct?"

"Yes, but I can leave immediately if you wish."

"No. He's been our honored guest this long. It can wait until your visit." He smiled. "Let him enjoy his last days."

Theron cast another glance at the sealed room. *We have come too far to be stopped now.*

Any obstacles in their path would share the same fate as Jake Carson. *They will be crushed.*

CHAPTER ELEVEN

MILO KEPPLER had never been an insomniac, and if the nights since Jana's arrival were anything to go by, he needed to resolve the situation fast before it started to affect his performance. The reason for his lack of restful sleep was obvious; thoughts of Jana consumed him. Ever since his conversation with Roslyn, two things plagued him.

Is there really someone out there who completes us?

What if I can't keep Jana safe?

Except failing to protect her wasn't an option.

He lay in the darkened barrack room, unable to switch his mind off. The snuffles and snores around him told him everyone else was asleep. Though how anyone could sleep with Janek snoring away in the corner like a buzzsaw was beyond him.

Milo.

He froze. The word came not from inside the room but inside his head.

Gods, I need to sleep. He rolled onto his side.

Milo. Can you hear me?

He sat upright, his heartbeat racing. *Jana?*

It couldn't be.

It was impossible.

Then how come I can hear you?

Sweat popped out on his brow, and a wave of nausea surged through him. *This isn't real.*

Does the fact I feel sick too make it more real for you? I don't know how I'm doing this. All I did was concentrate on you.

His breathing quickened. *Where are you?*

In bed, which is probably where you are, given how late it is.

There was a pause, and for one heart-stopping moment, Milo thought their connection had been broken.

Jana!

Still here.

What made you try this?

She gave an internal chuckle. *If other mates can do it, I didn't see any reason why we couldn't.* When she fell silent again, he waited, knowing there was more to come. *This is weird. I'm lying here, debating whether or not to tell you how I'm feeling.*

Milo closed his eyes and focused on the image of Jana that was never far from his thoughts. *I already know. You're afraid. I can feel it.*

It was no lie. He knew her heart hammered, causing her pain in her chest. He could feel how she wanted to flee from the sensations that swamped her.

Tell me what you're scared of.

Milo, I don't want to die. Her voice trembled. *I want to be home with my lodge. Having Mom make us a limitless supply of mussels, listening to my brothers argue over who can eat more while my father sits and smirks, then puts away enough that they're both humbled.*

Her words painted a picture in his mind, and his heart went out to her.

I don't want to die here in this awful place. I want to take your hand and introduce you to everyone in my house. My parents, my siblings, my grandmother. I want you to sit and eat with us. To... to....

Her sob cut through him.

I don't want to die.

Milo could have told her she would be okay, but it would have been a lie, because although he believed it once, now he didn't know for sure. And he knew she'd see right through him.

There was only one thing he could say to calm her.

Jana... I'm going to get you out of here.

Fuck, he could feel the flutter in her belly, could hear the hitch in her breathing.

That's it, honey. Don't give up. There's always hope.

But how? She sounded bewildered. *What are you going to do—set me free so the guards in the towers can shoot me? Walk out of here with me so they can shoot both of us?*

I don't know, all right? But I will find a way, I promise you.

There had to be a way. Because the alternative didn't bear thinking about.

Jana... try to sleep, sweetheart.

He didn't miss her cute little snort. *I could say the same to you. You feel as exhausted as I do.*

Then I'll try too. Okay?

Jana sighed. *All right, I'll try—for you.*

Good girl. Milo concentrated on his breathing, doing his best to take calm, measured breaths, forcing his body to relax.

Except his mind would not shut down.

Who in here would know anything about mates? Something that everyone—including me until a few days ago—thinks is a fairy tale?

Then it came to him. Jana had said she'd met someone in the camp who knew about mates.

It was as good a place to start as any.

Jana... you still there?

She laughed. *It's been less than a minute. What do you think?*

The guy you told me about... the one who'd met shifters who were mates. What's his name?

There was a pause.

Jana? Don't you know?

Of course I know.

Then what's the problem? Then cold swept through him. *Oh, I get it. You don't want to tell me because you think that'll put him in danger. Jana, you have to trust me. This may be the only way I can come up with—*

His name is Jamie Matheson. He hasn't been here all that long. Another pause. *And I know you won't put him in danger.*

Her confidence rang out, clear and true, and Milo knew he would never do anything to jeopardize that trust.

Thank you. Now, go to sleep. Again.

She chuckled. *Only if you stop talking to me.* Jana let out a happy sigh. *I love this. Being able to hear you, to feel you. It's the only thing that keeps me going. One day this will all be over, and we'll be free.*

Milo loved it too. But until he got an answer to his questions, he had no idea if the future Jana dreamed of would ever materialize.

If he'd even survive should anything happen to her.

JAKE STARED at the line of trees beyond the fence. "Something's coming."

Beside him, Seth froze. He followed Jake's gaze. "I don't feel anything."

"But I do." Jake shivered. "Trouble is, I can't tell if it's good or bad." He snorted. "Except in this place? Unfortunately, my money's on bad."

"Jamie's walking toward us," Seth said in a low voice. "Only he's trying not to make it *look* as if that's what he's doing."

Jake smiled. "The kid learns fast." He waited until Jamie was a few feet away from them. "Got your cards, Seth?"

"Sure." Seth patted the front pocket of his overalls. "What else is there to do in here?"

"Then let's sit and play." Jake squatted on the bare ground and beckoned Jamie. "Hey, you want a game?" It was their favorite way to avoid attracting too much attention.

"Sure," Jamie said with a shrug. "I was gonna get my nails done, but they'd double-booked me." He joined Jake and Seth on the ground, the three of them in a little huddle.

Jake chuckled. "That's my boy. Humor is the only thing that gets me through the day." He leaned back on his hands and watched as Seth dealt the cards. "Anything new to tell me?" he murmured.

"Not much. Except...." Jamie glanced at the compound. All the inmates were outside, the morning sunlight falling on them, a warm breeze stirring hair and clothing alike. "I'm being watched." He delivered the words in a whisper.

"By whom?"

"The captain of the guard."

Jake frowned. "And whatever did you do to attract *his* attention?"

"Are you kidding?" He gestured at his body. "I'm fucking gorgeous. *All* the men are watching this." He grinned. "And no, I'm not being serious. I can't think of any reason why he's got his beady eye on me, but I'm sure of it. I've felt his gaze boring into my back all morning."

Jake recalled the captain from their last camp. Sure, he was a Geran, but he didn't seem to possess the Pure Bastard gene that some of the guards exhibited. *What's his name? Yeah. Keppler.*

The same Captain Keppler who was heading their way.

"Don't look now," Jake whispered, "but we have company." He studied his hand of cards, snorting. "Gee, I'm sure glad we're not playing for money, because I'd be fucked."

Keppler came to a halt behind Seth, his eyes watchful. He pointed a finger at Jake and Seth, the other hand resting on his rifle. "I remember you two from the last camp. Tigers, right?"

Jake merely nodded. Seth said nothing but kept his gaze locked on his cards, Jamie too.

Keppler nudged Seth's shoulder with his knee. "Didn't you have a boyfriend back then?"

Seth scowled. "Still do. All you did was force us to be apart."

Jake flashed him a warning glance.

Keppler cleared his throat. "So is he your boyfriend—or your mate?"

Holy fuck. Jake jerked his head up and stared at Keppler.

Things had just gotten interesting.

Seth put down his hand and twisted to meet Keppler's intense stare. "Not that it's any of your business, but yeah, he's my mate. Well, one of them."

Jake expected to see surprise or shock reflected in Keppler's features. But Keppler bit his lip, gazing at Seth with something that seemed a lot like….

Hopefulness.

You're seeing stuff that isn't there.

Keppler cleared his throat again, and Jake's skin prickled.

Whatever was coming, this was part of it.

"What would happen if your mate died? To you, I mean."

Ice crawled over Jake's skin. "You bastard. How cold-hearted do you have to be to threaten someone's mate?"

Keppler paled. "What? No. That isn't what I meant at all. I need to know about this… connection."

Seth frowned. "I don't know, all right? And I hope to God I never know."

Jake's anger reduced itself to a simmer as he stared at the handsome captain. "What interests me is why you're asking."

All Jake's senses were screaming at him that Keppler was hiding something. He opened himself up, focusing on Keppler's stiff posture, his parted lips.

When the answer revealed itself to him, numbness crawled through Jake's body.

Holy fuck didn't cover it, not by a long shot.

"You've got a mate, haven't you?" Jake kept his voice to a whisper.

Keppler's reaction was instantaneous. He spun around and strode toward the barracks, his back ramrod straight, his gait stiff.

Seth turned his head to watch the captain's departure. "What the hell just happened?"

Jamie threw down his cards. "That was going to be my question too."

Jake stared after Keppler. "Now we wait."

"For what?" Seth gave him an inquiring glance. "Dad? What's going on?"

"We need to keep an eye on Captain Keppler."

THE TECHNICIAN was in the middle of removing electrodes from Jake's and Seth's temples when the guards entered the experimental block. The techie gave them a sweeping glance. "I'm almost done here." Then he went back to wiping the skin, removing the glue.

Jake's senses went on alert, and he caught Seth's eye, giving him a meaningful glance. He addressed the waiting guard.

"We really don't need an escort. We know the way to the compound by now."

All he wanted to do was sleep. The afternoon's testing had dragged on longer than usual. But he couldn't escape the feeling sleep was not in the cards.

At last the technician straightened. "They're all yours."

The guard inclined his head toward the door. "Outside."

"Well, seeing as you asked us so nicely...." Jake was done being polite. It changed nothing. He trudged into the hallway, Seth behind him. When they got outside, his suspicions were confirmed when the guard indicated the reeducation block.

"That way."

Seth frowned. "We haven't done anything. Why can't we go to our block?"

The guard indicated the reeducation block again, only this time with the barrel of his rifle.

There was nothing to do but follow instructions.

They crossed the compound, the guard walking behind them.

"I don't like this," Seth muttered.

"Me neither, but we don't have much choice, do we?" They climbed the wooden steps into the block to find another guard waiting by the door that led into the main room.

"In there." He pointed with his rifle.

"Has anyone ever told you what a great conversationalist you are?" Jake asked, keeping a straight face.

The guard scowled. "Huh?"

"Yeah, I didn't think so." Jake went into the room, stopping when he saw it was already occupied.

Jamie sat at one of the tables.

A trickle of unease slid down Jake's spine. "What's going on?"

The door closed behind them.

Jamie stood. "Do you have any idea why we're here?"

"Not a clue." Jake walked over to him, his pulse racing. After hours of jumping through hoops, he was too tired to try and fathom it, but that didn't stop his stomach from clenching.

The door opened again, and a guard walked in, carrying a box.

"Sit down." He headed for the front of the room.

"Why are we here?" Seth demanded. He flopped into a chair, and Jake pulled out the one next to it. Jamie resumed his seat.

The guard regarded Seth with an impassive expression. "You already know the answer to that. How did you get the gun?"

Jake froze. "What gun?" He stared in disbelief when the guard removed a revolver from the box. "How could we get our hands on a gun? Unless one of you got careless."

"Where did you find it?" Seth was pale, and Jake understood the panic he was undoubtedly feeling.

What are the penalties for being found with a weapon? Not that Seth would have done such a thing.

The guard replaced it in the box. "Same place we found this." He held up a compass, then glanced at Jake. "Under your bed." He stared at Jamie. "And what about this, from under *your* bed?"

Jamie's jaw dropped when the guard showed him the wire cutters. "No fucking way."

"You may as well tell us everything. You're obviously planning an escape." He sneered. "You must know how futile this is. You wouldn't get more than three feet before you got a bullet in the back."

Jake folded his arms. "None of us have any idea what you're talking about. Because if you found those under *our* beds, one of you planted them there." He tilted his head. "Did you search the entire block, or was it just our little part of it? And if that was the case, how did you know to look there?"

"We got a tip from an informant."

Jake leaned back. "Then I'd suggest your informant has it in for us. We're being framed."

That earned him another sneer. "Yeah, well, you *would* say that, wouldn't you?"

"I'll take it from here." Captain Keppler stood at the back of the room. "Leave the box. You can stand guard outside. I'll call if I need help. But I don't think that will be necessary. We can be civilized." He stared at Jake, Seth, and Jamie. "Isn't that right, gentlemen?"

Jake arched his eyebrows. "I know *we* can be—I'm not so sure about you, however." He waited until the guard marched out of the room and Keppler closed the door behind him. Jake stood, his arms folded. "This is complete and utter bullshit."

Keppler walked slowly toward them. "I know."

His admission took the wind out of Jake's sails. "You *know*?"

Keppler regarded him with faint surprise. "Of course."

"Then you know who *did* put them there?" Before Keppler could answer, Jake darted forward, reached into the box, and grabbed the gun.

"Carson."

Jake ignored him. He held the revolver in both hands and focused his attention on it. *Come on. Don't let me down now.*

"Drop it. And it isn't loaded."

Jake turned to face him. "And you would know that, wouldn't you? Because *you* put it there."

What the fuck was going on?

Keppler nodded. "It was the only way I could get to talk to you without arousing suspicion."

"What?" Seth gaped at him. "Are you—"

Jake held his hand up, and Seth quieted. Jake stared at Keppler. "But why?"

"I need your help."

Jamie let out a derisive snort. "Okay, that's a new one."

Jake glanced at him. "It seems my sons have inherited my sarcasm."

"I'm being serious." Keppler pulled out a chair and sat, gesturing for Jake to do the same.

"How can *we* help *you*?" Seth asked.

Jake studied Keppler. "You *do* have a mate, don't you?"

He gave another nod. "Except there's a problem. She's one of you—an inmate."

Seth widened his eyes. "Wow. That's a tricky one. Good luck with that. And yeah, my heart bleeds for you. Now let us out of here."

"Wait." Jake turned to Keppler. "Okay, you have my attention. How do you expect us to help you?"

"This is a trap," Jamie protested. "Don't fall for it."

Jake's senses were telling him otherwise, and he trusted them.

He gave Keppler a pointed glance. "Well?"

"I… I want to contact the Fridans. I want to tell them how to find this camp so they can liberate it, the same way they did in Bozeman and Texas."

Seth's eyes were huge. "You expect us to simply *give* you this information? Jamie's right. This is a trap. Why should we?"

Keppler's eyes were as wide as his. "Because if you don't, Jana is going to die."

"That's her name?" Jake kept his voice low. Keppler seemed to be under a lot of strain. When he nodded, Jake tilted his head. "How is she going to die?"

"That part doesn't matter. You need to trust me that it's a probability. And I can't do a thing to change it, because it's out of my jurisdiction. The only way I can save her is for the Fridans to take this camp and set everyone free."

Jake frowned. "But you're a Geran."

"Yes, but an enlightened one. Just because I'm a descendant of Ansger, that—"

"Wait." Seth's jaw dropped. "Really?"

"Yes, but that doesn't mean I should follow blindly if I don't like the road I found myself on. Can you believe that?"

"*I* can," Jamie piped up. "I found myself on that same road, so I took a detour."

Keppler regarded him with interest. "And?"

"What I've learned since then brought me new understanding about what's really going on. Unfortunately, it also brought me to this place, because you caught me trying to help the Fridans."

Keppler's eyes held genuine anguish. "Then will you help *me*? We have to move fast. I don't know how long we have before—"

"I get it," Jake interjected. "But there's one flaw to your plan. I don't know how to contact the Fridans."

Keppler's face fell. "Oh. I see. Then the situation is hopeless."

"I might be able to help you," Seth blurted. "I could get a message to Aric. He's my mate."

Keppler gaped at him. "You can do that?" Seth nodded, and Keppler's eyes shone. "Thank you."

That was all it took to convince Jake of his motives.

"But I can go one better than that." Jamie smiled. "How would you like the address where to find one of the Fridan groups?"

"Seriously? Where are they? Is it far from here?"

Jamie chuckled. "That assumes I know where *here* is."

Keppler hesitated for one second. "We're in northern Maine. Northern Aroostook County, to be exact."

Jake grinned. "I always liked Maine." He glanced at Jamie and nodded. "Give him the address."

Keppler handed Jamie a notepad and pen, and Jamie scribbled quickly. "When can you contact them?"

"I'm overdue for leave. I'll go this weekend. I've already put in for it," Keppler told them.

Jake studied him. "But will you be coming back?"

"That will depend on how swiftly they can put together a mission. Jana… Jana said there should be three of us."

Seth nodded. "Aric is with our mate. I haven't yet met him in the flesh—only in my dreams."

"There *is* one thing you need to think about," Jake said. "You convinced us. How do you know you will convince them?"

Keppler smiled. "Because I have a few aces up my sleeve." Before Jake could ask what they were, Keppler raised his voice to call in the guard. He gestured to Jake, Seth, and Jamie. "I don't know what's been going on here, but I think this evidence has been planted." He leveled a hard stare at the guard. "Maybe you need to keep a watchful eye on these three."

"Yes, sir."

Keppler stood. "Okay, you can take them back to the compound."

Jake made sure his back was to the guard before mouthing *Good luck*. Keppler was going to need it.

CHAPTER TWELVE

IT WAS the last interview, for which Hashtag was profoundly grateful. His brain was screaming at him that it was well and truly done for the day. He'd spent a whole week in a small room at the Chicago barracks, seated on what had to be the most uncomfortable chair ever made, with the worst coffee he'd ever tasted.

I've gotta tell H and Dellan about that. They have to do something.

So far he and Saul had seen about sixty potential recruits, with a lot more to come. About half had been shifters, not that Hashtag was surprised anymore to learn the military was peppered with them. Horvan was the prime example, after all. So there were obviously mechanisms—and people—in place to protect shifters who wanted to serve. Most of the ones he and Saul had interviewed so far had made the grade.

One most definitely had not, and that had been down to Saul's instincts. Hashtag had been prepared for possible infiltrators, but to have one show up was confirmation that the enemy was following their business *way* too closely for comfort. Saul had gone through the motions, asking the usual questions and revealing nothing, and when he was done, he thanked the candidate—*what was his name? Simon something*—and told him they had more people to see. Once the door closed, Saul had let out a loud snort.

"They must think we're fucking stupid."

Hashtag peered at the file on the table. "On paper he looked perfect."

"Yeah, *too* fucking perfect. And he said all the right things." Saul regarded Hashtag with interest. "What did your senses tell you?"

"Honestly?" Hashtag grimaced. "He gave me the creeps. Couldn't put my finger on why, exactly. I only know I didn't trust him." He cocked his head. "He was one of the Gerans who wanted to *join the cause*, right?" He got why Duke didn't want to share that piece of information with them, in case it prejudiced them. *It makes us rely on our instincts.*

Thank fuck their instincts were shit hot.

One more to see, and then it would be back to the house, ready to chill for the weekend. Hashtag kept thinking about diving into the cool waters of the lake and stretching out on Dellan's patio with a cold beer—once he'd taken his allergy meds.

Fucking pollen.

The door opened, and Crank came in. "You not done yet?"

Saul laughed. "I thought you were waiting for me at the house. You said something about being ready…."

Crank snickered. "I figured I'd show up here so we could get the party started early. I'm sure we can find a flat surface somewhere."

Saul snorted. "Since when did *you* ever require a flat surface?"

"Good point," Crank acknowledged. "So I'll sit back here and wait. I promise, I'll be quiet as a mouse."

Saul grinned. "Quiet is not in your vocabulary. That's part of the reason Vic brought up getting a ball gag for you."

Crank glared at him. "Sure, share *all* my secrets, why dontcha?"

Hashtag burst out laughing. "You think that's a secret? Aw, how cute."

Saul waited until Crank was seated before pressing the intercom button. "Send in the last candidate, please. Then you can call it a day."

"Yes, sir."

Saul glanced at the list. "Eve Duncan. Shifter. She's yet another one who looks great on paper."

Hashtag glanced up as Eve entered the room. "Whoa. Not only on paper."

Saul chuckled. "Stop thinking with your dick," he whispered.

He'd nailed it. Hashtag was *totally* thinking with his dick.

"That's okay, it's how most men do their thinking," Eve said as she walked toward them.

What the—

"Their single brain cell can't handle more than one thing at a time." She grinned smugly. "And for the record, I can recommend some great ball gags. I have a catalog at home, plus a drawer full of them, all tried and tested."

Hashtag's jaw dropped.

"Shifter hearing is better than a human's," she informed him with a sweet smile. "So are our other senses. And so we're clear, I'm here to do a job, not looking for a barely adequate roll in the hay."

"I… I… I'm sorry," Hashtag sputtered.

"That you said it, or that you got caught?" Her eyes sparkled. "Or are you apologizing for your… equipment?"

His cheeks burned. *Goddammit.* No woman had *ever* taken him to task—and done it so expertly. So why did he find it so fucking hot? There was a trace of an accent, and dammit if that wasn't hot too.

He couldn't help but stare at her. Eve was tall, maybe five eleven, her dark brown hair pinned up at the back. There was an Italian air about her. He liked the confident way she crossed the floor to them, the line and breadth of her shoulders, the straightness of her back. As she drew nearer, he took in her dark brown eyes, her sun-kissed complexion, her chin that she raised as she gazed at them. The kind of woman who'd look amazing whether she was on the catwalk or carrying an M-16.

And *totally* Hashtag's type.

Yeah, maybe I'd better let Saul lead on this one. Hashtag would have signed her up on the spot, but for all the wrong reasons. *I'm only here for balance anyway.* It wasn't exactly a good-cop/bad-cop scenario—his role was to ask questions designed to help them gain insights into each candidate while Saul sifted through their resume and asked about their military experience.

Saul gestured to the chair facing them. "Please, take a seat."

"Thanks. And thank you for the compliment. I'd better make sure my performance is as perfect as my resume."

Saul arched his eyebrows.

Okay, *that* was funny.

Hashtag gave her a nod, and she returned it. Eve sniffed a couple of times, her nose wrinkling, before giving Saul her attention. Hashtag leaned back and listened as Saul did his thing.

Well—*half* listened. He was far too busy trying *not* to stare at her and her insanely adorable twitching nose.

Talk about distracted. Hashtag put that down to his libido. It had been months since he'd gotten any, with no one—male *or* female—catching either his eye or the attention of his cock.

Eve had his undivided attention from the minute she walked into the room, and Hashtag's boner was showing no signs it planned on subsiding anytime soon.

True to his word, Crank remained silent the whole time, his attention focused on the proceedings.

"Anything you want to ask?"

Hashtag flushed when he caught Saul's amused stare. *Busted.* "You're doing fine," he mumbled.

Saul chuckled. To Hashtag's surprise, he closed the file in front of him and leaned forward, hands clasped on the table, his gaze fixed on Eve.

"Okay. On paper you look good—except you already know that, don't you? You make all the right noises too."

She raised her eyebrows at that but said nothing.

"Now let's talk about what's *not* in here." He tapped the folder with his forefinger.

Eve blinked. "Excuse me?"

"I can see you started your military career in 2005, aged eighteen. It's also obvious you were on track to make rank. But then there's a gap, from 2015 to the present to be exact. Now while it doesn't go against you, I can think of a number of reasons why that might be. Except… you list yourself as single, you have no dependents…." Saul folded his arms. "You weren't working for the US military, were you? And you *definitely* weren't working with the Fridans. I checked."

Hashtag froze. *She's a Geran?* Obviously her appearance had fouled up his senses, because he really hadn't seen *that* coming. *Damn.*

"No, I wasn't. I served with the Geran military until a few months ago." Eve looked Saul in the eye, her gaze unflinching. "And I *was* going to tell you, by the way. I wouldn't hide something like that."

He nodded. "Now tell me the whole story." Saul spoke in a low, even voice, and Hashtag admired his capacity to keep cool.

Eve relaxed a little. "My parents are Gerans, as is my brother. He also serves in their military. He was the one who persuaded me to enlist."

Saul huffed. "I bet that went down well." Hashtag gave him a puzzled glance, and Saul shook his head. "I've met a few women over the years who served in the Geran military. Let's just say the potential for rising through the ranks is pretty nonexistent."

Eve snorted. "You can say that again. When he first suggested it, my brother made out that it was exactly like the human military. It didn't matter if you were male or female—*all* ranks were on the table." She shrugged. "He was my brother. He wouldn't lie to me, would he? So I applied."

Saul stroked his finger along his bearded jaw. "What happened? Because I'm guessing your brother lied his ass off."

"He lied like a cheap rug." She gave another snort. "It wasn't so much a glass ceiling as a concrete one. My superiors seemed less concerned about my military prowess and *more* concerned about what they could gain if they had me join their breeding program."

"What are you?" Hashtag blurted. His nose itched, and he rubbed it.

"I'm a gorilla."

He let out a snort. "Well, I don't have to ask why they wanted to do that, do I?"

"So they reneged on their side of the deal," Saul continued. He frowned. "But you still stayed put for six years."

Eve stared at him in silence before letting out a sigh. "You're right. Because I believed what they told me. I was helping—in my own small way—to prepare for what was to come."

"And what was that?" Hashtag sniffed, and Saul passed him a box of tissues.

"It was common knowledge. We were increasing our numbers, ready for the day when shifters would take their rightful place."

Hashtag guffawed. "That would be with your foot on the necks of all humans, right? And you *know* we're both human, don't you? I'm sure those excellent shifter senses of yours told you that the second you walked into the room."

Eve fell silent again, except for several sniffs.

"You got allergies too, huh? They suck." Hashtag pushed the box of tissues toward her. "I think your need is greater."

"Let's get back to the interview, shall we?" Saul focused his attention on her. "You're here, so something clearly changed your mind."

She bit her lip. "Events took place this year that challenged my beliefs."

Saul cocked his head. "The raids on the schools?" Hashtag could understand that. According to what Aelryn had told Horvan, it seemed to have shaken a lot of people's beliefs.

Eve nodded. "I think they tried to suppress the facts, but word got out." She shivered. "Those poor kids.... What they did was horrific, both the teachers and the parents. And then I heard about the camps, how they'd left shifters to their fate, how they'd told them the Fridans would kill them all." Her face tightened. "That wasn't right."

"But you still think humans are inferior," Hashtag pressed. For some reason, knowing Eve's stance was important.

I want to believe she's different. He was clueless as to why it should matter to him.

106

Eve studied her clasped hands. "I have to be honest. All those years of indoctrination tell me yes, but what if the stories I've been hearing are true? What if humans are our ancestors? How could they be inferior to us if we came from them?"

Fuck, it was so tempting to put aside his doubts.

Then Hashtag thought about his friends—hell, his *family*—who might be at risk if they let her in.

He stood and walked around the table to where she sat. "Let's cut to the chase. Why should we trust you? What's to say you're not still working with *them*?"

Eve gazed up at him and sniffed, her brow furrowing,

"Answer the question, please," Saul said in a firm tone.

She locked gazes with him. "It's true, I've done things I'm not proud of. Things *no one* should be made to do. But I did them because I *believed* in what they were saying—until I found out what they were doing in the shadows. Suddenly everything I'd thought was good and right became dark and sinister. So I resigned. Told them some crap about wanting to start a family. They weren't happy about it, but I wasn't going to change my mind." Eve bowed her head. "It's okay, I get it. You'd have me on your team because I'm a damn good fighter, and you need as many of those as you can get, but—and it's a big but—you'd never trust me. And there's nothing I can do about that."

The anguish in her voice cut through Hashtag like a scalpel. He laid his hand on her shoulder, unable to refrain from doing so. "Hey...."

Eve gave another sniff, and her eyes widened. "Who *are* you?"

He chuckled. "You got amnesia or something? I'm one of the guys who's been asking you questions for the last half hour."

At the rear of the room, Crank chuckled too.

She shook her head. "No, I mean, who are you to *me*? There's this strange smell about you, that—"

"He has a smell?" Saul interjected. He blinked. "Kinda spicy and sweet, all at the same time?"

She gaped at him. "How did you know that?"

Hashtag turned to stare at Saul. "What she said. Because you lost me. What does the way I smell have anything to do with this?"

Saul grinned. "Oh, Hashtag, my friend. Your life is about to get really interesting." He glanced at Eve. "Do you have any idea what's going on?"

"You didn't answer my question." Eve didn't break eye contact. "Tell me how you know that."

Saul leaned back. "Because I smell that same smell—every time I'm around my mates."

Crank jerked his head up, his eyes round.

Eve's mouth fell open. "Mates?"

"Before you say mates are a myth, I should point out that he has two," Hashtag volunteered. "One human, one shifter. And he's not the only one. I know of at least two more...." He frowned. "What do you call it? A throuple? A triad?" The interview had taken a weird turn, and he was struggling to keep up.

"Mates?" Eve repeated, her brown eyes huge. She lurched to her feet. "No. No. This can't be real."

Hashtag threw his hands in the air. "Will *one* of you tell me what's going on?"

Saul stood. "How does she smell, Hashtag?"

"How does she—what the fuck kinda question is that?"

Saul pointed to Eve. "Go on. Take a good sniff." When Hashtag didn't move, Saul gave him a mock glare. "Consider it an order from a superior, soldier."

Hashtag rolled his eyes. "Fine." He turned to Eve. "Ma'am? Do you mind if...? I mean, is it okay if...? Aw fuck."

She chuckled. "I do like a man who understands consent." She tilted her head. "Yes, go ahead."

He leaned in closer to Eve and sniffed.

Holy fuck.

Her scent made him shiver and sent all the blood rushing south. He ached to touch her, kiss her.

Protect her.

He swallowed. "What the fuck is happening to me?"

Eve's eyes glistened. "Then it's true."

"*What's* true?" he demanded.

She smiled. "You're my mate."

What in the holiest fuck of fucks was she—

Then he froze as her words sank in, something unfurling deep in his belly, sending heat racing through him, along with a voice that was yelling one word over and over again.

Yes. Yes. Yes.

Hashtag forced himself to breathe deeply, portraying a calm exterior. Inside, he was torn between doubt, denial, shock—and exhilaration.

"If you say so." How he kept his voice from trembling, he would never know.

Eve seemed to have recovered her self-control. "I do." She stood tall, her eyes level with his. "So let me put all my cards on the table right now, because I don't want there to be any misconceptions."

"Me neither." That voice in Hashtag's head was telling him to stop talking and *kiss* her, for fuck's sake.

"I'm not one to defer to *anyone*, do I make myself clear? I've lived my life by my rules, taken care of myself, and I *refuse* to allow anyone to think they can control me."

Lord, she was magnificent when she was determined. Even her voice was a turn-on.

Hashtag smirked. "I have no problem whatsoever with you controlling me." What shocked him was how quickly his mind assimilated this new situation.

I have a mate.

Then he reconsidered. *Just the one? Oh dear Lord.*

She erupted into a coughing fit. When it stopped, she glared at him. "I'm not talking about sex."

He smiled. "Neither am I."

Eve widened her eyes. "You're not serious."

"I certainly am." Hashtag grinned. "And if we have *another* mate out there? I hope it's a guy."

"You what?" Crank hollered.

Hashtag twisted to look at him. "I'm bi, baby."

Crank's jaw hit the floor. "Since when?"

"Since… well, pretty much forever."

"But I thought you were straight. Hell, we all did."

Hashtag shrugged. "Have you *ever* known me talk about my conquests? Hmm? I can tell you the answer. No, you haven't, because I keep my sex life to myself. Except for Horvan blabbing about the whole tongue thing." He grinned. "But now my secret's out, I can reveal the truth. I *love* taking it up the ass."

"You never told me that."

"Because knowing *you*, you'd think you'd be man enough to give it to me."

Crank snickered. "I would have thought *exactly* that."

Hashtag guffawed. "Yeah, no. It takes a real man to make me submit. You're too much of a bottom."

Crank glared at Saul, who held up his hands. "Hey, I never said a word."

"I hate to interrupt all this masculine banter," Eve said loudly, "but can we get back to the part where I discovered I have a mate? Because having even *one* mate is absolutely huge."

"I wouldn't call it huge," Crank said with a chuckle. "But it *is* pretty impressive, if I—"

"Crank." Saul's voice had an edge of steel to it. "A word of advice? Do *not* describe another man's… equipment in my presence, okay?"

Crank's cheeks pinked. "Oh. Yeah. Right."

Hashtag couldn't take his eyes off Eve. "You're right. This *is* huge." He smiled. "Not to mention exciting as hell."

Part of him was yelling *Are you fucking* kidding *me? You're gonna roll over and* accept *all this?*

Another part couldn't wait to see where this would lead.

Saul sighed. "I think you'd better come with us," he told Eve. "We obviously have a lot to talk about." His phone buzzed. "I might as well take this. We're done here anyway."

"We are *so* done." Hashtag grinned. "And she is *so* in."

"I am?" Eve beamed.

"Fine, she's in. Besides, you'd kill me if I said no, right?" Saul clicked on Answer. "You're okay, we're done. What's up?" He listened, and Hashtag took advantage of the moment to take Eve's hand in his.

"Does that work for you? Coming with us, I mean."

She chuckled. "You think I'm letting you out of my sight? Besides, I have, like, fifty-million questions to ask."

"You and me both."

"And top of the list is… what tongue thing?"

Hashtag merely grinned.

"We're all going home," Saul announced as he finished his call. "That was Brick. Apparently we're about to receive a visitor." He paused. "And he's a Geran."

CHAPTER THIRTEEN

HASHTAG STABBED his finger against the glass. "Hey, we passed Hollingworth Candies."

"You want us to stop so you can buy your new girlfriend some chocolate-covered cherries?" Crank asked from the front seat, with a grin.

Saul turned right onto W 151st Street. "Too late now. I'm not going back."

Eve tapped Crank on the shoulder. "And is Saul *just* your boyfriend?"

Saul chuckled. "She got you there."

"All right. I apologize. You're way more than his girlfriend."

Eve smiled. "Apology accepted."

"And I was thinking of getting some chocolate chips for Mrs. Landon. You know, the ones she puts in the cookies?" Hashtag retorted. "That's where she buys them."

Eve arched her eyebrows. "Okay, I have a couple of questions. Who is Mrs. Landon, and where are we going?"

"To the home of a shifter called Dellan Carson," Saul told her. "Except it's more like HQ for the group."

"The barracks are only about twelve miles from the house," Hashtag added.

"And is that where I'll be living? At the barracks?"

Crank snorted. "Seeing as your mate lives at Dellan's place, I don't think that would be a likely scenario. One or more of you might have something to say about that."

"Do you take *all* your recruits to HQ?"

"Nope." Saul glanced at her in the rearview mirror. "You're the exception."

"Shouldn't that be *exceptional*?" Crank said with a snicker.

"It's a big house." Hashtag smiled. "And if you want a room to yourself—at least at first while you come to terms with the situation—that's fine. You can have my room, and I'll bunk up with Roadkill." Not that he wanted her in another room, but these were weird-ass circumstances, and he had to tread lightly.

I don't want to piss her off. Who in their right mind would piss off a gorilla?

This has to be a dream. Any second now, I'm going to wake up in bed, hearing Horvan, Dellan, and Rael fucking like bunnies above my room.

Except he *really* didn't want it to be a dream. He'd watched as the team found their mates. He'd seen how their love reflected in their eyes. He'd never admit it to anyone, but he desperately wanted that for himself. To be loved? Needed? Wanted.

Please let this be real. I think I'd die if it wasn't.

"Which leads me to another question." Then Eve returned Hashtag's smile, and it was as if sunlight filled the SUV. "By the way, you scored major points."

"I did?"

She nodded. "That bit about giving me my own room. You didn't assume."

"Wow. I'm seeing a whole new side to you, Hashtag." Crank grinned. "I don't even recognize you."

Hashtag gave him the finger. He gazed at Eve. "Ask your question."

"Hashtag… is that really your name?"

Before he could respond, Crank butted in. "No, but that's what everyone calls him, and maybe he likes it that way. I know if anyone called me by *my* real name, I'd flatten 'em." He twisted in his seat to stare at Hashtag. "I don't think I even *know* your real name."

He snorted. "And that's the way it'll stay." He held his hand out to her, and she took it. The light touch connected them, and with it came a sense of calm.

Eve gazed at their joined hands. "This still feels so… fantastic."

Hashtag said nothing. She'd nailed it.

Saul gave a snort. "Wait until you hear Hashtag's voice inside your head. First time that happened? It freaked me the fuck out."

Crank smacked Saul on the arm. "I don't hear you complaining now when we—"

Saul glared at him. "And you can stop right there."

Eve gaped at them. "You're mates? Okay, now the comments make sense. But I don't understand. You're human."

Saul chuckled. "Yeah, welcome to *our* world. Our mate is a Greenland shark."

112

"Can we get back to the voices part?"

"It seems once mates find each other, they can communicate using telepathy."

Eve stilled. "Seriously?"

Crank peered at Hashtag. "Why don't you give it a try?" He grinned. "You could tell her what you *really* think of her and we'd be none the wiser."

"He doesn't have to," Eve retorted.

Hashtag took a deep breath and stepped out of his comfort zone. *And what if I want to?*

Eve jerked her head in his direction, her eyes wide, and he smiled. *You have beautiful eyes.* Funnily enough, they reminded him of a photo he'd seen once of a gorilla. Its eyes had captivated him with their intelligence.

Her face lit up. *Thank you. And you have beautiful... muscles.*

He chuckled. *Glad you like 'em.*

And I can't wait to see them in all their glory.

Hashtag's dick perked up about a nanosecond later, and he groaned internally. *Can you not say stuff like that? We're almost at the house, and I am not gonna walk in there sporting a hard-on.*

She laughed, and even inside his head, it was a bright, joyous sound. *One of the drawbacks to being male. Suck it up, buttercup.*

"I get the feeling we've suddenly become surplus to requirements," Crank remarked with a smirk.

Eve glanced at the passing landscape. "Seems like a great place to live." Then she grinned. "Wow. Look at *that* house. It's more like a mansion. God knows how many bedrooms that place has."

"Five," Hashtag told her with a smile. "And eight bathrooms."

Saul turned left onto the driveway that curved through lush green lawns to the house, the lake visible behind it.

Eve gaped. "*This* is HQ?"

Saul chuckled. "Awesome, isn't it? Crank, Vic, and I share a room, but Dellan is building us a house down by the lake. I think they're laying the foundations next month."

So you don't mind staying here for a while?

Eve chuckled. *Gee, I dunno. I mean, I guess I could slum it here for a while.*

Thank God. She had a sense of humor.

Saul drove toward the six-car garage and parked in front of one of its white doors. Dellan came out to greet them, blinking when Eve got out of the car. Crank went over to him, and Hashtag would have given anything to overhear *that* conversation.

He leaned closer to Eve and whispered, "That's Dellan. Tiger shifter. His mates are Rael, who's a lion, and Horvan, who's a bear. Horvan and Saul are our joint team leaders. Me and Horvan, we go way back, along with Crank and Roadkill."

"I'm guessing you're the tech guy," she murmured as they approached Dellan.

"You got that right. Crank can fly anything that'll stay up in the air, and Roadkill, he's our driver. They're good guys in a fight too. They've had my back plenty of times."

Eve turned her head to gaze at him. "They're your family."

Hashtag nodded. "And just as precious to me as my own flesh and blood."

"They're *mates*?" Dellan's voice rose.

Hashtag laughed. "And here we go again. This is getting to be a regular thing."

He couldn't wait to introduce his family to his mate.

Still feels so fucking strange to be saying that.

Eve chuckled. *Tell me about it.* She frowned. *Am I going to hear your thoughts* all *the time? And vice versa?*

Hashtag put his hand at the small of her back. *Horvan says there are ways around that. I'll get him to sit down with us and share.*

With each passing minute, he grew more accustomed to the idea that he wasn't a single guy anymore. What shocked him was how much he liked that realization.

They went inside, and Hashtag took Eve into the kitchen to meet Mrs. Landon, who beamed at her.

I guess it must make a nice change to have another woman under this roof, after dealing with seven or eight guys all the time, depending on who's around.

Horvan came through the patio doors, wearing nothing but a pair of shorts. "Dellan's making this up, isn't he?" Rael was behind him, struggling into a pair of sweats.

Hashtag laughed. "Good news sure travels fast around here. Did we interrupt something?"

"They were playing outside," Dellan told him with a twinkle in his eye.

Horvan narrowed his gaze. "Bears don't play. I was getting some exercise."

Rael snorted. "You were trying to steal my ball, you mean." He went over to Eve. "You are *very* welcome here, Eve." He glanced at the others. "And *some* of us will have to watch our language from now on. Won't we, Crank?"

That raised a few chuckles.

"Oh please." Eve rolled her eyes. "Trust me, *I* can turn the air blue sometimes too. Don't treat me like some delicate flower, because I am *so* not that."

Hashtag didn't think he could have found a more perfect mate.

"Where's Roadkill?" he asked.

"Downstairs in the gym with Brick and Aric." Rael smirked. "Except I don't think Aric is working out—he's having a good time enjoying the view."

"Brick is a polar bear," Hashtag told Eve. "And his mate Aric is a kitty. Their other mate, Seth, is a tiger, but... he isn't here."

"He's being held in a camp," Horvan stated. "But that's why I asked you to get back here. He's been in touch. We're to expect a visitor sometime this weekend. He didn't know when, exactly, only that he is definitely coming."

"A Geran, you said?" Hashtag frowned. "What else do we know about this visitor?"

"Oh, not a lot," Horvan said lightly. "Except that he's the captain of the guard at the camp where they're holding Seth, Jake, and Jamie."

Hashtag stared at him. "You have *got* to be fucking *kidding*. And he's coming *here*? Why, for fuck's sake? How does he even know about us?"

"Seth told Aric that we need to listen to this guy. He said it would be to our advantage. So we'll hear him out, okay?" Dellan swallowed. "Besides, he might have news about my dad."

His dad?

Hashtag squeezed Eve's hand. *Long story. I'll tell you later.*

Voices grew louder, and Brick, Roadkill, and Aric walked into the kitchen. Roadkill grinned when he saw Hashtag.

"About time you got here. There are a couple of beers in the fridge with your name on them." He blinked when he saw Eve. "Hell-*o*. And who are you?"

"Meet Eve Duncan, our latest recruit, but more importantly, Hashtag's mate," Crank announced with glee. "And yeah, you heard that right."

Hashtag wanted to laugh at Roadkill's stunned expression. "Believe me, I was as shocked as you. But it's true."

"And he'd better stay on her good side, because she's a gorilla," Crank added. "So I guess we all know who'll be wearing the pants in *their* relationship." He cackled.

Roadkill dropped his towel over the back of a chair and strolled over to her, his hand outstretched. "Then I'm delighted to meet you."

Eve took his hand—

And gasped.

"What's wrong?" Hashtag noted her pallor, the way she trembled. "Eve?"

She sniffed. Sniffed again. Then she moved in closer until her body was almost touching Roadkill's.

"Eve? What's going on?"

She turned her head toward Hashtag, her eyes wide, her lips parted, and whispered one word.

"Mate."

Roadkill let out a strangled noise and took a step backward. "What the fuck?"

"Holy cow." Crank's eyes bulged. "Does *everyone* around here have a fucking mate?"

Hashtag's brain could not compute. Because if Roadkill was Eve's mate, that meant….

He shook his head slowly. "No. No. Uh-uh." He stared at Eve. "You've got it wrong. He's one of my squad mates."

She nodded, regaining a little of her usual color. "And now he's *another* type of mate."

Horvan cleared his throat. "Everyone out of here. I don't care where you go—give them some space." Then he turned and walked out the door, the others following.

Hashtag had never witnessed a room empty so goddamn fast.

He sank into a chair. "This is not happening."

Eve frowned. "I know it's a shock, but…. Didn't you tell me he's like family to you?"

"Yeah, I did, didn't I?"

"Then is it too much of a stretch to accept he's *more* than that?"

Roadkill's gaze went from Eve to Hashtag and back to Eve. "You're serious."

"There's one way to prove it," Hashtag announced. "Tell me what she smells like."

"What she…. Are you fucking nuts?"

"You heard right." Hashtag breathed deeply. "So take a good sniff, and if she *doesn't* smell like sugar and spice and all things nice, then maybe she's wrong. But I'm starting to doubt it."

Eve took a step toward him and offered him her neck.

Roadkill was like a statue. "This is fucking crazy."

"Just *do* it, all right?"

He leaned closer and gave a cautious sniff. His nostrils flared, and his face flushed. He took another sniff, only this time he brushed his lips against the golden skin under her earlobe, and *fuck* if that wasn't the hottest fucking thing *ever*.

Eve shivered. "My mate."

Roadkill straightened. "Oh my God." His gaze met Hashtag's.

There was only one more piece of proof needed.

Hashtag stood and crossed the floor to them. "I'm only guessing about this, but maybe now the three of us know who we are to each other, that's triggered something. So why don't we find out?"

"What are you talking about?" Roadkill demanded.

Hashtag placed his hand on Roadkill's arm. "Don't move, okay? Just let me…." He leaned in, buried his face in Roadkill's neck, and breathed him in.

Mary fucking Mother of God.

"Oh fuck," Roadkill whispered.

Eve cupped Roadkill's face with one hand, and Hashtag's with the other. Hashtag watched as she claimed Roadkill's lips with a fierce kiss, and the soft moan that escaped his buddy went straight to Hashtag's cock. Then it was his turn as Eve kissed him, and even though it was a fleeting, chaste connection, he felt it all the way down to his toes.

"Now kiss each other," Eve instructed.

Hashtag jerked his head around so fast, he was sure he'd gotten whiplash. "What? No way."

She narrowed her gaze. "Did I *ask* for your opinion? Kiss him."

The strength of her voice, combined with the order, made his knees weak.

Okay, so he loved being dominated, but it wasn't something he ever talked about. To anyone.

Eve already had a handle on him, and it was both disconcerting and heady as fuck.

"Let's get this over with."

The whining catch in his voice surprised the hell out of him.

Roadkill leaned in, moving slowly. So, so slowly.

Fucking tease.

Then their lips brushed, and every single synapse in Hashtag's brain was suddenly alive. He was on fire, imagining himself sandwiched between Eve and Roadkill. Some inner voice screamed that was a *really* bad idea, but was drowned out by another that told him in no uncertain terms to keep doing what he was doing, but without clothing.

Hashtag knew which one he wanted to listen to.

Okay, this got interesting. Eve grinned. *Never had a threesome before.*

Hashtag registered the shock that reverberated through Roadkill. *Holy fuck. I can hear you.*

He chuckled. "Yeah, it's surprising how fast you get used to that part." Eve's words sank in, and he realized she was right. It wasn't too big a stretch after all. And give him his due, Roadkill was awfully easy on the eye in a hot Asian, midthirties, fit but not overly muscled kinda way.

What was endearing as fuck? The brief encounter had steamed up Roadkill's glasses.

Not as steamy as it's gonna get when all three of us are naked.

Then he remembered that where his mates were concerned, there was no longer such a thing as a private thought.

Roadkill smirked. "I always loved seeing your ass in the shower. Can't wait to be inside of it." Soft lips ghosted Hashtag's neck before he let out a throaty chuckle. "Bet you're tight as hell."

Hell no.

Hashtag stepped back. "No. Absolutely not. I am *not* letting you fuck me."

Roadkill laid a warm hand on his shoulder. "You make it sound as though you have a choice."

"And you *did* say it would take a real man to make you submit," Eve added.

He glared at her. "Not helping," he ground out.

Roadkill's eyes gleamed. "Oh, he *said* that, did he?" His raw chuckle made Hashtag's cock stiffen. "Trust me when I say you'll be on your knees for me quite often."

Warmth flooded him, and his mouth suffered from an excess of saliva. The hairs rose on his arms and nape, and his breathing quickened. A pleasurable shiver rolled through him, and his fingers tingled with the need to touch Roadkill.

All it had taken were a few words from Roadkill to make Hashtag want to drop down in front of his friend.

His mate.

Another shiver trickled through him. "Yes, sir," he murmured.

Roadkill's hand was gentle on Hashtag's cheek. "Good boy."

Eve laughed. "Oh, I can see the three of us having *so* much fun together."

And now she said that? Hashtag could see it too.

"And *I* can see we have a lot to talk about," he said at last.

Saul had nailed it. Hashtag's life was about to get really interesting.

HASHTAG SAT on one of the patio chairs that surrounded the fire pit, a bottle of beer in his hand. Eve was in the kitchen with Dellan and Mrs. Landon, and by the sound of their laughter, everyone was getting along like a house on fire.

Didn't see this coming. Then he smiled to himself. *Neither did Roadkill. Wow. I can still hear you when you're out there. This is wild!*

Yeah, the sooner he talked with Horvan about that mental lockbox thingy, the better. It was getting very noisy inside his head.

"Okay if I join you?"

He jumped at the sound of Horvan's deep, quiet voice. "Sure." He indicated the nearest empty chair. "Funny. I was just thinking about you."

Horvan sat, nursing his own beer bottle. "So... you and Roadkill. Mates."

"Yeah. Who would've thunk it?"

And it still feels so fucking surreal.

Horvan leaned forward, elbows balanced on his knees, the bottle swinging between them. "And you never felt any *kind* of pull toward him?"

Hashtag wasn't sure he knew how to answer that.

Both Roadkill and Eve shared that same intoxicating scent, but it was more than that. He'd always admired Roadkill's body, slighter than his own bulk. The musky odor that clung to him after they finished a hard workout. The way he smiled.

Was that attraction? Did he have the hots for Roadkill even before he knew what it meant? Now that he was aware what they were to each other, he could think of a thousand different things he'd noticed about Roadkill that he never bothered to catalog about any of the others. The timbre of his voice had vibrated all the way to Hashtag's core on more than one occasion.

Then he recalled his pangs of jealousy whenever he'd seen Roadkill go off with a woman. Hashtag had always believed it had been because he'd felt the woman should've wanted *him.*

And now, with the benefit of hindsight?

Maybe he'd been jealous of *her.*

He took a swig from his bottle. "Not only is this all new, it's opened up a whole different dynamic."

"What do you mean?"

"I don't know how things work with you three—and I don't wanna know, okay? It's none of my fucking business. But... I'm happy giving *and* receiving, if you get my drift."

"Between us? You just described Dellan, whereas Rael? Total bottom."

"And you're a total top, right?"

Horvan chuckled. "Got it in one." He cocked his head. "Do I take it Roadkill is also a top?" Hashtag nodded, and Horvan smiled. "Then everything works out perfectly for the three of you, doesn't it?"

Hashtag took a long drink from his bottle before speaking. "Honestly? I'm not sure. From everything Eve says—and she hasn't said all that much—it sounds like she's a total top too. And it *should* upset me, but... I dunno. It doesn't. I feel as though I've finally found what I've been searching for my whole life."

Horvan arched his eyebrows. "So if you never get to top again?"

He shrugged. "I want to say I'd be upset, but I can't. I understand I don't know fully what it means, but they're my mates, and I want to give them the world." He thought back to that conversation, and heat flushed through him.

"What's on your mind?"

Hashtag coughed. "That dynamic I was talking about? There's something about Roadkill that makes me want to—"

Horvan's eyes gleamed. "Submit? It's something I'm used to. When the three of us shift, there's a distinct pecking order. Dellan submits to me, Rael submits to both of us, and yeah, that gets carried over into our sex life. But it's okay to submit." He smiled. "Roadkill and Eve are two lucky people. They get you for a mate." The smile morphed into a grin. "They also get something else that makes me jealous."

He frowned. "What?"

Horvan chuckled. "They get to be on the receiving end of that talented tongue of yours."

Hashtag scowled. "Can we forget about that part? I mean, that was a lifetime ago."

"When you were young, single, and horny as fuck." Horvan's eyes grew warm. "And now you have two people in there who would crawl through fire for you. As you would for them."

Hashtag's breathing hitched. "I would."

Horvan stood. "Of course, it does make your job a lot more awkward."

"What do you mean?"

"I'm lucky. When I go on a mission, my mates are safely out of harm's way, waiting for me to come back to them." He frowned. "Well, except for that one time when they ignored my instructions. But *your* mates aren't civilians—they're fighters. And we're about to go into battle." He looked Hashtag in the eye. "You need to ask yourself if you can focus when you're in the thick of it, knowing *they're* in the thick of it too."

Shit.

CHAPTER FOURTEEN

HASHTAG LAY on the lounger, staring up at the ink-black night sky strewn with stars. "Makes you feel so insignificant, doesn't it? All that vastness, and here we are, tiny little ants crawling over the skin of a giant blue-green marble floating in space."

"How many beers have you had tonight?" Roadkill's voice brimmed with amusement.

"Just the one." He'd wanted to keep a cool head, because *fuck*, there was such a lot to consider.

Eve spoke softly off to his left. "One day and everything changes."

That was the opening Hashtag had been waiting for.

"Let's get closer to the fire pit." The air had a definite chill. He got up and headed down the stone steps that led to the patio chairs. Behind them, the house was quiet; everyone else had gone to bed.

Which is where I should be at this hour.

Roadkill chuckled. Now *you're talking.*

He caught Eve's giggle as she joined him.

"We haven't *stopped* talking since the two of you walked through the front door," Roadkill reminded them as he strolled over to the fire pit. The flames lit up his face, reflecting in his glasses.

"Both out loud *and* inside our heads," Eve added, holding out her hands to warm them. "That mental lockbox Horvan and Dellan told us about.... Have either of you tried it yet? I mean, have you tried to hide your thoughts?"

"Not yet," Hashtag admitted. "Maybe tomorrow when I'm not so tired. And we *still* need to talk. This is important."

Eve studied him. "Yeah, I can feel that. What's on your mind?"

Hashtag stared into the orange-yellow flames. "There's a reason a lot of military guys stay single. Well, two, actually. Having a partner can be a distraction, and bad guys can see that as a weakness to be exploited." He grimaced. "Saul, Vic, and Crank learned that the hard way." He glanced at Eve, then Roadkill. "But *we* have a totally new situation. What happens when we're on a mission? How am I gonna concentrate when I'm worrying

122

about you two? Because losing either of you is gonna have consequences. You're more than partners." He swallowed. "I asked Dellan what happens when someone loses a mate. His answer wasn't helpful. He said he didn't have a clue. *Then* he added he hoped he never gets to find out."

"Now wait a minute." Roadkill stared at him. "Did you ever worry about me *before* when we went on missions? And tell the truth."

Hashtag didn't have to think about it. "No, I didn't."

"And why not?"

"Because I know you can take care of yourself," he admitted.

"Exactly." Roadkill's smile was as warm as the firelight that danced on his skin. "Nothing's changed. Well, except for one thing. When we go out on missions, we've got radios, mics...." His eyes gleamed. "We don't need any of those. And that means we'll be aware of each other. If something happens to one of you, I'll know about it in a heartbeat, which *also* means I can respond faster."

Eve nodded. "What he said. You're both good at what you do. You wouldn't have gotten this far if you weren't." She smiled. "Well, so am I, and I happen to think we make a pretty formidable team."

Hashtag smiled too. "You and Roadkill are rocking the pretty part, at any rate."

Roadkill shuffled his chair closer to Hashtag's. "So I'm pretty? You *have* noticed me, then?"

He chuckled. "Course I have."

"So that means we can hit the sack now?"

Eve snickered. "What he said."

Hashtag threw his hands up in the air. "Look, I'm *trying* to do the right thing, okay? We just found out we share a profound connection. That doesn't give us carte blanche to jump on each other's bones." He gazed at them. "I want to get to know you guys."

Eve got out of her chair, walked over to him, and crouched in front of him, the firelight providing her with a golden aura as it backlit her hair. "I love that you're trying to do things the right way, to be a gentleman. And if it was any other time, and you two were any other people, I'd say sure, let's take the slow path. But let's be honest. Thanks to this connection, we already know each other far more intimately than couples who've been together decades."

"But you have this overwhelming feeling that time isn't ours to do with as we please," Roadkill interjected. "I feel it too."

Eve nodded. "Yes. I can't help it. I know you said you'd give me space, privacy… but what if that's not what I want?" She sat back on her haunches, and Hashtag's nostrils filled with the scent of her, the essence of her that turned him inside out, upside down, back to front. "Question. Have you both had a ton of relationships?"

Roadkill snorted. "Yeah, right. The lifestyle precludes that."

"Same here." Hashtag shrugged. "You get used to taking what you can get."

Eve tilted her head to one side. "Not exactly satisfying, is it? I know how you feel. And I'm tired of meaningless sexual encounters designed to merely scratch an itch. I want something *real*." She stood, moving between their chairs, and took their hands in hers. "And something tells me I'll have that—with you. So sure, if you really want, I'll find a room of my own. Just be prepared for the consequences. Both of you."

Roadkill blinked. "Hey. *I* was going to suggest we all share one room, so don't lump me in with him." He turned his head to give Hashtag a beseeching glance unlike any other he'd given in all the ten plus years Hashtag had known him. "Quit being so noble and do what your heart is telling you to do."

Hashtag knew exactly what his heart wanted. *Maybe he's right.* Then Eve's words registered. "Be prepared for the consequences, you said. What consequences?"

Eve stared at him, and the silence that fell pressed in against him.

When he felt a hand on his cock, he glanced down to find—

Nothing.

But I can feel it. Soft, warm fingers stroked his length.

"Feels good, doesn't it?" Eve murmured.

"How… how are you doing this?"

"I'm imagining how it feels to stroke your dick." She grinned. "Actually, it feels *damn* good. So go to your own bed by all means. But you're going to know exactly what I'm thinking about all night long until it has the desired effect. And that's both of you in my bed. Me in your arms." She expelled a breath, and the invisible hand was gone. "I've just found my mates, and I want them to hold me, caress me, kiss me. If you want to wait to make love, okay. I can deal. But I really don't think you want that, do you?"

Hashtag knew when he was fighting a losing battle—one he didn't want to win in the first place. "No, I don't."

"Then let's stop talking and go upstairs so we can get to know each other a whole lot better."

"As soon as we get the practicalities out of the way," Roadkill said in a decisive tone. "Not knowing how it works with shifters, but do we need condoms?"

"I'm good to go." She glanced at him. "Besides, do you have any?"

Roadkill shook his head.

"And I don't either," Hashtag added.

Eve peered at them. "Have either of you fucked bareback before? I'm asking because if you get as many physicals as I do, you know if *you're* good to go too."

Heat rolled over Hashtag in a slow tide, and his hole tightened at the thought of Roadkill's shaft sliding bare into him, nothing between them.

Holy fuck.

Roadkill grinned. "I don't think we need to continue this conversation, do you?"

"Hell no." Hashtag stood up, Roadkill with him, and still holding hands, Eve led them toward the house.

It was cool inside as they climbed the stairs. Hashtag's heart was pounding, but he knew Roadkill's was hammering too. Eve tightened her grip on their hands.

"Don't be scared," she whispered. "You've shared plenty of experiences in the past. Well, this is a new experience, and if my instincts are correct, it's going to feel amazing." She paused at the top step. "Whose room are we going to?"

"Mine," Roadkill told her. "It's got more space, not to mention a bigger bed than Hashtag's." He pointed to the door. "That's it." He led the way, opened it, and went inside.

"I think this is what happens next," Hashtag said as he lifted her into his arms and carried her across the threshold.

Eve pressed her cheek to his. "And *this* is where I tell you that a gorilla can lift something that weighs two thousand kilos, which is over ten times their body weight and equivalent to about thirty humans."

He chuckled. "Then you get to carry *both* of us in next time."

AS SOON as the door closed, Roadkill's imagination went into overdrive.

I think Christmas just came early.

Eve chuckled as Hashtag lowered her onto the bed. "As long as neither of *you* do." She cocked her head. "Or is this something I should know about? Is a stiff breeze all it takes to pull your trigger?" Her eyes were bright.

Roadkill laughed. "I'm all about the stamina, baby. And right now, stiff is the perfect description." He watched as she unclipped her hair, letting it fall in long dark bronze waves that framed her face and tumbled onto her shoulders. He loved her leanness, her toned muscles, the set of her jaw.

Hell, he loved every bit of her.

Fuck, you're beautiful.

Eve smiled. "You're easy on the eyes too. But I'm curious." She pointed to Hashtag. "What do you think of our mate over there?"

He stared at Hashtag, drinking in the sight of the man he knew so well—his strong jawline, the clear blue eyes that sparkled when he laughed, the permanent five o'clock shadow because Hashtag hated shaving every day, the spiky haircut he hadn't changed in years. Roadkill already knew by heart what lay beneath Hashtag's jeans and tight tee. He'd seen it enough in the shower.

He smiled. "Hashtag? He's as hot as you are." He chuckled. "It's like standing in front of a buffet and not knowing where to start."

"I think *I* know." Eve gestured to him and Hashtag. "So you two have never—"

"Never," Hashtag blurted.

"Not even a threesome where you shared a woman—or a man?"

"Not even that."

"And you've been buddies for how long?"

"Ten years, give or take," Roadkill told her.

Eve nodded. "So you've fought together, shared quarters. I'm going to guess you've both had a few women in your time." She glanced at Hashtag. "And by the sound of it, you've had a few guys too."

Roadkill jerked his head in Hashtag's direction. "Wait—what? You're bi?"

Eve blinked. "You didn't know, did you?" She peered at Roadkill. "Have *you* ever been with a guy?"

"Uh-uh."

Hashtag gaped at him. "Then what was all that stuff you came out with downstairs? Was that just bravado? Because you sure sounded like you knew what you were talking about."

Roadkill shrugged. "So I've looked at your ass. Hey, I like asses. But I've never stuck my dick in one." He flushed. "Well, in a guy's, at any rate."

Eve snorted. "I shouldn't think it's all that different from a woman's." Then she smiled. "Okay, that settles it." She shuffled back toward the headboard and leaned against the mound of pillows. "This first time is all about you boys."

Roadkill blinked. "What?"

"And where do *you* fit in that scenario?" Hashtag demanded. "Because after that trick with your hand on my cock, we all know you want this as much as we do."

"Oh, don't you worry about me. We'll get around to that soon enough. And now I know Roadkill's into anal?" She grinned. "Taking both of you at the same time went to the top of my bucket list."

Oh dear Lord. Roadkill's shaft was like steel.

"But not tonight," Eve added with a smile. "This time is all about you two, connecting in a whole new way. And as for me? I get a front row seat."

"You're gonna sit there and *watch*?" Roadkill couldn't keep his incredulity out of his voice.

Eve gave him a sweet smile. "Think of me more as a… facilitator." She pointed to Hashtag. "Now kiss him, and make it good enough to curl his toes."

"Are you always this demanding?" Roadkill asked with a grin.

"Honey, you have *no* idea. But judging from what I heard downstairs, you'd give me a run for my money." She paused. "Now make him yours."

Roadkill smiled. "Yes, ma'am." He crooked his finger. "Come here."

Hashtag stood in front of him, and Roadkill didn't hesitate. He cupped Hashtag's nape and pulled him in for a no-holds-barred kiss, going deep, loving the groans that escaped him.

"Oh Gods, he likes that," Eve gasped. "More."

Roadkill had no intention of stopping there. He kissed Hashtag roughly, his hands all over those wide shoulders, the broad back, the narrow waist, loving the feel of hard flesh beneath his fingertips. He slid his hands lower to squeeze that firm ass.

Roadkill leaned in. "You want me in there, don't you?"

"Yes." The word was almost a moan.

He arched his eyebrows. "Forgotten already?"

Hashtag blinked. "Yes… sir."

Roadkill grinned. "That's better." He molded his body against Hashtag's, feeling hardness that was easily the equal of his. He rocked against Hashtag's erection, loving the soft noises that only added to the need pouring from him.

He took a step back, severing their connection. "Undress me. Everything comes off."

Hashtag's fingers trembled as he removed Roadkill's clothing, especially when he got down to his briefs, where his cock strained against the black cotton, the head already poking above the waistband. Hashtag's light touch on his dick only served to ramp up Roadkill's desire.

"Take 'em off," he instructed.

Hashtag slowly lowered the briefs, revealing Roadkill's erection an inch at a time until at last it sprang free, pointing to the ceiling.

"Wow." Eve's voice sounded awed, and Roadkill felt way taller than his five feet and seven inches. "Talk about packing."

Hashtag grasped the hem of his own tee, and Roadkill frowned. "Did I say you could?"

The tremors that rippled through Hashtag sent a clear message.

Holy fuck, he's really digging this.

Roadkill spread his feet apart. "On your knees. Suck it." He caught the hitch in Eve's breathing, but his hearing only confirmed the thoughts that filled her head.

If this is what it's going to be like every time....

I know! The delight in Eve's voice lit him up inside. Then Roadkill groaned when Hashtag gave the head of his cock a hard suck.

"No hands," he instructed. "Just your mouth." He cupped Hashtag's head and gave a leisurely thrust before going deeper.

So thick. So fucking long. Hashtag's eyes were huge as he swallowed more and more of Roadkill's shaft.

Roadkill smiled. "Good boy. That's it, take it." He pulled free and smacked the head of his dick a couple of times against Hashtag's cheek before sliding it once more between his lips. "Take your cock out. Show me how hard this gets you."

Hashtag fumbled with the zipper, shoving his jeans over his hips, his shaft bobbing up. Roadkill loved how it curved to the left, precum descending from the slit in a glistening trickle.

This is amazing. I feel everything that you do. Watching you adds to it all. Even her thoughts had a breathless quality to them.

"*Now* you can get undressed," Roadkill told him.

Hashtag's grin was a thing of beauty. "Yes, sir." He stood and discarded his clothing in the blink of an eye, his erection evidence of his arousal. Roadkill took a moment to admire the deep vee that led from above Hashtag's hips to his pubic hair, the flatness of his belly, the smooth skin in direct contrast to his stubble-covered jaw.

He drew Hashtag to him, unable to ignore the siren call of that mouth, desperate to taste those lips again.

"Get his hole ready," Eve instructed.

Roadkill grinned. "There's lube in the nightstand drawer."

Eve chuckled. "Uh-uh. Don't prep him with your fingers. Use your mouth."

What the—

"I... I...."

"You've never done that?" Eve laughed. "So you're okay sticking your dick in a hole, but not your tongue?" She cocked her head. "You ever had your ass eaten?" He shook his head, and she chuckled. "The thought turns you on, though, right? That much I can tell."

Roadkill couldn't hide a damn thing from her, and he knew it.

Eve gave him a triumphant smile. "In that case... eat his ass. Jump to it, baby."

Then he realized Hashtag was already on the bed on his hands and knees, back arched, ass tilted, his knees wide.

Roadkill snorted. "Oh, so you like that idea too, huh?"

Hashtag twisted to glance at him over his shoulder. "Yes, sir." He raised his chin, and Eve kissed him. She gazed along his body, smiling.

"Still enjoying the view?" Roadkill asked.

"I'll enjoy it even more when I see your face buried in his crack."

Roadkill shook his head. "You're one bossy woman."

"And you wouldn't have me any other way."

Ain't that the truth?

Roadkill stood behind Hashtag, pulled his cheeks apart, and gave a cautious lick over his pucker.

"More," Eve said before claiming Hashtag's mouth in another heated kiss.

Roadkill swept over Hashtag's hole with a flat tongue, his hand on Hashtag's dick, tugging it as he licked and sucked.

Eve's eyes widened, and she stroked Hashtag's hair. "Holy hell, you like that, don't you?" Then she chuckled. "Scrap that—you both do."

It was one hell of a revelation for Roadkill too.

Hashtag moaned, and Roadkill grinned. "Let's see if he likes this." He brought the flat of his hand down *smack* on Hashtag's ass, and there was no mistaking his reaction. Another moan fell from Hashtag's lips, but the groan of pleasure that filled Roadkill's head was even louder. Precum was still dripping onto the comforter in a steady trickle.

He's ready.

I was ready at first lick, Hashtag groused.

"Flip over and scoot up the bed a little," Roadkill instructed. Hashtag rolled onto his back, and Eve hooked her arms under his pits to hoist him toward the headboard until his head was in her lap. She bent over to kiss him while Roadkill grabbed the lube and slicked up.

Eve's right. I know there were no surprises on your last physical. Roadkill grinned. *I saw the results, remember? Just like you saw mine. And it's been months since—*

"For fuck's sake, hurry up and put it in me," Hashtag cried out.

Roadkill climbed onto the bed, knelt at Hashtag's ass, and eased into his body, unwilling to rush. He wanted to savor this, to burn the moment into his memory. *Our first time.*

Hashtag's gaze met his, and he nodded, mouth open.

Roadkill bit his lip. "So tight," he murmured.

"So deep," Hashtag murmured back.

"I can go deeper," Roadkill said with a grin.

Hashtag's eyes flashed. "Do it." Roadkill filled him to the hilt, and Hashtag's eyes rolled back. "Aw fuck." Eve stroked his chest and stomach while Roadkill settled into a steady rhythm, hips rolling as he moved in and out, at times withdrawing completely, then spearing his dick deep into Hashtag's body.

Eve's hand was on Roadkill's thigh. *How does it compare to fucking with a condom?*

He laughed. *No comparison. This is awesome. It's feels as if....* He struggled to find a suitable analogy. *It's like I'm swimming in you, and it's warm, and comforting, and....* Roadkill bent down and kissed him. *I love it.*

Hashtag's hand was on his neck, his gaze fixed on Roadkill's eyes. *I love it too.*

Eve leaned over, grasped Hashtag's ankles, and pulled them toward her, rolling his ass up off the bed. Roadkill leaned forward, his lips meeting Eve's in a slow kiss while he picked up the pace, driving his shaft all the way home, relishing the noises that poured from Hashtag's mouth, the sensations that assaulted Roadkill, leaving him in no doubt as to how much Hashtag was loving every fucking minute.

He wrapped his hand around Hashtag's cock and worked it in time with his thrusts, hips bucking now, not languid but impassioned, not fluid but frantic, his own orgasm within sight.

"How do you feel?" he demanded as he fucked Hashtag with deep strokes.

"Full," he moaned.

Roadkill withdrew, his gaze locked on Hashtag's face. "Whose hole is this?"

"Yours."

He froze, the head of his dick pressing against Hashtag's hole. "What?"

"Yours, *sir.*"

He smiled. "Better." Then he hooked his arms under Hashtag's knees and fucked him hard and fast while Eve tugged on his cock, the pair of them working together to push Hashtag over the edge. Roadkill's harsh breath mingled with theirs, and then they were there, Hashtag's come coating Eve's hand as Roadkill pulsed into him, his head bowed.

"Kiss me?"

Roadkill couldn't ignore the entreaty in Hashtag's voice, and he took Hashtag's mouth in a fierce, primal kiss. A second later, Eve's lips met theirs, and they shared a different kind of kiss, one that filled Roadkill with a quiet joy.

It was a weird moment. He withdrew from Hashtag's warm body, yet *he* was left feeling empty. As he sat back, he caught his breath at the sight of his own spunk trickling from Hashtag's body, his hole contracting as he pushed it out.

That is the hottest thing I have ever seen.

A sight Roadkill wanted to witness again. And again. And again.

Hashtag snorted. *If you think I'm letting you back in there tonight, think again. We're talking recovery time here.*

"Oh my God." Eve laughed out loud. "If you'd told me a week ago I could have this much fun without even taking my clothes off, I'd have said you were nuts."

"So imagine how good it's going to be when you do." Hashtag expelled a long breath. "Just give me time to get my breath back."

Eve traced the line of his spent dick with her finger. "It's not your breath I'm interested in." Then she scooped up some of his come and tasted it.

"Feed me some of that," Roadkill asked her.

Eve swiped her fingers across Hashtag's belly, then held them to Roadkill's lips. He sucked on them, his dick twitching when he caught the soft moan that escaped her.

Hashtag chuckled. "You two are gonna kill me, aren't you?"

Roadkill let out a happy sigh. He'd assumed his life would take a predictable course, and in one day all his assumptions had shattered into a million tiny fragments.

Ready to be molded into an entirely new life that promised to be way better than anything he could have imagined.

CHAPTER FIFTEEN

HORVAN FOUND Dellan on the couch in one of the living rooms, his legs curled under him and a pot of coffee sitting on the table beside him. Dellan stared out the window where the first rays of sunlight had caught the treetops.

Dellan turned his head as Horvan approached. "Hey. There's coffee if you want some."

Horvan sat beside him. "How long have you been down here? I didn't hear you get up."

"I couldn't sleep." He raised his gaze to the ceiling and smiled. "Unlike Rael. He amazes me how he can shut out the world the way he does."

Horvan poured himself a cup. "Suppose you tell me what kept you awake." He didn't like the air of unease that clung to his mate.

"I was thinking, I guess. Couldn't shut my mind down." Dellan shook his head. "Yesterday certainly gave me plenty to occupy my thoughts."

Horvan didn't have to ask what that meant. Hashtag and Roadkill were like brothers, had been for more than a decade, and to learn their connection went way deeper than that? There was a rightness to it. As for Eve, she'd walked through that door and Horvan's band of brothers had suddenly gained a sister.

A pretty awesome sister at that.

Dellan rested his head against the seat cushion. "We know nothing about mates, do we?"

He gave a wry chuckle. "Oh, I wouldn't say *that*. We know one thing—they seem to come in threes. And so what? Maybe that's how it's supposed to be."

Dellan stared at him. "You mean three is the norm?"

Horvan nodded.

He pondered for a moment. "You might have something there. A triangle is *the* most stable shape, isn't it? And while threesomes occur for different reasons—to spice up a relationship, to bring in something that's

133

lacking in the original partners—sometimes they can be a little… wobbly, you know, with not all the sides equal. But with mates, it isn't like that." Dellan pointed toward the ceiling. "Take Saul, Vic, and Crank for example. Crank came along after Saul and Vic had been together for years, but if you ask him if he feels as though he's an add-on or a third wheel, he'd laugh at you. He *knows*, balls to bones, that he's meant to be with them, just like they're meant to be with him."

"I don't think musing about mates would've deprived you of hours of sleep," Horvan remarked. *Come on, baby, tell me what's hurting you. Let me in.*

Dellan returned his gaze to the window, his face tight. "Alec…."

Aw shit.

Horvan felt the pain that lanced through Dellan. Ever since Saul had told them about his torture at the hands—or rather, claws—of Alec, the result of the Geran's experimentation with one of Dellan's offspring, Horvan knew it had to be on his mind. *No one wants to think they're created a monster.* He waited for Dellan to say more.

"Once I learned about the enforced mating—and God knows how many times they brought shifters to that fucking cage in more than a year—I accepted the truth. Somewhere out there are probably untold numbers of little Dellans and Dellanettes."

Horvan couldn't hold back his smile. "That sounds cute as fuck."

"It does, doesn't it? Except then you remember why they came into being, and suddenly it's not so cute after all. But Alec? He's in a whole different league. From what Saul told me, he's… an impossibility. A bio-engineered freak. A Geran killing machine." His face contorted. "But I have to find him, if only to discover if…."

"If what?"

Dellan's eyes were full of pain. "If he can be saved."

Aw fuck.

Horvan put his cup on the table and held his arm out wide. "Come here."

Dellan didn't hesitate, shifting across to rest his head on Horvan's chest. Horvan wrapped Dellan in his arms, holding him close enough that he could feel Dellan's heart beating.

"Remember what Saul told us? How he described Alec? He said it was as if the lights were on but no one was home. He also said Alec didn't speak, not once. That he didn't show any emotion."

Dellan craned his neck to peer at him. "But maybe he can be... deprogrammed?"

Horvan stroked a finger under Dellan's bearded chin. "We won't know that until we find him." Then he pressed his lips to Dellan's forehead. "But I don't think you should get your hopes up. It'll only hurt more if they're smashed."

"At least you said *if* and not *when*." Dellan sighed. "I want my dad."

"I know. And when this guard gets here, we'll know more." He hoped.

I hope so too.

Horvan chuckled. *I'm getting forgetful in my old age. I didn't hide that thought.*

Dellan's eyes twinkled. "Anyone who can fuck me through the mattress twice in one night is not old by *any* stretch of the imagination." He returned his head to Horvan's shoulder. "About our visitor.... We're going to have to keep an eye on Brick."

"You noticed that too, huh?" When Aric had informed them of the visit, Horvan hadn't missed Brick's mottled face, the veins on his neck straining against the skin, his clenched hands.

"Hey, I'm with him on this one. This guy is one of the bastards in charge of keeping my dad, Seth, and countless others prisoner. How many seconds do you think Brick will wait before ripping his arms out of their sockets?"

Horvan snorted. "Two—if we're lucky."

"Exactly. So if this guy is as important as Seth says, we have to let him speak. And that means keeping Brick on a tight leash until we've heard why the fuck he's come to us."

"Seth didn't tell Aric that part?"

Dellan shook his head.

Horvan bit his lip. "I don't think they make a leash strong enough to restrain a pissed-off polar bear."

"Remember the other day when we called Doc? Well, something he said got me thinking."

"Too much thinking, not enough fucking," Horvan remonstrated.

Dellan gave him a light swipe on the arm. "I'm being serious. He reminded me that I connected with Rael in a dream. And that led me in a new direction."

"You got no sleep at all, did you?"

A shrug. "Not much."

"Okay, tell me about this new direction."

Dellan ran his hand over Horvan's chest. "Aric said they wouldn't split up Seth and my dad at the camp."

"Maybe because they're father and son?"

He snorted. "As if they'd care about that. But what do we know about Seth? He's a tiger, like Dad. *And* he has psychic abilities. So... what if those abilities are inherited? What if I found my way into Rael's dream because *I* inherited those same gifts?"

Horvan stilled. "Whoa there. Where are you going with this?"

Dellan sat up. "I want to try."

"Try what?"

"I don't know. Experiment? See if there's anything *else* I can do?" He huffed. "Surely Doc's network of shifters has *someone* who's into psychic research."

Horvan saw the light. "You want to see if you can find Alec."

Dellan nodded.

"Then we'll try."

Horvan would do anything to bring his mate some peace.

HASHTAG HAD a grin that would not quit. Unfortunately, everyone knew what had put it there. At least Roadkill and Eve appeared as goofy as he did.

Scratch that. Eve appeared to be as cool as a cucumber.

Does nothing ruffle her feathers? Then he thought back to the previous night. *Nope, not a goddamn thing.*

"I'm going to grab some time in the gym before lunch, while it's quiet," Eve told them. She arched her eyebrows. "Either of you going to join me?"

"Give me five minutes and I'll be there," Roadkill replied.

"Me too." Hashtag tried not to stare at Eve's ass as she walked away from them.

Those shorts could have been molded to her. The strip of golden flesh between shorts and crop top, the long, tanned legs.... Every inch of her called to him.

"Hey." Roadkill pinched Hashtag's arm. "Mind out of the gutter. Horvan wants a quick meeting, remember?"

He guffawed. "Don't forget I can see exactly where *your* mind is. And no, we are *not* fucking on the weight bench. Dellan would kill us. Do you have any idea how difficult it is to get lube out of the leather?"

"Spoilsport," Roadkill muttered. Then he grinned. "I'll get Eve to work her magic on you."

Yeah, he was a pushover where she was concerned.

"I can't believe what we did last night," he murmured.

Roadkill chuckled. "Well, you sure seemed enthusiastic." His eyes gleamed. "And you? Talk about a dark horse. I had no fucking idea you had a domination kink." He grinned. "This is going to work out great." He inclined his head toward the stairs leading down to the basement. "She was a revelation, wasn't she? She looks like butter wouldn't melt, and then we discover—"

"She's demanding as fuck."

Roadkill rolled his eyes. "Tell me about it. She even had *me* doing things I would normally balk at."

He grinned. "Yeah, I noticed. You didn't seem all that into it when she told you to eat my ass."

"I was wrong, okay?" Roadkill sighed. "You were fucking delicious." He leaned in closer, his breath tickling Hashtag's ear. "And even tighter than I imagined you'd be."

His words sent heat racing through Hashtag, and all he could think about was Roadkill's cock driving into him.

"Tell you what. After dinner tonight, why don't the three of us go down into the media room, pick a movie, and have a date night?"

Hashtag stared at him. "What—no plans for another night of hot sex? Who are you, and what have you done with Roadkill?" Not that he minded. The ache in his ass was a glorious reminder that Roadkill's dick was definitely out of proportion in comparison with the rest of his body.

He let out another sigh. "You were right, okay? We need to spend time getting to know each other. We've got a head start—we need to let her catch us up."

Hashtag moved in and kissed him on the lips. "I love it. Let's go tell her."

"Sure—*after* we've fucked on the weight bench."

Hashtag was still chuckling as they headed for their meeting.

Seems like some things don't change.

Thank God.

CRANK DIDN'T begrudge Hashtag and Roadkill a little happiness, but if he had to glance up one more time and see that damn *cat who got the cream* expression, he was going to lose his shit.

You know you won't do that. You're missing Vic, that's all, like I am. And seeing the three of them brings it home.

He turned his head to find Saul regarding him with a warm smile. *Yeah. Snapchat isn't cutting it. Can't feel his mouth on my dick that way.*

Horndog.

You know it.

He said he'd be home soon.

"Taxi pulling up," Hashtag called out, peering at the cameras on his laptop screen.

"Is it Vic?" Crank's heart lurched into a higher gear.

Roadkill took a closer look before giving Crank and Saul a sympathetic glance. "Nope. Sorry. It's some guy in jeans and a hooded jacket, and he's got a bag."

"What does he look like?" Aric asked from the small couch where he and Brick sat in a tangled heap of arms and legs.

He seems so small when he's next to Brick. Then again, so do most people.

Saul gave a mental snort. "Polar bear? House kitty? You do the math."

Hashtag peered at the screen. "Dirty blond hair, scraggy beard...."

Aric sat upright. "That sounds like the guy Seth described."

Brick was up and off the couch in a heartbeat. He paced a little, scraping his fingers across his scalp, the veins visible on his muscled biceps. Aric was at his side in an instant, his hand on Brick's thick forearm, his gaze trained on his large mate.

Hey, Saul? Better watch Brick. This could get ugly real quick.

Saul glanced at him. *You got it.*

"Let him in, Roadkill," Horvan said from the wide two-seater couch where he sat with Dellan and Rael. Roadkill headed out of the room.

The stranger's arrival sent a current of electricity through everyone, and Crank noticed how all heads turned in the direction of the door.

"Remember what Seth said." There was a note of warning in Horvan's voice. "We need to hear him out."

Good man. Horvan clearly knew the score too.

"And maybe bear in mind not *all* Gerans are the bogeyman?" Eve suggested. "Present company included." That earned her a hug from Hashtag.

The door opened again, and Roadkill walked in. "I've searched him. He's clean."

A tall man followed him. He was maybe in his early thirties, with a shock of hair brushed up from his forehead. And judging by the way his gaze darted around the room, by the way his hand shook, he was nervous as hell.

"You've got a fucking *nerve*," Brick bellowed as he charged across the room, grabbed the guy by the throat, and slung him against the wall.

"Brick, no!" Aric yelled as Hashtag, Saul, and Horvan grabbed Brick's shoulders and tried to pull him away from the guy. Crank joined them, and even with four muscular men, they couldn't divert Brick from his mission to kill the son of a bitch.

"Brick." Aric stepped between Brick and his quarry, both hands on Brick's broad chest, his face upturned to look Brick in the eye. "Please, baby."

Listen to him, Crank urged silently.

Aric reached up to curve his small hand around Brick's cheek. "Brick... please...."

Brick gave a loud sob and crumpled into Aric's arms. Horvan and Saul helped him into a chair. Aric wrapped his arms around Brick's large frame, shivers racking his slight body.

The guy stood trembling. "What the hell?" he croaked.

Horvan arched his eyebrows. "Well, what the fuck did you expect? We know where you work—"

"Except I hardly think 'work' describes what *you* do, *Captain*," Crank interjected with a sneer.

Horvan glared at him before addressing the guy. "You have his mate incarcerated in your fucking camp. Did you *really* expect him to invite you in and offer tea and scones? Are you *that* delusional?" He paused. "What's your name?"

"Milo Keppler. And I don't understand how you can—" Milo expelled a breath. "Seth told you. I still don't understand how he managed it, but he said he would." He glanced at their faces, freezing when he caught sight of Dellan.

Then he walked over to him.

Crank and Hashtag were at Milo's side in a heartbeat, and Roadkill was behind him.

Milo was still shaking as he stared at Dellan. "You resemble your father."

Dellan made a choking sound. "He's okay?"

"He's fine. Well, he *was* the last time I saw him." Milo paused. "He gave me a message for you. He said, 'Tell Dellan I can't wait to see him again, and I'm sorry I didn't bring him back a present from Italy.'"

Tears trickled down Dellan's cheeks, and Horvan and Rael held him.

Horvan stared at Milo. "Seth also told us to listen to you." He let go of Dellan and stood. "Now tell us how you knew where to find us. Because Seth doesn't know that." He turned to peer at Aric. "Unless you told him?"

Aric shook his head, not letting go of Brick.

"I was given this address by Jamie Matheson," Milo announced.

Dellan was on his feet in an instant. "Jamie's there too?"

He nodded. "And he's okay."

"So why are *you* here?" Brick ground out.

Crank was relieved to see Aric's gentle hands were working their magic.

"I want the Fridans to liberate the camp." Milo sounded a little breathless.

"As easy as that," Saul said with a snort. "Sure, why not? We've got nothing better to do than organize a raid on a camp whose location is a freakin' *mystery*."

Milo gaped at him. "I'll give you all the details you'll need. Coordinates, routines, numbers...."

"And why would you do that, soldier?" Eve snarled, her voice harsher than Crank had heard it so far. She folded her arms across her chest and glared at Milo.

Crank grinned. Eve was gonna fit in just fine.

Milo blinked. "I know you, don't I?"

She nodded. "We met about seven years ago. You were the rising star, I recall. Now answer my question. Why would you waltz in here—into what amounts to the enemy's HQ—and betray everything you've been fighting for? And yes, I'm doing exactly the same thing, but I've got a damn good reason for doing it. What's yours?"

"My mate Jana is in that camp," he blurted. "And if you don't help, she'll die."

All the color drained from Eve's face. "You... you have a mate too?"

He frowned. "You mean...."

"Why should we believe a word you say?" Roadkill hollered.

"Because you won't only be saving Jana—you'll be saving Seth, Jake, and Jamie." Milo's gaze swept around the room. "And if you want more incentive to trust me... how about the fact that I know the location of every Geran compound on the planet—including the main camp."

Chapter Sixteen

It took Horvan less than a second to realize few members of his team were buying what Milo was spouting, not that he could blame them for that; it was a fantastical idea.

And Saul was leading them, gimlet-eyed. He folded his arms, his jaw set. "This is a plot. We throw all our forces at these camps, and guess what? They're waiting for us."

"But what about the mates part?" Horvan was determined to be the voice of reason, especially because no one else seemed to be keen on the role.

Seth said to listen to him.

Crank rolled his eyes. "What about it? The Gerans *know* about mates. Hell, they tried to convince Saul that Vic and I were already mated, and that was a fucking lie." He pointed at Milo, who despite his size and build, shrank back, trembling. "All that shit you came out with? It's nothing but a line, designed to make us believe you."

"Hey, now wait a minute." Aric's cheeks were red as he glared at Crank. "Seth told me he was coming here."

"That still doesn't mean we should just roll over and take his word as gospel," Brick yelled. Then his eyes went wide, and he clutched Aric to him, burying his face in Aric's hair. "I'm so sorry, baby. I didn't mean to yell at you. I'm angry and frustrated, but I should never take it out on you."

Horvan's heart ached for them. *This business has to end, and soon. It's tearing too many people apart.*

Aric managed a chuckle. "It's fine. Seth tells me all the time how frustrating I can be. He's said I could make a nun curse."

Brick didn't crack a smile. "Maybe Seth was duped into believing this shit, but it doesn't mean we have to be. And let's not forget, he's a fucking Geran."

"And?" Eve's eyes flashed. "So was I, but I didn't see you kicking *me* out the door."

142

"That's because you're different," Brick retorted. "You're Hashtag and Roadkill's mate."

Her eyes bulged. "So?" She pointed at Milo, her hand shaking. "*He's* someone's mate too, and the thought of losing her has driven him to this. Do you have any idea what he must have gone through to resort to coming here?" She swallowed. "Because *I* sure do. I always thought my job was what I lived for. I truly believed what we were doing was right, that this is the way it was supposed to be."

Milo nodded, his face pale. "I felt the same way. Until I met Jana, I thought we were doing the right thing."

Horvan felt the shock that reverberated through Dellan before he even opened his mouth.

Aw shit.

"The *right thing?*" Dellan snarled. "How is taking a scared one-year-old kid and turning him into some kind of monster the right thing? They made him *murder* people in cold blood, for fuck's sake. Including Brick's family. So right now, Brick's lost his parents, his mate…. But I'm *really* glad you had an epiphany, Milo." His voice was heavy with sarcasm. "Pity you couldn't have had it before it affected you."

Then Dellan was out of there, Rael chasing after him, and Horvan couldn't help but sag with relief. Dellan had been seconds from shifting and pouncing on Milo. He could see the images in his head of what Dellan wanted to do.

And if he had attacked Milo, would I have stopped him—or helped him?

Milo stared after Dellan, rubbing his chin and blinking. "Monster? What's he talking about?"

Unless Milo was a supremely accomplished actor, it appeared—to Horvan, at least—as though he didn't have a clue.

His voice low, Horvan filled him in on Alec, with Saul adding a word or two.

Milo recoiled, his eyes wide and staring. "Oh my God. I didn't know. You have to believe me. This is the first I've heard about it." His Adam's apple bobbed. "There has to be some way I can convince you that what I'm telling you is true." He stilled. "I can hear her thoughts in my head."

Saul huffed. "The Gerans know about that too."

Stalemate.

Except….

Dellan? Can you come back here, please?

When there was no response, Horvan tried another tack. *Rael? I need him. Do what you can.*

There was a pause. *I'll try. I've only just got him to calm the fuck down. Please. I know he's hurting, but this is important.*

Horvan gestured to the couch. "Take a seat, Milo. There's something I wanna try that might help resolve this situation."

Milo's eyes reflected his incredulity. "I don't see how you can." He snorted. "After hearing about Alec, *I* sure as hell wouldn't trust me. We're at an impasse." Nevertheless, he did as asked.

"Maybe, maybe not." Horvan jerked his head toward the door as Dellan entered, Rael behind him. "Come here, baby."

Dellan walked over to him, his face blotchy, and Horvan held him for a moment.

"You said you wanted to know if you've inherited any of your dad's abilities. I think we should find out."

"What do you want me to do? Read his mind?" Dellan was as incredulous as Milo.

"No, of course not. All I'm suggesting is that you sit down with Milo, and… open yourself up to the possibilities. See what you can sense."

"Your dad trusts me," Milo blurted. "Why else would he have given me that message for you?"

Horvan squeezed Dellan's hand. "You can only try."

Dellan squared his shoulders. "I'll give it a go, okay?" He smiled when Horvan kissed his cheek. "I'll expect more of that when I'm done." His eyes twinkled. "*And* I'll expect to feel those lips in *way* better places."

"You'll get it, I promise."

Rael chuckled. "And my lips will be joining in on the action too."

Horvan sensed resignation, but there was something else too, a trickle of anticipation.

He wants to do this. He wants to see where it leads.

Dellan sat next to Milo. "This is new, okay? I don't even know if anything's going to happen. But Horvan's right. I have to try. Give me your hand." Milo stared at him, and Dellan let out a sigh. "Look, I know I blew up just now, but I had my reasons. And fortunately for you, I've gotten past the point of ripping your head clean off your shoulders. Well, mostly." He stilled. "By the way, what are you?"

"A gorilla."

Eve's breathing hitched.

Dellan managed a chuckle. "Okay, maybe the whole head-ripping thing might not have worked." He held out his hand. "We're going to have to try to trust each other. Are you willing?"

Milo sucked in a deep breath and took it.

"Don't try to think of something specific, okay? I only want to see if I can sense anything." Dellan closed his eyes.

Horvan didn't dare breathe. It wasn't until that moment that he realized how much he wanted to believe Milo.

This could be a game-changer. The break we needed. Not that he let Dellan see that thought. Horvan didn't want him under any more pressure. He even tried to shut out Dellan's emotions, to give him the space and privacy to attempt this.

Horvan glanced around the room. Hashtag, Roadkill, and Eve stood together: Eve kept staring at Milo, and Horvan got the sense that she too wanted to believe him.

Brick watched from the doorway, Aric in front of him, Brick's arms crossed over Aric's chest in a protective gesture. *This has to be hurting them.*

Crank and Saul stared too, and Horvan knew this had to be hardest on Saul: the Gerans had put him through hell, and this was probably bringing it all back with a vengeance.

Then Dellan opened his eyes and let go of Milo's hand.

Horvan was at his side in a heartbeat. "Well?"

Dellan shuddered out a breath. "Well, that was… interesting."

Rael knelt beside him. "What did you feel?"

Dellan shivered. "He's in torment. His mate, what he's learned about the Gerans…." He fixed Milo with a steady gaze. "I believe you."

"Thank God," Milo croaked.

Dellan turned to gaze at Saul. "And before any of you suggest I'm saying that because my dad is involved… no, that isn't true." He shook his head. "That was so strange. It wasn't so much that I could *see* anything—it was mostly emotions—but I could feel Milo, feel his pain, his despair…."

He returned his attention to Milo. "Your love for Jana. That was the strongest feeling."

"What's happening to Seth, Jake, and Jamie?" Brick blurted. "Tell us. You owe us that much."

Milo hesitated before speaking. "On his arrival, Jamie was kept apart from the other detainees for—"

"*Detainees?*" Brick let out an explosive snort. "Call 'em what they are—prisoners."

Horvan flashed him a warning glance. "Not helping, Brick." He spoke in a low but firm voice. Brick had the grace to flush. Horvan gave Milo an encouraging nod. "Finish answering his question."

"He was kept apart for two months. And no, I don't know why. Seth and Jake.... They've spent a lot of time in the experimentation block, being tested."

"Tested for what?" Dellan demanded. "What the fuck are they doing to them?"

Milo glanced at Aric. "Seth didn't tell you any of this?"

Aric shook his head. "No, but I can guess why. He probably didn't want me to worry."

Milo cleared his throat. "They're conducting tests to determine the full range of Seth and Jake's psychic abilities. So far they're the only two subjects."

"Holy fuck." Cold crawled through Horvan's body. "We've got to get them out of there. Where's this camp? This has to be our priority."

"Northern Maine. Northern Aroostook County, to be exact. The nearest town is Allagash, population two hundred thirty-seven. The site was chosen for its remoteness. We're talking one road in or out."

"And where do your superiors think you are now?" Horvan inquired.

"On leave for a week, sitting out on a beach, sipping cocktails, and getting laid. I'm due back a week from Monday."

"Then we'd better make good use of you while we have you. Let's take this to the office," Horvan suggested. "I have about a million questions."

"I hope I have all the answers." Milo stood. "I don't suppose I could have some coffee? I sure could use some."

"I think we can manage that," Rael told him. "I'll bring it to you."

Horvan led the way out of the living room, Dellan and Milo following.

"Wait up. I'm coming too," Saul yelled after him.

He chuckled. "Yeah, Mr. Joint Team Leader. Get your ass in gear. We need you."

146

If Milo could provide detailed information about the camps, Horvan was going to break all records for the fastest assembling of a team.

Dellan, we're gonna bring your dad, Seth, and Jamie home.

BRICK COULDN'T sit still. All he could think about was Seth.

Are we really closer to finding him?

He had a few million questions of his own, ones that only Milo could answer. As the minutes ticked by, he got up and went outside. He needed to expend some energy, and the lake provided the perfect solution. Unfortunately, shifting wasn't possible. The houses on the other side of the lake might not be all that close, but he was certain they'd easily spot a polar bear taking a dip in the calm waters.

"I should be in there," he muttered.

A small hand closed around his. "No, you really shouldn't." Aric's voice was gentle. "Let them do their thing."

Brick couldn't miss the wave of fatigue that rolled over Aric. "How much sleep did you get last night?" He'd been aware of tossing and turning on the other side of the bed.

"Not much." He sighed. "Okay, none."

Brick did a quick mental assessment, then grabbed Aric and lifted him into his arms before carrying him out of the room, heading for the staircase.

Aric chuckled. "Okay, two things. My legs still function, and where are we going?"

"To our room to cuddle up and take a nap. It's better than sitting around down here, waiting for something to happen. They could be hours yet. Someone will yell when there's news." He climbed the stairs, holding Aric against him as though he were fragile and precious.

Fragile, no. Aric had been through stuff Brick didn't even want to think about, and he'd survived. As for precious, he was all that, and more.

"You still don't trust Milo, do you?"

Brick lowered him onto the bed. "No, I don't. He's a Geran. What's that saying about a leopard never changing its spots?" He kicked off his shoes and lay on the comforter, spooning Aric. "Now close your eyes. Even half an hour is better than nothing." Brick kissed his shoulder. "Please, baby."

Aric didn't answer, and it was only after registering the change in his breathing that Brick realized he'd fallen asleep almost instantly.

Sleep, pretty kitty. The world's still gonna be here when you wake up. Unfortunately.

ARIC KNEW it was a dream, but he didn't care. Seth was holding him, kissing him. He felt warm and alive, and that was good enough.

"I have one complaint. I can't smell you in my dreams."

Seth chuckled. "Yeah, I noticed that too. So... has Milo arrived yet?"

Aric relayed the morning's events. "It wasn't pretty." He shivered. "I thought Brick was going to kill him."

"How is he?" Aric caught the note of concern.

He paused to open a mental lockbox. He didn't want Brick peeking in and seeing his thoughts. "Fraying at the edges, to be honest. I worry for him. For his mind."

Seth sighed. "Brick has experienced so much loss at the hands of the Gerans that his reaction isn't unexpected. You need to tell him.... Milo is the key to freeing us. Brick has to play nice for a while longer."

Aric noted Seth's furrowed brow. "Something's wrong."

"Not *wrong*, exactly.... There's something going on here. It's a kind of electricity. I can feel it. They're getting ready for a visit."

"What kind of visit? Who's coming, the president?"

"Some VIP or other. Jake's been listening hard all day, trying to find out what he can. From what he's gleaned, this big shot is arriving this weekend, and yeah, he might as well be the president for all the preparation they're doing."

Aric knew he should be paying careful attention, but he was more interested in the feeling of being in Seth's arms. "Can't wait until we can do this for real."

"Me too, baby."

Aric smiled. "Brick calls me that. I like it."

Seth froze. "Sorry, but I've got to go. I'll try again tonight, okay?" He kissed Aric on the lips. "Take care of our mate."

"You know I will." Then Seth was gone, and Aric woke up with a start. Brick enfolded him in his muscular arms, and Aric sighed.

"You dreamed of Seth, didn't you?"

He nodded, then repeated Seth's message.

Brick made a low grumbling noise. "I guess I can play nice, if he's that important."

"Brick? Aric?" That was Hashtag. "Quit jerking each other off and get your butts down here."

"I should be so lucky," Brick muttered.

Aric had a feeling that once they got Seth back, they wouldn't see beyond their bedroom door for at least a week.

Maybe two was nearer the mark.

They hurried downstairs and followed the sound of voices into the living room. Everyone was there. Horvan and Saul stood by the fireplace, talking, and Rael and Dellan were busy pouring coffee.

Horvan arched his eyebrows when he saw Brick. "Glad you could join us." He surveyed their faces. "Okay, I've gotten through talking with Duke and Aelryn. We're gonna need every team we can mobilize if we're gonna liberate the camps. They assure me that if we put a plan together, they'll get us the manpower we need—which might be more than ever before, now Vic's spreading the word. Aelryn's talking to the west coast leaders. Well, as soon as he can get them all to wake up."

"How many camps are there?"

Horvan flashed Milo a glance before answering. "About two hundred."

Aric's gasp was echoed around the room. *So many?*

"They're everywhere," Milo added. "I don't have precise coordinates for all of them but I can get them."

Hashtag let out a low whistle. "Now I understand why we're gonna need to mobilize everything we've got." He peered at Eve. "Did you have any idea of the number?"

She shook her head.

"How many inmates are there at the Maine camp?" Brick asked.

"About one hundred fifty, with an armed force of around seventy, give or take. The camp is fortified, with towers along the perimeter."

Saul snorted. "Goddamn concentration camp."

"There's an airfield too," Milo told them. "You'll have to take that out first."

Horvan nodded. "Our biggest problem is surprise. The camp is out in the open, with an airstrip to the east. There are trees on two sides, and it's built on land in the loop of a river, the Saint John. That's their water supply."

"So we could launch an attack from the trees, the river, or both," Brick suggested.

"Yes. We can target buildings using drones, but we wanna minimize loss of life. That means a night raid. Milo is going to draw us a plan of the camp, showing the barracks, the sleeping quarters, the lot." Horvan stared at Hashtag. "It's a fair bet the camp won't be visible on the regular sites, so you're gonna need to hack that satellite again."

Hashtag gave a sharp nod. "I'm on it."

Eve blinked. "I'm mated to a hacker?"

"Hashtag? He's the best. And that satellite H mentioned? He neglected to say it was a US spy satellite." Roadkill grinned. "And *now* you know why Dellan has a fucking huge antenna in his backyard."

Hashtag buffed his fingernails on his shirt, and Eve chuckled. "Consider me impressed."

"So when do we go?" Roadkill demanded.

"As soon as we've got enough bodies. Milo goes back in a week, and he'll stay in touch, informing us of any changes. And when we do raid the camp, he'll be captured along with the rest of the guards. Gotta make it look right."

"Hey!" Aric's skin tingled. "There's something you need to know." He told them about the VIP visit the following weekend.

Horvan glanced at Milo. "You know anything about this?"

He shook his head. "It must be a recent thing. Did Seth say who's coming?"

Aric frowned. "I'm trying to remember."

Saul snorted. "I bet it won't be that bastard Fielding. Can't see *him* setting foot in a camp." His face contorted. "More's the pity. What I'd give for five minutes with that fucker."

"Fielding?" Aric froze, his eyes wide. "But that's him. That's the name Seth mentioned, I'm sure of it. Their VIP guest."

"And he's going to be there in a week's time?" Dellan jerked his head to stare at Horvan. "H…."

Horvan got his phone out and stabbed at the screen. "Duke. Change of plan. … Yes, I know we only just finished discussing this, but something's come up that we can't ignore. … Duke, you need to pull out all the stops on this one, call in every favor you're owed. … Why? Because we're going in next weekend." Horvan listened, grinning. "Yeah, I know, I'm a pain in the ass, but you gotta trust me on this one. You remember that fucker who tortured Saul? Who is probably the same guy who had Anson Prescott torn apart, by the way. Well, he's gonna be there." Horvan's eyes gleamed. "Yeah, my thoughts exactly. Fielding's about to learn payback is a bitch."

Dellan shuddered, and Rael put his arm around him. "If anyone knows where Alec is, it'll be Fielding."

"And you think he'll volunteer that information?"

"Probably not," Brick said. "But we can be pretty persuasive." His smile sent a chill through Aric.

He was glad his information had provided impetus, but he wasn't about to lose sight of the goal—to free all those poor shifters.

To bring Seth, Jake, and Jamie home.

CHAPTER SEVENTEEN

BY THE time Saturday evening arrived, Crank had gotten over his initial mistrust of Milo, although he wasn't ready to welcome him with open arms. No matter what had brought him to them, he was still a fucking guard, a Geran.

Let it go.

Crank jerked his head in Saul's direction. Saul stood by the fire pit, a bottle of beer in one hand. *Let what go?*

I know you don't like him—hell, no one's asking you to do that—but Horvan was right. This guy can turn the tide for us.

Crank swallowed. *I look at him, and I see the bastards who—*

Saul was at his side in a heartbeat. "Hey. I'm here, aren't I? I'm alive. So what if I have a few scars?" He smiled, his eyes twinkling. "I've got you and Vic to kiss 'em better."

"You're telling me you're totally okay with him helping us?"

Saul shrugged. "Totally? No. But if he's for real—and Seth and Jake think he is—then I've got no reason to hold a grudge. He wasn't one of the bastards who tortured me. He's just another shifter who made the situation he was in fit the narrative he'd been told. That's what true indoctrination is, right? The Gerans fed him—and many like him—all that stuff to make them think what they were doing was right."

Crank gazed in awe at his mate. "You're amazing, do you know that?"

Saul grinned as he leaned in to whisper, "So you keep telling me every time I make you come." He chuckled. "I have my moments."

"Is this where you two have been hiding?" Horvan walked over to join them.

Crank snorted. "Does it *look* like we're hiding?" The others filed outside until every seat was occupied, with some of them sitting on the low circular wall that surrounded the fire. The sun had set, and the sky was shades of pink and purple, reflecting on the calm surface of the lake.

"I should get going," Milo murmured before taking a drink from his bottle.

Saul arched his eyebrows. "And go where? We still have a lot to talk about."

"There's a spare bed in the basement," Dellan remarked. "You're welcome to stay."

"He can have my old room," Hashtag announced. He grinned. "Seeing as I'm now sharing with this lummox." He nudged Roadkill with his elbow.

Roadkill gave him a mock glare. "Come out with more comments like that and you'll regret it."

"Oh yeah? And what are you gonna do about it?"

Crank was used to their banter, but now it had a different quality, an intimacy that laced their words.

"It isn't a case of what I'll do—it's what I *won't* do." Roadkill's eyes gleamed. "If you get my meaning."

Hashtag froze. "I'm gonna shut up now."

Eve laughed. "Very wise."

"But he *is* right," Roadkill added. "It's a better room than the one downstairs."

"If you're sure."

Crank got the feeling Milo was the one who wasn't sure, and a wave of guilt swept through him.

I haven't exactly made him welcome, have I?

Saul put his arm around Crank's waist. *And* that *is why I love you.*

Crank gave a mental chuckle. *I noticed you kept that thought between us.*

To his surprise, Saul put his bottle on the wall, took Crank's hands in his, and then glanced at their friends—their family. "I love this guy. And this is me putting it out there in case anyone was wondering."

Roadkill snickered. "Okay, we got the memo. So long as we don't have to watch you putting out. There are some things you can never unsee, you know?" That earned him a ripple of laughter.

"Can we be serious for a minute?"

Part of Crank wanted to tell Horvan no, they couldn't. "Can't we sink a few beers and leave it at that?" There had been enough tension that day, and all he wanted was to kick back and enjoy the canopy of stars over their heads.

Wow. That last part was beautiful.

Crank narrowed his gaze. *Tell anyone, and you're a dead man.*

"A *few* beers?" Eve stared at them in mock horror. "Oh gods, please tell me my mates aren't lightweights."

"She drinks, she fights, and she looks amazing." Hashtag beamed, his chest puffed out. "We are lucky dudes."

Roadkill gave a soft chuckle. "Preach."

Crank sighed. "Sure, we can be serious."

Horvan leaned forward, elbows on his knees, his gaze fixed on Milo. "Tell us about the camps."

"What do you want to know?"

"What all those shifters did to end up in them, for one thing," Saul commented.

Brick snorted. "They're prisoners, isn't that obvious?"

"Yeah, but *why* are they prisoners?" Crank demanded. "For political reasons? Are they anarchists? Activists?"

"Let me ask *you* a question." Milo took a drink. "Do the Fridans know how many shifters are on this planet?"

"No," Horvan replied. "I don't think anyone's ever researched it."

Milo nodded. "Well, the Gerans have—and they came to a conclusion. The world needs more shifters."

"Can't argue with that," Horvan acknowledged. "Humans outnumber us, but I guess that's the way it's always been."

"Where you and the Gerans might disagree is the type of shifters we need more of. The ones in the camps have traits the Gerans want to replicate: strength, agility, dexterity, intelligence…. Hence the breeding program."

"So you're saying you only incarcerate the crème de la crème?" Saul gave Milo an incredulous stare.

Crank shook his head. "That doesn't fly. What about all the shifters they abandoned in the Bozeman camp? They were gonna shoot them all."

Milo stilled. "How many shifters were left there?"

"About a block full," Dellan told him.

"Well, the average is about one hundred fifty detainees, so I'd assume they…."

"They what?" Rael stared at him. "Say what you think."

"Look, the breeding program was nothing to do with me, okay? But if they were trying to create better, stronger, faster shifters, then I'd guess some genes weren't passed on." His cheeks grew red. "And I had no idea they'd left instructions to eliminate the remaining shifters. I was already in Maine at that point."

"I don't know whether to feel insulted or fortunate," Aric announced. "So my genes didn't cut it, huh? Then again, if they'd taken me along with Seth and his dad, Brick might never have found me."

"I'd have found you," Brick stated quietly. "Even if I had to scour the fucking planet."

Aric flushed and kissed him on the cheek.

"Until I met Jana, I believed we were simply breeding more shifters to even the balance, but now?" Milo's face contorted. "She made me question why the Gerans were forcibly breeding shifters, and I didn't like where that question led me." He leaned back. "Your friend, Jamie Matheson—"

"He's my half brother," Dellan said quietly.

Milo blinked. "I didn't know. While it's true Jamie could've ended up at the camp because they caught him, he's also a tiger, and they can't get enough of the big cats."

"Which is why they left Aric." Brick gazed fondly at his mate. "House kitties don't make good killers."

Crank snorted. "You won't be saying that the next time he sticks you with those murder mitts."

"But that's not why they've got Seth and Jake, is it?" Dellan's voice rang out.

"No, I don't think so. They're the icing on the cake. That's why the scientists are doing so much testing." Milo scanned the faces of the people sitting around the fire pit. "I know how it sounds."

"You mean, as if they want to use Jake and Seth's abilities to their advantage. Make them into some kind of weapon." Dellan was pale.

Milo broke eye contact, lowering his head.

"You're seeing everything differently now, aren't you?" Eve said in a gentle voice.

"And then some." Milo swallowed. "How could I have gone along with all this?"

"Because you believed what they'd been telling you since you were old enough to listen." Crank stared at Milo, unable to miss his discomfort. Except he couldn't leave it there. "Something I don't get. If there are about one hundred fifty inmates and seventy guards, why don't the prisoners just shift and kill the fuckers? No offense intended."

"None taken. And all the guards are armed."

Dellan shook his head. "No, there's more to it than that." He turned to Rael. "Think about what happened to me. I was in that cage for a year, and I couldn't shift—except when they forced me to."

Rael nodded, his face tight. "We figured they'd drugged your food... something to prevent you from shifting."

Dellan cocked his head to one side. "So what if all the shifters in the camps are drugged in the same way?"

Horvan scowled. "I don't like this. Drugs to suppress a shift, drugs to force a shift.... I need to talk to Doc about this. Because once we get all the inmates out of there, we have to check 'em out. God knows how the drugs have fucked 'em up."

"And if you asked any of the people who set up the camps, they'd probably tell you the end justifies the means. I believed that—once." Milo's Adam's apple bobbed sharply. "Not anymore." He stared at Horvan. "This mission you're planning... I want in."

"Me too," Eve piped up.

Saul chuckled. "You've got no choice, Duncan. This is what you signed up for. Speaking of which, there's a training session at the barracks tomorrow. We'll get to see you in action. No denying you look good on paper."

Her eyes sparkled. "In real life? I'm even better."

Roadkill snorted. "I'd say you don't suffer from a lack of modesty, but my instincts tell me you're probably telling the truth."

She widened her eyes and gave him a mock glare. "'Probably'? Oh, you are *so* in for it tonight—baby." Hashtag guffawed, and she flashed him a glance. "Sure, laugh it up now—pay for it later."

You know, I almost feel sorry for them. Crank peered at Saul with a grin. *Almost.*

"I'm going too, right, H?" Brick's voice was quieter.

To Crank's mind, the fact that Horvan didn't reply right away was telling.

Brick let out a loud snort. "Don't even think about keeping me here. And if you order me not to go, I'll go anyway. Besides, you need me."

Horvan sighed. "Everyone is going. I need my best team."

"Does that include me?" Aric gazed at him.

"And what would *you* do on a mission? Lick 'em to death?" Then Crank grimaced. "Mind you, a cat's tongue feels fucking awful, the way it rasps—"

"Not helping," Saul muttered.

"Excuse me?" Milo glared at them. "Can we get back to the part where I said I wanted to be on the team for this one?"

Horvan met Milo's gaze, and Crank winced. He knew that look.

Milo isn't gonna be a happy bunny.

Horvan took a deep breath. "You need to go back. You're more use to us at the camp."

"No!" Milo's voice was strident. "I want to—" A phone buzzed, and he pulled it from his pocket. Milo stared at the screen in obvious dismay. "Well, crap."

"What's wrong?" Horvan asked.

Milo huffed. "Seems like you're going to get your way. This is from the camp. They want me back. Tomorrow. They've canceled all leave because of the inspection next weekend."

"And there's our confirmation right there," Saul muttered.

"Right." Hashtag got out of his chair. "Before you go, I'll give you a burner phone so you can stay in contact with us. All messages will be encrypted."

"But I want to fight," Milo protested.

"I get that," Horvan replied. "But you can do more on the ground."

Eve got up and went over to Milo, crouching beside him. "Besides, how does it feel being parted from Jana?" She covered his hand with hers.

Milo stared at it. "You've nailed it, of course. I knew I had to come here, but the thought of leaving her there... unprotected...."

"Then follow orders, soldier, and go back to Maine." Horvan gave him a forthright glance. "But stay in touch, okay? Just don't put yourself in danger to do it."

"You can leave in the morning." Crank grabbed a bottle of beer from the ice-filled bucket and handed it to Milo. "Tonight you spend with us."

See? That's my man. Even in Crank's mind, he could hear the pride in Saul's voice. *You can let it go.*

Crank gave Saul a slow smile. *And tonight I'll kiss every one of your scars.*

As long as you do it all over again when Vic gets home.

Vic....
I want him home. With us. I hate that he's so far away.
Saul nodded. *Me too.*
I want to see him before....
Before what?
Crank stared at him. *Before we go off on this mission.*
It's going to be fine.
Crank had been on enough missions to know better than to take anything for granted.

CHAPTER EIGHTEEN

SAUL CHUCKLED as he watched Dex Peters hit the floor of the training room for what had to be the umpteenth time. "You thought this would be easy, didn't you?" He'd asked for volunteers to put Eve through her paces, and Dex's hand had shot up in a heartbeat, even though she had four inches and about ten pounds on him.

Even I'd think twice about tangling with her.

Except he had an advantage over Dex—he'd read Eve's file.

"She caught me off guard," Dex protested, a little out of breath.

Saul grinned. "Nah, she's been wiping the floor with you since I gave the go-ahead."

Eve stood over Dex, her face flushed, eyes bright, hands on her hips. "You *sure* you don't wanna shift?" That edge of amusement in her voice told Saul one thing.

Eve was enjoying herself.

The door opened and Crank ambled in. For a man as muscular as he was, Crank moved with a fluidity that never failed to impress Saul.

It also got him hard as a rock every single time.

And he's all mine. Well, mine and Vic's.

"Horvan says you need to get your ass—" Saul arched his eyebrows, and Crank coughed. "Excuse me, *sir*, but you're wanted in a meeting."

"Fine. I think we're done here. Aren't we, Dex?"

Eve extended a hand and hauled Dex to his feet. "No hard feelings?"

He huffed. "Just my ass that aches like a bastard from being dropped on it one time too many. Maybe we need to get padding for the floor."

Crank guffawed. "Next thing you'll be wanting is a bed in here so you can lie down and recuperate."

Dex's face reddened. Then he chuckled as he shook Eve's hand. "You're all right, Duncan." He glanced at Saul. "You might've warned me."

Saul raised his eyebrows. "Why? When you go on a mission, you don't have a clue who you'll be up against. You have to deal with the unexpected." He pointed at Eve and smirked. "Meet the unexpected."

"Yes, sir." Dex gave a nod to Saul and Crank, turned, and headed for the door.

Eve sauntered toward Saul, that gleeful light still evident. "So is that it? Or is there someone else you want me to work over?"

Saul smiled when Crank brought a finger to his lips and snuck up behind her with all the stealth of a tiger stalking its prey. "No, I think that's it, especially if I have a meeting to—"

A second later Crank pounced, and Eve ended up on her back, glaring at him. "Hey!"

"Now tell her why you did that," Saul told him.

Crank smirked. "To show her there's always someone better, and that she can't ever let her guard down. Plus, it was fun."

Eve propped herself up on her elbows and let out a chuckle. "Yeah, okay, it was fun for me too. Next time I'll know better."

"You'd better." He stared back at her. "Okay, so you were bigger than him. That means dick around here. Size isn't everything. Having smarts is what really counts, and not being afraid to fight dirty."

She sighed. "I get it." Crank held out a hand to her, and she hooked her leg around his calf, bringing him down with all the grace of a wounded buffalo. Then she sat astride him, grinding her ass against his crotch. She grinned. "Who says I'm afraid to fight dirty?"

Saul snorted. "Crank, get up. You're enjoying that far too much."

"I will. Just… gimme a minute."

Eve performed another slow grind, and Saul laughed out loud. "I tell Roadkill and Hashtag about this and I know one gorilla that's gonna get her ass smacked." He gave Crank a pointed stare. "I thought we're supposed to be in a meeting?"

Eve stood and helped him to his feet.

"Yeah, H wants both of you in the briefing room." He glanced at Eve. "I like the way you fight."

She snickered. "I know what else you like."

Crank gave Saul a sheepish grin. *Sorry.*

Saul snorted. *No, you're not. And just because we're mated, that doesn't mean she isn't sexy as fuck.*

Crank grinned. *As long as you know the only ones in my heart are you and a certain Greenland shark.*

Saul and Eve followed him out the door and along the hallway. The main building at the Romeoville barracks comprised two training rooms, two meeting rooms, and a cafeteria and kitchen. From the sand-covered yard outside came roars and hollers as Troy had the guys working on their combat tactics.

Eve inclined her head toward the sound. "I should be out there."

"Uh-uh. H needs you." Crank glanced at her. "Plenty of time for that later." He pushed the door open, and they filed into the briefing room. Horvan stood at the head of the table, large sheets of paper spread out in front of him. To his right was a guy Saul recalled having met when Horvan and Aelryn's teams had swooped in to save his ass. Brick, Hashtag, and Roadkill were there too, along with a familiar face.

"Hey there, Doc." Saul greeted him with a wave. "When did you get in?"

"Horvan picked me up at Joliet Airport, after he'd dropped off Keppler. He's been filling me in on what you've learned."

"Doc's assembling the medical team for us." Horvan gestured to the man at his side. "This is Johan, one of Aelryn's top men." He pointed to one of the sheets of paper. "This is what Hashtag found using the satellite. Milo's drawing of the compound matches it exactly, only now we know what these buildings are. So gather round and take a look."

Crank and Eve joined the others who stood at the end of the table.

Horvan pointed to the thin pale line that ran from east to west, ending in a large gray square. "This is their airstrip, and it's long enough to deal with jets. We can easily land the Chinooks on it when we're ready to take all the inmates outta there."

"I didn't know we had Chinooks," Roadkill commented.

"You don't—we do," Johan informed him with a smile. "We've also got a mobile center of Operations. We'll have all the headcams and mics online, so we'll be able to monitor the whole shebang from one vehicle." He gazed at Hashtag. "Horvan says you're the best tech guy he has. You'll be in Operations with our guys."

Hashtag's face tightened for a second, then relaxed. "Yes, sir."

It didn't take a genius to know what had just gone through his mind. Saul gave him a sympathetic glance. "I know, you wanna be in the thick of it, but this is a huge operation. Our most powerful weapon is intel, and that means we need our best on it. And like the man said, that's you."

"And it's not as if you have a problem following orders. Right, soldier?" Horvan stared at him.

Hashtag straightened. "No, sir."

Horvan smiled. "That's what I thought. We're assuming Fielding will arrive by plane, so we'll take out whatever transportation we find there, mainly because we don't want him to leave." That earned a few snorts. "The buildings include a science block, what Milo called a reeducation block—basically where they conduct interviews or keep prisoners isolated—four barracks for the guards, five sleeping quarters for the inmates... you get the idea."

"We've been going over the information Milo gave Horvan," Johan continued, "and we think we've come up with a plan of attack. I'm going to lead Aelryn's forces. We'll be Team B."

"And Saul, you'll be in charge of our troops, Team A," Horvan concluded.

Saul peered at the map. "How many men are we taking?"

"We think fifty should be enough, but we're waiting on any last-minute information from Milo."

Johan sighed. "It had better be enough. What with all the missions currently being conducted around the globe, it's all we could scrape together."

Saul perched on the edge of the table. "What are the variables?"

"We know there are usually about seventy guards at the camp, but we don't know if they're going to bring in more men for this goddamn inspection, or if Fielding is bringing his own team with him." Horvan scowled. "We also don't know when he arrives exactly, or how long he's staying at the camp. He could be planning to be there less than twenty-four hours for all we know." He glanced at Eve. "Have you had much experience of camp inspections?"

She frowned. "Two that I can recall, but they were both different. One was a last-minute visit with no warning, and that put the wind up the camp commander."

Hashtag frowned. "Put the wind up? What does that mean?"

"It's a British phrase meaning scared the bejesus out of." Eve rolled her eyes.

Then Roadkill stilled. "Wait. You're British?"

"I was born in the UK, but my parents moved here when I was ten years old."

"Is that why you don't have a strong accent?"

She laughed. "My parents would disagree with you on that one. I was involved in intelligence work, so I needed to learn to speak like an American. My natural voice? Definitely not like this."

"Then what do you really sound like?" Hashtag demanded.

Eve locked gazes with him. "Why do you need to know? Got a thing for Brits?"

That flush told Saul she'd nailed it.

Hashtag huffed. "Well, fuck. That's just great."

"What's wrong?" Eve demanded.

"Now I have to learn another language."

Roadkill shook his head. "What the fuck are you talking about? It's still English."

He gave a goofy smile. "Yeah, but English never sounded that good. And you know what this means, right? We have to learn to like tea and drink it with our pinkies up. I'm too old to learn new shit like that."

Eve chuckled. "Trust me, baby, you're not. I've got *all* kinds of things I'll want you to learn for me."

Hashtag's cheeks pinked. "You think you could talk British tonight? You know, when we're—"

"Excuse me?" Saul glared at them. "Would it be okay with the three of you if we focused on the present situation? Leave the flirting for the bedroom, for fuck's sake." He stared at Eve. "Back to what you were telling us about surprise inspections."

She flushed. "There was no time to put on extra guards, not that we were undermanned. I think he stayed a total of two hours."

"And the other time?" Saul inquired.

"We knew the VIP would be staying a couple of days, so we had accommodations ready for him. And then we all tried not to look as if we were walking around on eggshells the whole time he was there."

"So they've got a week to get ready for Fielding's visit." Saul nodded. "Then let's hope Milo moves fast if there are any changes that'll affect the mission."

"And speaking of the mission...." Horvan pointed to the map. "Okay, here's Allagash, roughly nineteen miles to the east of the camp, along the

Saint John River. The Canadian border is about thirteen miles to the west. There's a forest to the north of the camp, and the river meanders around it." He pointed to a spot east of Allagash. "This will be Johan's entry point: Northern Aroostook Regional Airport, about forty-four miles from Allagash. He and his men will land there, where they'll have transportation waiting. They drive to Allagash, cross at Dickey to the northern side of the river, then follow the Old River Road all the way to the camp." He paused. "Except we don't go all the way."

Crank snickered. "That's not what *I've* heard about you."

Horvan rolled his eyes, then continued, pointing to the river. "Team B will approach the camp from the water in Rigid Inflatable Boats." Another pause. "Now, there are at least three civilian campsites along the river, so they're going to have to appear as if they're out on military maneuvers."

Eve peered at the map. "There's only the one road that goes to the camp?"

"Yes. The entrance to the compound is in the northeast corner, and there's electrified fencing around the perimeter. Obviously we can't approach the entrance, not without alerting them to our presence."

"Maybe we can."

Horvan stared at her. "I'm listening."

Eve leaned back in her chair. "Okay, I've worked in three camps so far, and they all had one thing in common: They were shit hot on security. So much so that any deliveries—ammunition, food, you name it—were always scheduled to arrive in the middle of the night. That way, there was never any likelihood of inmates trying to escape by clinging to the underside of trucks or climbing on top of them. Once they were in their sleeping quarters for the night, that was it. They were locked in. So the soldiers would unload the deliveries and send the trucks on their way without having to keep an eye out for wannabe escapees." She smiled. "If there's only one road in, then any delivery trucks will have to take that road." Her eyes gleamed. "Of course, if we hijack the trucks *before* they get to the camp...."

"A Trojan truck." Saul beamed. "I like it."

"And if there *are* trucks, then there's a schedule. Milo can check whether there are any deliveries planned for that weekend." Eve bit her lip. "I suppose it's too much to hope for."

"We can plan for our two-pronged attack—and if luck is on our side, then it becomes a three-pronged attack." Horvan smiled. "What do sailors say about plans being written in the sand at low tide?"

"If we *can* hijack the delivery truck, I think Eve should lead that assault," Saul declared. He glanced at her. "You up for that?"

She grinned. "Sir, yes, sir."

"Question." Roadkill drummed the table with his fingertips. "Milo said we'd need to secure the airfield. Drones?"

Horvan nodded. "We'll have Predators for reconnaissance, then use them for air-to-ground weapons. Once we're inside the camp, it'll be nonlethal ammo, unless we're fired upon. We'll have cover from a couple of Apaches too, once we're in."

"Pepper rounds?" Hashtag inquired.

"Yeah, .68 caliber."

Eve blinked. "Is that standard procedure?"

Roadkill shrugged. "Sure. They make the target cough, and the PAVA powder stings like fuck when it gets into contact with the eyes, nose, and throat, but they're still alive. Sometimes we use Byrna MAX, which is mostly tear gas. That brings 'em down for about forty-five minutes, long enough to get in, do our thing, and get out." He cocked his head. "Let me guess. In the Geran camps, the guards only use live ammo." She swallowed, and he sighed. "Figures. Don't get me wrong, there *are* going to be deaths, but our mission goal is getting the inmates out of there in one piece."

"What will happen to them?" Eve asked.

"There's space for them at the schools in Boston and Croatia," Johan told her.

"But... didn't you shut down the schools?"

Johan smiled. "Why do that when we can use the buildings? We have to teach these kids somewhere."

"For 'teach,' read 'deprogram.'" Hashtag murmured.

Johan nodded. "And that takes time."

"Wait—you kept them in the same schools?" Roadkill's eyes were huge.

"They're only bricks and mortar. What matters is that all those kids have a good home life and normal schooling. No indoctrination, just a solid education. Mind you, we did take the Boston kids to Croatia and vice versa. I don't think half those children knew what had been going on. By all accounts, they were treated well. But try explaining why your mom and dad don't want you to come home. And we couldn't leave them in the same buildings. That'd be like freeing people from the concentration camps and telling them the torture would end but they still had to live there. The point

165

I was trying to make is that there's plenty of space at the schools to house the inmates, and they'll be well looked after."

"But Jake, Seth, and Jamie will be coming home with you, surely," Doc remarked.

Horvan chuckled. "Of course they will. I like my balls where they are."

Brick snickered. "No one who's ever had a cat would underestimate them." He glanced at Crank. "And what are you grinning about, you doof?"

"Oh, nothing. I'm realizing for the first time what the phrase *pussywhipped* really means." He gave Horvan an innocent gaze. "And speaking of pussies... how come you managed to hold this meeting without your mates being here?"

Horvan sighed. "I had to promise them all the facts when I got home. Well, that and copious sexual favors." Saul let out a muffled snort, and Horvan eyed him with amusement. "Laugh it up, but your time will come. We will do *anything* for our mates, right?"

Saul glanced at Crank, and warmth flooded through him. "Yeah."

Horvan cleared his throat. "We're going to start moving the troops into the area on Tuesday. Time enough for several recces. Then as soon as Milo gives us the go, we'll be in and out."

"You know what will happen to him if they get so much as a whiff of what he's doing, don't you?" Eve's face was pale beneath the tan.

Horvan's expression grew solemn. "Yeah, we know."

"But it won't come to that," Saul announced.

Crank's eyes were warm. *Yeah, talk it into existence.*

CHAPTER NINETEEN

BRICK'S KIT bag sat by the bedroom door, all packed and ready for the flight the following morning.

Ready to take me a step closer to finding Seth.

"I don't need to tell you to be careful, do I?" Aric hugged his knees, the pillows piled high behind him.

Brick glanced at him. "The same way I don't need to tell you not to worry?"

He huffed. "I'd worry less if I was going with you. I'm not suggesting going up against the bad guys—I may only be a cat, but that doesn't mean I'm stupid—but at least I'd be at the base camp. You know, when you get back there with Seth."

Brick sat beside him, lifted Aric into his lap, and wrapped his arms around his mate's slim form. "Let's get one thing straight. You are *not* only a cat, you got that? You're smart, you're intuitive—" He kissed Aric's hair. "—and I know you were with me the last time in Texas, but that was different."

"How? How was it different?"

Brick stroked his back. "We were miles from their camp. We had more guys. I knew you'd be okay. This mission? It feels way more dangerous, and I want you safe." Aric stiffened in his arms, and Brick sighed. "I know, baby. You want to be around when we take Seth and Jake—and all the other prisoners—out of there. But we'll be bringing them back here, I promise."

Aric sagged against him, and Brick knew he'd seen sense. "Fine. I'll just give up sleeping until you're home with our mate." He sighed. "Waiting is gonna kill me, though. I want it to be the three of us, together."

"I know. I want that too." Then he chuckled. "Give up sleeping? That's supposed to make me feel guilty and change my mind? Sorry, but it ain't gonna work. Nice try, though." He planted another kiss on Aric's head. "And speaking of sleep, how about we hit the sack? I've gotta be up awful early in the morning."

"As long as you fall asleep holding me."

Brick smiled. "I was gonna do that anyway." He set an alarm on his phone, stripped down to his shorts, then climbed beneath the cool sheets.

"Wait!" Aric lurched off the bed and disappeared into their closet. He appeared a moment later, carrying a folded garment. Aric went over to Brick's duffel, opened it, and placed the item inside.

"What are you doing? I've got my packing down to a fine art."

Aric got into bed. "I wasn't packing any of your stuff—it was mine."

Brick arched his eyebrows. "One of your shirts wants to go to Maine? Does it need a vacation? Because I can think of far better locations."

Aric froze, his chin held high, his eyes unusually flinty. "One of my mates is about to go in, guns blazing, to save another. Or maybe to find his body. And all the while I'll be here, scared out of my mind, waiting to get a call from Horvan where he *might* tell me neither of you will be coming home." He was trembling. "Please, tell me what's funny here, because I'm not getting the joke."

Brick pulled him close. "I'm so sorry, baby. I was trying to lighten the mood. Please, forgive me."

Aric rested his head against Brick's shoulder.

"And as for why I'm sending you out with one of my shirts? You don't have a romantic bone in your body, do you?" He craned his neck to look Brick in the eye. "So you can smell it. You know, to help you remember who you are and who you belong with."

That was the sweetest fucking thing. Sweeter still seeing as Brick had told him he couldn't come.

"Thank you. I appreciate it."

Aric leveled a keen glance at him. "Use it to help keep your head on straight so you can find our mate. Okay?"

"Sure." This was all so weird. Aric was like a third the size of Brick, but he could make him feel loved and cherished. Something Brick hadn't had in forever.

And telling him how I feel before I go on a mission is no bad thing.

Brick pulled him close. "I love you. I hope you know that."

Aric smiled, then leaned in and gave Brick a kiss. "Just keep that in mind. It'll come in handy later." He wriggled until his back was pressed against Brick's chest, and Brick's nostrils filled with his delicious scent.

"You really think it's going to work?"

Brick made sure to lock away any doubts or misgivings before replying. He didn't want to spook Aric. Telling him nothing was ever written was not an option.

"We've got the best people. We've got Milo in the camp. Yeah, I think it's gonna work."

It had better. His mate's life depended on it, as well as Jake Carson's and Jamie Matheson's. Plus Milo's own mate had to be another priority since the man was risking his life to help.

Brick closed his eyes, relaxed his body, and waited for sleep. Except it took a while. He couldn't shake the notion that he'd just missed something important.

Go. To. Sleep.

He chuckled. *You're a bossy little kitty. Are you gonna be this bossy when you're waving me off in the morning?*

Aric rolled in his arms. "About that... I can't be there when you leave."

"Why not? It'll be the first time I go on a mission without you. You're telling me I don't even get a fond farewell?"

"No, you don't, because I'll cry, you'll get upset, and then you'll have Horvan being, well, you know... Horvan."

"Yeah, that makes sense."

Aric snuggled in. "Besides, I don't want you going off to fight remembering me with a blotchy face, red eyes, a wobbly lower lip, a—"

"Okay, okay, I get the picture." Brick kissed him. "In that case, I'll say my goodbyes in bed."

With extra cuddles.

"WILL SOMEONE stop that goddamn ringing?" Crank growled. He'd been having such a fantastic dream. He and Saul had been swimming with Vic, only Vic had shifted back into a human, and Crank's arms were suddenly full of a smooth, slippery, lithe body, Vic's legs wrapped around his waist while Saul kissed Vic's neck.

The same Saul who reached over him toward the nightstand. "It's your phone. Mine's on silent." He grabbed it, then nudged Crank. "Hey, sleepyhead. Wanna talk to a certain shark?"

That woke him up fast.

Crank sat upright in bed, and Saul clicked on Answer. Vic's handsome face filled the screen. From the background, it seemed he was in a hotel room.

"*There* you are." He froze. "Aw fuck. My time zones are all out of whack. Did I wake you?"

"Sure you did, but we'll forgive you." Saul tugged Crank closer, until both of them were on camera. "Hey, baby. How are you? Any news on when we're likely to get you back here?"

"Do you want the good news or the bad news?"

"Gimme the good news first." Crank rubbed his eyes.

Vic beamed. "I'm done. I'm coming home."

Crank let out a whoop, and Saul clamped a hand over his mouth. "Do I have to remind you what time it is? You'll wake everyone up. And seeing as we all have to be out of here in a few hours, they will *not* thank you." He grinned. "Awesome news."

"I'm gonna reserve judgment until I've heard everything," Crank groused. "What haven't you told us yet?"

"I got a call from Luciano Orsini. He's the archivist I went to see. He wants me to visit him again, so I'll stop off in Rome on my way back."

"You think it could be important?" Saul asked.

Vic hesitated before replying. "If I share something with you, I need your word that you won't tell a soul. Not yet at least."

It was as if someone had unloaded a glass of icy water all over Crank. "You got it."

"Me too," Saul added.

"Okay." Vic took a deep breath. "Orsini has an artifact that could shake the foundations of our world. I'm talking the shifter world, all right?" They nodded. "What if I told you I've seen evidence the two brothers weren't as diametrically opposed as we've been led to believe? And what if I *also* told you that whole part of our history might have been… manufactured?"

Crank gaped. "But… why the everlovin' fuck would anyone *do* that?"

Saul snickered. "Why does anyone start a war? Because they like war and the power that comes with it. So do you know why Orsini wants to see you?"

"He says another artifact has come into his possession, and I need to see it."

"That's all he's told you?" Saul frowned. "You sure you can trust this guy?"

Vic smiled. "Hell yeah."

Crank relaxed a little. "Okay, then. When's your ETA here? Only asking because we leave for Maine in the morning, and it looks as if we'll be gone a few days."

"I'll be in Homer Glen when you come home. Make sure you both come back with all your bits and pieces."

He grinned. "You like our bits and pieces."

Vic chuckled. "You know it. And when I get the two of you alone, I want *all* those bits at once."

Saul groaned. "Great. Now you've made us both horny as fuck. We need to sleep, dammit."

"Fuck first, sleep later." Vic's eyes sparkled as he held up a small bottle of lube. "I'll watch the first part."

BRICK WAS calm in mind and body, but then again, he always was when he dreamed of Seth. "Where are we?" The beach was long, the sand soft, and the breeze warm. Palm trees rose up, tall and majestic, and the air was filled with the sound of waves crashing upon the shore.

"Somewhere I went as a child," Seth told him. "And if I ever find out where it was, I'll take us there." He glanced at the clear sky. "I needed to be someplace that wasn't here. This is where my mind took me."

Seth's hand in his was the best part.

"We're coming for you," Brick told him in a low voice. "In a few hours' time, we'll be leaving here for Maine."

"When will you be here?" Seth's chest heaved.

"Sometime over the weekend. We won't know exactly until we hear from Milo." Brick squeezed Seth's hand. "But we'll be together soon. And once you're home with us, I'll keep you safe, away from harm."

Seth let go of Brick's hand. "And what if that's not what I want?"

Brick stared at him. "What do you mean?"

Seth wandered over to where pieces of driftwood lay in a heap and perched on a sturdy one. "How many camps are there?"

"A couple of hundred, maybe?"

171

He nodded. "Exactly. Who knows how long it will take to bring them all down? And I want to be a part of that."

Brick's heartbeat raced. "You want to fight?"

Seth shrugged. "Maybe not fight, but I want to work in Intelligence. I can be useful." He cocked his head to one side. "Will *you* give up fighting then? After everything they've done?"

Brick didn't hesitate. "Fuck no."

He nodded, smiling. "So we both want to do our part."

"And what about me?"

Seth laughed. "About time you joined us." Aric ran to him, and they hugged. "Hi, honey."

Aric took a step back. "I'm not a fighter. I don't have your gifts, so what do *I* do when you two are off God knows where?"

Seth put his arms around Aric. "You give us something to fight for."

Brick enveloped both of them and kissed Aric's head. "You give us something to come home for."

Then Seth smiled. "Besides, you'll have your hands full taking care of our kids."

Brick blinked. "Excuse me?"

Aric's smile reached his eyes. "We used to talk about having kids."

Seth kissed him. "You'll make an amazing Mom and Dad all rolled into one. So maybe this is something we should discuss—when Brick brings me home."

Aric peered at Brick. "I'm not going to wait that long. I need to know *now* if you like the idea."

Brick's head was full of the most delightful images: the cutest little polar bear cubs, tiger cubs rolling around on the grass, and adorable kittens mewling, all soft fur and huge eyes.

Seth grinned. "I think we just got our answer."

THERON ANSWERED the call on the second ring, and waited for the caller to speak.

"Vic Ryder is going back to Rome. To the archive."

He frowned. "Do you have any information as to why he needs a repeat visit?"

"No, sir. He got a call. That's all I know."

Theron didn't like this at all, not when it came hot on the heels of disturbing news from Germany. The tomb of Berengar, discovered only weeks ago. He didn't want to think about what would happen if word got out about what lay in that noble and ancient shifter's tomb, apart from his bones.

What I need is a distraction.

Then it came to him.

Theron smiled. "Vic Ryder is not going to make it back to his mates or his friends, do I make myself clear?"

"Understood, sir."

"I don't want him harmed, okay? He's far too valuable for that. Let me know when you have him and you'll receive more instructions."

"Yes, sir."

Theron ended the call. It was time to play his ace.

And while everyone is reeling from the news and demanding action, we employ misdirection and move swiftly to bury the truth before anyone has a chance to see it.

He gazed at the stone caskets behind the wall of glass.

And it will stay buried until the right moment.

When Gerans would cease to be the villains they were portrayed as and instead be hailed as a unifying force, bringing peace and harmony to all in a universe where every shifter knew their place.

Their superior place.

CHAPTER TWENTY

Tuesday

BRICK HAD to admit he was impressed.

"How in the hell did Duke lay his hands on a C-17? We're talking top of the line cargo aircraft." The belly of the steel beast held the troop of thirty or so men and women, plus the trucks and trailers that housed the medical equipment, night-vision goggles, food, rifles, tents, water.... Everything they'd need for the mission.

"I told him to call in every favor he was owed. Looks as if he did just that." Horvan sniffed. "Why does your bag smell like Aric?"

Brick smiled as he stroked a hand over his duffel. "He packed one of his shirts to remind me why I'm doing this."

Horvan returned the smile. "Okay, that's kinda cute, but seriously?" He wrinkled his nose. "He must've worn that thing for days." The plane hit turbulence, and he tapped his earpiece. "Is this gonna last long? … Okay." Horvan shook his head. "Pilot says we'll be out of it soon."

The sound of retching filled the air.

"Wizbang, you forgot to take your Dramamine again, didn't you?" Crank yelled. "Fuck, you do this every time."

"And you know I fucking hate it when you call me that, Crank. What's wrong with Wizbowski? Too many syllables for ya?" More retching followed.

Across from Brick, Saul passed a bag along the line of soldiers. "Here, give this to him."

Brick snickered. "Some of the best fighters I know are in this team, but they can't fight a queasy stomach." Another retching sound met his ears, only this was quieter—and closer to him.

Crank glanced around, frowning. "Who's throwing up now?"

"No idea." Brick snorted. "It sure wasn't me. Got the constitution of an ox."

"You mean a polar bear, right?" Horvan said with a smirk.

174

Crank got up and lurched across to them. "Okay, this is weird. The sound came from over here." He cocked his head, listening.

It happened again.

"I heard it this time." Horvan frowned. "Except it seems to be coming from your duffel, Brick."

Crank arched his eyebrows. "It seems your luggage doesn't like air travel. Better give it a Dramamine too."

Brick stared at the kit bag, a suspicion dawning. "Oh my God, he didn't." He loosened the straps and the cord and peered inside—to find a pair of beautiful gray eyes staring back up at him. The barf on his striped fur took away some of the cuteness and provided Brick with a reminder of why he was angry. "You little—" He reached into the bag, lifted out the tabby kitty, and held him up, Aric's front legs splayed and stiff, his tail down.

"Who's that, Brick? Your emotional support animal?" Dex hollered, chuckling.

Eve glared at him. "Shut up. That's his mate."

Horvan peered into the bag. "Hey, at least he threw up over *his* shirt."

Brick gave Aric a hard stare. *You are in so much trouble.*

Yeah, I got that part. Even his whiskers appeared dejected.

Now I know why you asked me to keep in mind that I love you. 'It'll come in handy later.' You were planning this all along. How did you breathe in there?

Check the bottom of the bag. You might find a few… slits. Aric flexed his claws. *And did you really expect me to stay at home? Dogs follow instructions—cats don't give a shit.* He barfed again.

"Great." Brick placed Aric on his lap, stroking a hand over the silky fur and sighing. *I've got you.*

Horvan handed Brick a wipe. "When we land, we'll find something for him to wear. Unless he packed more than one shirt in your bag, and I think you'd have noticed that." His eyes twinkled. "Let's face it. He'd be swimming in your fatigues."

A tremor rippled through Aric, and Brick gave him a mock glare.

It isn't that funny. And don't be too keen to shift. Just because you're my mate doesn't mean I'm not gonna put you over my knee.

Is that meant to scare me? Bring it on, big guy.

Brick fucking *loved* his feisty little mate, and although he'd never admit it, Aric had shown a lot of balls sneaking into his duffel.

Let this be a lesson to me. Never underestimate the kitty.

HASHTAG ADMIRED Eve's cool. She appeared completely unruffled. If anything, she seemed bored.

That's because I am. Can't wait to get off this thing and see some action.

Roadkill snickered. *You and me both.* He gave Hashtag a warm glance. *And you'll be watching over us from Operations, a kind of muscular guardian angel.*

Eve gave his hand a surreptitious squeeze. *I know it's not what you wanted, but—*

Hey, it's fine. Roadkill's right. Hashtag didn't want to think about being parted from them. He gazed at the team around him, some asleep, others reading, the rest talking in low voices. Then he noticed Doc Tranter's furrowed brow. The doc sat alone, hands clasped over his stomach. *I bet he makes an impressive elephant.*

Eve blinked. *Really? African or Indian?*

How would I know that?

She smiled. *By the shape of his ears.*

Then I wouldn't know, because no one's ever seen him shift.

Eve gazed thoughtfully at him. *He has the appearance of someone in a quandary.*

Hashtag had had the same thought. *Think I'll go keep him company.*

She smiled. *You're a good man.*

He left his place and wobbled across to the other side of the plane. "Hey, Doc. Can I join you?"

"Of course."

Hashtag dropped into the empty seat next to him. "I thought you said something about retiring, last time we spoke."

"I'll retire when we've done something about the Gerans. And when we've shut down these infernal camps and schools." Doc's face darkened.

He huffed. "And how long is that gonna take?"

"It's not something we can achieve quickly, that's certain, but even making a serious dent would be a good start. Right now it feels as if we've barely scratched the surface. I have to say, I'm worried what we're going to find at this camp."

Hashtag frowned. "Can't be worse than the last one. And that was only a few months ago."

"Sure, and since then we've discovered what the Gerans can do when they really put their minds to it."

"Well, I'm glad you're here." He peered at Doc. "You were friends with Dellan's dad, Jake, weren't you?"

Doc smiled. "Yes."

Something in that smile....

Hashtag leaned in. "So I guess the question is are you here for us—or for him?"

Doc turned to face him. "An astute question indeed. And to answer it, I'm here in my usual capacity, to patch up any of our troops who need it, but I'm also here because there are going to be a lot of shifters who will need medical—and psychiatric—help."

He blinked. "Psychiatric?"

Doc arched his eyebrows. "Think about it. A shifter is given a drug—without their consent—forced to shift, again without their consent, then forced to breed. There's another word for that, isn't there?"

Hashtag sighed. "Yeah, rape."

"Exactly. So how do you think all these shifters feel when they produce offspring who are then taken from them to be raised by adoptive parents and sent to schools to be indoctrinated? And let's not forget about the men."

On the other side of the plane, Dex snorted. "What do they have to complain about? All they did was take advantage of an opportunity to make little tigers, lions, panthers, whatever. And think of the positives. No child support."

Doc stilled, and Hashtag recoiled at the fury blazing in those usually cool eyes.

"Are you for fucking *real*, soldier?" he barked, and there was steel in his voice.

Dex froze, his eyes wide. "Sir?"

"How do you have the unmitigated fucking *nerve* to make forced mating sound like a good thing? Because from where I'm sitting, it's so far beyond awful, they'd need to invent a new word for it. Do you think they had any say in what happened to them? Who's to say any of them *wanted* to be fathers? Especially fathers to offspring that they'd probably never see."

Saul let out a growl. "It's a fucking good thing you're a better fighter than a thinker, Dex. Next time, put your brain into gear before you put your mouth into action. Otherwise, your section leader is gonna tear you a new one."

"Section leader?"

Saul gave him a cool smile that didn't reach his eyes. "Yes. Duncan's in charge of your section. Got a problem with that?"

Dex's face underwent a swift change, and he stiffened. "No, sir." He coughed, then buried himself in his book.

Hashtag placed his hand on Doc's arm. "You okay?"

Doc swallowed. "Sorry. I just saw red."

"Hey, no apology needed, Doc," Saul told him. "You did good."

Dellan leaned forward in his seat next to Horvan. "Doc's right, though. There are going to be a lot of questions once this is over."

"But how can we bring all this to an end?" Eve remonstrated.

Horvan gave her an inquiring glance. "Having problems seeing the long-term picture, Eve?"

She swallowed. "Yes, sir. We're facing all these camps, the schools…. If we're going to make any changes, then as a wise man once said to me, we shouldn't be afraid to fight dirty."

"We're about to get ourselves a VIP," Saul said. "A Very Important Prisoner."

Crank snorted. "I was thinking a Vastly Insufferable Prick, but hey, I can go with your version."

Horvan tapped his earpiece. "Copy that." He stood. "Okay, folks, your attention, please. We're about to land at Estcourt Station Airport, which is also the northern-most airport in Maine and less than a thousand feet from the Canadian border. We're gonna set up camp in the forest south of the airstrip. Some of you will be joining Team B, led by Johan Deerling, one of Aelryn's men. Once we get to the site of our camp, I want everything running like clockwork, you got that?"

There was a chorus of "Sir, yes, sir!"

"More troops and medics will meet us at the airport. Now just because we have a day or two before we see action, that does *not* mean you're all on vacation."

Laughter greeted his words. "Aw, shit. And I was gonna work on my tan," Crank quipped. He smirked at Brick. "I guess you'll still be able to."

Brick frowned. "Fuck that. I have a kitty to deal with."

Horvan scanned the faces of his men. "Study the map of the compound. Work in your teams. Every one of you has a specific job to perform. No one is redundant." He grinned. "And if you don't pull your weight, Brick's mate will leave a little gift in your boots."

Hashtag held his hand out to Aric, but stopped halfway. "Is it okay if I pet the kitty—I mean, Aric?"

Horvan chuckled. "Wise move, asking first. Aric's his mate, after all, and we tend to maim first and ask questions later if anyone touches our mates. That goes for Aric, too."

Brick didn't answer right away, and then he smiled. "I think it's okay just this once. Aric says it's fine too."

Hashtag scritched Aric behind his ears. "Hey, pretty kitty. You wouldn't shit in *my* shoes, would ya?"

Brick chuckled. "He says that depends on whether you brought a bag of Temptations with you."

Hashtag gaped. "Hey, kitty treats don't feature on my packing list."

Dellan grinned. "You'll know better next time."

Brick scowled. "There isn't gonna *be* a next time." He bent over. "You hear that, kitty cat?"

Aric rolled onto his back, presenting a very fluffy tummy.

Brick laughed. "Nice try. You're not forgiven yet."

Hashtag made his way back to Eve and Roadkill. "I suppose I ought to know what counts as a treat for gorillas."

She smiled. "Bring me a bowl of strawberries in bed and you'll be on the right track. Throw in some bamboo shoots and you're golden." She took his hand in hers. "You're not going to worry about me, are you? We talked about this."

He sighed. "Last time I was on a mission, I concentrated on getting the job done and going home at the end of it all. Now?" He gazed at Eve and Roadkill. "I'll do my best. Can't promise more than that."

If we weren't on this plane right now, I'd kiss you so fucking hard. Roadkill's intense stare sent heat curling through him.

That's probably a good thing. PDAs in front of this crew? Yeah, no.

Then the plane banked left, and Hashtag straightened.

Time to switch into fighter mode.

IF THERE was one thing Horvan admired about his team, it was their ability to hit the ground running, even before the sun had risen. Less than five minutes after reaching the site for the camp, the men got busy erecting tents in the predawn light, sorting out the portable generators and water supply and establishing a perimeter. The command tent was up in less than half an hour.

Hashtag had a quiet moment with Eve and Roadkill before he and about eight others went off in a truck, heading for the meeting point at Allagash with Johan and his team, about an hour and a half away. His job would be to get the drones airborne so they could get their first real-time look at the camp.

Horvan sent a coded message to Milo to let him know they were on the ground, while Doc did a briefing with the team of medics.

And now we wait.

Dellan entered the command tent, carrying a flask. "Flynn's in charge of food. He said you'd need this."

Horvan chuckled. "That man knows me too well." He unscrewed the cap and poured himself a cup of strong coffee. He sniffed. "Damn, that smells good."

"Saul said we're sending drones to look at the camp. Is that safe? Won't they hear them?"

Horvan sipped his coffee. "Drones usually make a distinctive buzzing or whirring noise, like an electric motor or a swarm of bees. But once they climb above a hundred feet from the ground, it's much less noticeable—for human ears, that is. That's why we're gonna have them cruise at a height of about twenty thousand feet. They'll appear like a speck in the sky. And Hashtag has orders to take his photos and be out of there as fast as he can."

Brick came into the tent. "Aric's asleep. We found him some fatigues, although it was tough with this crowd. We don't have any guys his size. Thank God for Eve and her safety pins. At least he's not gonna be performing any impromptu strip shows." His face clouded. "H, I'm sorry. I had no idea he—"

"Forget it. I know how these things go. Remember the raid on the Bozeman camp? When I discovered my mates had followed us?"

Dellan smiled. "And I also recall how useful we were. Aric will prove useful too, I'm sure of it."

Brick glanced toward the tent flap. "I'm hoping to hear Seth's thoughts. We must be close enough by now."

Horvan patted his arm. "We're going to get him out of there soon enough. Then you can hear his voice out loud." He smiled. "You get to hold him too."

Horvan's phone buzzed, and he glanced at the screen. It was from Milo. *Can we talk?*

He clicked on Call. "Are you safe to talk?"

"For the moment. I don't have any more news about Fielding's arrival."

"Then why are you calling?" Horvan's bare arms erupted into a carpet of goose bumps, and it had nothing to do with the chill morning air.

Something's wrong.

"Horvan, don't ask me how, but… they know you're coming."

CHAPTER TWENTY-ONE

HORVAN'S SKIN was like ice. "That's impossible."

"They *know*, I tell you. The camp commander told me last night. I had to wait for the first opportunity to call you. So now I have to ask. Who knows about this mission?"

He thought fast. "It can't be any of my team. I'd stake my life on it. Aelryn knows, of course."

"And who has *he* told?"

That was the question Horvan wanted answered too. "So what do you know?"

"They have no idea when you'll be here. They're waiting to learn what your schedule is, and once they know that, they're bringing in extra guards. The plan is that not one of you will live."

Horvan froze. "Waiting to.... But where are they getting their information from?"

"I don't know! All I'm telling you is the talk around here isn't about *if* you're coming—it's *when*."

Horvan had a call to make. "Let me know as soon as you hear anything, okay?"

"You got it." Milo disconnected.

Brick gaped at him. "*What* can't be any of the team? What information? What the fuck is going on, H?"

Dellan was pale. "The Gerans know we're coming. No specifics, just that."

Horvan's mind was already trying to come up with a logical answer. But there was only one possible conclusion, and he didn't like it one little bit.

He scrolled and hit Aelryn's number.

"I take it you're in Maine. So are we."

Horvan recognized the voice at the other end. "Scott, I need to talk to Aelryn, and it has to be a private call. I'm not talking about you—you're his mate, for God's sake. I mean no leaders, no counsel, *no one*, okay?"

There was maybe a second's hesitation. "I'll get him."

"And what are you going to tell him?" Dellan said in a low, urgent voice. "'Hey, Aelryn, you've got a traitor'? We can't prove that."

Horvan clutched his phone to his chest. "I think we can." He brought it to his ear.

"Horvan, what's wrong?"

He filled Aelryn in on Milo's call. The shocked silence that followed was no surprise.

This has to hurt him. One of his trusted people had just stabbed him in the back.

"Could it be one of your men?"

Horvan's heart went out to him, but there was no way to paint this in any other color. "No. Okay, so we have newbies, but Saul's vetted the fuck out of every last one of them." He wasn't about to mention Eve's past—time was of the essence, and besides, he didn't see how that could be possible, not with Roadkill and Hashtag as part of the equation.

"But it *can't* be anyone at this end. I'd know if we had that kind of snake among us."

Horvan forced himself to be calm. "Look, I've got an idea how we might learn the truth. We can't try it yet—we need to wait on Milo—but I think it'll work."

"Let's hear it."

"When we get the go from Milo, you call a Zoom meeting, and you inform your leaders—everyone you'd *usually* inform, all right?"

"With you so far."

"Then once we've worked out our timings, you email every leader—but *individually,* you got that?"

"I get it, but why?"

Horvan outlined his idea. It was a spur of the moment kinda thing, but it had worked for a friend of his. He was banking on it working for them too.

Screw that—he was praying it would.

"So what do we do in the meantime?" Aelryn demanded.

"What we were going to do. Get the drones up, do a recon, take pictures.... We follow the plan. We're still going in, remember? Only we'll do it when they're not expecting us."

"If you're right. And to be honest, I'm hoping you've got it all wrong and there's some other explanation."

Horvan would give anything for that to be true.

"One last thing. In any of your briefings, have you mentioned the source of our information?"

Please, tell me you haven't said a goddamn word about Milo. Because if that was the case Horvan didn't even want to think of the consequences.

"No. I simply told them we were acting on information received."

Horvan let out a sigh of relief. "Okay, good. Let's keep it that way."

Milo was their only hope now.

THE MOMENT he got the message to go to the camp commander's office again, Milo was on a mission to get his heart to calm the fuck down.

Don't let them be onto me.

Don't let them be onto me.

Don't let them be onto me.

He knocked at the door, his pulse racing.

"Come in."

Milo stepped into the small, cramped room. Everything about the commander was thin, from his tall, lanky form to his long face and long, sharp nose. He glanced up from his desk as Milo came to a halt in front of it and saluted.

"Keppler. Two things I need you to deal with."

"Yes, sir." Inside, he relaxed.

I'm still safe.

"Our VIP will be arriving Friday afternoon, by plane. It'll be your job to sort out sleeping quarters for him."

Milo removed his phone from his pocket and tapped the screen. "Certainly, sir. How many nights will he be staying? And will I need to accommodate any staff that might be accompanying him?"

"He'll be leaving here Monday morning." The commander peered at his monitor. "And he'll have two guards with him. I don't care if you have some of our men sleeping outside—he must be shown every courtesy and consideration, and that means providing him with his own room." He glanced at Milo. "Can you arrange that?"

"Yes, sir." Milo could sound confident when he needed to.

"Excellent. And now for the other matter...." The commander leaned forward, his long fingers steepled. "Who is our best marksman in your opinion? I need a sniper."

Milo frowned. "Walsh is good, sir, and so is Bradley, but for accuracy, I'd have to say O'Neill every time."

"That was my thought also. We've been asked by our VIP to perform a small task, for which we will require O'Neill's expertise. One of the prisoners is to be eliminated."

Milo gave him an inquiring glance. "I don't understand, sir. Why use a sniper for the job? Why not simply give the prisoner a lethal injection?"

"Because, Captain Keppler, our VIP wants to make an example of him. His instructions are that the prisoner will be taken out with a single shot while he's on the exercise yard. No one else is to be harmed. This is to be a lesson for the others. A little fear is no bad thing. A reminder that everyone is expendable."

"And when is this to take place, sir?"

The commander sat back in his chair. "Ah, now *that* I don't know yet. Apparently the timing has to be right. I'll know more when we receive further intelligence about the Fridan raid."

"We still don't know when they'll be making their move?"

He shook his head. "Although I have it on good authority that it will be within the coming week. As soon as I know, I'll share the details. You'll need to bring in reinforcements." He smiled. "They'll be walking into a trap, and not one of them will leave here alive." He glanced at Milo. "That'll be all, Captain."

"Sir." Milo gave a sharp salute, then stilled. "Excuse me, sir, but I'm missing one important detail."

"Which is?"

"The name of the prisoner to be executed?" Milo forced a chuckle. "O'Neill needs to know who to aim at, after all."

The commander laughed. "Good point. His name is Jake Carson." Then he frowned. "I'm not sure I understand the reasoning behind killing one of their most successful experiments, but I'm sure the powers that be know what they're doing. As they say, ours is not to reason why."

Milo gave another salute and marched out of the office, the following line of the quotation ringing inside his head.

Wasn't it something like 'ours is but to do and die?'

Except if Fielding got his way, it wouldn't be the Gerans who were dying, but the Fridans.

And Dellan's father.

He hurried out of the block and into the open air. It seemed incongruous to feel the warmth of the sun on his face, to see the clear sky above the canopy of trees, and to have to give the order to end a life for no reason that he could fathom.

Milo took a deep breath. *Jana? Can you hear me?*

A heartbeat later, her sweet voice was in his head. *Yes, Milo.*

I can't tell you when exactly, but I'm going to keep my promise. I'm getting you out of here. He swallowed. *And I'll be going with you.*

His career with the Geran military was about to reach an abrupt end.

Really?

He smiled to himself. *Really.*

When?

You'll know when it happens.

Everyone would know.

Milo waited until he was alone to send a message.

F arrives Friday PM. Leaves Monday AM.

Horvan's reply was swift. *Thank you. Will send details ASAP.*

He hesitated before typing again. *You need to know. F has given orders to execute Jake.*

WTF? When?

No clue. Seems it depends on your arrival.

With every second that followed, Milo could only imagine the pain Dellan was going through.

Not gonna happen. Not if we can help it.

Milo typed fast. *I'll send details as soon as I get them.* He pocketed his phone, then headed to the barracks.

He had to find space for a certain VIP.

Then he remembered. He had another job to do. Horvan wanted to know about the deliveries schedule.

Timing would be everything if this was going to work.

HORVAN WAS bone tired, but that didn't matter. The important thing was to discover who'd betrayed them.

He clicked on Call, and Aelryn's face filled the screen.

"You seem to be having the same issues I'm suffering from. Both of us need our beds."

Horvan snorted. "How does the saying go? Sleep is for the weak." He tapped the sheet in front of him with his pencil. He'd gone from a mass of scribbling to a neatly written plan. "Okay, the attack will be Sunday night. At least, that's what you're going to tell all your leaders, with the exception of Johan."

Aelryn studied him. "And when do we actually go in?"

"Early hours of Saturday morning, before dawn. We're gonna time it to coincide with the delivery. So three teams, not two."

Aelryn nodded. "So I share the false information with all my leaders, exactly as you described." His face hardened. "And then we wait."

"As soon as I hear back from Milo, we'll know which bastard sold us out."

"I'd better start putting emails together."

"Milo is also sending us files," Horvan told him. "Photos of every inmate and every guard, so no one can fool us by claiming to be a prisoner. I'll forward them to you for your team."

"Thank you." Aelryn grimaced. "I still cannot believe someone would do this."

"Hey, I feel ya. We were in the same boat for the first school mission. Brick, remember? They had his parents. And we all know how that ended."

Aelryn straightened. "I'll get to work. We'll be talking later, I have no doubt."

No doubt at all.

Rael came into the command tent. "You appear to be a man in need of some loving."

Horvan gave a weary chuckle. "You have no idea." He wrapped his arms around Rael's waist, his ear pressed to Rael's chest, listening to the reassuring beat of his heart. They stayed that way for a few minutes while Horvan let his mate's scent fill his nostrils, Rael's calm seeping into his bones. "I needed this."

Rael kissed the top of his head. "I know. Why do you think I'm here?"

"Where's Dellan?"

I'm with Aric. He had a dream where Seth told him we were about to walk into a trap.

Horvan sighed. *Tell him we're not. In fact, we're about to turn the tide in our favor.*

Rael pulled up a camp chair and sat beside him. "What's this plan of yours? You've been careful to shield us from it."

Horvan leaned back, stretching out his long legs. "One of my former military buddies retired a while back and took up writing as a hobby. Mostly about his experiences. But when he finished his first book, he decided to publish it himself."

Rael smiled. "Was it any good?"

Horvan grinned. "It was fucking awesome. But he had to learn a whole bunch of stuff along the way. One of the things he hated most was the way his book got pirated."

"That happens a lot, I hear."

Horvan nodded. "Okay, Leon had a team of beta readers. Military guys, mostly, who read what he'd written and gave their thoughts—stuff he'd missed, impressions, that kinda thing. All this was before it reached the publication stage, and he trusted these guys. But he also had an ARC team. That's Advance Reader Copy to us nonpublishing mortals. These were people who got sent advance copies, and their job was to write a review to boost the book's release. So before his *second* book came out—and to cut down on pirate copies—he had an idea."

"He thought one of his ARC team was uploading the book to pirate sites?"

"Yup. So what he did was this. He sent a copy to every ARC reader—but each copy had a slight variation. A different word here, a typo there. No two copies were the same. And he had a list of which reader got which version. So when the book released and ended up on a pirate site—"

"He downloaded it and checked to see which version it was." Rael chuckled. "That's inspired. Did it work?"

Horvan snorted. "No. None of the ARCs were uploaded. Someone obviously bought a copy on release and *then* decided everyone should read it for free. But it gave me the idea. Aelryn is emailing every leader our attack plan, but with one subtle difference—the timing of our initial attack varies from email to email."

"So when Milo gets back to us after he's seen the plan, we'll know who sent it to them."

"Exactly. And right now Aelryn is sending out our false plan to see who bites."

"Then we wait?"

Horvan sighed. "Then we wait."

Dellan strolled into the tent. "Then might I suggest you get a few hours' sleep in the meantime?"

Horvan huffed. "I would, but that camp bed ain't gonna fit all three of us."

Dellan smiled. "Who says we need a bed?" He started to remove his clothing, and Rael copied him.

"I hate to tell ya, boys, but I'm in no mood to fuck."

"That's fine, because we had something else in mind." One minute Horvan was looking at Dellan's lean naked body, and the next, a beautiful tiger stood there, joined seconds later by a gorgeous lion.

"Now you're talking." Horvan stripped and shifted, and the three of them lay down on the ground sheet, Horvan in the middle, his mates on either side, snuggled against him.

He could manage a few hours.

HORVAN'S NOSTRILS twitched, and he opened his eyes.

Time to shift, H. Because no way can those paws hold a coffee cup.

He chuckled and shifted. Dellan held out a cup to him. "Feel better?"

"Much." He drank the cup's contents, and Dellan took it from him. "I'll get you some more."

Horvan reached for his fatigues. "How long did we sleep?"

"Put it this way. Tuesday is almost over." Rael handed him his boots.

Horvan's phone buzzed, and he grabbed it. "Milo," he told Rael. "And?"

He scanned the message. "Looks as if it worked." He called Aelryn, who answered after two rings. "Good evening."

"Is it?"

Horvan sighed. "No, it isn't. I hate to be the bearer of bad tidings, but it worked. Which means… you've got a traitor."

"Seems that way." Aelryn's grave tone sent a shiver through him.

"What will you do if you find the person?"

Aelryn sighed. "Even though there's been no formal declaration, we *are* at war with the Gerans. This act compromises our people. That means there's only one thing we *can* do. Execute them."

CHAPTER TWENTY-TWO

Wednesday

AELRYN KNEW he should be out there in the camp with his men as they prepared for the mission, but his heart felt too heavy.

How can I be positive and upbeat with this weighing me down?

He still couldn't believe it. He'd known Rudy Myers for decades. They'd fought together, rejoiced together, celebrated their victories, commiserated over their losses, and talked into the wee small hours, setting the world to rights, more times than Aelryn cared to remember.

I trusted him.

I loved him like a brother.

To discover his treachery was the most painful blow—and the bitterest pill to swallow.

What went wrong? Why did he lose faith?

The one thought that went around and around, tormenting him, making his heart sink even further?

How could he do this to us?

The tent flap opened, and Scott came inside. *I heard you right across the camp.* He walked over to Aelryn, stood behind him, and put his arms around Aelryn's shoulders.

Aelryn forced a smile. *I'm still getting used to this.* The telepathic connection had been a recent development, and after months of being with his mate, he had to wonder why now. Not that he was complaining. It added an extra level to their relationship, especially during intimate moments.

I know him, heart, body, and soul. And loved him just as much.

Scott sighed. "Rudy's here. He arrived about five minutes ago."

That was all it took to banish such thoughts from Aelryn's mind and chase away the momentary lightness Scott's presence had brought.

"Show him in. Then leave us, please."

Scott's breath warmed his ear. *If you need me....*

Aelryn reached up to caress Scott's cheek. *I'll call. But I'll be safe. I know him.*

He swallowed. *At least, I thought I did.*

Scott left him, and Aelryn stood, his back rigid as he pushed aside sentimentality and affection.

Time to be the leader he was born to be. A leader worthy of his bloodline.

Rudy Myers stepped inside the command tent, and Aelryn noted his hesitation, his sweeping gaze that took in his surroundings, the sharp bob of his Adam's apple.

Rudy was nervous—unless Aelryn imagined it.

He pointed to one of the chairs that had been set up for his briefing with Johan. "Sit down."

Rudy blinked. "No greeting? No explanation for why you sent a truck to collect me at too damn early o'clock? Why am I here, Aelryn? I'm not part of this mission. At least, I *thought* I wasn't." His lips twitched. "Did I miss the memo?"

"Why are you here? I'll give you the short answer." Aelryn fixed him with a steady gaze. "You gave details of this mission to the Gerans."

His eyes widened. "What? Of course I didn't. Why would—"

"Please, don't try my patience," Aelryn interjected, one hand raised. "We have proof. Undeniable, solid proof. But before I give the order to have you taken from here and... dealt with, I want to know one thing: Why?"

Rudy's eyes were like saucers. "'Dealt with'?" All the color slid from his face.

Aelryn stared at him. "This isn't an action that requires a slap on the wrist, or even a formal reprimand. Surely you knew what would happen if you were found out."

Silence.

Aelryn could almost hear the cogs clicking in Rudy's head as he undoubtedly went through every conceivable response, every possible denial. Then Rudy crumpled, his broad shoulders sagging, his shaved head bowed. "I wasn't thinking about the consequences of my actions," he whispered.

"Then what *were* you thinking about? Apart from helping the enemy to thwart our plans, of course."

Rudy raised his head, and tortured eyes met Aelryn's gaze. "My only thought was… my mate. His survival."

Oh, by the gods….

Aelryn froze. "You found your mate? When was this?"

"A month ago. But… it's complicated."

He sat in the chair facing Rudy and leaned back, arms folded. "Tell me. Everything."

"Now isn't the time to—"

"You are not leaving this tent until you've told me." Aelryn scowled. "It's no secret I have a mate. I need to know this isn't some ploy to gain sympathy." Except he didn't believe that. He *knew* Rudy. "And you'd better make it convincing. Because if you're treated the way *all* traitors are treated, what happens to your mate? Think about how much he'd suffer without you."

"At least he'd be alive to do it!" Rudy snapped. Seconds ticked by, and at last he sighed. "This might be the only chance I get. Okay, then. Last month, I was in New York…."

RUDY HAD to admit the exhibition was fascinating. He'd thought Colchis was a figment of some screenwriter's imagination, the place where Jason and his Argonauts went to find the golden fleece. He'd had no idea it was a real location, a place of ancient tombs and documents….

Call yourself a history teacher? For shame.

The Institute for the Study of the Ancient World at New York University hadn't been his idea of a tourist spot—a friend had recommended it—but so far he'd spent a few hours gazing at the artifacts and reading the displayed information.

Then his senses went on alert.

Someone's watching me.

He turned and scanned the room. There were only three other people present. Two of them were peering into a glass cabinet.

The third, a tall, imposing man, was staring at Rudy, lips parted, eyes wide.

What the hell?

Then Rudy froze as the most delicious scent tickled his nostrils. He couldn't tear his gaze away from the man with the buzz-cut dark hair, a firm jawline, and the bluest eyes Rudy had ever seen.

Eyes that were locked on his.

A rhythmic thud filled Rudy's head, the sound of a beating heart. Except it wasn't his—it was the stranger's.

What the fuck is going on?

Rudy walked slowly, as if in a daze, not stopping until he was barely an inch away. His nostrils filled with that same aroma and something else. A spicy, warm scent that Rudy associated with sex.

He's attracted to me.

Rudy was experiencing that same thing. Heat barreled through him, blood surged south, and his fingers itched to touch, explore, penetrate....

The guy's breathing hitched. "I thought it was all lies."

"What was?"

"The concept of mates. And yet here you are, so real." The man touched Rudy's face with tentative fingers, and *holy fuck*, electricity shuddered its way through Rudy, his synapses firing, his body burning with need.

Then his words sank in. "Mates?"

A voice in his head shouted *Yes, yes, yes.*

"My name is Valmer Cooper."

"Rudy Myers." Gods, the urge to kiss him was all-encompassing.

Valmer's nostrils flared. "If you tell me you're straight, I'm in real trouble. Because the things I want to do to you right this minute...."

Shit. Rudy's dick reacted. "Maybe we should share lists. Except I'm not in a hurry to get arrested for indecent exposure—or worse."

Valmer groaned. "My hotel is half an hour from here."

"Mine's closer."

"Then what are we waiting for?"

RUDY LAY with his head on Valmer's shoulder, tracing invisible lines over Valmer's chest with his fingertips, loving the shivers that rippled through him when Rudy brushed over his nipples.

Rudy had never had sex like that in his life, not even with partners he'd shared years with. The intimacy he and Valmer had achieved in just a few hours left every relationship Rudy had ever had in the dust.

"This is crazy," he murmured.

Valmer chuckled. "Beyond crazy."

Rudy dipped his finger into Valmer's navel before heading south, reaching the tight curls of his pubic hair, his dick lying limp to one side, yet reacting to the slightest touch. "You're real."

Another chuckle shook Valmer. "I think we've proved that three times already, but I'm game for a fourth attempt." He peered at his crotch. "Or I will be. Gimme a few minutes." He laughed. "I haven't gone more than three rounds in one night since I was in my early twenties."

Rudy craned his neck to stare at him. "And I've never fucked a guy's brains out when all I knew about him was his name." He snorted. "Except that one time, and it was a sex party, so that was okay, right?" He pressed his lips to Valmer's chest. "You could be an ax murderer for all I know."

Valmer cleared his throat. "Not an ax murderer. That much I can confirm."

"But what *are* you?"

He smiled. "I'm a cheetah."

Rudy grinned. "Whoa. A sleek, fast kitty. I like it."

"What about you?"

"Nothing so impressive. I'm a golden retriever."

His eyes lit up. "Now I know why I prefer dogs." Valmer pulled Rudy closer, until Rudy could feel every beat of his heart.

Then Rudy's senses went on the alert again and unease trickled through him. "What's wrong?"

Valmer blinked. "How did you—stupid question. So let me ask you another. Why were you at the exhibition?"

"I'm a history buff, but recently I've become interested in ancient history."

He nodded. "Me too. I studied it." He paused. "How much do you know about *our* history?"

Rudy managed a one-shoulder shrug. "Not much, but then again, I don't think anyone knows much. Beyond the tale of the two brothers, of course."

Valmer shivered. "I know more than I ever wanted to know. More than it's *safe* for me to know, I'm certain of that."

Cold crawled over Rudy's skin.

Valmer rolled onto his side to face him. "There's one important detail neither of us has shared, and I'm beginning to think that was deliberate."

Rudy suddenly knew where Valmer was headed, and cold reached his extremities.

"So?" Valmer propped his head up with one hand. "Fridan? Geran? Or do you follow neither?"

Icy fear swirled in Rudy's belly, making him afraid to answer, but he had to.

This is my mate.

He took a deep breath. "Fridan."

Valmer nodded, and for a few brief seconds Rudy felt relief. Then Valmer spoke, obliterating his hope. "Geran."

Rudy couldn't breathe. *No. No. This can't be right.*

Valmer sighed. "Maybe we both knew instinctively, and we were afraid to say it out loud."

"But that doesn't change a thing," Rudy blurted. "You're my mate."

Whose views had nothing in common with his own.

"And now you're trying to figure out how we can make this work, given that we're on opposing sides."

Rudy swallowed hard. "I have to admit, it doesn't make a lot of sense."

Valmer stared at him before flipping onto his back and hauling Rudy on top of him. He cradled Rudy's nape, gazing into his eyes. "I know something that could change everything. Not our mate bond—I don't think anything could do that. I've known you for all of, like, five minutes, and it already feels like a lifetime. No, something else. Something huge." He cupped Rudy's cheek. "Ansfrid and Ansger. Whatever stands between us started with them."

"Their split, you mean?"

Valmer went quiet for a moment. "Suppose I were to tell you…," he began slowly, then clammed up.

"Don't stop there. Please." Rudy's heart pounded.

Valmer studied his face, and every second that passed only served to compound Rudy's intensifying, overwhelming fear. "Suppose I were to tell you that everything you believe—everything we *all* believe—was built on lies?"

Rudy's fear swelled from a stream to a raging torrent. "You're frightening me."

Valmer kissed him on the lips, and the sweet embrace took away a little of his anxiety. "I was a student of ancient studies, the history of language, the arts, literature, even the first written records of civilization. You might have heard of one of my classmates. Sarah Delaney?"

Rudy blinked. "The archaeologist?"

He nodded. "We became friends. What's more, we've stayed friends. I've even visited her on some of her digs. Well, she contacted me a week ago to tell me she'd unearthed something extraordinary. A tomb—an ancient shifter's tomb, to be exact."

"Whose?"

"His name was Berengar, and the tomb was found in Germany. Sarah was so excited. Actually, they'd need to invent a new adjective to adequately convey her emotions. She called me a few hours later to tell me all about it. And the next day? She opened the tomb."

Rudy's stomach clenched. "What did she find?"

"She only gave me hints. But she also said she'd called the shifter archive in Rome."

He did the math. "These hints... did they have anything to do with what you said to me? About everything we believe being built on lies?"

Valmer nodded. "The day after she called, the dig was closed down."

"And you think that was because of what Sarah found in the tomb?"

"I know it was."

Rudy stared at him. "Then tell me what *else* you know!"

The horror in Valmer's expression froze the marrow in Rudy's bones. "I can't. Because if I did that, you'd be in danger."

Rudy gaped at him. "You can't know that."

"Oh, can't I? Let me tell you what I *do* know. After that last phone conversation with Sarah, I tried to call her back. Only I couldn't reach her. She'd disappeared." Valmer's face tightened. "It's as if she never even existed. And the tomb? It was covered up again."

"With everything still inside it?"

"Hell no. Sarah told me arrangements had been made to remove its contents. That was the last message I had from her."

Rudy sat upright and grabbed his shirt.

"What are you doing?"

"I know someone who might be able to help." Aelryn would know what to do.

"No!" Valmer grabbed Rudy and held him close. "Please, you mustn't."

"Give me one good reason why."

"Ever since Sarah disappeared, I haven't been able to shake the feeling that... I'm being watched."

Rudy stared at him, letting his senses do the talking.

He didn't like what they told him.

"You're serious."

Valmer nodded, then kissed Rudy's forehead. "Yes. And if I'm right, they can't know about you. I can't lose you."

Rudy couldn't bear the idea of losing him either.

His stomach chose that moment to growl, and he managed a chuckle. "I think you're about to lose me to hunger. I'm starving."

"I'll order food for us. Just promise me you won't put yourself in danger. Please, Rudy."

There was no way he could ignore the entreaty in Valmer's voice. "Okay, I promise." For the time being at least. When he got Valmer to a place of safety, however?

All bets were off.

They lay in bed, cuddling, talking about anything but the elephant in the room. When the knock at the door came, Valmer pulled on a robe and went to let in the server. Rudy caught the aroma of rich sauce and roast chicken, and his belly grumbled in anticipation.

"Hey, don't I know you?" Valmer's voice rose. "Wait—you—"

The popping sound that followed reminded Rudy of a champagne cork. From around the corner came the server, a white napkin draped over his arm—

Where a gun pointed at him.

"Don't."

It was the only word he got out before pain speared into him and he knew no more.

Rudy opened his eyes.

I'm not dead. He felt weak, however, robbed of all energy. Darkness surrounded him, and there were no clues as to his whereabouts. His ears told him he was not alone. In fact, he was certain someone was behind him.

"Where am I?" Rudy yelled, his heartbeat racing.

"That doesn't matter." The voice came from in front of him, deep and smooth—and filled with menace. "What *does* is who you are, and how valuable you are."

Rudy went with a bluff. "I think you've got the wrong person. I'm a history teacher. Nothing valuable about me."

A rich chuckle made him go cold. "I'm sure Mr. Cooper would disagree with that statement. Don't bother lying, Mr. Myers. You think we don't have files on every Fridan leader? And don't think about trying to shift, either. You can't. We've made sure of that."

Then everything he'd heard was true.

Ice filled his veins. "Where is Valmer? What have you done to him?"

"He's safe. And he'll stay that way—as long as you do exactly what we tell you."

"Not good enough," Rudy ground out. "I can't operate unless I have proof he's still alive."

There was a pause. "Will live video be sufficient? Once a day?"

It would have to do.

"What do you want from me?" As if he couldn't hazard a guess.

"You're going to keep us informed of any Fridan missions, discoveries…. Because if we find out you *didn't* share, he dies. If you tell anyone what's happened, he dies. And so far we don't know what effect losing a mate can have on someone. It's tempting to kill him just to find out." The gleeful note in his voice sent shivers down Rudy's spine. "But like I said, you're too valuable. As long as you give us the information we require, he'll stay alive."

"I'd ask for your word on that." Rudy's voice quavered. "Except I wouldn't believe you."

Harsh laughter filled his ears. "Ha. Neither would I. So now it's time for you to leave us."

"I don't suppose I get to walk out of wherever this is under my own steam?"

Another chilling chuckle. "You suppose correctly."

Something sharp scratched his neck, and he was out like a light.

"I WOKE to find myself in my hotel room. The manager said I'd been brought there by ambulance, and that I was suffering from shock." Rudy's face grew glum. "You know the rest."

"And did they give that to you? The live video?"

199

He nodded, his face contorted. "The first one, he'd been beaten. Badly. His eyes were swollen shut, and his lips were chapped and bloodied. But as soon as he heard my voice, you know what he did? He screamed not to help them. *Don't tell them a goddamn thing.*"

"But you agreed."

"Yes. Every time I saw him, the damage was worse than the time before. They told me that as long as I helped them, they wouldn't kill him. At least not outright. But if I refused, they would beat him to death while I watched."

"And yet he was one of their own." Aelryn couldn't hide his disbelief—or disgust.

Rudy nodded. "And if they find out I've told you...."

"Especially if they discover you've passed on false information."

Rudy stared at him. "What?"

"The information you leaked to them? It isn't true."

"But... there's a mission. You're here. It's happening."

It was Aelryn's turn to nod. "Yes, it is—only not when we *told* you it was. We had to know who was passing them information." The implications weren't lost on him.

They had to be all too clear for Rudy.

His face was the color of milk. "And when they find out I lied to them? They'll kill Valmer."

"Not if you convince them we changed our plans at the last minute. A spur of the moment decision. Because you're going to keep doing exactly what you've *been* doing. Only now, you'll pass on vetted information."

"Aelryn, I...." Rudy swallowed.

"What is it?"

"I got the impression I wasn't the first Fridan they'd had spying for them."

That wasn't too much of a shock. Vic Ryder had said much the same thing in a recent message.

"And... I didn't just tell them about the mission."

Aelryn froze. "What else?" When Rudy didn't answer, Aelryn lost it. "What *else*? You tell me *now!*"

"I told them about Vic Ryder, how he was visiting all the team leaders."

Oh gods.

"Are they keeping tabs on him?"

Rudy nodded. "I think so. But... what reason would they have to harm him?"

Aelryn could think of one reason. Vic's mission was to convince leaders of the very real threat the Gerans posed.

And they won't like that.

Rudy might have put Vic in harm's way.

Horvan will need to know. And Vic's mates.

"What will happen to me? You... you're not going to...." Rudy's voice shook.

"No." Aelryn sighed. "I *was*, but now I know the truth? I've been asking myself what *I'd* do if I were in your position, and if I'm honest.... Where my mate is concerned, my emotions get the better of me." He fixed Rudy with an intense gaze. "I'm not sure Vic's mates would be so understanding."

Rudy winced. "They'll tear me apart."

"They might be inclined toward leniency—but *only* if Vic comes out of this alive. Besides, you've provided us with vital information. Once this mission is completed, our next task will be to discover what was in that tomb—and exactly what the Gerans don't want *anyone* to see."

CHAPTER TWENTY-THREE

Thursday

VIC STRODE along the Via del Banco di Santo Spirito, heading for the Sant Angelo Castle bridge for the second time, his thoughts fixed not on his meeting with Orsini, but on his mates. Crank had sent several messages grousing about the food in the camp, but Vic took those with a grain of salt. Crank was a regular omnivore. Saul called him a human garbage disposal unit, and Vic had to admit he pretty much nailed it. One night back in Homer Glen, Roadkill had filled him in on all the horrendous things they'd gotten Crank to eat over the years, and Vic had been both appalled and impressed.

Not long now.

He knew Saul would be up to his neck in preparation for the mission. He was leading the biggest team, and Vic pitied the men under his command. He imagined Saul would be a tough son of a bitch who demanded nothing but the best from his team.

Yeah, Vic was proud as fuck of both his mates.

Saul had said the team would be heading back to Illinois on Saturday, and Vic wanted to be ready for them. That meant only one thing—lube, lube, and lube. He'd actually gone online to see if a fifty-five-gallon barrel was readily available. It was hard not to order one.

Or two.

As he drew closer to the gates, his progress was impeded by two men in suits, and Vic's senses went on alert.

"Mr. Ryder?" The taller man flashed him a polite smile. "If you could accompany us, sir."

Shit. This isn't good.

Vic frowned. "I don't know who you are, you've shown me no identification, and I have a meeting. So if you'll excuse me...." He tried to swerve around the men, only to feel what was undoubtedly a gun poking

202

into his back. The person holding it was close enough that Vic could feel his body warmth.

"Don't cause a scene, Mr. Ryder."

Vic wanted to wipe the smug smile from that fucker's face. "Where are you taking me?"

"We have a car waiting. After that, our plans need not concern you."

Looks like I have no choice.

He followed the two men to the Palazzo Alberini. They went through the hallway and emerged into an inner courtyard where a black van awaited. The side door slid open, revealing another man who beckoned him, a gun in one hand.

"Get in."

"Seeing as you asked so politely." Vic climbed into the back seat, and before he could get another word out, something sharp pricked his neck.

"Pleasant dreams, Fridan."

SAUL CAME to a dead stop in the middle of his run, unable to stop the shivers that coursed through him. He bent over, struggling for breath.

Crank.

I know. I felt it too. What the fuck was that?

Saul turned back toward the camp and broke into a run. *Only one explanation.*

Holy shit. Vic's in trouble.

Saul headed for the command tent. *I'm going to see Horvan.*

On my way.

The camp was a hive of activity. Weapons checks, equipment, tech…. Nothing would be left to chance.

Except Saul couldn't think about the mission.

What's happening to Vic?

If those bastards hurt him….

Gods help them.

VIC OPENED his eyes. He was bound, arms behind the chair back, ankles tied to its legs. The first thing he registered was the faint hum of the AC. The air temperature was cool, the lighting limited, but enough to see the wide chair across the room from him. He squinted, trying to get a better look at its occupant.

"Welcome to my home."

It was a cultured voice, smooth and low.

It was also menacing as fuck. Vic's balls wanted to shrivel up and retreat into his body at the sound.

"I don't suppose you're going to tell me where your home is located." The words came out as a croak, and he cursed his dry throat. No way did he want to appear afraid of this guy.

Except he was, and he had no idea why.

The man in the chair gestured with one hand, and someone stepped closer, holding a glass with a straw. Vic sucked on it greedily, relishing the cool water. When it was withdrawn, he cleared his throat and stared at the dark figure before him.

"Who are you?"

"Don't you know?" A light flickered, illuminating the speaker, and Vic sucked in his breath.

This was Someone. He sat straight in his chair, legs crossed, hands clasped in his lap. His expensive-looking suit fitted him perfectly, but what drew Vic's attention was his face.

His eyes. They were dark, catching pinpricks of light.

Vic was being studied.

Whoever this guy was, he was old. And intelligent. Not only that, he was dangerous.

Vic took a breath. "Well, you're not Fielding." No trace of a tremor in his voice.

He frowned. "And how would you know that?"

Vic managed a shrug. "I've seen him."

"I doubt that." The man stilled, eyebrows arched. "Wait. Of course. If Saul Emory saw him, that means you did too." He smiled. "My name is—"

"Theron," Vic blurted, recalling his conversation with Orsini.

It had to be.

Theron arched his eyebrows once more. "Very impressive indeed."

"Now tell me why I'm here."

That thin smile was as creepy as his voice. "You're about to be a pawn in my ongoing game. An important piece, in fact." His eyes glinted.

"You're going to provide me with the perfect excuse to declare war on the Fridans—legitimately."

Vic didn't like the sound of that at all.

"They'll find me," he ground out.

Theron shrugged. "Anything is possible." He leaned forward, his dark eyes focused on Vic. "But all they'll find is a corpse." Vic froze, and Theron chuckled. "Oh, not immediately. We have to prove you're still alive, don't we? And you will be—until your time runs out."

Vic wished his thoughts could reach his mates, but he had no idea where he was, or how far away they were.

He was still going to try.

Saul. Crank. Can you hear me?

CRANK WANTED to throw his fucking useless phone across the tent.

"He isn't answering."

"I got Aelryn to call Orsini at the archive," Horvan told him and Saul. "Vic never showed this morning. Orsini received a handwritten message telling him Vic had changed his plans. Orsini thought nothing of it—until Aelryn phoned."

"Vic's in danger, and we don't have a fucking clue where he is."

"They wouldn't keep him in Rome." Saul paced.

"And what makes you think that?" Crank demanded.

"I don't *know*, all right?" Saul's face was mottled. "I'm as much in the dark as you are. But my instincts tell me they'll want him closer to home. And while we have no idea where *home* is… what's the most powerful nation in the world?"

"The US?" Crank frowned.

Saul nodded. "So doesn't it stand to reason that it's also the nation with the most shifters—and therefore the most powerful leaders? Aelryn's here. Why shouldn't the bad guys be here too?"

"If we could hear him, we'd know that for sure," Crank surmised. "I don't think even Vic can send his thoughts from another continent."

"That's what I've been waiting for all freaking day."

Crank forgot his mate was an ex-Delta, a military leader, a man no one would want to cross, and put his arms around him. "We're gonna find him, you hear me? He's coming back to us."

Because the alternative was unthinkable.

Saul's forehead met his. "I want him back *so* badly," he whispered.

"I know, babe."

Horvan coughed, and Saul glanced at him. "Breathe one word of this and—"

He smiled, his eyes glistening. "One word about what?" His phone buzzed. "It's Aelryn." He clicked Answer. "Hey. You're on speaker. I've got Saul and Crank here."

"Okay, there's something you need to know. The Gerans have contacted Fridan leaders to say they've taken Vic hostage."

"But why?" Saul hollered. "Why him?"

"There's more. They say they'll exchange him for a Geran that we have in custody."

"Then fucking exchange them!" Crank bellowed.

"You don't understand." Aelryn's voice was strained. "It's all lies."

"Do they have him or don't they?" Crank was in serious danger of losing his shit.

"They have him—they sent a video—and before you ask, he looked fine. Not a scratch on him, okay? But… they're demanding we release Valmer Cooper."

"And who the hell is he?" Saul sounded as close to the edge as Crank.

"He's one of their leaders. And there's only one problem. We don't have him—the Gerans do."

Horvan's eyes widened. "Come again? You just confused the fuck outta me."

"They've taken him because his mate is a Fridan leader."

Horvan expelled a long breath. "A leader… who's one of your team. Would he be the same leader who informed them of our impending attack? *Now* I get it."

"Well, I don't," Saul retorted. "Why are they offering to exchange Vic for this Valmer? How can we exchange someone we don't even have?"

"Exactly." Fatigue laced Aelryn's voice. "And if we say, 'Hey, we can't do that because we don't have him' it'll be seen as a refusal."

"Giving them the excuse they need to go on the offensive—to launch an attack." Horvan sounded pissed.

"Then what'll happen to Vic?" Crank's gut was in turmoil.

"That we don't know," Aelryn admitted.

Horvan peered at his screen. "Aelryn, I'll call you back. Milo's trying to get in touch. This could be important."

"I'll be here." Aelryn disconnected.

Crank started pacing until Saul grabbed him. "Hang in there, okay?"

"Doin' my damnedest, but fuck, it's hard."

Just let me hear Vic's voice. Just once.

Horvan held up a hand, and they fell silent. "Milo, what's the news?"

"There's been a change of plan with regards to Fielding."

Crank stilled, his gaze locked on Horvan.

"He's still coming, right?" Horvan's brows knitted.

"Yes, and his ETA is still Friday afternoon. But it seems he'll be leaving here Sunday morning."

"You mean he doesn't wanna be around when we attack." Horvan snorted. "Too bad he's gonna get a front row seat."

Dellan burst into the tent. "Milo," he called out. "Dellan here. What about my dad? Do you have any idea when they intend taking him out?"

"No, but—" There was a pause. "—would you say Fielding is the kind of man who'd want to be there when they pull the trigger?"

Horvan let rip with another derisive snort. "Fuck yeah. Let us know if there are any more developments, Milo."

"I will. And I'll email you with the final arrangements." He hung up.

"That fucking bastard." Saul's mouth was an ugly line.

Horvan scraped his hand over his bald head. "Okay. We go in Saturday morning as planned, and we take Fielding alive. Because if anyone will know where Vic is, it's him." His phone buzzed again, and he groaned. "Now what?" He stilled. "It's Aelryn again."

"Something else you need to know," Aelryn said quickly. "Once this is over, we've got another mission—to find the contents of a tomb. I'm not going to explain it all now, just to say this could be crucial to every shifter on the planet."

Crank jerked his head to stare at Saul. *What the fuck?*

Saul shook his head. *Beats me. But Aelryn doesn't strike me as someone prone to exaggeration.*

"Aelryn, if you hear any news about Vic...." Crank's throat tightened.

"I'll let you know, of course."

Horvan pointed at Crank. "You're our best sniper. Fielding's *your* target. But you'll be using tranq bullets, okay? We want that fucker alive."

"What makes you think he'll talk?" Aelryn asked.

Dellan's grim expression was so unlike him it sent cold inching through Crank.

"We'll make him talk."

CHAPTER TWENTY-FOUR

Friday

HORVAN WAITED until Saul gave him the nod before moving to stand in front of the men and women who'd squeezed into the command tent. Behind him was a white screen, and Dellan was in charge of the laptop, the images ready. Low chatter filled the air, but what was noticeable was the absence of laughter. After three days of exercises and preparation, these guys were more than ready to get into the action.

That was fine in Horvan's book. He wanted every last one of them to be focused on the briefing.

"Okay, guys."

That was all it took to gain complete silence.

"We go in before dawn tomorrow, and we have only two goals—to remove every last prisoner unharmed, and to capture a Tier One personality. I repeat, *capture*. We need this guy alive." He gestured to Saul, who joined him at the front.

"We've had eyes on the enemy camp since we got here, and everything we've seen so far confirmed our intel." He glanced at Dellan. "This is our target."

On the screen a detailed sketch of Fielding's face flashed up.

"We don't have photos of this guy, but believe me, this is as close as it gets to a likeness. I should know. I've seen him, and it isn't a face you could easily forget." Saul straightened. "So here's what you all wanna know. Mission time from incursion to extraction is to be no longer than thirty minutes."

That didn't cause a ripple. The team was used to tight schedules.

"Every one of you will have facial recognition software linked to your headgear cams. We have photos on file of all the prisoners *and* the guards and other personnel. So check *everyone*. There will be no guards claiming to be prisoners, you got that?"

"Affirmative," Crank muttered.

Horvan had no clue how Crank and Saul were holding it together. Vic had to be in their thoughts constantly, and if it had been Rael or Dellan in the hands of the enemy, Horvan knew he'd be sorely distracted. To their credit, Saul and Crank both put on a brave front. Vic's capture wasn't common knowledge, and they were keeping it that way.

Let's pray Fielding knows where Vic is.

As for him sharing that knowledge? Horvan would leave that interrogation to Saul and Crank. *And if he won't tell us what he knows, we might need to lock him in a room with Brick for a while with a reminder that he was responsible for them holding one of his mates. I hope he enjoys pain.*

"Crank is in charge of taking down our target. He's one of only a few who've seen this guy." Saul scanned the faces before him. "Under no circumstances is lethal ammo to be used on this target. Crank will be armed with tranq bullets."

Horvan stepped forward. "Dawn is at oh five twenty-eight, so infiltration is set for oh four hundred. We've timed it to coincide with the scheduled arrival of a delivery truck. We're gonna hijack it to gain entry to the camp."

"Yeah, about the delivery guys…. Do we eliminate them?" Dex asked.

Horvan frowned. "They're not the enemy. According to our source, they just work for the delivery company."

Dex frowned. "The Gerans let humans on the base? I didn't think they'd be happy about that."

"Of course they're happy," Crank retorted. "Weak humans serving strong shifters? What's wrong with that?"

Dex huffed. "I see your point."

"You've all been assigned your teams," Horvan continued. "So listen up. Team A will be led by Saul and Brick. You'll be approaching the camp through the forests to the north and west. Your first tasks are to take out the perimeter guard towers on those sides and secure the airfield. We're gonna need that for evac."

"Team B will be led by Johan Deerling, and they'll be approaching in RIBs on the Saint John River that runs along the south of the compound. Hashtag's already with Johan's team, and he's in charge of drones. He'll be our eye in the sky."

Murmurs of appreciation followed Saul's words.

"Team B will take out perimeter guards to the south and east." Saul gave the nod to Eve, who rose to her feet. "Duncan will lead Team C, along with Roadkill and Crank. They'll be waiting on Old River Road to intercept the delivery truck. Then they'll drive to the camp."

Horvan glanced at Dellan, then pointed to the screen. "This is the map of the compound. You've all seen it. Well, now we can confirm locations." He indicated the upper righthand corner. "This is the gate. One way in, one way out. Now get this. *No one* is to make a move until we have confirmation that Team C is inside the camp *and* has control of the gate. They'll take out the guards on duty and cut off the power to the electrified fence. Once they're in place, no one gets to leave the camp. Our trucks will be waiting at the gate to bring us back here."

Saul indicated the blocks to the northeast corner. "This is the medical block, and this is the experimentation block. Doc Tranter and his medics will go in with Team A, and their job is to seize all records, drugs, tech...." He paused. "Okay, here's the bad news. We know the Gerans have developed a drug that can suppress shifts. And the good news? Thanks to our source, we know where this is stored. Once the guards have been incapacitated with tranq darts, we intend using this drug on them. We don't want any of them coming round and shifting on us." He pointed again to the screen. "These five blocks contain the prisoners, roughly thirty to each block. I want every last one rounded up and moved toward the airfield to await evac." He pointed again. "These four blocks are the barracks, housing roughly seventy guards. We use flash-bang grenades and gas bombs to gain entry. Both lethal and nonlethal ammo are authorized, but get this—lethal ammo only to be used if you're fired upon. And once the perimeter guards have been immobilized, all teams will mop up any remaining guards. All weapons will have HK417 laser flashlights, and all headgear will have thermal vision eye pieces."

"Where's Fielding gonna be?" Crank asked.

Horvan pointed to one of the barracks. "In here. He's been given a room to himself. His bodyguards are in with the regular guards. Dellan, next photo, please." Milo's face filled the screen. "Now, memorize this face. This is Milo Keppler, captain of the guard. Under no circumstances are any of you to use lethal ammo on this guy, you got that?"

"Why are we sparing this dude?" a voice called out. "He's a Geran, isn't he?"

Horvan glared at the speaker. "He's the reason we have all the intel we do. And it's been confirmed by another source. I don't have to tell you guys, intelligence is the most powerful weapon we have. We don't want them to know Keppler's our mole, so don't treat him any different, okay? Tranq him if you have to, for appearance's sake. But when we leave, we bring him with us."

"Two Apache helicopters will control the sky," Saul continued, "and three Chinooks will land on the airfield to evac all the prisoners. They'll be flown to the forward operating base in Brunswick." He surveyed the faces before him. "We have two goals, remember. Rescuing the prisoners and taking Fielding alive."

"Once the Chinooks are out of there, we come back here, take down the camp, and load everything into the C-17," Horvan announced. "Rendezvous at Brunswick to refuel before heading back to Illinois."

"Are we sending Fielding to Brunswick too?" Eve asked.

"Yes, but he goes in one of the Apaches, with Crank," Horvan replied. "Aelryn has made plans to take the rescued prisoners to several safe places where they'll be cared for. Well, most of the prisoners. Three will be coming home with us." He smiled at Dellan.

Finding Jake, Jamie, and Seth was gonna make for some emotional reunions.

"What about the guards?" someone asked.

"Leave 'em where they drop. They aren't our concern once we've got what we came for." Horvan grinned. "I'm sure their superiors will have a lot of questions for them."

"Hey, H. Does the kitty have its own headgear and weapon?" someone called out. That earned him a few chuckles.

A snort came from Brick. "The kitty has built-in weapons. They're called claws. And he'll be staying right here."

"Okay, that's it. Briefing over." Horvan put his hands on his hips. "Get some sleep, because we're up awful early, and I want you all bright-eyed and bushy-tailed."

The soldiers stood and filed out of the tent while Dellan disconnected the projector, leaving the team leaders behind.

"H, I'm gonna go spend some time with Aric," Brick told him.

Horvan gave him a sympathetic glance. "Not long now and you'll all be together." He waited until Brick had left before sighing. "He's still a mess. He'd better keep a lid on it tomorrow."

"I'll watch out for him," Saul told him. "I could do with something else to keep my mind occupied." He grinned.

Crank huffed. "Like your mind isn't already overtaxed."

"I don't have to worry about you, do I?"

Crank smiled. "No, sir. I'll be just fine." He glanced at Eve. "We're gonna give those delivery guys a change of cargo."

"It'll be you and me up front," Roadkill reminded him.

"I'm not ready for bed yet," Eve held her hand out to Roadkill. "Want to take a walk and look at the sunset?"

"I could do with a little romance." Roadkill chuckled. "And seeing as I can't share your cot bed—not without attracting a lot of unwelcome attention at any rate—I'll take all I can get."

DELLAN PUSHED the three cot beds together. "I guess there have to be some perks to being Joint Team Leader. Getting to sleep alone in the command tent is one of them."

Rael dumped the sleeping bags onto the beds. "You call these things a perk? I think we were more comfortable sleeping on the ground sheet. At least then there wasn't a steel frame poking me the whole night."

Dellan laughed. "No, that was Horvan's dick, but I can see how you could confuse the two."

Horvan rolled his eyes. "We'll be back in our own bed soon enough. You can put up with one more night."

Dellan walked over to the tent flap and stared out into the inky blackness. No light pollution made for a gloriously starry night, the pinpoints of light as numerous as a sprinkling of salt on a layer of black velvet.

"Hard to believe we're so close to Dad and Jamie," he murmured. He knew without turning that the reassuring warm hand on his shoulder was Horvan's. Dellan leaned back, breathing in the smell that reminded him of home—of love.

"You'll see them tomorrow."

"Yes, but that's the scary part. The last time I saw my dad, I was seven years old. I know what he looks like, sure, but…." His throat tightened.

"But you won't know him," Horvan finished.

"We'll have so much to learn about each other. And it makes me nervous."

Rael joined them. "Don't be. He's probably just as nervous. He's about to meet his sons-in-law."

Horvan blinked. "Excuse me?"

"Well, how else would you describe us? Okay, so we don't have a piece of paper, but we'll be together for as long as we live."

"Maybe longer," Dellan mused. "I'm holding out for an afterlife."

Horvan's arms enveloped him, and he leaned against that broad chest. "I don't have to remind you that you're staying here tomorrow, do I?" Horvan's voice was a reassuring rumble that reverberated through Dellan.

"But—"

"But nothing," Horvan interjected. "This is going to be dangerous. I don't want you within a mile of that camp." He tightened his arms around Dellan. "Can't risk losing you. Either of you."

Rael reached up and stroked Horvan's cheek. "We know. But you have to understand why Dellan wants to be there."

"Doc will take care of Jake and Jamie." Horvan's voice brimmed with confidence, and that went a little way to easing Dellan's aching heart.

"Just bring Dad back to me. Bring both of them back."

"CAN I sleep with you?"

Brick frowned. "You think that's such a good idea?" He glanced at the tent's other occupants, most of whom were already out of sight beneath sleeping bags. Okay, they were a diverse crowd, and Lord knew they'd seen plenty of shenanigans over the years, but he didn't think they were ready to share a tent with two guys sleeping together.

Aric rolled his eyes. "I don't mean like this. Can't I shift and curl up with you?"

He smiled. "I guess we can do that." He liked the idea of having a warm fuzz ball snuggled against him.

Brick.

He froze. *Seth?*

Thank God. They've been running nonstop tests for the last two days. God knows what they're trying to discover. Where are you? It must be someplace close.

Brick wanted to weep with relief. *We're not too far away. And we'll be there early tomorrow.*

I'll be awake. And waiting. Want me to spread the word? I can do it quietly.

Brick thought fast. *Only if you trust them. We don't want anyone telling the bad guys we're coming a day early.*

Okay. Now... where's my favorite kitty?

Aric snorted. *Waiting to get a word in. And I'll be waiting too.*

Gods, I want to hold you both so much.

Brick wanted that too, but he had to stay focused.

Soon, baby. Now try to get at least a few hours' sleep. We'll be there before it gets light.

I'll know when you're near. And I'll be the one wanting a hug. He chuckled. *The rest of what I want will have to wait until we've got some privacy.*

Beside him, Aric's face flushed.

With everything going on around them, their first time together had completely slipped Brick's mind. And thinking about it on the eve of a mission was *not* a good thing.

What do you expect? You've got two virgin mates. You think that's something they're gonna forget? What are you, delusional?

Yeah, what was he thinking?

Aric? One last thing. This VIP who arrived today... we've already met him.

We have? Who is he?

There was a pause. *Remember in Bozeman? The guy you called Scary Man?*

Brick couldn't miss the violent tremors that racked Aric's slim form.

Oh shit. I hoped I'd seen the last of him.

Brick, you need to take this guy out. I mean it. He just reeks bad news.

Brick would do whatever it took to keep his mates safe.

Unfortunately, taking him out would have to wait.

They needed that bastard.

CRANK LAY on his back, staring at the roof of the tent above him, a single light hanging from it. "I can't hear him."

On the cot bed beside him, Saul let out a sigh. "Me neither."

He swallowed. "I can't do this. Sorry, but this business with Vic is eatin' me alive."

He caught the sound of a zipper, and a moment later, Saul lay beside him, making for a cozy fit but welcome as fuck. Saul slid his arm under Crank's neck and pressed his forehead to Crank's. "You *can* do this. You're gonna find Fielding before anyone else, and you're gonna take that fucker down. Because if anyone knows where Vic is, it'll be him."

Crank closed his eyes. "But what if we can't find him?"

Saul gave him a gentle kiss. "We will. Because the alternative is unthinkable."

ROADKILL GAZED up at the millions of stars twinkling in the jet-black sky. Their camp was maybe seventy feet away, and no noise reached them. Trees stood around them, their canopies black against the sky, shadows that blocked the stars. "We should be asleep. We're out of here before everyone else." At his side, Eve chuckled, and he turned to gaze at her. "What's funny about that?"

She let out the cutest little snort. "Hashtag."

"You heard him? How come I didn't?"

"Because he told me to give you something from him."

"But why is that a secret?"

Eve sighed heavily. "He wanted it to be a surprise." She glanced around them. "Which is why we're standing in the forest."

"Huh?" Then Roadkill's breath caught in his throat as Eve knelt on the ground in front of him and unzipped his pants. Gentle fingers released his cock from his shorts. As her lips touched it, a shiver ran through him, but it wasn't because of what Eve was doing. This was something else.

Your nipples are sensitive, aren't they? Hashtag sounded as if he was enjoying himself.

What? Roadkill found it difficult to concentrate.

This is a very different kind of scene. While she's sucking you, I'm going to make you squirm.

And how are you going to—holy fuck! There was a tongue in his ass. A tongue. In his freakin' *ass. How are you doing this?*

They were going to make him come in record time.

Remember when Eve let us feel her pleasure? Same basics. I might not be there with you, but it doesn't mean I can't play too.

Roadkill groaned. "In case I forget to tell you... I love my surprise."

Eve chuckled. *Okay, this is awesome. I get to suck and talk at the same time.*

Focus, soldier, Hashtag admonished.

Sir, yes, sir.

DOC WALKED around the camp, enjoying the sounds of night birds, the breeze stirring the leaves on the trees, the occasional noise from the airfield a mile from their camp. Sleep had eluded him so far, and while he knew this wasn't an uncommon occurrence, he put the root of his insomnia down to one thing.

Or should that be one person?

He'd been thinking a lot lately about Jake Carson. Remembering him when they'd first met. Their conversations. His laughter. The light in his eyes.

He disappeared before I could tell him how I felt.

Except Doc would never have done that. Jake and Miranda were happy. Anyone could see that. Why would he do anything to spoil that?

When he learned Miranda had died, he looked her up. He still felt the circumstances surrounding her death were suspicious and that the Gerans were implicated.

Then his mind returned to thoughts of Jake.

I'll see him tomorrow.

What do I say to him?

He couldn't reveal the truth. Besides, he'd fallen for Jake a long time ago. Who was to say he'd feel the same way when they met again?

No, I can't tell him. But I can renew our friendship.

After all these years, Doc would take that as a win.

CHAPTER TWENTY-FIVE

Saturday

SAUL TAPPED his mic. "You seeing what I see?"

Brick's reply was immediate. "No one at the airfield. We got guards in the towers, though. I make it three in total on the north and west perimeters. Not moving." He snorted. "They could be asleep on duty." He let out a low chuckle. "Time for their wake-up call."

Saul gave a signal to the seven men on his left, their features concealed by camouflage face paint, and they crept out from beneath the cover of the trees and moved stealthily toward the north fence. He signaled to his right, and the second team moved out, heading for the west fence. Finally, three men moved swiftly in the direction of the airfield.

"Doc, you ready with your team?"

"Copy that."

"Then let's go."

Saul and Brick followed the first two teams, Doc and his medics behind them, until they were crouched in the dark at the base of the fence.

And now we wait.

HASHTAG'S VOICE filled Eve's ear. "Truck's on its way. ETA about two minutes."

"Copy that." She tapped her mic. "Get ready. Roadkill and I are going to move into position. Wait for Crank's signal." She slipped off her body armor and moved out from behind the bushes where she, Roadkill, Crank, and a team of ten men had been hiding for the last fifteen minutes. Eve lay down in the road, and Roadkill crouched beside her, his own armor stashed with Crank.

"They're almost here," she told him.

"I can't hear them."

Eve grinned. "Shifter hearing, babe. The fucking best." Then headlights pierced the darkness. "Showtime." Roadkill waved his flashlight in the air, and the truck rumbled to a halt a few feet away from them, the beams falling on Eve's prone body.

The driver stuck his head out the window. "What's going on? Is someone hurt?"

"We were hiking north of here," Roadkill called out. "We got lost. We've been walking most of the night. Then my girlfriend took a tumble. Her leg's hurt pretty bad."

The passenger door opened, and a guy in overalls got out. "We're heading to a military base not far from here. They'll have a medic who can help, right? Is it safe to move her?"

Crank gave the signal, and Dex stepped out from his hiding place and closed in on the driver, his gun pointed at the guy's head. "Hands off the wheel, nice 'n' easy. Get out of the truck. Leave the keys in the ignition."

"You got it, you got it." Judging by the note of panic in his voice, the driver wasn't going to pose a threat.

Roadkill pulled his weapon on the passenger, who raised his hands in a heartbeat. "Fuck, don't shoot. This is my first day on the job."

Eve bounced to her feet, pulling her gun from where she'd stowed it in the waistband of her pants, and the rest of the team emerged from the bushes. They made short work of tying up the two men before placing them at the roadside.

"You can have your truck back when we're finished with it," Eve told them, while the team got busy unloading all the food and supplies from the back. Crank brought out her body armor, then climbed into the truck behind the wheel, wearing a denim jacket. Roadkill joined him.

Eve crouched in front of the two men. "What do you actually know about this place you're delivering to?"

The backup driver rolled his eyes. "Fuck, lady, I don't know shit, only what this guy told me."

"And what was that?"

"Only that it's some supersecret hush-hush military base, and if we talk to anyone about it, prison will be the least of our worries." He swallowed. "Look, lady, me and the wife? We've just had a kid, and I need the money."

She straightened. "When we bring the truck back, you hightail it out of here. Trust me, you won't want to be around when the shit hits the fan. And there's going to be an awful lot of it flying around here."

Time to go, hon.

Eve climbed into the back of the truck with the rest of the team.

"Okay, next stop is the camp. Not a sound, guys." She tapped her earpiece mic. "Let's go, boys." She clung to one of the side bars used for securing loads, her heart pounding.

First mission with this group, and Saul had given her a team to lead.

No pressure.

You're doing great, sweetheart.

A wave of relief mingled with appreciation swept through her. *Thanks, babe. Wasn't nervous until now.*

And you know once we get in there, everything will be automatic. You've got this.

She smiled to herself. There were definitely benefits to having mates.

I've got my own secret cheerleaders. My mental support buddies.

Who would always have her back.

That's right, hon. Just think of us as your mental bra. We'll always give you support in all the right places.

Eve groaned internally. *Guys? I* really *didn't need that image.*

"WE'RE AT the gates," Crank told Eve in a low voice. "Thermal imaging shows two guards. No one else nearby." The truck's headlights bounced off the metal barrier that barred their way, illuminating two guards armed with rifles. Crank took a moment to remove his headgear before stopping the truck and lowering the window. "Morning. Except it isn't."

One of the guards approached the truck, a flashlight aimed at Crank's face, then Roadkill's. "Hey. Haven't seen you two here before." His tone made it sound as though the experience wasn't a pleasant one. Vic always said how much he loved the way Saul and Crank smelled, yet here was this asshole, wrinkling his nose as if they were covered in shit.

"Yeah, we only started with the company this week. Told us we had an 'early delivery.'" Crank air-quoted, wearing a suitably grumpy expression and acting as though he hadn't noticed the guy's manner.

The guard laughed. "Sounds as if you drew the short straw. I think I drew the same one. Fourth time I've done this shift in two weeks. Someone around here obviously doesn't like my face."

Okay, maybe he wasn't all *that* big an asshole if he was attempting a little conversation. Then Crank reasoned that being a slightly less obnoxious shifter than the rest of them didn't alter the balance a whole lot.

He raised his gun and aimed it. "You wanna know something? *I* don't like your face either. So put down your weapon before I rearrange it with this." Roadkill got out and took down the other guy with a tranq dart.

The guard lowered his rifle, and Crank gave a nod of approval. "Now raise the barrier, and kill the power to the fence." When the guard hesitated, Crank aimed for the dead center of his forehead. "Did I stutter? Drop the weapon and do as you're fucking told."

The guard did as instructed, and Crank followed him to the small control booth, his gun in the guy's back. "Make a wrong move and I paint this closet with your guts, you got that?"

"Got it." The guard pressed one switch and the barrier rose into the air. Then he pressed another and a loud beep sounded. "That means the fence is off." He reached toward another switch.

Crank shot him in the neck with a tranq dart. "Unfortunately for you, I know that's the alarm." He waited until the guard had dropped to the ground before tapping his earpiece mic. "Saul, Johan, we're in business."

Roadkill drove the truck through the gate, and Crank went around the back to open the doors. One by one, the team got out, and Crank pointed in the direction of the barracks.

First task was to take down every last fucking guard.

They crept through the darkened compound, and Crank heard other sounds, cutting metal, muted shots....

"Team A is in," Saul told him. "Doc is heading for the medical and experimentation blocks. Airfield is secured."

"Copy that."

"Team B is in," Johan reported. "We're through the fence and the guards are down. Repeat, the guards are down."

"Copy that." Eve's voice filled his ear. "Team C in position at the barracks."

Time to kick ass.

Crank waited until all teams had converged on the barracks before opening the doors to the nearest block and throwing in the flash-bang grenades, followed by the gas bombs. The brilliant white light illuminated the interior briefly, and he signaled the teams. "They're coming out." He pulled on his mask, dove into the block, and kicked in the door closest to him.

In the ghostly light of the thermal imaging camera, Fielding could be seen out of bed and reaching toward his nightstand.

Crank didn't hesitate. "Oh no you don't, you fucker." He fired the gun and the dart pierced Fielding's neck, then another in his thigh, before swiping him with his arm and dropping him onto the bed. Fielding tried to remove the dart, but the damage was done.

"You won't… get away… with—"

Crank rolled his eyes. "Would you just shut the fuck up?" He swung again, and this time Fielding went flying, out like a light. "Tier One target acquired," he said into his mic. From all around came shouts as the guards swarmed out to be met with force. Every *pop* meant another guard out, which was fine by him.

"Get Fielding to the airfield. The Chinooks are on their way, and once it's no longer needed for air cover, one of the Apaches will land. You go in that," Saul told him.

"Copy that." Crank hoisted Fielding onto his shoulder and strode out of the block, through the still forms of guards who lay on the ground, unconscious.

"Barrack two secured," Johan messaged.

"Barrack three secured." That was Roadkill.

"We've got unfriendlies trying to escape through the windows in barrack four," Eve yelled. "Be on the lookout."

"Copy that," Johan replied. "Deerling to Air Control, you copy this?"

The air was filled with the sound of whirring blades. Spotlights pierced the dark as the Apaches hovered above the compound, and shots rang out.

Crank wasn't about to mourn the deaths of a few idiots. Shit, if they ran, they had to take the consequences.

Crank tapped his mic. "Doc, you hear me? How we doin' with locating the drug?" Fielding wasn't that heavy, thank God, and the airfield was in sight. The drone of Chinooks spoke of their imminent arrival.

"Acquired. Medics on their way to you with shots. Enough for all guards, if we need them."

"Copy that. And save a shot for Fielding. I don't know what kinda shifter this bastard is, and I don't wanna find out." Two tranq darts would take down a human—he wasn't so sure about shifters.

"Head for the sleeping quarters. We've got one hundred fifty prisoners to get the fuck out of here," Saul told them.

"Copy that. Meet you there," Brick called out.

Crank smiled to himself. *I know who* you're *looking for.*

BRICK OPENED the door to the first sleeping block—and stopped dead to find silent figures standing close by.

Waiting.

Then his arms were full of a lithe, warm body. "I told you I'd have them awake and ready."

Brick's knees buckled, and he cupped Seth's face, kissing him on the lips. "We'd better save this for later, okay? Let's get you someplace safe first." He peered at the faces lit by his flashlight. "We're gonna head to the airfield. Anyone unable to make it that far?"

"We're all fine." The guy's voice was deep. "And more than ready to leave this fucking place."

Brick glanced at him, and knew in a heartbeat who was speaking. "Jake Carson, I presume. Dellan's the spitting image of you."

Jake's face broke into a huge smile. "You know Dellan?"

"Can this wait?" Saul interjected. "We've got three Chinooks standing by, and we don't wanna keep 'em waiting."

Jake chuckled. "Isn't it always the way? You want a helicopter to whisk you out of here, and then three turn up at once."

"Where's Jamie?" Saul demanded.

"Not in this block."

"We'll find him. In the meantime, stay close to Brick. You guys aren't going in the Chinooks—you're coming with us back to our camp." Saul smiled. "Some people there who can't wait to see you."

Brick led the prisoners out, Seth by his side, Jake close behind them, and all around them was noise and smoke that drifted in the breeze, raised voices and the *throb-throb-throb* of blades. From behind the building, a lone figure emerged, a rifle pointed in their direction, and as soon as Brick registered its owner as the enemy, he aimed his gun.

"Give it up," he commanded.

The guard made no reply, but as soon as Brick heard the click of the safety, he acted instinctively and fired a single shot to the heart.

The guard dropped like a stone.

He tapped his earpiece. "We missed one. He's been taken care of." Then he realized Seth was staring at him. "Hey, if I'd known for certain he was one of the ones who treated you badly, he wouldn't even have gotten a warning. I played nice."

Jake chuckled. "If this is you playing nice, I'd hate to see you when you're pissed."

Brick hurried them along, stopping only when he encountered a prisoner who'd fallen, clutching his leg. He glanced at Jake. "Head for the airfield while I see to this guy. Seth, go with him."

Jake nodded, then took the lead, Seth beside him.

Brick crouched down next to the injured man. "Can you stand?"

The guy shook his head. "You might have to carry me."

Brick took a good look at his face, then tapped his earpiece. "Hashtag, you getting this?"

"Copy that. Enemy. I repeat, enemy."

"Copy that." Brick didn't hesitate. He fired a tranq dart into the guy's neck with a snort. "Nice try." He pushed the man out of the path of the oncoming stream of prisoners, then dashed toward the airfield, where Johan and others beckoned them up the rear ramp into the belly of the helicopters. As each Chinook was filled, it rose into the air, heading southeast.

Three trucks stood on the tarmac, and Brick pointed to them. "They're for us." Then he saw a familiar face and his gut tightened. Jamie was there.

Not now. Seth grasped Brick's hand. *You can explain it all to him later if you want, but right now let's get away from this place.*

But it's my fault he got caught.

And because he did, he found his dad, so enough guilt, all right? You've both been through hell. It's time to leave it behind and move on. Another squeeze of Brick's hand. *You've got other things to think about. Two mates, actually.*

And the start of his new life.

SAUL TAPPED his earpiece. "Crank, where are you?"

"In the Apache, on my way to the FOB in Brunswick. Fielding's come round, but he's had his shots and he ain't goin' nowhere." A chuckle. "He ain't sayin' much either. I gagged him."

"Meet you there. And Crank? Don't lay a finger on him, okay?"

Crank snorted. "Now would I do a thing like that? Not until he's answered a few questions first. Over and out."

Saul was going to ensure Crank wasn't left alone with Fielding. Not that Saul hated the idea of a little retribution for the pain and suffering he'd endured on Fielding's orders, but the bastard had information they needed.

He tapped again. "Anyone seen Milo Keppler?"

"Copy that," Eve came back. "He's in one of the Chinooks, and he's with his mate."

"Great. Where are you?"

"Heading back your way. I had to return a truck."

He smiled. "I bet that was a relief for the drivers. Okay, let's head back to the camp, pack it up, and get the fuck out of here."

Then on to Brunswick where a certain Geran had a lot of explaining to do—and a location to reveal.

DELLAN DRANK what had to be his third cup of coffee since Saul and the men had left. He'd been surprised Horvan hadn't gone with them, but he and Aelryn remained in constant contact, watching the mission unfold via drone camera. Horvan assured him that so far it had been textbook, but that hadn't alleviated Dellan's nerves.

Horvan stuck his head out of the command tent. "The trucks are on their way back here with the troops." When Dellan stared at him, he smiled. "And your dad, Jamie, and Seth."

Then he heard the sound of the trucks' engines, and he could hardly breathe.

The trucks rolled into camp, and someone flicked on the perimeter lights they'd set up. The guys piled out, talking loudly and laughing, and for Dellan, it felt like a rerun of the Bozeman mission, the same sense of exhilaration that it was over and everyone was home alive.

He stilled. *At least, I* assume *they—*

No injuries or fatalities. For us, anyway. They never saw us coming. Horvan sounded pleased as fuck.

Dellan breathed a relieved sigh. *Thank goodness.* He watched as the trucks emptied, and couldn't help smiling when Aric all but flew across the camp and into Brick's arms. Judging by the way Brick wouldn't let go of the guy at his side, Dellan reckoned it had to be Seth, and the joy shining from their faces brought a lump to his throat.

I guess I can meet my new half brother later.

Then his heart lurched at the sight of a familiar face.

Dad.

Jake spotted him a split second later, and his eyes went wide. He broke into a run, and Dellan hurried over to meet him halfway. They came to a stop a couple of feet from each other, and it was as if neither of them knew what to do next. Then Jake held his arms wide, and Dellan ran into them, tears streaming down his cheeks as Jake enfolded him, a warm, solid body that felt so fucking *real*.

"I can't believe you're here," Dellan croaked.

It didn't matter that he was almost forty years old. It didn't matter that he was male and *everyone* knew men weren't supposed to cry. His dad was sobbing too, his tears wetting Dellan's cheeks, and if his dad could cry like a fucking baby, then Dellan could too.

"Do I get one of those?" a tremulous voice asked.

Dellan turned his head and smiled at his half brother. "Get your ass over here." He and Jake pulled Jamie into a hug that seemed to stretch into minutes.

You hug them all you want. Horvan sounded a little croaky too. *Plenty of time for introductions later.*

Dellan didn't want to let go of either of them, for fear it would somehow break the spell, and he'd wake up back in Homer Glen in the house his stepdad had built for his mom, his dad nothing but a distant memory.

I'm not going anywhere.

With a shock, Dellan realized the voice in his head was that of his dad. What the fuck?

CHAPTER TWENTY-SIX

THAT SHOCKED expression was all it took to confirm Jake's suspicions.

"I guess the apple doesn't fall too far from the tree." He'd wondered if Dellan shared his gifts. Well, he had his answer.

"I only found out I could do stuff like that when I met Rael. He's one of my mates. The first time we met, he heard my voice in his head. And then I spoke to him in a dream. But I thought that was because of the mate bond." Dellan bit his lip. "Apparently not."

Jake's heart skipped a beat. "You look like me, but when you did the lip-biting thing a moment ago? Lord, you remind me of your mother." His breathing hitched. "Dellan, is she...." He didn't want to voice the fear that wound tightly around his heart.

Dellan's face contorted, and that told him everything. Pain lanced through Jake's chest.

Oh, Miranda.

"I hate to break up the reunion," a deep voice rumbled. "But we need to get back to our camp and onto a plane." The guy was huge, with broad shoulders and an equally broad chest.

"This is Horvan, my other mate," Dellan informed him.

Jake smiled. "I have a severe amount of catching up to do. And you're right. This conversation can wait."

He was in no hurry to have his heart broken.

THE C-17's engines droned, but Jake pushed the noise into the background. Dellan hadn't left his side since they'd boarded the trucks, and that was fine by him. He didn't want to let his son out of his sight for an instant.

A lot of the soldiers around him were asleep, and Jake imagined that was a combination of a very early start and downtime after the mission, not to mention adrenaline crash. They were an impressive bunch. Jake was awed at how quickly they'd moved to free all the inmates, with very little loss of life.

His gaze fell upon Brick. Seth had fallen asleep in his arms.

"He hasn't had much of that the last few days," Jake murmured to Dellan. "He's wiped out." He paused. "You do know he's—"

"Your son, and therefore my half brother? Yeah, I know. I found that out when we rescued Aric from the camp in Bozeman."

Jake smiled. "Love that kitty." Aric was presently curled in Seth's lap, his eyes shut tight. What made Jake smile even more was the fact that even in sleep, Aric was in contact with both his mates. His paw was now resting on Brick's arm, where earlier his tail had been draped over it.

"We were so relieved when we learned Jamie was with you and Seth." Dellan sighed. "I think we turned his life upside down." He glanced farther along the plane's interior. "I think Brick is avoiding Jamie."

"Why would he do that?"

Dellan frowned. "Because Brick was the reason they caught Jamie. He's the reason Jamie ended up in that camp. The Gerans took his parents hostage, saying they'd release them if Brick provided information. Except we think they pretty much killed them right off the bat."

Jake frowned. "Yeah, that sounds about right. Then Brick needs to talk to Jamie, and soon. I can understand why he'd feel responsible, but as Jamie told me, they would have caught him at some point, regardless. How did he phrase it? 'Did I like being caught? No. But I found my people, and I can't be angry when I'm so fucking happy.'" Jake couldn't wait a moment longer. "Tell me about your mom."

"She... she died about a month before the Gerans took me."

Jake fought the urge to weep. "Did she... did she ever remarry?"

"Eventually. She had you declared dead seven years after you disappeared. I was only fourteen at the time, but I remember one thing. Everyone had to convince her it was time to move on. She was certain you'd walk through the door, a suitcase in one hand, a bag containing gifts from Italy in the other."

"She hung on in there, didn't she?" Knowing Miranda, she would have only resorted to that if there was no hope of his return.

"Visiting the lawyer to go through the paperwork? It devastated her. She was working as a barista—one of three jobs—when she met Tom Prescott. They married a while later. He took care of her. He was a good guy." Dellan snorted. "Can't say the same for his son, but Anson got his in the end."

"How did she die?"

Dellan's face tightened. "I don't know. Doc doesn't think it was natural causes, though. He thinks the Gerans got her out of the way, because once I was drugged and unable to shift back, she'd have known about it and tried to find me."

Doc sounded like a very astute man. "He may well be correct in that assumption. I take it he *is* a doctor?"

Dellan smiled. "Yes. He was a military doctor. That's where Horvan met him. And when they rescued me, they called in Doc Tranter to check me out." He glanced at Jake. "He told me he knew you and Mom."

Jake stilled. "Nicholas? Do you know where I can find him?" His heart pounded.

"You'll see him when we get to Brunswick. He's with the inmates we rescued."

That sent Jake's heart into overdrive, until he forced himself to breathe more evenly.

It's been a long time. You don't know anything about his life. He could be happily married. Hell, he could be a grandfather.

"I'm gonna go sit a while with Jamie." Dellan squeezed his knee, then stood, a little unsteady on his feet.

"He'd love that. He's talked about you so often." Jake watched as Dellan made his way along the plane to where Jamie sat with Rael, Dellan's other mate.

Still can't believe they found each other. When he and Miranda first met, Jake didn't even know there was such a thing as mates, but after listening to Seth, he had a feeling she hadn't been Jake's. Not that it mattered. He'd loved her from that day forward. Nicholas had been a good friend. He was also incredibly sexy, a fact Jake was sure Miranda hadn't overlooked when she'd given him a push in Nicholas's direction.

I wonder if age has diminished his appearance—or improved it.

Either way, Jake was about to find out, and the prospect of meeting him again was enough to give him butterflies.

Horvan came over and sat beside Jake. "How're you doing?"

"Better now that I'm a free man. It's been a while." He peered at Horvan. "I understand you're the man who freed Dellan."

"Yes, sir."

He chuckled. "*Sir?* Damn, that makes me feel old. Call me Jake, okay? Did you know he was your mate when you rescued him?"

229

"Yeah." Horvan smiled. "That episode was just one shock after another. I met Rael and discovered mates were real. Then he told me *he* had a mate, and that logically, Dellan would be my mate too." He sighed. "Which made it imperative to get him the fuck out of that cage."

"I'm looking forward to getting to know you." Jake trusted his instincts, and right then they were telling him Dellan's mates were good men.

"Once we get to Brunswick, a medic will check you out." Horvan's eyes glittered. "I imagine there's a certain elephant shifter who'd be keen to draw that straw."

Yeah, Horvan was pretty astute.

"Did you capture any of the guards from the camp?"

Horvan cocked his head. "Capture? Hell no. We left them there to face the music when the Geran powers that be discover we breezed into the camp, grabbed Fielding—who we're sure is a big noise—and took every last fucking inmate with us. The camp commandant won't be put in charge of a parking lot, once they've finished hauling him over the coals. We did bring one guard with us, though."

"Milo Keppler?"

"Yeah."

Relief swamped him. "Then he's safe. Thank God. Is he with his mate?"

Horvan nodded. "We owe him a lot. It was thanks to him that we knew about your imminent execution."

Jake froze. "My what?"

"Fielding gave orders that you were to be shot. Today, probably, while he had a ringside seat."

Ice surrounded his heart. "That cold-hearted excuse for a— Why? Why go to the trouble of testing me six ways from Sunday only to have me taken out?"

"Maybe he saw you as a threat."

"Me?"

"Specifically, your... talents."

Jake stilled. "Oh. Okay, you might have something there. I'm pretty sure that's why they've kept me alive and imprisoned so long. So what's the thinking? He was going to eliminate me before I could use my gifts to... what, discover something?"

"I'll introduce you to Aelryn. He's a Fridan leader, and he wants us to go searching for a tomb, of all things, that he says could be important."

Horvan scowled. "I should think Fielding wouldn't want you finding out about his nasty little secret weapon."

"What secret weapon?"

He sighed. "You're not gonna like this. The Gerans' breeding program included Dellan, all the while he was in that fucking glass cage. And... well, they took one of his children, a boy, and...."

"And what?" Jake listened in growing horror as Horvan told him about the grandson he had no idea existed.

The grandson who sounded like a fucking abomination.

Jake swallowed. "Where is Alec? Do you know?"

Horvan shook his head. "No one does. But *you* might be able to find that out. Because once we get to Brunswick, there's gonna be an... interrogation you might wanna be part of. If you feel up to it. I know you've been gone a long time, and maybe all you want to do is rest, relax, and reconnect with the people in your life. No one would blame you for that."

"Feel up to it? Questioning that...." Cold fury surged through him. "I'd consider it payback. Just let me at him."

"There's something else." Horvan pointed to two guys sitting together, both of them muscular and menacing. "That's Saul Emory, joint team leader, and the guy on his left is Crank, one of my team and a damn good man. They're human, but their mate is a shark shifter. And he's been taken by the Gerans. We don't have a clue where he is, and they've given us some bullshit about exchanging him for a Geran captive that we don't even have. But Fielding might know where he is, or at least have an idea where to start looking."

Jake stared across the plane's interior to where Seth lay sleeping. "You might consider bringing Seth in on the interrogation too."

Horvan nodded. "Two heads are better than one, don't they say? So two psychics have gotta be a force to be reckoned with."

Jake was now a man on a mission—to delve into Fielding's mind and learn everything he could. He had a grandson to save—if Alec could be saved—and a lot of secrets to uncover. It was time to unravel this whole bunch of bullshit, and starting from the top seemed like a very good idea.

He also had to get to know the man his son had become.

NAVAL AIR Station Brunswick in Maine had been officially decommissioned in 2011, Horvan told him, but Aelryn had taken it over about two years ago. The original aircraft hangar had burned down, leaving only the main buildings. By the time the C-17 landed on the airstrip, buses were waiting on the tarmac, ready to take the former inmates to a place of safety once they'd had a medical checkup.

It was easy to spot where Fielding was being kept: The building had armed guards on the doors.

Is that to keep him from getting out, or us from getting in? Jake imagined Brick would love to spend a few minutes with Fielding.

He didn't think Fielding would be so happy about it, however. He'd be lucky to escape with his limbs intact.

"Dad?"

Jake gave himself a mental shake. "Sorry. I must've zoned out. Did you say something?"

Dellan smiled. "I said I don't think we'll be here long. Aelryn's got food waiting for everyone in the main building, and as soon as you get the all-clear, we'll be back in the C-17, on our way to Homer Glen, in Illinois."

"Is that where you live?"

"It was the house Tom built for Mom, and it's your home now, for as long as you want to stay. Jamie's, too. And if we don't have the room, we'll add on to the house."

"Don't go to any trouble on my account," Jake admonished. "You have your own life to lead with your mates. You don't want me hanging around."

Dellan blinked. "Are you *kidding*? Less than five months ago, I discovered you weren't dead after all. Then I missed you by I don't know how long when Horvan raided the camp at Bozeman. *Then* I find out you're in the same camp as Seth and Jamie. Dad, what makes you think I'm ever going to be ready to be parted from you again?" He grinned. "Sorry, but you're stuck with me."

"And if I suddenly have my own life… someone to love… what then?"

Dellan cocked his head to one side. "In those circumstances, yeah, I *might* be willing to let you move out, on the proviso that you visit—often."

Jake smiled. "Just checking. And as for visiting? You'll be sick of the sight of me." He inclined his head toward Fielding's makeshift jail. "I'm not leaving here until I've had the chance to question him."

"Horvan said as much. Fielding isn't going anywhere, and thanks to the drugs he probably proposed and produced, he can't shift." He snorted. "Bet he's regretting that now. Doc made sure he got a taste of his own medicine."

Jake watched as one of Horvan's team approached the guarded building, carrying a tray containing a bottle of water and a plate of food. Once the door opened, however, a small, lithe furry shape darted across the tarmac and went inside. Seconds later there were shrieks of mingled pain and rage, accompanied by a caterwauling that was so loud, it hurt the ears.

"Get this fucking cat off me!"

That had to be Fielding.

The soldier appeared in the doorway, carrying the calico kitty, who was hissing and spitting, and even at a distance, Jake could see the blood on its claws. He didn't blame Aric, not for one nanosecond, not after the way he'd treated Seth.

Brick strode toward the soldier, hands held out, and Aric was deposited into them. Brick stroked his back. "Feel better now?"

The soldier hollered toward the main building. "Can we get a medic in here, with a first aid kit? We're gonna need sterile wipes and wound dressings. Maybe even stitches."

Brick chuckled. "Hey, you did good, kitty."

There was something else Jake couldn't miss.

I never knew until this moment that a cat could look so smug.

"Ready for your checkup?"

His heart hammered at the sound of that voice, older now, but unmistakably that of Nicholas. Jake turned to see him, aware of appearing older than his sixty-two years, the lines created by years of being subjected to the tender mercies of the Gerans.

How must I seem to him? Nothing like the young man I was the last time we met.

Then he realized he wasn't the only one who'd aged, who'd suffered. Nicholas's eyes glistened. "Hello there. It's so good to see you."

Now. Now.

Jake's heart thumped. "Tell me. Are you married?"

Nicholas blinked. "Er, no."

"Seeing anyone? Involved with anyone?"

233

His lips twitched. "Not exactly the greeting I expected after all this time, but I'll roll with it. No, there is no one. Not even a cat."

"Then I'm sorry, but I can't wait a moment longer." Jake let go of his fears and took Nicholas in his arms.

Nicholas gave a jolt. "You're either about to kiss me or get me in a headlock." The expression of longing in his eyes threatened to unravel Jake where he stood. "Lord, I hope it's the former."

That was all the invitation Jake needed.

He kissed Nicholas, not holding back, and a moment later, Nicholas's arms were around him, and Jake's kiss was returned, tenfold.

"Whoa," Nicholas said when they broke the kiss, both of them breathing hard. "You don't waste any time, do you?"

Jake kissed his forehead. "After the last thirty-one years? I intend to never waste a single second of what time I have left."

That included sharing what he'd discovered all those years ago. The sooner the shifters of the world learned the truth, the better.

Nicholas cupped his cheek. "I still need to give you a quick physical, but when that's over, I'm done. I'm not about to leave your side."

If Jake had his way, that was where Nicholas would stay for the rest of eternity.

I lost one love—I'm not going to lose another.

CHAPTER TWENTY-SEVEN

"SO WHAT'S the status?" Duke asked.

"Mission accomplished," Horvan told him. "All prisoners accounted for. Five Geran fatalities. They were the only ones who put up resistance. And we got Fielding."

"Excellent. What's the plan?"

"I'm sending the team back to Illinois in the C-17, with Roadkill in charge. And then they get a week's leave." That included Doc, although Horvan had an inkling where he'd be spending his time. After witnessing that kiss he and Jake had shared, he had to wonder where it would lead them.

"Sounds as if they've earned it. One question, though. Why aren't you going with them?"

"I've got a little unfinished business here. I'll let you know when we're ready to make a move."

"Who's staying with you? I need to know how many bodies to accommodate when I send transport for you guys."

"Twelve."

"Noted. I'll try to make it a plane with seats this time."

Horvan snorted. "You're all heart."

"That's why you love me. Now go deal with your unfinished business." Duke hung up.

Horvan shook his head. He and Duke went way back, and yeah, he loved the guy like a brother. Which was no bad thing, seeing as they co-owned a business.

Roadkill entered the room. "You wanted to see me?"

Horvan nodded. "The team is heading back to the barracks, and you're going with 'em. Hashtag and Eve too. You can break the news that everyone's got a week's leave."

Roadkill grinned. "Does that include Hashtag and Eve?"

"No, but you get to stay at Dellan's place until we return. That means Mrs. Landon's cooking, uninterrupted use of the hot tub… and privacy."

His grin widened. "Sir, yes, sir."

"Tell Hashtag to get working on all those locations Milo gave us. We need to pinpoint every last Geran camp." Horvan smirked. "A little homework for when he's not busy with other pursuits."

Roadkill cocked his head. "Where *is* Milo?"

"In a Fridan safe house in Boston, waiting to see Jana as soon as she gets the all-clear. Johan said he was making noises about wanting to fight with us."

"Well, we know we can trust him. *I'd* work with him."

"Yeah, so would I, but we might need to convince some of the team. You've only got to whisper *Geran* and their hackles rise."

"Do you blame them?"

Horvan stared at him. "What if we could bring an end to all this?"

"All what? The war that's waging, even though no one's actually declared one?"

"Not just the war. I'm talking about the deep divisions between shifters."

Roadkill blinked. "What do you know that the rest of us don't? Because that sounds like pie in the sky. Only *your* pie sounds like it comes with ice cream." His stomach rumbled. "Great. Between thinking about Mrs. Landon's cooking and pie ala mode, I'm hungry."

Horvan chuckled. "Well, save me a slice. Anyway, I can't tell you much—because I don't have the answers right now—but I *can* tell you that's what we're working toward." Horvan peered at him. "Is that something you'd like to see too?"

"Gee, let me think." Roadkill rolled his eyes. "In a fucking heartbeat, H. There are enough human conflicts going on in the world right now to keep us employed until the Rapture. Taking shifter battles out of the equation? Feeling safe again? I'm all for that."

He smiled. "Me too. Now go home. Make the most of having the house to yourselves, because we'll be rolling up to the front door before you can say skinny dipping in the hot tub." He patted Roadkill on the back. "And in case I haven't said it yet, I think it's fucking awesome that you, Hashtag, and Eve are mates."

Roadkill beamed. "It is, isn't it? And now I'll go tell them the good news." He hurried out of the room, passing Aelryn on his way in.

"Just the man I wanted to see." Horvan inclined his head toward the former office building that was serving as Fielding's temporary jail. "Who's going to talk to our prisoner?"

"I thought you and I were the obvious choice."

Horvan nodded. "I have a couple of suggestions. I think Saul should be in there too. He'll want any info Fielding can give us about Vic, plus I wanna rub that fucker's nose in the fact that they didn't manage to kill him despite giving it their best shot. Well, their best shot fell *way* short of the mark."

Aelryn huffed. "I couldn't agree more. Anyone else?"

"Yeah. Jake Carson and Seth Miles."

Aelryn's eyes gleamed. "Anyone would think you were trying to rattle our... guest."

"Yup. Think it'll work? Because Fielding must've ordered Jake's execution for a reason. And if the bastard won't talk, then we have a plan B."

"I think having them in there might give us an edge."

"I wanna be in there too, H." Brick spoke from the doorway, his eyes glinting.

"No." Horvan's gut clenched at the idea of denying Brick what he so desperately wanted, but he knew he was right.

"Hey, I was—"

"I said no. And if you were thinking clearly, you wouldn't ask. Besides, you'll hear everything that's said, right? Seth will be there."

Brick glared at him. "But... he... he...."

Horvan's heart went out to him. "I know, Brick. But face facts. Do you *really* think you could sit across the table from him and *not* shift and tear him limb from limb? Well?"

One glance at Brick's tight features was all the answer Horvan needed.

"So what's gonna happen to Fielding?"

Horvan gazed at Aelryn, who frowned. "We haven't decided yet. Let's wait until we see how cooperative he is—or isn't."

Horvan let out another snort. "My money's on the latter."

"If Seth's gonna be in there, you *know* I'm gonna be close by," Brick informed him.

Horvan knew. If one of *his* mates was in the same situation, he'd be a hot mess.

Brick sighed. "Think I'll go stroke a kitty. It might even bring down my blood pressure. They say cats can do that." He turned and walked away.

Brick needed a whole *heap* of cats. Not that Horvan could blame him. Fielding had cost him so damn much: his parents, the constant fear for both him and Aric, holding Seth prisoner. Of everyone, Brick had been the one who'd had the most crap heaped on him. Horvan knew without a doubt that if the opportunity arose, Brick would seize it. And Horvan wasn't sure he would want to stop him.

Horvan met Aelryn's glance. "So when do we get this show on the road?"

Aelryn gave a thin smile. "No time like the present."

THE FORMER office building comprised one main room, a couple of storerooms, and a restroom. Fielding had been kept bound to his chair except for when he'd hollered to use the bathroom or when he ate. All the windows were locked, and there were two doors, both of them guarded by two of Aelryn's men, who let no one approach.

After Aric's little unannounced visit, they were on the watch for kitties too.

Horvan and Aelryn walked into the main room, followed by a soldier who stood in front of the door, his rifle held across his chest.

Fielding sat in what had been a wide office chair, his ankles bound, wrists tied to the armrests with rope. He appeared to be in his sixties, although that meant nothing. Some shifters were much older than their looks.

Vic, for instance.

He gazed at them with belligerence, jaw set, cool eyes locked on their every move as they sat down facing him. Fielding glanced over their shoulders to the armed guard with unconcealed amusement.

"One guard? That's all you're bringing along for protection?"

Horvan arched his eyebrows. "What makes you think he's here for *our* protection?"

That earned him a blink, but Fielding recovered quickly. "Neatly played, Mr. Kojik."

Horvan pointed to the Steri-Strips on his face. "Besides, it seems as though you could use a little protection. I mean, *someone* has to guard you from the kitty, right?"

"And if you hadn't bound me, that cat would have none of its nine lives left," Fielding retorted with a fierce scowl.

Horvan wagged his finger. "Not something you should say out loud around here. You never know if one of his mates is listening. They might not be as tolerant as me."

Fielding arched his eyebrows. "Not a word I'd use to describe you. You see, I remember you. The last time we spoke, you were in some remote cabin with your mates and several thugs, while I was busy cleaning up Anson Prescott's mess."

Horvan breathed evenly. "Yeah, I remember you too, except you haven't quite got your facts straight. Last time we spoke, you were *making* a mess of him—not that you sullied *your* hands on a human. No, you let a gorilla take care of that little task for you, until Anson shot him unexpectedly, and then you left what remained of them both for the Chicago Police Department to find."

Fielding ignored him and stared at Aelryn. "I know *your* face from my files too. Aelryn, isn't it? A direct—"

"We're not here to talk about my lineage," Aelryn interjected. "We wish to find two shifters, and—"

"You dragged me away from a camp full of them. You could have taken your pick." He smirked.

Horvan snarled. "Vic Ryder. Where is he?"

Fielding raised his eyebrows. "Vic who?"

The door opened, and Saul strolled in with an easy air Horvan envied. *He's one cool customer.*

"Having memory problems, Fielding? You asked me to access the shifter archive—you know, the one Vic controls? You told me Vic and Crank had already bonded, which was a fucking lie, but I won't hold that against you because we *all* bonded eventually." Saul dragged a chair over and sat in front of Fielding. "So... where is he? Did *you* give the order to have him taken?"

Fielding gazed at him with an expression of mild surprise. "You're asking *me*? Why should I know? And by the way, let me congratulate you, Mr. Emory. I thought I'd seen the last of you."

"Where are you keeping Alec?" Saul spoke calmly in a low voice, hands clasped between his knees.

"And who is Alec?"

Saul rolled his eyes. "Wow, dementia is certainly playing havoc with your memory, Fielding. Alec, the young boy you had carve me up like a fucking turkey? Believe me, *I'm* never gonna forget him."

"He's Dellan Carson's son, Jake Carson's grandson, and Seth Miles's nephew." Aelryn tilted his head. "You do recall those names, don't you, *Mr.* Fielding? I mean, you could hardly forget Jake Carson, could you? The man you were going to have executed today?"

Fielding widened his eyes. "I find it very interesting that you are in possession of that piece of information."

"You might as well tell us, because we're just gonna keep at you until you do." Saul folded his arms. "Where are Vic Ryder and Alec?"

"How tedious." Fielding did his best to straighten. "Very well. Alec is where you'll never find him. I'd hazard a guess that he isn't all that far from Mr. Ryder. In fact I'd wager Alec is going to be making his acquaintance very, very soon." He gave a bright smile. "So I hope you said all your goodbyes."

Horvan let out a growl. "You fucking—"

Aelryn laid a hand on his arm, then gave the guard a nod. He opened the door, and Jake and Seth walked in. They pulled two chairs to join Horvan, Aelryn, and Saul, and sat, their faces impassive.

Fielding reacted instantly. He became very still. "Why are they here?"

Aelryn regarded him with a neutral expression. "I invited them. Do you have a problem with that? They're here to help us with our… questioning." He gave Fielding an inquiring glance. "Is there something wrong? You're a little pale. Surely their presence doesn't disturb you?"

Fielding recovered enough to manage a shrug. "Why should it?"

Then Jake lurched to his feet, and Fielding shrank back in his chair.

It looked as if Plan B was a go.

"I've heard every word so far, and you know what I've learned? This guy isn't going to talk." Jake's words dripped with contempt. "All *he's* going to do is dance around with words and waste our time." He went over to where Fielding sat, leaned forward, and gripped the armrests. "So why not go straight to the source of all the information we need?"

Fielding quirked one eyebrow. "You have *another* Geran to interrogate? My, you *have* been busy."

Horvan wasn't fooled. The tremor in Fielding's voice, the way he wouldn't look Jake in the eye, the sweat that popped out on his brow….

Jake smiled. "You're going to tell me everything I want to know."

Fielding snorted. "Me? I doubt that." He swallowed.

"You won't have much choice in the matter, because if you won't *give* us what we want, I'll just have to take it. From your head."

CHAPTER TWENTY-EIGHT

FIELDING FEIGNED indifference. "Your mind-control tricks won't work on me. I can shut you out."

Jake arched his eyebrows. "You can try. Some of your scientists at the camp tried that too. Want to know how that went? And while we're on the subject... *mind control*? Seriously?" He rolled his eyes. "Why would I even *want* to do something like that?" He leaned in closer until his face was barely an inch from Fielding's. "No, *my* specialties are psychometry and clairvoyance, although I do have other skills." He smiled. "You know what psychometry is, don't you, Fielding? Of course you do. And you're about to get firsthand experience of it." Jake glanced at Saul and Horvan. "Hold him still, please."

They moved to either side of Fielding's chair and grabbed his arms, although he struggled to free himself. Jake placed his fingers on Fielding's temples.

Fielding glared at him. "It won't work. What makes you think I'm going to cooperate?"

"You really don't know how this works, do you? Who says I need your cooperation, anyway?" Jake narrowed his gaze. "Do I need to gag you? It's bad enough that I have to be this close to you." He closed his eyes, and a surge of emotion assaulted his senses, so strong he could almost smell it.

Interesting.

"He's afraid."

"What's he afraid of?" Aelryn asked.

Jake concentrated. "Me... and...." He opened his eyes. "Who's Theron?" Fielding's gasp mingled with Aelryn's, and Jake grinned. "I think I just hit a nerve."

"You're on the right track," Aelryn confirmed. "Theron is a person of interest."

Jake closed his eyes, shutting out the sight of Fielding's contorted features. "I can see him. He's... old. But there's nothing frail about this guy. Power rolls off him in waves."

242

"Where is he?" Horvan demanded.

Jake frowned. "He's in a long room with a vaulted ceiling, like it's underground someplace. Somewhere old. Can't see much except...." He scowled. "Try and kick me out of this memory all you want, Fielding. It won't do you any good. You can't hide from me."

Fielding's muted whimper told Jake he knew it too.

Jake walked through the hallways of Fielding's mind. "I'm in another room. Same place, I think. There's a bed but little else. Someone's sitting on it. A boy." Jake stared at him. "Such a blank expression." It sent a chill coursing through him. "Green eyes, bronze-brown hair." Those eyes....

"Looks as if he's maybe ten?" Saul asked.

"Yes. Wait—no. He's older than that. He could be in his teens. Who is he?" Except he already knew, and the knowledge gripped his heart in an icy hand.

Saul let out a sigh. "You're seeing your grandson, Alec. And if you're right, then... he's aged since I saw him."

Jake froze. "But if he's Dellan's son, and taking into account how long the Gerans had him imprisoned in that cage..." It didn't compute.

In real terms, he couldn't be more than two years old. What the fuck did they do to him? More importantly, how could they do that to a child? Scrap that—he had to have been still little more than a baby when they did whatever they did. Jake wanted to grab Alec and cradle him, to run with him as far away from that bland room as they could get.

A calm voice in his head dragged him back on task. *Later. There's stuff you need to discover.*

Jake took a deep breath, forcing himself to think clearly.

"I don't know where he is. Not yet." Then he was walking back to that first room.

Something important in here.

"Can you see Vic?" Jake couldn't miss the anxious edge to Saul's voice.

He sighed. "There are limits to what I can see. If it's not in Fielding's memory, then no." And right then, Fielding's memory was fixated on a door.

So what's in there?

"The room has a walled-off section with a door in it. Walls of glass. I can see stone caskets." He stilled. Familiar caskets.... Jake pulled back and looked Fielding in the eye. "You know about the Missal of Godwin, don't you? Theron saw it at the archives."

Fielding froze. "No. Get out of there."

"What's that?" Horvan asked.

Without breaking eye contact, Jake answered him. "The oldest document we have about shifters—well, to date at any rate. It was written in 1050. I saw it in the archives in Rome. It mentions the brothers. I also saw other artifacts, but that was where things got interesting." Fielding moaned, and Jake moved in closer, his fingers pushing into the flesh of Fielding's temples. "You don't like me looking at this, do you? Why does Theron keep these caskets from prying eyes? What do they contain? More forgeries?" He stilled. "Or maybe not. Maybe they're the real thing."

"Search his memories for Berengar," Aelryn suggested.

Fielding jerked beneath his fingertips, and Jake smiled. "Jackpot. Who is Berengar?"

"An ancient shifter whose tomb was recently discovered. Whatever they found in it, the Gerans want it to remain hidden."

The fear Jake had sensed when he first touched Fielding had blossomed, creeping through his body like corruption.

"You're afraid of Theron, aren't you?" Jake said softly. "Whatever Theron is hiding, he's not just keeping it from the Fridans, but the Gerans as well. He doesn't want *anyone* seeing it." Then Jake froze as the memory of a conversation came to him, as clear as if he'd been present at the time. "You asked Theron why he hadn't destroyed whatever's in there when they were first discovered."

Fielding's eyes widened.

Jake nodded. "He told you they may yet prove useful." Then he recited Theron's reply, word for word.

I can understand your confusion. Why keep something that would lead to peace when we wish to sow nothing but discord and chaos? But the day will come when we have won this war. The Fridans will be nothing but a memory, and all shifters will be bereft. Then it will be time to 'discover' these artifacts. Then we'll tell everyone that we never knew. How could we? The truth had lain hidden, undisturbed for centuries. Can't you just hear the words? 'But now we can see that all shifters and humans must work together, as they were meant to. We must strive to forget what has passed and live in peace and harmony.' After all the bloodshed and heartache, such words will ensure no one seeks to resurrect the past, and we shall live out our days the way we always intended—as the rulers of all.

Fielding stared at him openmouthed, his upper lip curling back, his face twisted in a grimace.

"Now I *really* want to see what Theron is hiding," Aelryn murmured.

Saul's voice broke through. "Fielding said wherever Alec is, Vic is there too."

Jake removed his fingers, straightened, and glanced at Seth. "I think a little Remote Viewing is called for."

Seth nodded, his eyes bright. "I need something of Vic's. Something personal."

"I'm on it." Saul glanced at Aelryn. "Can you take over here?"

Aelryn grabbed hold of Fielding's arm, and Saul was out of there.

Jake resumed his task, taking a moment to retrace his steps in Fielding's mind. "I saw some of your handiwork at the archive. Well, not yours, but I'm sure it was a Geran who produced it." When Fielding didn't react, Jake cocked his head to one side. "Surely you haven't forgotten? Ansger's comments to Ansfrid about what would come of mixing with humans? Because I haven't. Those words are burned into my brain." He closed his eyes and recited the text Orsini had read to him more than thirty years ago.

For so long as you choose to mix the blood of humans and versipelli, my brother, you will bring about our destruction. Mankind is weak, but we are strong. Mankind's place is beneath our feet, but our destiny is to rule. Mankind has tried to eliminate us already, and your weakness for their company would bring us to the brink of extinction. You have chosen your path, my brother, and I have chosen mine. Peace is not the answer, only war. And if you continue along this path, then my war will be against not only mankind, but against you, and any who choose to follow your example.

Horvan made a choking sound. "Oh gods." Then he paused. "Wait— what do you mean, handiwork?"

"They produced an artifact, one that supported the tale of the brothers' split. Except it wasn't real." He glanced at Horvan. "What I just read to you

245

wasn't real. I was able to tell Orsini that much. The last thing he said when I left him was that he would get it dated."

"Orsini spoke of this," Aelryn confirmed. "And you were correct. The document dates back to the early nineteen hundreds."

Jake blinked and jerked his head in Aelryn's direction. "Is he still alive?"

Aelryn smiled. "Yes. And he's still the archivist."

"Then we're going to need him. If we can get him to leave the archive." There was a mystery to be solved in those stone caskets—wherever they were—and Orsini would be key to cracking it.

Aelryn frowned. "Can you search for any memory of Valmer Cooper?"

Fielding twitched again, and Jake chuckled. "He knows that name too. Who is he?"

"A Geran. He might even be a leader."

Jake closed his eyes, focusing once more. "He's there, with Theron." Jake frowned. "I don't understand. If he's a Geran, why have they had him beaten? Why are they holding him?"

"As leverage. He's definitely there?"

"Yes." Jake had a ton of questions, but they would have to wait. He delved a little deeper, aware of the fatigue crawling through him, making him ache.

I'll have to stop soon.

Fielding had become very still, and Jake's instinct went on alert.

What is it you don't want me to see?

"You've killed many times for your master, haven't you?" he murmured.

"Well, we know about Dellan's stepbrother, Anson," Horvan commented.

Fielding let out a whimper, and Jake saw what he'd tried so hard to hide. He froze, his limbs heavy as lead, pain lancing through his chest. "I ought to shift and tear you apart where you sit."

A hand touched his shoulder, and Jake knew it was Aelryn. "Jake, what have you seen?"

Tears trickled down Jake's cheeks, and he did nothing to impede them. "He killed my wife. Injected her with something. Then he stood there while she died." He pushed the memory aside, unable to watch Miranda's beautiful face as it contorted in agony.

Nicholas was right.

It was one thing to suspect it, but quite another to know it for certain. Jake struggled to get back on track. "There's another death. A scarred man with long gray hair and dark eyes."

Aelryn's breathing caught. "Is the scar on his neck?"

"Yes."

"What can you glean about him?"

"He gave the Gerans information about your activities." Jake stiffened. "He was the one who told them about me visiting the archive."

"Raderan Milos, a Fridan leader. He committed suicide about twenty-eight years ago."

Jake scowled. "That was no suicide." Fielding shivered, and Jake gazed at him, seeing to the heart of his unrest. "You're afraid of what Theron will do when he learns what you've revealed to us."

"Theron is an important Geran leader," Aelryn told him.

Jake shook his head. "I hate to contradict you, but he is *the* leader." And suddenly he was out of energy. He broke contact with Fielding, shaking and beyond exhausted. Fielding slumped in his chair, his eyes closed.

"You need to rest." Horvan's voice was kind.

Jake managed to shake his head again. "Not yet. Have to find Theron's residence. Because that's where all the answers are." Fielding chose that moment to open his eyes, and Jake recoiled from the look of stark hatred.

"I hope you're proud of yourself," Fielding said with a sneer. "You just mind-raped me. You say you're all benevolent, but you'll get dirty when the need suits you."

Jake blinked, then recovered. "No, you're wrong. A good man will do whatever he has to in order to protect what's his. All this? It never would have happened if you'd been a normal person. But *no*, you had to be a murderer, killing people who got in your way, people you had no more use for. It wasn't mind-rape. It was stopping a monster." He snorted. "But I *will* say this. Thank you."

Fielding's eyes bulged. "For what? I did none of that willingly." He sounded as tired as Jake.

"I'm not thanking you for that. I'm thanking you for thirty years of pushing me, testing me, trying to work out the limits of my abilities. Because it forced me to push the boundaries of those limits. My psychic talents were pretty good before you took me. Your treatment of me made me hone them, develop them." Jake gestured to his body. "You made me into the psychic you see before you. And now? I'm going to be the engine of your undoing. Not just you—*every* Geran who believed the lies you spun." Jake turned to Horvan. "Now get me away from this bastard. I've had about as much of him as I can stomach."

How he got back to the cot bed Nicholas had procured for him, Jake had no idea, except that Horvan had had a hand in it somehow. Jake dropped like a stone onto the bed, arm thrown over his eyes.

"I can't thank you enough." That was Aelryn.

Jake huffed. "Don't thank me yet. Save it for when you *really* have something to thank me for."

"Are you okay?"

"No, but it'll pass." He swallowed. "Where's Horvan?"

"I'm right here."

Jake's stomach clenched. "He was right, you know."

"Fielding? Right about what?"

"What I did just now? It was cruel and unusual. I tortured him."

"But *you* were right too." Horvan's tone was gentle. "You did what you had to do to stop a monster. You said it yourself. He would *never* have told us any of that, not in a million years. And we needed to know—to save lives." There was a pause. "If you still feel the same way when this is all behind us? There's always therapy. It's saved me a few times. And maybe if I shared that with more people, they'd get help instead of carrying all that baggage around with them, weighing them down, dragging them deeper into some mental mire that seems inescapable."

Jake peered at him. "Okay, I didn't expect that." He smiled. "My son got real lucky with his mates."

Horvan returned his smile. "We're the lucky ones."

Crank stood at the foot of his bed, holding out a stainless-steel ring. Jake stared at it.

"What's that?"

"It's not important," Crank replied with a cough. "Saul said you wanted something of Vic's so Seth could do his thing."

Saul appeared next to him. He rolled his eyes. "I said a cock ring wasn't appropriate."

"Hey, you said something personal. How much more personal can you get?"

Next to the bed, Horvan chuckled. "I'm dying to know what you're doing with Vic's cock ring, but you know what? I can live without knowing."

Jake propped himself up on his elbows. "Anyone else want to join us? Should I sell tickets?" Then he saw Seth at the foot of the bed. "Okay, good. You're supposed to be here. Your turn."

Seth took the cock ring from Crank and held it in both hands, eyes closed. Silence fell, until all Jake could hear was the drone of a plane taking off in the distance.

Then Seth froze. "I see a man. He's shortish, very slim… he seems very young."

"That's Vic. Has to be. He looks about twelve." Crank's breathing hitched. "He's alive?"

"Yes. He's locked in what appears to be a storeroom." He paused. "He appears to be okay. Quite calm."

Jake sat up. "Seth? Expand your horizon. See beyond the walls. You can do it." His skin tingled and his heartbeat raced.

Seth frowned. "Wow. It's… it looks like a castle. There's a stream around it."

"Are you talking about a moat?" Aelryn asked.

Seth nodded. "Yeah, that's it." He paused. "There are people working here. I can hear them talking, but… they sound a little strange." He frowned. "I *think* they're British, but it's the weirdest accent. I'm having trouble understanding them."

Jake gaped at him. "You tracked him all the way to the UK? You are *awesome*."

Seth flushed. "I think that's the farthest I've managed so far."

Saul leaned forward. "Can you repeat what you're hearing, *exactly* as you hear it?"

"I think so."

Saul pulled his phone from his pocket and stabbed at the keyboard. "Eve? I want you to listen to Seth, then tell me where this UK accent is from." He snorted. "No, I haven't heard it. I'm just cutting out the middleman and coming directly to you. Putting Seth on now." He held out the phone, and Seth repeated the strange-sounding words. When he finished, Saul brought the phone to his ear. "Well?" He listened for a moment, then grinned. "You beauty. Thank you." He finished the call. "Okay, that narrows the field a bit.

Eve says we should be looking in Lancashire, in the north of England. And if Vic is there, so is Alec."

"And the contents of Berengar's tomb," Aelryn added.

Saul peered at Seth. "If we find photos of castles in Lancashire—"

"With a moat," Crank interjected. "They gotta have a moat. Can't be all *that* many of them, right?"

Saul speared him with a glance. "Okay, photos of castles in Lancashire—with a *moat*—you think you can identify the one you saw?"

Seth nodded, and Jake's chest swelled with pride.

Saul met Horvan's gaze. "Then it's Google time."

Aelryn gave Jake a sympathetic glance. "Get some rest. We're going to need you."

"We need Orsini too," Jake reminded him. "Give me an hour to recharge my batteries and I'll make the call."

"And Fielding?" Horvan inclined his head toward the block where Fielding was stowed.

Aelryn smiled. "He's going to be my guest a while longer. I don't think he'll be in any hurry to return to his master, do you?"

Judging by what Jake had felt while he'd crawled through Fielding's mind during the last half hour, Aelryn had nailed it.

And speaking of crawling, Jake was in dire need of a shower after that. He felt soiled.

At least now they had a name. A target.

One line of that conversation gave him hope.

Theron is hiding something that could lead to peace.

Whatever it was, Jake was going to help bring it out of the darkness and into the light.

Keep Reading for an Exclusive Excerpt from
Mysteries, Menace, and Mates
Book #4 in the Lions & Tigers & Bears series
by K.C. Wells
Coming Soon from Dreamspinner Press

CHAPTER ONE

ARIC WAS fast coming to the conclusion that hearing his mates' thoughts was both a blessing and a curse. Sure, he loved knowing they were safe, that they were thinking about him. *Who wouldn't love that?* And while it made keeping secrets more awkward, he could get around that with the mental lockboxes Horvan had told them about.

The last half hour, however, had been nothing less than torture.

Okay, so they were safe. The mission to liberate the Maine camp was over and the inmates had all made it out alive. Better than that—they were all on their way to someplace where they could be safe, and it wouldn't be long before whoever was left got shipped out, heading back to Illinois or wherever Aelryn's base was located.

What tortured Aric was one man.

Well, one monster.

Aric had sat in the sunshine, and despite its warmth, his blood had run cold every time Fielding opened his mouth, every time Jake revealed some new atrocity.

How could Seth stomach it?

In the camp, Aric had lost count of how many times he'd seen Seth all weak and wobbly after coming back from their goddamn tests, but still doing his best to care for Aric. *And how did they treat him once they'd separated us?* Once Seth was too far away for Aric to feel his distress, his exhaustion. Even when he'd seen Seth in his dreams, Seth had hidden his fatigue.

And then there was Brick. He would have heard Fielding's interrogation too. Aric had known countless nights when he'd lain beside Brick, conscious of the inner turmoil Brick couldn't hide.

He's already suffered so much. This is making it worse.

All Aric wanted was to hear Fielding's fate. Execution by firing squad would be just fine, and Aric wouldn't draw the line at aiming a rifle at the son of a bitch. He was a crack shot—he'd grown up around guns on his dad's farm—and having that bastard in his crosshairs might go some way to healing the pain.

Yeah, right. As if they'd let me.

And that right there was the problem. Aric felt useless as fuck.

I want to help my mates, to help them *heal.* Except what could he do? *I'm not a polar bear. I'm not a big cat. I'm a freakin' house cat, and that means I can't overpower anyone, I can't run fast, I can't take down bigger animals....* All Aric had going for him was his brains, and his recent attack on Fielding should have proved to everyone that underestimating him was a big mistake.

The base felt empty. Aelryn's people were all but gone. The medics had done their job and checked out all the prisoners, so now they were heading out too. Doc hadn't left, though, not that Aric was surprised. Right then he was with Jake, and Aric thought nothing short of an atom bomb would drive him from Jake's side.

Jake looked a little older than the last time Aric had seen him, before they'd sent him to Maine. Gods knew what the Gerans had subjected him and Seth to.

Fielding was part of that. Yet another reason to plant a bullet in his brain.

Aelryn, Horvan, and Saul were deep into planning... whatever they were planning. There'd been whispers, something about artifacts, a tomb... it all sounded a little surreal. Aric's chest had swelled with pride to learn Seth had been a part of whatever it was they'd discovered.

Eve, Roadkill, and Hashtag had taken off in the C-17, along with the rest of Horvan's team, and were on their way back to Illinois. Aric longed to go there too but was torn between yearning to start his new life with Brick and Seth, and needing closure. He'd walked around the base's perimeter three or four times, trying to calm the muddle of thoughts and fears that fogged his mind.

So far, he'd had little success.

"Ready to get out of here?"

He jumped at the sound of Brick's voice and turned. Brick and Seth strolled toward him, and he ran to them. Brick's strong arms enfolded him, and Aric breathed him in. Seth's hand was on Aric's back, a welcome connection.

"Can we go now?" Aric asked.

"Soon," Brick murmured. "We're almost done here. We're just waiting on H and Saul. They've let Jake sleep a little longer. He was wrecked."

Aric kept his cheek pressed to Brick's chest. "So what happens to Fielding?" He managed to keep his tone nonchalant, except he knew that wouldn't work around his mates.

Sure enough, Seth stroked Aric's hair. "That hasn't been decided yet."

Aric stiffened. "They can't just forget about him."

He wouldn't let them.

"Hey, no one's said that will happen," Brick said in a low voice. "But right now Aelryn and Horvan have a mission to plan, and they might need him."

Aric pulled away from Brick. "I don't think so. I think Jake and Seth got all they're going to get out of him."

Seth huffed. "You may be right."

"And if we're at war," Aric continued, his heartbeat quickening, "that makes Fielding a war criminal."

There was only one way to deal with those.

Brick sighed, gazing at him with compassion. "We're trying to stop this war before it even starts."

"Brick? H wants you," Crank hollered across the tarmac, beckoning him. "And Jake's asking for Seth."

Seth chuckled. "No rest for the wicked." He kissed Aric's forehead, then he and Brick strode to where Crank stood.

"Hey, Seth!" Aric shouted after him. When he turned, Aric smiled. "You don't have a wicked bone in your body."

Seth grinned. "Maybe, maybe not, but I get a wicked *boner* when I think about a certain kitty cat. And if we're lucky, we'll *both* have a wicked bone in our body when we're alone with Brick."

Aric could feel Brick getting hot at the thoughts Seth was sending out, not to mention the delicious thrill they sent through Aric, but he shoved his desire somewhere deep.

Right then he had to think clearly, and the last thing he needed were images of Brick's dick taking up space in his head.

Just how big does that dick get?

He watched Brick and Seth until they were out of sight, then hurried over to the hangar where Brick had stowed his combat gear while they waited for whatever transport was going to take them out of there.

His heart pounded, and his mouth was dry as a bone at the thought of what was about to happen.

What he was about to do.

Aric made sure no one was around as he snuck into the hangar. Brick's combat harness lay next to his duffel bag, and Aric saw the M17 handgun in its holster. His hands shook as he picked it up. The manual safety was on. Aric removed the magazine and checked the bullets.

Don't think about it. Just do it.

He stuffed the weapon in the waistband of his combat pants, hidden below the baggy shirt they'd found for him to wear. Then he scanned his surroundings for the prop he needed.

There it is.

Aric grabbed the first aid box and headed out into the sunshine. He leaned against the hangar wall and assessed the situation. The guard hadn't moved from his position in front of the building where Fielding was being kept, and there was no one else in sight.

Now all Aric had to do was make his move.

The sun was at its highest point when another soldier came out of the hangar, a tray in both hands, and walked toward the makeshift jail.

Perfect.

Aric ran across to him. "Hey."

The soldier came to a halt midway between the hangar and Fielding's temporary prison. "You need something?"

Aric pointed to the tray, which contained a plastic bowl covered in foil, a plastic spoon, tortillas, a snack-size packet of peanut butter, a bag of mixed fruit, and a bottle of water. "Is that for Fielding?"

"Yup." The soldier grinned. "And no, you can't spit in his cheese tortellini."

Aric grimaced. "Oh my God, is this one of those ready-to-eat meals I've heard the guys talking about?"

He chuckled. "Sure is. Fielding should count himself lucky he isn't getting the curry chicken I asked them to give him. It was cruel and unusual punishment, they said, because he'd end up shitting through the eye of a needle." He gave Aric an inquiring glance. "Well? Did you want something, or are you just delaying me so his food gets cold?" His eyes twinkled. "Because gee, that would be tragic."

It looked as if Aric wasn't the only one who held Fielding in pretty low esteem.

Aric held up the First Aid kit. "I was going to change his dressings. I might as well take him his food and save you the trip." His heart hammered.

Say yes. Say yes.

The soldier chuckled once more. "Wait a sec. Weren't you the one who gave him the wounds in the first place?"

He bowed his head, looking suitably ashamed. "Yeah, but I'm feeling bad about it now. The medics have all gone, Doc's busy with Jake, so I said I'd do it. I do have a little first aid training." That wasn't a lie, but then again, he had no intention of delivering any aid.

The opposite, in fact.

"Well, okay then. Knock yourself out." The soldier handed him the tray. "I'm not about to argue with you, especially as you'll save me from having to get too close to him again." He shuddered. "That guy gives me the fucking creeps with the way he stares, like he's looking into your head."

Aric thanked him and waited for him to head back to the hangar before approaching the building.

The guard glanced at the tray, then Aric. "You been conscripted?" he said with a smirk.

"Just helping out, delivering his food and changing his dressings," Aric replied, holding up the first aid kit again.

The guard nodded. "Okay. Knock when you're ready to leave, and I'll untie him so he can eat. Just no shifting this time, okay? I thought you were murdering him last time. All that screaming…. How much damage can kitty claws inflict anyhow?"

Aric snorted. "He's still alive, isn't he? So not enough, obviously. And I won't shift. You've got my promise."

What Aric had in mind wouldn't require shifting.

The guard didn't open the door right away, however, but regarded Aric for a moment. Aric tried to keep his cool. His heart was beating so fast, he was sure the guard could hear it. Finally the guard nodded. "I guess you'll be safe enough. He can't shift, and while he might give some pretty impressive glares, *they* won't harm you." He opened the door, and Aric went inside.

Fielding sat in the same office chair, his ankles and wrists secured with rope. He glanced at Aric with disdain, his lips curled into a sneer. "Well, if it isn't the kitty cat again. Come to inflict more damage?" There were four Steri-Strips on his forehead and cheeks, and his hands were all scratched up. Fielding peered at the tray and shuddered. "What muck are they giving me now? It should come with a health warning."

"You don't need to worry about that." Aric's voice shook. "Food's going to be the least of your worries." He put down the kit and the tray, then approached Fielding's chair. His fingers trembled as he unfastened the rope around Fielding's ankles, then his wrists. Aric stepped back quickly and pulled the handgun from its hiding place, pointing it at Fielding with as steady a grip as he could manage.

"Why have you cut me loose? And what are you doing with that?" Fielding looked almost amused.

Aric raised the gun a bit higher. "Taking back my fucking dignity. Taking it back for all of us who you hurt, tortured, and killed. You can't be allowed to live."

Fielding sneered again. "You? You don't have the guts. You're a weak, pathetic little thing. The only reason we kept you was because we wanted Seth to comply." His smile was cruel. "If it wasn't for him, you would have been one of the first to be culled."

"Well, this weak, pathetic little thing is going to end you." Aric spoke clearly, not bothering to mask his thoughts.

Come on, Brick. I need you.

Aric pulled the trigger and the gun clicked. He did it again with the same result.

Fielding smirked. "See? Pathetic." And before Aric could take a breath, Fielding lurched out of the chair and grabbed the gun, knocking Aric to the floor. "Are you so stupid you didn't realize the safety was on?" He moved his thumb, and smiled. "But it's off now, not that I need it to finish you. I can do that with one hand, but I'm not going to waste time killing you. Especially since you might have some use after all—as a shield." He grabbed Aric around the throat and squeezed. "How many guards outside?" He released his grip a little, and Aric coughed.

"One," he croaked. "Everyone one else is inside."

Now would be a good time, Brick.

Fielding nodded. "Armed, of course." He dragged Aric to the door and opened it a crack, the gun raised. Then he shoved Aric through the open doorway, aiming at the guard, pulling the trigger—

And nothing happened. Fielding's shocked expression was almost comical.

Then a ferocious roar shattered the silence, and Aric scrambled to his feet, his heart thumping. Somewhere, Seth cried out, "Don't shoot him!"

A solid mass of white fur crossed Aric's field of vision, barreled into Fielding, and shoved him out of sight, accompanied by Fielding's shriek. Thunderous noises filled the air as heavy paws slammed the ground, and Aric winced at the sound of Brick's deafening roar as he hurtled after Fielding.

I have to see.

He turned in time to watch Brick slam a hefty paw into the side of Fielding's face with enough force to snap his neck. Fielding dropped like a stone, but Brick wasn't done. The air was filled with noises that curdled Aric's blood: The scream that was cut off, the gurgle of blood, and the crunch as Brick bit through bone and cartilage. He closed his jaws around Fielding's throat, and by the time he was through, Fielding's head was hanging by its tendons.

Aric jumped when arms encircled him.

Easy, baby. Only me.

Aric turned away from the sight of blood staining Brick's maw and buried his face in Seth's chest. Seth held onto Aric, his hand on Aric's nape. *Trust me, you don't need to see any more.*

"Hey!" Brick yelled. "Can I get some help here? Got some trash that needs scraping off the tarmac."

Then there was the sound of boots thudding on concrete and raised voices.

"What the fuck?" That was Crank.

"Here." That was Horvan. "Wipe yourself off with this." A pause. "Good thing we found out everything we needed, huh?"

"He was going to kill Aric!" Brick retorted. "And the world's a better place without that fucker. What's going to happen to him? What's left of him, at any rate."

"Aelryn will find a deep, dark hole to bury the POS in, where no one will ever look. That's one grave that won't get a marker."

Aric. Turn around.

There was no way Aric could ignore Brick.

He turned to be greeted by the sight of a naked Brick, a bloodied towel in his hand.

Brick was glaring.

"Why would you go after him with my gun? And I *know* it was loaded."

"Yeah, it was." Aric reached into his pocket and withdrew the bullets. "Now you can put them back."

Seth gasped. "You set him up. You knew Fielding would go for the gun, and you made sure we knew what you were doing."

"Of course." Aric glanced at the tarp-covered lump on the ground. "Fielding haunted Brick's dreams. I wanted to give Brick the chance to kill him, to rid us of him forever." What surprised him was how the memory of what he'd just seen, what he'd heard, was fading with every second, as if his mind didn't want to hold on to it a moment longer and was already into the process of expelling it.

Aric was fine with that.

Brick pulled Aric to him. "I've already talked to you about putting yourself in danger. What the hell do I have to do? Put you over my knee and swat your ass as a reminder?"

Seth coughed. "Uh, Brick?"

Brick's head snapped toward him. "What?"

"Okay, so this isn't the time, but, ixnay ethay unishmentpay alktay. Aric likes a little pain with his pleasure, so you're not exactly helping."

Brick narrowed his eyes. "What the hell does that mean?" he demanded, his deep voice reverberating through Aric.

Seth sighed. "I swear, *no one* remembers classic pig Latin anymore. I had to teach Aric so we could talk in the camp when I was too tired to show him my thoughts." He met Brick's gaze. "It *means* exactly what it sounded like. Aric likes a little pain with his pleasure, so threatening to spank him? That isn't a deterrent."

Brick's mouth fell open. "He... what?" Then he frowned. "Wait, I thought you two haven't—"

"That's right, we haven't. That doesn't mean I didn't get to see something in Aric's head once when we were jerking off. And we did share fantasies."

"Hey, will you quit giving away all my secrets?" Aric growled. He had to admit, the conversation helped ease his tremors, even if it was the most surreal thing ever, with Fielding's remains only feet away from them.

He'd been Aric's definition of a bad guy while he lived, and dead, he was fast becoming nothing but a bad dream.

Right on cue, a couple of guys appeared, and Aric didn't break eye contact with Brick, because that was way better than watching them clear away what was left of Fielding.

Brick bit his lip. "Fantasies? Okay, that's hot. Still…." He ran a thumb over Aric's face. "You're going to look so beautiful in our bed, all spread out, needy for me. For us." His voice cracked.

Aric smiled. "We can't wait to be there with you. Although…."

Brick stilled. "Although? There's an *although*?"

Aric glanced at Seth, who nodded.

Time to tell it like it is. And talking about what lay in their future was way better than thinking about what had just happened.

"Well… you see… Seth and I? Zero interest in topping, which means basically we're going to work you to death in bed, because it'll be up to you to satisfy us both." Aric smiled again. "Don't worry, though. I've been stocking up on multivitamins to give you energy." When Brick arched his eyebrows, Aric nodded. "Seriously. I gave Crank my shopping list. He thought it was hilarious."

Brick laughed, something Aric hadn't heard much of, but what he sensed in Brick was even better. He'd seen it all: the fear, the crippling loneliness, the pain at the loss of his parents. It was as if that bright laughter had broken the chains holding Brick's heart hostage.

What flowed from Brick was love.

Then Brick's arms closed around him. "Don't worry. I'll fuck you both into a coma every day, and that's a promise."

Seth snickered. "He doesn't know a lot about cats, does he?"

"Apparently not, but now we're together again? There's plenty of time for us to learn."

Brick raised Aric's chin with his fingers. "But if I can be serious for a minute? This is the last time you pull a stunt like this, kitty. Got me?"

Aric knew what that meant.

He craned his neck to look Brick in the eye. "If it helped you to move on? I'd do it again in a heartbeat."

Brick chuckled. "What do I always say? Never underestimate the kitty. And I'm deadly serious."

"You're deadly, I won't argue with that," Seth murmured.

Brick towered over Aric. "You *will* be doing therapy."

It wasn't a request.

Aric stuck his chin out. "I don't need it. I'm fine." *See me? You just ripped Fielding apart, and I'm still here. I'm not cowering under my blanket.*

He was made of strong stuff.

Brick scowled. "That's bullshit, and you know it. And it's no use you arguing. This is nonnegotiable."

"Listen to him." Seth's voice was gentle. "You'll need someone to talk to."

Brick stared at him. "Excuse me? This involves you too. Both of you will be seeing someone."

"But we don't *need* to talk to anyone," Aric protested. "We can talk to you."

"What he said," Seth added.

Brick pulled him closer. "Sweetheart, you're more than welcome to talk to me. Anytime. But I'm not a professional. I'm more of a kill first, ask questions later kinda guy. You need someone who can empathize with you. And I'm not big on empathy."

"This is such bullshit," Aric muttered. "I won't need therapy."

"And yet, you're gonna do it and you'll go into it with an open mind."

"Why?" he demanded.

Brick slid a finger over Aric's cheek. "Honestly? Because I think the real you is hidden beneath all this stuff you've been dealing with." He kissed the tip of Aric's nose. "I love you, and I'll love you even more once the rest of you shines through."

Aric knew when to give up a fight. Then he realized he could play this game just as well as Brick. "Then you're going with us." He folded his arms. "And like you said, this is nonnegotiable."

Brick smirked. "Or what?"

Aric gave him what he hoped was a suitably smug smile. "Or we won't put out."

"Considering we have yet to do anything, that sounds like cutting off your nose to spite your face." Brick drew himself up to his full—and very impressive—height. "Don't forget who's in charge here."

Aric could fight dirty too.

"And don't *you* forget, you're not alone. We need you, just like you need us. It's ridiculous for you to think you can get through this alone." He batted his eyes. "Please, Brick? Do it for us?"

"What he said," Seth added.

Aric could sense the battle of emotions taking place inside his mate. Finally Brick sighed. "Fine. But if I agree to this, what's in it for me?"

Aric arched his eyebrows. "Two very happy mates. What more do you need?"

He could see the moment Brick relented. Brick pulled them both close. "Okay, but I want sex. Lots of it."

Aric grinned. "Whenever, wherever. Just say the word."

Brick gave a satisfied smile. "Then we'll go together. How does that sound?"

Seth chuckled. "Like I want to be home to collect on a blowjob reward. When do we leave this place?"

Aric closed his eyes and breathed in the heavenly scent of his mate. Then he caught the tail end of a thought.

"Wait just one minute. You said Horvan and Aelryn had a mission to plan. *What* mission?"

K.C. WELLS lives on an island off the south coast of the UK, surrounded by natural beauty. She writes about men who love men and can't even contemplate a life that doesn't include writing.

The rainbow rose tattoo on her back with the words "Love is Love" and "Love Wins" is her way of hoisting a flag. She plans to be writing about men in love—be it sweet and slow, hot, or kinky—for a long while to come.

If you want to follow her exploits, you can sign up for her monthly newsletter:

http://eepurl.com/cNKHIT
You can stalk—er, find—her in the following places:
Email: k.c.wells@btinternet.com
Facebook: www.facebook.com/KCWellsWorld
KC's men In Love (my readers group): http://bit.ly/2hXL6wJ
Amazon: https://www.amazon.com/K-C-Wells/e/B00AECQ1LQ
Twitter: @K_C_Wells
Website: www.kcwellswrites.com
Instagram: www.instagram.com/k.c.wells
BookBub: https://www.bookbub.com/authors/k-c-wells

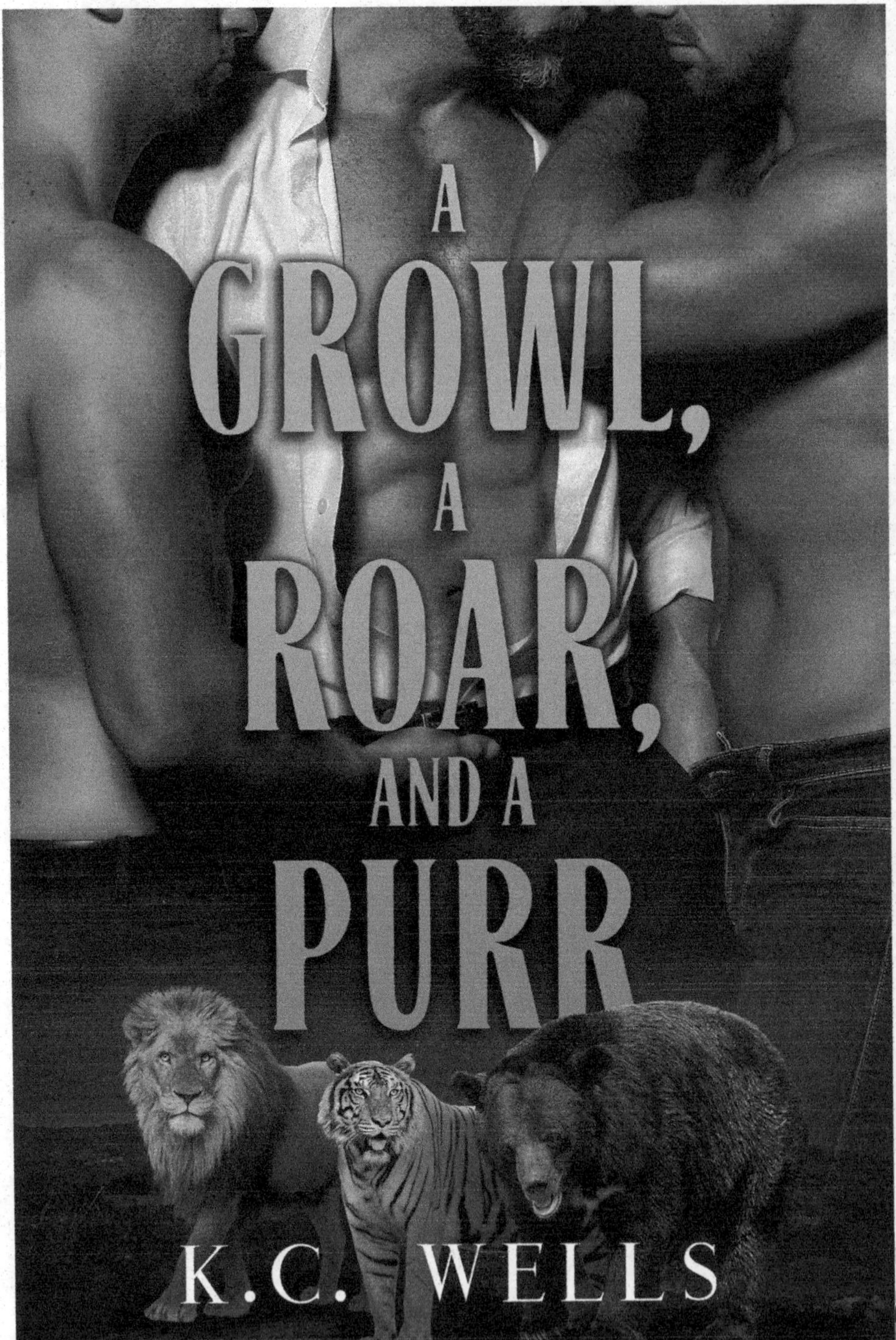
A
GROWL,
A
ROAR,
AND A
PURR
K.C. WELLS

Lions & Tigers & Bears: Book One

In the human world, shifters are a myth.

In the shifter world, mates are a myth too. So how can tiger shifter Dellan Carson have two of them?

Dellan has been trapped in his shifted form for so long, he's almost forgotten how it feels to walk on two legs. Then photojournalist Rael Parton comes to interview the big-pharma CEO who holds Dellan captive in a glass-fronted cage in his office, and Dellan's world is rocked to its core.

When lion shifter Rael finds his newfound mate locked in shifted form, he's shocked but determined to free him from his prison... and that means he needs help.

Enter ex-military consultant and bear shifter Horvan Kojik. Horvan is the perfect guy to rescue Dellan. But mates? He's never imagined settling down with one guy, let alone two.

Rescuing Dellan and helping him to regain his humanity is only the start. The three lovers have dark secrets to uncover and even darker forces to overcome....

Scan the QR code below to order

A SNARL, A SPLASH, AND A SHOCK

K.C. WELLS

Lions & Tigers & Bears: Book Two

As part of a military team, Crank needs to keep his head on straight. His unit depends on it. So the recurring sensual dreams he's having—the ones featuring a shark shifter with dark brown hair and eyes—really screw with his focus. Especially since the shifter is a guy.

Greenland shark shifter Vic can't stop thinking about Crank, a human military guy he met when Vic got called in for a consult. Crank seems handy with anything that flies, and Vic would be happy to have him at his back, in more ways than one. And that's a problem—firstly because Vic's in love with his boyfriend, Saul, but also because Crank is sarcastic, irreverent... and straight.

The problem comes to a head when Saul discovers Vic has been dreaming about a man who isn't him. Saul does not share. But when Crank starts invading Saul's dreams too, he has to reassess his feelings. His life may depend on it.

Exploring the growing connection between the three of them will have to wait, though. The upcoming mission demands the team's full attention. They're about to discover something huge, and they have badly underestimated the enemy....

Scan the QR code below to order

IN HIS SIGHTS

K.C. WELLS

His psychic powers could help find the killer—unless the killer finds him first.

SECOND SIGHT 👁 BOOK ONE

Second Sight: Book One

Random letters belong on Scrabble tiles, not dead bodies. But when a demented serial killer targets Boston's gay population, leaving cryptic messages carved into his victims, lead detective Gary Mitchell has no choice but to play along.

As the body count rises, Gary gets desperate enough to push aside his skepticism and accept the help of a psychic. Dan Porter says he can offer new clues, and Gary needs all the insight into the killer's mind he can get.

Dan has lived with his gift—sometimes his curse—his entire life. He feels compelled to help, but only if he can keep his involvement secret. Experience has taught him to be cautious of the police and the press, but his growing connection to Gary distracts him from the real danger. As they edge closer to solving the puzzle, Dan finds himself in the killer's sights....

Scan the QR code below to order

IN PLAIN SIGHT

K.C. WELLS

A headless body hidden
from sight—can his
psychic powers bring
the killer to light?

SECOND SIGHT BOOK TWO

Second Sight: Book Two

Detective Gary Mitchell and psychic Dan Porter are now investigating cold cases that are literally falling from the sky—a headless body in 2006 and a carpenter who fell from a roof two years ago.

The first case leads them into dangerous territory. The second feels like a dead end.

But what if they're connected?

Gary has a lot of balls in the air—his work, his new relationship with Dan, his personal quest to discover more about his brother's murder.... And the more he looks into these two cases, the more convoluted the path becomes.

Everyone is hiding something, and some people would do anything to make sure Gary and Dan don't uncover the truth.

Dangerous territory indeed.

Scan the QR code below to order

OUT OF SIGHT
K.C. WELLS
Something from the past might well destroy the future.
SECOND SIGHT BOOK THREE

Second Sight: Book Three

Detective Gary Mitchell and psychic Dan Porter have a new cold case to tackle, and new leads to research in the hunt for Gary's brother's killer. Their life in Boston has settled into a comfortable rhythm.

But when forensic discoveries in a recent robbery gone wrong share similarities with their three-year-old cold case, all they can do is follow the evidence—and Dan's gift—which leads them in an unexpected direction, way out of their comfort zone.

Gary and Dan find themselves in a shadowy world where they can trust no one, with unseen opponents who want them to back away from their investigation—and suddenly they're in a race they have to win.

Because if they don't, the consequences could be more far-reaching than they could possibly imagine.

Scan the QR code below to order